Acclaim for
I Should Be Extremely Happy in Your Company
by Brian Hall

"Fills in the blank pages of the Lewis and Clark journals, offering marvelous character studies . . . Hall, a spellbinding prose stylist, writes with the kind of ethereal poetic sweep found in the historical novels of Michael Ondaatje and Wallace Stegner. With consummate skill he weaves the true 1804–06 journey with a deep psychological probe of his enigmatic characters' mindsets. . . . A seamless narrative flow earmarks this hybrid book as approaching the status of classic American literature."
—Douglas Brinkley, *Los Angeles Times*

"Magnificent . . . Hall has created a novel as full of surprises, wonders, and revelations as the journey itself. . . . No contemporary novelist I know of inhabits the minds and hearts of his characters more convincingly than Hall and, in a sense, we as readers live and die with them . . . the finest novel I've ever read on the Lewis and Clark expedition and the best history-based fiction I've encountered since *Cold Mountain*."
—Howard Frank Mosher, *The Denver Post*

"The relationship between Lewis and Clark, and . . . the way Hall depicts the volatile interactions of the white men and the Indians they meet during their journey, are like prisms with an infinite number of facets that you can turn over and over in your hand forever. Like real human relationships, they're endlessly, inexhaustibly fascinating."
—Laura Miller, Salon.com

"As a novelist, Hall is con_____ined: the blank pages in Lewis' jou_____, the unresolved contradictions b_____est pleasure of this novel stems _____ncipals, distinguishing not just thei_____ different visions of a world in rapid flux . . . Sacagawea's surreal vision of a world blended with native myths and tribal history provides the novel's most haunting moments, conveying a strikingly un-Western way of thinking about time and reality that can't be captured in even the most sensitive museum diorama. Here's literature that saves one of the greatest American moments from the pastel palette of mythology."

—Ron Charles, *The Christian Science Monitor*

"[Hall] tells the tale from many points of view. This pass the talking stick strategy gives the book a delicious gossipy feel . . . the great triumph of *I Should Be Extremely Happy in Your Company* lies in its fantastic reconstruction of the day-to-day logistics and life of the expedition . . . Hall gives white–Indian relations the full complexity the subject deserves . . . he has a keen eye for colorful historical detail."

—Bruce Barcott, *The New York Times Book Review*

"With lyricism, humor, and psychological acuity, Hall envisions not only the 1804 expedition and its aftermath but the explorers' response to a wilderness that defies description, let alone calculation . . . artful layering and flawless pacing transform a monolithic legend into a quixotic, heartbreaking story, one you enter rather than salute."

—Anna Mundow, *The Boston Globe*

"Combining fine prose with a factual foundation, Hall produces a stunning tribute to the upcoming two hundredth anniversary of the Lewis and Clark expedition. . . . A tour de force . . . it deserves to be a hit."

—Ellen Emry Heltzel, *Chicago Tribune*

"Breathtaking . . . An intimately compelling, and unraveling expedition in-and-of-itself, a revelatory narrative that juxtaposes the imaginations and inner dialogues of its characters against the wild exteriors of war, death, the onslaughts of nature, slavery. Above all, it is an exploration of the echoing, haunted interiors of loneliness, specifically the ghostlike loneliness of Lewis . . . the agonizing emotional journey Hall details is matched by his brilliant description of the pair's physical travels. This is not the exterior run-with-the-river-hounds so many historians give us."

—Nasidijj, *The Raleigh News and Observer*

"A brilliant reconstruction of the expedition braced by some learned guesswork about the explorers' various demons . . . in the way of the best historical fiction, the novel extends our understanding of the past while steering clear of the treacherous shoals of presentism . . . his tale brims with imagination and intelligence."
—Gregory McNamee, *The Washington Post*

"There are more than a million and a half words in the comprehensive journals of the Lewis and Clark expedition. Brian Hall sounds like he has read them all . . . Hall's magnum opus of a historical novel makes hugely enterprising use of firsthand accounts of the pioneering journey . . . fascinating, multifaceted . . . detailed, intense . . . Hall tries to penetrate and examine Lewis and Clark lore by creating strong narrative voices for the major players in this much-examined event. In the process, he is able to fill in the gaps."
—Janet Maslin, *The New York Times*

"Packed with erudition and wit, the book feels like a cross between *Son of Morning Star* and *The Right Stuff*."
—Carol Doup Miller, *The Seattle Times*

"The gem of 2003's Lewis and Clark bonanza . . . Hall swings for the fences here . . . his round-robin approach to narrating gives us a truly panoramic view of the West as it was then, from both white and Indian perspectives . . . Lewis has been alternately portrayed as a hero and a villain. Hall allows the great figure the imaginative space to be both: horrified by the indignities perpetuated in the name of expansion, and yet determined not to let anything stand in his way."
—John Freeman, *TimeOut New York*

"This is a dense, rich, impossible story, enhanced both by our knowledge that it is true and by our desire to know more about these two explorers than mere facts can ever tell us."
—Anne Stephenson, *USA Today*

"Hall raises mere tragedy to a portrait of the human soul lost in an eternal wilderness that can never be explored, discovered, bought or sold: the very mystery of life."

—Bill Roorbach, *Newsday*

"Delightful . . . Few larger-than-life heroes have ever been rendered more human and endearing than these two comrades."

—Tricia Springstubb, *The Cleveland Plain Dealer*

"Audacious . . . Hall's book is a close study of the truths most legends ignore."

—Sherryl Connelly, *New York Daily News*

"Hall's wonderfully written account is the best fictional treatment of the expedition we have. It represents the finest contemporary historical fiction."

—William H. Leckie, Jr., *St. Louis Post-Dispatch*

"Takes the novelist's license and goes where no historian can. It requires a leap of faith, a suspension of disbelief, as all fiction does, but it rewards it amply, filling the voids of character and experience as imaginatively and plausibly as they can be."

—John Gamino, *The Dallas Morning News*

"Hall offers a more convincing view of the expedition and some tantalizing projections of what might have been . . . he does not concentrate on a linear telling of the entire trip; instead, he examines key parts of the expedition from the imagined viewpoints of five members . . . the effect is disconcerting to anyone used to narrative history, but ultimately a joy to read."

—Peter Sleeth, *The Oregonian* (Portland)

PENGUIN BOOKS

I SHOULD BE EXTREMELY HAPPY
IN YOUR COMPANY

Brian Hall is the author of two previous novels, most recently
The Saskiad, and three works of nonfiction. His journalism has
appeared in publications such as *Time*, *The New Yorker*, and *The
New York Times Magazine*. He lives in Ithaca, New York.

Brian Hall

I SHOULD BE
EXTREMELY HAPPY
IN YOUR COMPANY

*A Novel of
Lewis and Clark*

PENGUIN BOOKS

PENGUIN BOOKS

Published by the Penguin Group

Penguin Group (USA) Inc., 375 Hudson Street, New York, New York 10014, U.S.A.

Penguin Books Ltd, 80 Strand, London WC2R 0RL, England

Penguin Books Australia Ltd, 250 Camberwell Road, Camberwell, Victoria 3124, Australia

Penguin Books Canada Ltd, 10 Alcorn Avenue, Toronto, Ontario, Canada M4V 3B2

Penguin Books India (P) Ltd, 11 Community Centre, Panchsheel Park, New Delhi–110 017, India

Penguin Books (N.Z.) Ltd, Cnr Rosedale and Airborne Roads, Albany, Auckland, New Zealand

Penguin Books (South Africa) (Pty) Ltd, 24 Sturdee Avenue,
Rosebank, Johannesburg 2196, South Africa

Penguin Books Ltd, Registered Offices:
80 Strand, London WC2R 0RL, England

First published in the United States of America by Viking Penguin,
a member of Penguin Putnam Inc. 2003
Published in Penguin Books 2004

1   3   5   7   9   10   8   6   4   2

PUBLISHER'S NOTE

This is a work of fiction. Names, characters, places, and incidents either are the product
of the author's imagination or are used fictitiously, and any resemblance to actual persons,
living or dead, business establishments, events, or locales is entirely coincidental.

THE LIBRARY OF CONGRESS HAS CATALOGED THE HARDCOVER EDITION AS FOLLOWS:

Hall, Brian, 1959–

I should be extremely happy in your company : a novel of Lewis and Clark / Brian Hall

p.   cm.

ISBN 0-670-03189-5 (hc.)

ISBN 0 14 20.0371 9 (pbk.)

1. Sacagawea, 1786–1884—Fiction.   2. Lewis and Clark Expedition (1804–1806)—Fiction.
3. Charbonneau, Jean-Baptiste, 1805–1885—Fiction.   4. West—(U.S.)—History—To 1848—
Fiction.   5. Lewis, Meriwether, 1774–1809—Fiction.   6. Clark, William, 1770–1838—Fiction.
7. Shoshoni women—Fiction.   8. Explorers—Fiction.   I. Title.

PS3558.A363 I13 2003

813'.54—dc21   2002066376

Printed in the United States of America
Set in Bulmer
Designed by Francesca Belanger

For Dave and Laurie,
co-historians

And Sarah C.—
trickster, guardian

I fear O! I fear the weight of his mind has overcome him, what will be the Consequence? What will become of ~~my~~ his papers?

—Letter of William Clark, October 28, 1809

CONTENTS

Prologue

Another night of sleep fleeing from him. Not one of his desolate nights, but too replete, anticipation and hope lifting him from his camp bed and carrying him into the adjoining chamber, where, with lamp lit and the open window breathing moist air and distant murmurs of first returning geese, he spread out the maps again, and opened the books, and he lowered himself into them, going away.

A drawing-room convention in Washington City's nascent society was to describe, to feminine titters and barks, one's first appalled sight of the national swamp, accompanied by an ironical phrase recalling some refinement of Philadelphia life. However, when Meriwether Lewis thought back to his own initial view, from the Georgetown heights—felled and stripped trees, acres of mud, log huts—what he principally remembered feeling was delight. It had been the 1st of April, and for a moment he had indulged the fancy that he was being played a fool by the men of his company; they had gulled him into believing he must give up his contented army life for that of a citizen, and then had led him, winking behind his back, to another encampment. Alas, the future had lain in the middle ground: the cluster of new brick townhouses, the buildings of War and State, and of course the President's House—Washington's Palace, Hoban's Folly—larger, it was said, than any British governor's mansion of the quondam colonies. A good Republican, Lewis had hated the House on the spot. But now that he had lived in it for two years, he must concede inwardly that he was rather fond of it. Why was this? It amused him, for one, that it was not finished, that the imposing exterior yielded on inspection (something the public could perform every day, as Mr.

Jefferson kept the doors open) a cheerless accretion of half-empty and entirely empty rooms, many of them mere shells. The House was an allegorical monument to the vanity of pomp and royal pretension. Furthermore, Lewis liked his own quarters: two small enclosures framed in lumber and sailcloth, standing at the south end of the cavernous, unplastered East Room, where they recalled a tent raised in a grove of barkless trees.

Lewis did not always enjoy society, and he had had to endure a good deal of it in his official capacity as the President's private secretary. But the House was so large that, except at dinner, it was possible to feel isolated in it, even when citizens were somewhere off in an unused room, admiring or deploring the appointments, or the lack of them. Alone in his canvas cabinet, a painted chair and writing desk the only marks of civilized life, his guns in a corner, a view south down the tussocky slope to the wilds of the Potomac shore, Lewis felt uncrowded, and he valued that extremely. At the other end of the House, Mr. J was similarly sequestered in his library. Lewis knew that the President, like him, often wanted to be left alone, a mark of the sympathy that (Lewis flattered himself) had grown up between them. As the President had remarked to him one night as they perused maps on the long library table, the west wind rattling the windows and the servants, as usual, so invisible as to be sprites, they were like two mice in a church.

Lewis's habit was to rise at half past four and go hunting. One refinement of Philadelphia, to be sure, was the lack of tree stumps in the thoroughfares, a Washington phenomenon that made walking in the dark treacherous. But say what one might about Franklin's city, Lewis doubted a man could get up at Front and Chestnut and within an hour bag a pheasant, a deer, or with luck, a bear. Only the wolves and the Indians were gone from the woods of Washington City. Lewis would bring the meat himself to the presidential kitchen by seven, secured to his back, Indian-fashion, by hoppas straps of sinew.

He had unhesitatingly accepted Mr. J's offer of the position of secretary, out of reverence for the man and a consciousness of his duty, but he had little savored the idea of being an amanuensis. To his surprise, he had discovered that the President had no need of one. Mr. J wrote all his own correspondence, copying the letters himself in a press. He kept his own weather diary, correspondence log, account books, and a variety of other vade mecums, such as his garden book, in which he had recorded the date of planting, budding, and fruiting of every tree, shrub, vegetable, grain, and flower on his farm since 1766. It would not be far from the mark to say that, other than his daily ride and twice-daily ingestion, Mr. J lived at his writing desk. As Lewis, therefore, was not really a secretary, he had spent a number of sleepless nights on his camp bed, by his open window, engaged in the tedious mental round with which he was tediously familiar, viz., asking himself, first, what he *was*; and second, why Mr. J might have chosen him.

Was it possible that his mere presence was the thing desired? Did two mice in a church simply make better society than one? There had been a sentence in Mr. J's letter offering him the position: *You would of course save also the expense of subsistence & lodging as you would be one of my family*. Lewis had begun to wonder if he was justified in seeing more in that than a reference to domestic economy. Mr. J had only his two daughters. Delightful and accomplished ladies they were, the jewels of any social setting; but surely all men longed for a son. Lewis shied away from the thought as presumptuous. Yet Mr. J had been so kind to him, so generous. In the past two years, they had seen more of each other than of anyone else. Lewis remembered how, as a boy, with his father dead, he would be lurking at the edge of some mysterious celebration involving Meriwethers, Lewises, and Jeffersons, and the great man of Monticello would engage him in conversation, pepper him with questions about his rambles and his woodcraft, or later about his schooling. Not a son, no; but perhaps the sort of youthful companion that Mr. J enjoyed, a bright and educable interlocutor. The thought made Lewis uneasy. Mr. J liked his young fellows lively, a touch irrepressible. He valued conversation above all, and Lewis lacked that sort of flair. What in a boy might seem forgivably tongue-tied, a fetching rose-cheeked incapacity, in a man was taken as arrogance. When Lewis had one of his black fogs upon him, he felt doubly oppressed that he was not being a serviceable protégé to his patient mentor.

At times like those, the dinners were a torment. His presence was expected, and he could not flee to an obscure perch below the salt, as the President's table had no such position. Rating both good food and good conversation extraordinarily high, Mr. J viewed dinner as an approximation of the perfect society, and thus he enforced at his famous oval table his republican ideals with especial vigor. The servants were even more than usually invisible. A rotating dumbwaiter set in the wall allowed Mr. J with a movement of his hand to conjure provisions as though directly from the Tree of Life. He had his host's chair, but no others were assigned; following the pell-mell seating, as this minister and that diplomat clashed in quick mute fury over the right-hand place and the loser went awandering among the now-taken seats like the outcast Jew, Lewis not infrequently found himself between the highest-ranked guest (were rank in this paradise admitted) and some illustrious personage of an allied, or worse an opposing, faction. Thus he could never predict, as he approached the oval rack, whether his torture would be to act the shuttlecock, or the buffer nation, or the oily conduit of false compliments. But whatever his role, it was invariably a speaking one—this republic had universal suffrage—and as he dragged the words one by one out of the mud at the back of his throat, he seemed almost to see them land, filthy and malodorous, on the white linen before him. Across the crystal and the plate and the exquisite French wine, always, were Mr. J's pale eyes.

Lewis knew in his heart that he might learn to be as irreverent and gay as the President could desire. No one perceived that he often did laugh inwardly, because he had been habituated at an early age not to show it. Or nearly—his mother had once said, when he was in the throes of a secret hilarity, that when he pursed his lips like that he looked an intolerable prig. Alas, his amusement had been at her expense, so he could hardly have explained the expression. Habits were very devils, and he hacked at this one, this instinctive reserve, but it was like striking one's image in the mirror, with blow returned for blow.

In any case, although his renascence as a blithe spirit and jokesmith still lay off in the effortful future, Lewis's fogs had lifted the previous summer, with the merciful appearance, as on angel wings, of Mackenzie's account of his overland voyage from Hudson Bay to the Pacific Ocean. Mr. J had heard of the upstart Canadian's feat in January; he'd ordered the man's book at his first leisure in Monticello, in June; received and devoured it in July; had Lewis read it the same month; determined on an American expedition to head off British pretensions in August; and chosen Lewis for its leader in September. Those nine months had accomplished a different and better birth.

Alone in his canvas cave in the cool late-winter night, he breathed down on the map spread open to him. A license, nay, a *duty* to run away. A miracle! The map was Arrowsmith's latest projection of North America; Lewis and the President had been discussing the new information it contained on the trans-Mississippi west. But as Lewis sat uncrowded in the lamplight, what made his heart beat high was not what was on the map, but what wasn't. His eye followed the line of his proposed route, the Missouri River, west and north, to where it stopped just above the 45th parallel and just beyond the 100th meridian. *The most Northern Bend of the Missouri River,* the map said. And: *Villages of the Tall Indians and Manders.* Beyond, to the west, was virgin linen, marred only by the dotted lines of conjectural river courses, looking like the footprints of a man lost in a vast field of snow. If the dinner table was Mr. J's paradise, this blankness was Lewis's. Five hundred thousand square miles, newly created, as it were, still awaiting the separation of its lands from its waters, still awaiting its Adam. *Blue Mud Nation. Long Hair Nation. Stone Indians. Tall Indians. Blackfoot.*

Lewis's eye wandered back east to the point at which the known Missouri stopped. That was where the true adventure would begin. And at that place, curving across the dotted footsteps, as though to block access to Paradise, was written the name of another nation: *Snake.* Lewis's mouth twitched, tugging down at the corners. At this moment, doubtless, he looked an intolerable prig.

water speaks

Shouts.

This one ducked, twisting away from maybe arrow or head crusher, touched earth and threw looks around. One thumb was galloping, pointing back to the turtle rock. The middle river there had become spitting white-water and out of the spray were born horsemen, raging forward. They were not people.

This one lunged into the redberry bush, away but the wrong way, slowed down by thicket. She thrashed through to the grass and ran. She was going to die. Where was camas flower, where was rides ahead?

Climbs the hill thundered past. His horse fell bleeding. Cracks in the air like spring ice breaking. Black weapons. Climbs the hill got up and sat down again. Blood on her legs. She ran. This one was still a child.

Horsemen were riding down the slope across the camp river. Were they dog-eaters? Hardskins? This one dodged, dropped, sprang. She reached the shed-fur trees and plunged in, snaking down between deadfall, falling on someone's legs: small frog, who kicked. A lightning crash of horses, a war shriek. An arrow burrowed, white bits flew. This one was running again, crazy, out of the woods toward the river. Camas flower, save her. This one was going to die.

A sandbar, a shoal. She jumped. She ran through the water. Behind her, water drummed. Water glittered, bright white. This one died.

—born again on a trotting horse, her cheek slapping the back of a strange-eater: blackshoe or hardskin, dog-eater or headcutter. If this was the end, it was only the beginning.

This one died.

The sound spoke in her head again, mouthed by spirit. Now maybe it would happen. Father's sister, frog jumps in, had come back from the hardskins, but the other captives, never. They died even if they didn't die, gone to a different place, renamed.

Her neck burned and her scalp on one side felt torn. Her arms were cinched around the strange-eater's waist. She could not feel her hands.

This one died. Spirit had been saying it to her all her life, full of meat or starving, feeding fire, scraping a skin, or wondermaking with the sinew webbed between her hands, twitching her salmon fingers to make the pronghorn run and the small children gape. Her mother, camas flower, said this one smiled when she first heard thunder, and that meant she would live long, but she had never believed it.

She smelled blood.

Spearing salmon, or palming them out of the weir basket to shiver on the riverbank, it would sound in her ears. *This one died.* How died? Spirit never said. Speared like salmon or goodfish? Thrown high and left gasping in some other air she couldn't breathe? Or when she was stripping the inner bark of a sticky-tree in the hunger moon when the yellowflower seeds and sharpberry cakes and roasted ants gave out, working the fibers in her teeth, keeping them long in the mouth so they would lie dreamless in the stomach. *This one died.* Of starvation? But she could not see that. Her band was weak, but only the old people, the stayers behind, had starved to death, and this one would not live to be old.

Her neck hurt. She shifted upright. The strange-eater's elbows accepted her as alive by lifting and falling, a bird settling its wings. The cords hurt her wrists, but she pushed that away. There was blood on her legs, not her blood. There was a woman's scalp on the horse robe, not her scalp. Where was camas flower?

When her father, two bears, was killed and they tied him in elk skin and took him into the hills and lowered him on the long thongs into the crack in the rocks, one thumb said people did this to their dead because those ones had to fly like arrows. You pulled the new arrow through a rock chink to smooth it straight, and the soul of two bears rising through the cleft would fly straight, he would not miss.

But fly where? People talked about that place but said different things.

Some said the spirit went straight up to Wolf's house. But sees the morning· said when he died his spirit only went up a little way, then stopped and looked back at his dead body lying on the ground, then went underground and visited Father before returning to his body so he could live again for a while. Wondering at these things, this one had looked down into the crack where her father had disappeared and heard floating up from the dark, *this one died.*

It was straight-sun time. Half a morning had passed since the attack. Other horses in front and behind, other people. Two riderless horses. One of them was one thumb's. Maybe that one was dead. The strange-eater behind her had a face painted pink like a snaproot flower. This one wondered how he mixed that color. She saw jumps once. And another boy, weir runner, tied to white eye's second horse, not moving. A woman, too, farther back: cloud. That one was bloody on the head, slumped, eyes rolling.

When she heard *this one died,* she felt no fear or sorrow. It was merely a thing that happened, as death happened, walking by, choosing, another story to pass on, and she was someone looking back, maybe she was her spirit looking down on her dead body. Maybe her spirit would be stuck when this one died, looking back at the body, not flying up to Wolf's house or underground to Father, and she would become a ghost in the hills at night. She thought of what people sang to the dead, to keep them from becoming ghosts, what one thumb sang when her father was lowered into the crack in the rock.

> *Reach a good land.*
> *Don't come back.*
> *This is not a good land.*
> *It is old.*
> *It is good for you to go.*

The strange-eaters were crossing the hills toward sunbirth from the plain of three rivers. The buffalo hunt trail. This one scanned the lower hills behind, the far plain of shed-fur trees and berrying places. No sign of pursuit. She had counted fourteen strange-eaters, every one with a black weapon. If camas flower or white elk skin or rides ahead or small moon were alive, she hoped those ones were fleeing toward sun-entering, reaching blue crow's camp, telling the others, mourning, *those ones died.*

The strange-eaters were heading for the pass to the buffalo hunt river, which meant they were not hardskins or blackshoes, who would go cold-ward. They might be dog-eaters or headcutters, or even birds. These ones were tall, like the birds that people traded with on the black rock plain. The birds always had metal, and these ones wore ring metal, and their arrowheads were knife metal. The birds usually did not attack people, but they had black weapons and people did not, so sometimes a band attacked, she had heard. But these strange-eaters did not wear the white chalked skins of birds. The men clacked and warbled to each other. It sounded like the bird speech she had heard on the black rock plain.

Her strange-eater had turned several times to look back. His face was charcoal with yellow-earth eyes. He pulled a brown mottled ball from his food bag and put it in his mouth. It looked like a grassbird's egg.

They stopped in the dark over the pass where the buffalo hunt river came from warm country and turned toward sunbirth. The strange-eaters tied and picketed the people. They left a strange, good grease on the ground in reach of teeth. They had let these ones drink from the river and had not beaten any or forced open smells good or cloud, and they made a fire nearby and sat on the opposite side, ignoring them, letting them talk.

—They are birds, this one offered to the others, mainly smells good.
—This is bird country and they are not hiding their fire.

Besides herself, there were two women and four boys. Smells good had become a woman in the grass moon past, cloud was two or three winters older. Cloud had been hit with a head crusher. She lay huddled on her side, not speaking. The four boys were young: jumps once, thorn, drops the robe, weir runner. No one had seen what had happened to weir runner, but that one had a welt on his crown, black blood in his ears, a smashed and leaking hand. His child eye was blood-red. He mumbled spirit words. He puked what this one chewed and tongued into his mouth.

—They eat eggs whole like crows, this one said.
—Those aren't eggs, smells good said. —They're bonegrease and yellow-flower seeds. I ate one.

You ate one. —They speak like birds.
—They don't look like birds, walks slow.
Walks slow. This one's name. But in her thinking, she was water speaks.

She remembered one thumb saying they were called birds because they used to fly from people. But not anymore, not since the Small Man sickness, not since the black weapons came from the sun-men. Water speaks looked across the fire at the happy faces of the birds. No one in their party had been killed. And this one had counted twelve stolen horses. The birds would be big back at their camp, maybe speakers.

And whose scalps were they bringing? —Climbs the hill is dead, water speaks said.

That one sat down in front of her and the blood spraying from the back of his head got on her legs. Or was it the horse's blood that flew? The horse fell one way, climbs the hill the other, and this one ran between. —And I think one thumb.

—One thumb was galloping away, smells good said. —Up the slope above the camp river.

—But the birds were coming down the slope.

—No, they were coming across the middle river.

—And also down the slope.

Smells good said nothing.

—I saw them, water speaks said.

—I saw, too. They came across the river. One thumb went up the slope.

—They have his horse.

Thorn said stick jammer was killed on top of him. —I saw one thumb get into the shed-fur trees.

Not up the slope. But water speaks only said,—I was in the shed-fur trees. With small frog.

The arrow. —Small frog is dead.

—That was the second attack, when they came into the trees, said smells good.

—Second?

—After they put more round arrowheads in the black weapons.

—But I saw them crossing the middle river and then I ran to the shed-fur trees and they came in right after.

Smells good laughed. —How do you think you reached them? Those trees are ten arrow shots from where we were picking berries.

Water speaks did not answer. Smells good was right. But this one had run that distance like one arrow shot. She had flown somehow.

—Camas flower? she asked.

No one had seen. Jumps once thought she was across the camp river gathering wood when the birds came. He had seen four ways run down. That one was dead. Jumps once had been caught in the bushes with small wolf and root digger and the strange-eater had cut the throats of those-both.

Drops the robe could tell them nothing. He only cried. He was young.

This one ran. The arrow popped in her ear, burrowing. Climbs the hill fell one way, the horse another, and she ran between. Smells good laughed. How do you think you reached them, walks slow?

She woke, roused with the others by the birds at first light. Her hands were left free so she could drink from the river and shit. Finished, she signed to her strange-eater, How many scalps?

Eleven.

Her face showed nothing. Climbs the hill, stick jammer, maybe one thumb. Small frog, four ways. Small wolf, root digger. Three men, two women, two boys: seven. Four others.

Before sunbirth they were mounting their horses. As her strange-eater turned to tie her hands, this one signed, Are you a bird?

He said something to pink face. Those-both laughed. He mounted and hauled her up. He kicked; his horse bolted. Off balance, this one reached for him, but he threw his arms out and flapped, cawing like a crow. Clawing at him, like a crow, she fell.

Her strange-eater would not give her a knife to cut her hair for the dead, maybe not wanting her to chop off fingers—his own salmon finger was missing, for some brother or parent—because if he was planning to sell her that might lower her price. The second night, her hands tied behind her, she took pleasure in gouging her cheeks against a sharp rock, pleasure at honoring the dead and spoiling his goods. Smells good did not scar herself, and water speaks hated her for it. Weir runner's arm swelled and the red people-eater fingers reached along it to catch his spirit, and on the third morning that one was dead. The birds took his skins and dragged his body away from the river. They left him unstraightened, to fly badly.

Squatting unwatched for a few moments in the dim light, water speaks rubbed pellets of her shit in the cuts on her face. Those ones grew hot in the next days, curling yellow lips outward, her mourning mouths, reeking of dead teeth, speaking to the dead. Her strange-eater pushed her face in the river until she breathed water and he smeared grease and black weapon powder on the cuts, and this one wiped the grime off against his tunic as he rode and regouged herself against his raccoon-claw fringe until he stopped his horse and throttled her and tied her sideways across the horse he was leading, where her head smacked against the horse's ribs until her skull felt small and the pain in her neck brought child's tears to her eyes.

On the fourth night, smells good was not picketed with the others but walked away from the fire with her strange-eater. For the first time water speaks cried, unseen in the night, the three boys huddled asleep and cloud in some other world, her eyes watching the movement of spirits, maybe Small Man, beyond sight in the dark, shooting his poisoned arrows into her. At first light the birds were laughing, all except smells good fucker. That one had waked at moonrise with a bloody lump on his head and found smells good gone. He and pink face rode off to search for her while the others went on. The searchers caught up that night. They had not found her.

How do you think you reached them, walks slow?

Water speaks had run, as smells good now was running. Water speaks could run as fast as smells good (ask others, faster) but smells good was smarter. That night water speaks did not cry, but urged on smells good, singing in her mouth, seeing her hiding in the sandbar arrow-trees during the day and running across the open in the dark, reaching the buffalo pass by lost moon time and crossing back to people country.

The birds and their captives continued toward sunbirth down the river valley. On the warm side were bluffs and scattered sticky-tree. This one knew that people long ago used to come here to hunt, and farther to the big muddy river and coldward to where the headcutters ran from them, but never in her life had any of her band come farther than four or five days beyond the pass toward sunbirth from the three river plain, and then only with other bands of people, or with shaved heads for protection, or with birds, when they agreed. The birds who traded on the black rock plain called this elk river. In signing, it was yellow stone river.

On the seventh day one of the outriders rode in fast, and the birds held their black weapons ready, but the band that came up the valley were not enemies. Her strange-eater signed to her that those ones were bellies and the bellies laughed. The belly sign might mean hardskins, or coldward headcutters, or undergrounders. Hardskins raided her band often. Undergrounders lived beyond the birds on the big muddy river. Coldward headcutters lived along the reed river beyond the hardskins. Crow flying said all of them were signed bellies because they used to pat their bellies, whining. Those ones were all starving beggars before they got black weapons.

These bellies were not hardskins, this one thought. They dressed like birds, with red shields and white skins and hair to the ground. The two parties did not use signs, but clacked and warbled at each other. They made shade, and smoked and spoke while the sun moved two hands. When the bands remounted and parted, thorn and jumps once were carried away by those ones. Four of the belly horses came with the birds. Two belly mothers would have sons to replace lost ones. The boys stared back at this one as they were carried away. She was the only one who might tell them what to do, what to remember. —The salmon stream! Toward sun-entering! was all she could think of in the hard moment. They grew smaller, staring back. The horses turned warmward into the hills, and they were gone.

Two days later her party left the river and struck straight toward sunbirth. They had passed beyond the edge of any world this one had heard of. Above the hills was a dry grassland, flat like a stretched skin. She did not like it. It was bigger than the black rock plain, like walking on the sky upside down. She saw a bush she didn't understand. The land was beginning to speak a strange language. It was only her and cloud and drops the robe tied together in the night, and water speaks was surprised to see the same stars above this place, and cloud said *ha'a* low, over and over: *yes, yes*. A spirit was teaching her the long way.

The band descended into more hills, their clay sides war-striped in blues and blacks and reds. There was power here. This would be something to tell people, if this one ever made it back. They climbed again to a plain. On the thirteenth day, they dropped into a broad suntrack valley, and that night one of the birds rode ahead. The next morning, the birds painted their faces black, and after straight-sun this one saw ahead a larger valley, with many trees in the bottom. She saw the haze of a big camp, then she heard the dogs, then runners came to meet them, grown men so poor they had no horses.

They hopped and whooped. At last the throng came in view. Singing women raised the eleven scalps on poles and paraded, as people would have done (as water speaks had heard) back in the time when people were strong enough to take scalps. Birds pressed close, and this one stared through them, turning them to ghosts who could not reach her.

Later, she would remember little except the noise. Her only clear memory was the moment she realized she had been wrong all along. When she saw the river: wide as five or six arrow shots, brown as skin. The big muddy river. So her captors were not birds. That was why her strange-eater had laughed, and also those ones who took the boys. Those others were the birds. These thronging ghosts, these were the bellies of the muddy river, undergrounders, who had sometimes raided other people bands (she had heard), but never hers, whose name was all she knew. They were mysteries like the sun-men. She didn't know whether they forced open captured women like the shaved heads, or roasted them like the headcutters, or ate them like the red-haired people-eaters of the caves. Or—*undergrounders*—buried them alive.

This one died. She pushed the thought away. That was shameful, like the tears.

Summer.

This one sat under a skin awning on a sapling mat raised man-high above the cornfield and sang, they thought, for the corn. The corn liked company. In the next field an undergrounder girl sat on another scaffold, singing, half asleep in the heat, and water speaks, pausing, could hear some of her strange speaking: I see you . . . hidden path . . . your robe. A love-boy song. This one hit sticks together and threw stones at the blackbirds, so the undergrounders would see she understood that part of the task. Otherwise she ignored the corn, for which we-people had no word. She sang what spirit spoke, wrapping her old life around her like a robe in winter. No one could understand what she said. She sang her band, tall grass, and the cold streams, and the mountain winters that aged you. She saw her old life more brightly than when she had lived it, as dreams of meat were bloodiest in the hunger moon. She was hungry for her salmon stream.

When all the tribes of the earth were born, only we-people were washed by Coyote. Other tribes hated we-people for this, but it made them tougher than their enemies. They would endure like thorn, crippling the feet of tribes that stepped on them.

This one had waked once and been washed in a we-people's birth hut, on the bank of the salmon stream flowing coldward between the mountains. Camas flower said that while she labored the spring thaw was on and as she crouched in the birth hut at the struggling point she heard the water outside speak encouragement in her mother's voice. So the girl was water speaks, until once on a march to a snaproot slope she fell behind and turned the wrong way and red tongue came back looking for her. Then she was walks slow. She did not walk slow, but it was foolish to say that. She had walked slow once, and it was a part of her. But the water, too, had spoken, and spirit, when it spoke to her, felt like water, ungraspable and gone, not like the furred weight of wolf or hare the young men saw when they fasted.

If this one got back to her salmon stream, they would give her a new name. Walks far, maybe. She pushed the thought away.

—Face warmward and hold up your making hand, one thumb had told her. —You will see in your hand the land of we-people, the tall grass band of the buffalo-eaters. The thumb pointing toward sunbirth, low down, the humped one, is the buffalo on the plains. The first finger is the tall grass valley on the sunbirth side of the pass: grass finger. The finger in the middle, mountain finger, is the ridge dividing our land into sun-entering-flowing salmon rivers and sunbirth-flowing buffalo rivers. The third finger is root finger, for the camas and snaproot slopes below the ridge. And the smallest finger is salmon finger, for the stream below the slopes that keeps us alive.

Spirit had spoken this to one thumb, because when he was a boy a horse bolted and pulled the thumb off his making hand, so he carried the mystery on his body, the bad times of we-people, of no buffalo. When this one's father's father hunted buffalo, the tall grass band spent part of summer and fall ranging far on the sunbirth side of the mountains, and their enemies ran from them, and they spent winters on the plain of three rivers, where many buffalo came. But then Small Man shot his sickness arrows, and his wounds festered, and skin came off in sheets, and children lay in piles, and bands rotted in their huts. Then their enemies got black weapons and the buffalo disappeared from the three rivers. Now the hunt did not begin until the frost moon, and as soon as the tall grass band had enough to survive the winter, it came back to hide in the mountains. That was why water speaks was born in a spring thaw by the salmon stream, instead of in buffalo country, and why she was born in a brush hut instead of a skin hut. The hardskins had stolen their skin huts. Unless it was the blackshoes that time.

She remembered the raids in her own time, the one near beaver's head on blue crow's camp by the blackshoes when two bears' older brother (this one's bigfather), wolf tooth, was killed along with his son, chalk; and the raid at the pebble-root place three winters ago when two bears was killed and they lowered him wrapped in elk skin into the cleft in the rock. That was the hardskins.

One thumb said,—If you put your making hand on your chest, salmon finger points to your heart. The buffalo may fail, but the salmon do not. We were salmon-eaters before we were buffalo-eaters. Some strange-eaters cut off that finger when they mourn for their dead, but we do not.

Sitting behind her strange-eater on the horse that first day, this one saw him putting the egg in his mouth, she saw the stump of his salmon finger, and she thought of the women in the Coyote story who cracked the eggs with their toothed cunts. Coyote tricked them in the dark with an elk thighbone and they broke their teeth on it, and then he fucked them and that was how all the tribes were born. This one wondered, watching the egg go into her strange-eater's mouth, if he would use her like a woman.

And all the tribes were born from the broken cunts and the women washed all of them, except we-people. Coyote washed we-people. Small people, tough, running from their enemies, living in brush huts. This one saw the arrow burrowing. She felt herself running, crazy, to the river. In her bird-watching hut, she closed her eyes. She offered spirit her two blue beads.

The salmon stream was the heart of the world and the people who lived there, her people, the tall grass band of the buffalo-eaters, were washed by Coyote. Nearby were other bands of buffalo-eaters: red shell band, thorn band, high-water band. Toward sun-entering from the salmon stream, in the high mountains, were the broken shoes, who were bow-horn-eaters, horse-eaters, bandless and dangerous. Warmward were the twoleaf people and the black rock plain and at the far edge of the plain was earth's cunt, the bed of the great snake that woke and wrapped the mountain until it melted. Beyond were the dirt people: pinenut-eaters, hare-eaters. All these were we-people. Beyond them were the strange-speakers. Coldward two days and over the mountain were the shaved heads. Toward sun-entering from the shaved heads, through long mountains with little grass for horses, were the mealy-root-eaters, who had so many horses they would trade a good one for ten baskets of salmon. They lived on a river that flowed into a bigger river that flowed into a big bad-tasting water. Toward sunbirth was the buffalo country, now overrun with blackshoes and hardskins and headcutters and dog-eaters, all enemies, all with horses and skin huts, all with black weapons.

And beyond them all, a summer's journey, lived the sun-men. It was from the sun-men that the black weapons came. No one in the tall grass band had seen a sun-man. Now this one had seen five, ten. Something to tell if she returned. Her name, saw the sun-men, maybe.

The sun-men's father was Knife-Metal Man, who had only sons, so the sun-men traded their black weapons for women. The birds on the black rock plain had told two bears that the sun-men they traded with on the muddy river had skin as white as ashes, but the sun-men water speaks had seen were no lighter than mealyroot-eaters, or the undergrounders who honked like geese half a morning down the muddy river. She wondered at this.

Birds—she threw a stone and a cloud of them rose briefly and settled. She threw more stones. Crazy. She climbed down from the scaffold and ran between the rows flapping her arms, yelling. The cloud rose higher and part of it sheered off to settle in another patch. She carried more stones up into the brush hut. She was glad when her stones hit the corn, glad when the birds settled again. They were Coyote's birds, his own black weapons troubling the undergrounders' Corn Mother, breaking her teeth and fucking her.

No one in the tall grass band had ever seen a sun-man, but they had traded for his metal when they could.

Pot.

Knife.

Ring.

Sometimes a bird would trade a black weapon, or a person would steal it. The yampa-eaters traded horse bits they said came from the mountain sun-men, who lived far warmward. But the mountain sun-men would not trade black weapons. No one knew why not.

Two bears had a black weapon, and water speaks remembered him and crow flying and climbs the hill and the older men sitting in the brush shade and talking about it. Knife-metal was stronger than pot-metal or ring-metal. It was so strong it could not be worked. Yet somehow the sun-men worked it.

It had so much weapon power, it tasted like blood. But it was also weak, with its own Small Man sickness. Knife-Metal Man was strong, but he was also weak, and Wolf could outsmoke him. When Knife-Metal Man tried to smoke as much as Wolf did, he puked and died. Black weapons were strong, but they stopped smoking without the round arrowheads or the black powder. Two bears had his empty black weapon on his horse robe the day the round arrowhead went through his neck, and his weapon was taken along with his horse, and both were fed now by a richer tribe.

Like spring ice breaking, the sound. It sizzled between the hills. And the back of climbs the hill's head came off, like mystery, like a dream. Climbs the hill fell one way and his horse the other, and this one ran between. Or had she confused it with the horsemen coming across the river on one side and the other horsemen coming down the slope on the other, and she running between? And how had the shed-fur trees come to her so fast? She had run like a hare and was chased down a narrowing path, horsemen on the slope and horsemen crossing the river, forcing her toward the trap at the end, the shed-fur trees that came up so fast. And small frog, her older sister, between the deadfall, and water speaks falling on her legs, and the arrow.

The horsemen had the black weapons, but an arrow was good enough for short range, into the face of an almost-woman with no shield. And the white bits that flew looked different in her different dreams. Sometimes eye matter, sometimes cheek bone, sometimes teeth.

This one had wondered, watching her strange-eater eat his egg, what would be done to her: knifed or burned or traded or forced open or adopted. Revenge was taken when called for, ghosts were comforted, enemies' fear of you maintained. If it came to that, to beating to death or a knife in the throat or slow burning, this one had hoped, with a feeling of standing outside herself, that she would behave well, and that her spirit, when ascending and pausing to look back, would not be caught by her, called out to, distracted, but would be free to turn again and rise to Wolf's house. If that was where spirits went.

But no raiders had been killed, and the women that gathered around them as they came to the camps did not have cropped hair or bleeding legs. During the scalp dance, her strange-eater gave her to a woman who led her to one of the small hills and took her inside it through a hole. Bonegrease and crushed strange leaves were applied to her cheeks, and this one let the salve remain. Her cuts had opened wide, the pulsing hot flesh had crowded into the gap. She would have good, ugly scars.

The woman who had taken her was her strange-eater's sister. There was a younger sister, and the man they shared, and the sisters' mother, and a young boy and a baby girl. They set her to work. They had metal knives and awls and axes, and metal pots, and their beds were raised off the ground and were warm with buffalo robes. Their lives were easy. The man did not come and fuck her during the nights. This one was a child.

In the tall grass valley there were times of being alone, at a root place, or tending a weir, moments of her and spirit and no one to say her name so that, nameless, she floated. But not here. She felt lost in the crowded camp, legs and bellies pressing into her, hills almost touching, dogs underfoot. The undergrounders made the hills they lived in, like muskrats. Tree trunks held up the earth. Around the camp was a tree-trunk fence this one had first thought was a line of dead trees along an old streambed. The undergrounders could cut down such large trees because they had knife-metal axes.

They had no salmon. Sometimes they ate wolves and foxes. Sometimes they ate coyotes. They had a feast of dog. They ate things she had never seen before. Corn was a stiff reed that grew toothed cocks. There were yellow and green berries as big as her head that grew on vines and tasted like sweet roots. There were fat soft seeds like grubs. When dog or wolf or coyote was in the stew this one would not eat it.

It was a camp you could not pack up and move like skin huts, or leave and build again like brush huts, and that was crazy. Their enemies always knew where they were. They feared the headcutters that lived warmward. There was a dead headcutter set up in a corn patch and shot at for practice. They traded with the coldward headcutters. They called those ones yellowlegs. They were friends with other undergrounders living in two camps nearby who honked like geese. They fought with a tribe down the river they signed big earrings, for the big glass beads those ones knew how to make.

Their sign for we-people was one she had seen before, a finger weaving forward. Crow flying had said it was for the grass we-people wove to make their huts (when their skin huts were stolen). One thumb had said it was for the salmon swimming up the salmon stream. The undergrounders thought the sign meant snake.

In spring, the ice on the big muddy river broke with the sound of climbs the hill's head coming apart. By then, this one could understand many undergrounder words, but her face showed nothing. She signed when necessary and did what she was told and did not speak. Old mother and two sisters did not beat her and the man did not fuck her and they let her eat from the stew pot when there wasn't dog or wolf or coyote in it. They thought (she thought) she had a little crazy spirit in her. But not so crazy as crazy woman, who once had been cloud. Crazy woman had been given to a beggarly womanless man whom she yelled at in the narrow spaces between the huts with a white-eyed fury, foam spotting the chin of her fresh-bruised face.

They lived underground, and buried their spare food underground, and the women spent the spring and summer digging in the ground. They did everything in the ground except bury their dead, which they raised up in the sky. It was strange to see, the ravens tearing at the wrapped bodies on the scaffolds, a fluttering away of a tatter in the wind, the cone-fall of a bone-heavy piece to the ground.

Older sister spoke of Corn Mother, who must be an old one, or crazy herself, since she would not take care of her corn children but made the undergrounder women do it. What kind of spirit had no power?

Crazy, not speaking, this one was put in the cornfields in the summer to watch for birds with the younger girls, away from the crowding bellies, where she could sing about their craziness under a skin maybe stolen from her people, and hear the watery sound of cornleaves rustling under the weight of Coyote's blackbirds.

Small frog had been seen because of this one. This one fell between the deadwood on small frog's legs, and small frog kicked, and she rose from the waist as she kicked, and the arrow took her in the face as she rose.

This one sang: —Die, corn.

The undergrounders called her *tsakakawia*. It meant bird girl, bird woman. Maybe because as a crazy snake and a scarred mute she was only good for chasing away birds. Maybe. But the other bird girls who laughed at her maybe did not know why hanging branch came back from the fall raid with the name bird rider. Maybe they said he fell on we-people like a war eagle on a snake. They did not know that water speaks had named him, that the morning after the raid she had signed the question to him, Are you a bird, and he had imitated a crow on his horse and the other men had laughed. By the end of the trek, they were calling her bird woman, his woman, as she knew by a sign pink face made to her the last night, as he put his palm on her unready cunt. (She thought he would break her teeth then, but he didn't.) This one had fought bird rider and been tied across a horse's back for two days, like a man's woman who had run away and had to be brought back bundled like a sack of dried fish.

This one was no longer walks slow, because there was no one left to call her that. Crazy woman never spoke to her between the earth huts, turning away with a flash of white teeth grinding. And drops the robe, adopted by a changed-man, was too young, that one was forgetting the salmon stream, the tall grass valley, that one was becoming an undergrounder.

This one might as well be tsakakawia.

And she had, it might be said—a strange thought, but she was alone now, floating in strangeness—named herself.

THE SECRETARY
[1803]

1

Only diligence made order. Only vigilance maintained it. Every generation was tested. Meanwhile, the world waited, unwinking, for a moment's chance to wreck and destroy.

A river killed his father. The Meriwether house at Cloverfields was hushed, Lewis lurked, five years old. His mother and his aunts went into the room he was barred from, with linen, steaming decoctions. They came out with chamber pots that also steamed. "Rivanna," they said. To Lewis, that was the long name for river. He had helped an older cousin fish from the Rivanna bank, he had thrown sticks far across its waters, he had learned to swim in it. The chamber pots reeked, like summer-cooked rivermud. "His horse was drowned," the women said, hurrying through the rooms, stoking the fire. Sparks flew up the chimney. And now the river was drowning the rider. He had brought it into the house with him, he had swallowed river water that rose in his lungs. His lungs were in flood, and he was swept away.

Lewis hardly knew the man. Like all the good men, he had been off fighting the British. Until he was seven, Lewis lived in a world of women and cowards, and the occasional British sons of bitches who raided them. He understood the redcoats' own cowardice later, not then. At the time, colorful on their chargers, the officers had been fearful and large; burning crops and dispatching turkeys at a gallop had seemed impressive. What he also understood later was that the British had killed his father, not the river. William Lewis would not have attempted to cross the Rivanna in flood, in November, except that his family leave was over and the war called.

Another thing a young boy could not understand: whence new fathers came, and why he had to pretend to know one when he had barely learned to recognize the other. John Marks wasn't a bad man, he had fought the British, too. But Lewis's mother soon gave him children of his own, and Lewis had a father of his own, somewhere down the river with his horse. Much later, during his schooling, Lewis read in a play about funeral baked meats coldly furnishing forth the marriage tables, and a flush of intimate distaste passed through him. The prince's complaint was valid, even if his antics were childish. Lewis's mother, Lucy, had waited all of six months. Her relatives, the Meriwethers, hastened to say that haste was both called for and customary, adducing the practical needs of the landowning widow. In other words: Thrift, thrift, Horatio! If marriage was thrift under another name, Lewis thought he could be thriftier on his own. Certainly the baser needs were more economical outside matrimony. The negro giantess into whose presence he'd been squired at the shrinking age of sixteen required only a quart of whiskey to make her glad. Lucy Meriwether Lewis Marks and her sisters always said afterward that William Lewis on his deathbed had made her promise to remarry. Perhaps that was true. Or perhaps the women had prognosticated it from the steam off the man's sputum.

Lucy Marks was a formidable woman, everyone agreed, and Lewis would be the last to argue. She shot as well as he did, was a better botanizer, and possessed more book learning. She could run a plantation at greater profit than any of her husbands or sons. When displeased, she had a way of looking through you that made you doubt your own existence. She could make you want to please her to a degree that made you displeased with yourself. Lewis from early on took the Indian's way out, and went hunting. The Lewis plantation, Locust Hill, lay along Ivy Creek, seven miles west of Charlottesville, in the first abrupt hills of the Virginia piedmont, at the edge of arable land (Lewis's uncle Nicholas held it lay just beyond it); within half an hour's march were wooded slopes that ax and plow would never touch. By the age of nine, Lewis knew the ravines well enough to negotiate them by starlight, and if he had been permitted to do as he pleased, he would have lived as nocturnal as the owl, coming out of the woods only to drop game on his mother's table. He had new terrain to learn when John Marks decided to try his hand at farming in Georgia, and brought along his family. A few Meriwether uncles and cousins went as well. The colony was on the Broad River, in open country of white oak, chestnut, and pine. Lewis disliked the climate, but the hunting was good, and the local Indians livened things up, as they hadn't yet agreed to give up the land. Still, this was a Marks and a Meriwether venture, and he was a Lewis. Locust Hill was waiting for him.

It was his mother's respect for books that opened the way back. There were no good tutors in Georgia, so at thirteen Lewis returned to Virginia, where his uncle engaged him one. To Lewis's surprise, he found he liked learning: Thucydides, Plutarch; Shakespeare, Milton; grammar, mathematics. There was something about memorizing a datum or a Latin declension that increased his precarious sense of mastery over the world. (Whereas farming accomplished the opposite.) Meanwhile, his mother was punishing him for his escape north by not writing to him, even when, in his adolescent loneliness, he fairly begged.

His punishment back was: he got good and used to it.

When John Marks succumbed to the logic of his appointed role and left Lucy Marks a widow again, she wrote to Lewis's older sister, Jane, that she wished to return to Locust Hill. She told Jane she was depending on Lewis to come down and organize the move of her and her household. By then, Lewis was seventeen. Just two months previously, he'd written to his mother of his contentment with his schooling, and his plans for two more years. *Every civility is here paid to me, and leaves me without any reason to regret the loss of a home of nearer connections.* If he brought her back with the three children— his younger brother Reuben, plus Marks's two whelps—he would have to give up his studies to assume the care of the family, which did not suit him at all. He wrote to her regarding her proposed disruption of his life, *I will with a great deal of cheerfulness do it, but it will be out of my power sooner than eighteen months or two years.*

The only thing out of his power was a prayer of thwarting his mother's will. She made it known to her brother Jack. Uncle Jack wrote letters to Jane. Jane dinned her mother's voice into Lewis's ears. It was all in the feminine vocabulary of anxiety, weakness, fears; but what it was, was commands. What it was, behind the tear-bright eye, was the glint of steel. Lewis would not bear it; he would not prolong his agony, when the end was foregone. Six months after his expression of token resistance, he wrote his mother blandly that he had happened to learn from Jane that she was anxious to return. *This together with my sister's impatience to see you has induced me to quit school and prepare for setting out immediately.* His education was over.

He brought his mother back and became a farmer. Now it was his turn to be the paper proprietor of a plantation while Lucy Meriwether Lewis Marks mostly ran it. They had two thousand recalcitrant acres. They had twenty-four slaves, who did the work of ten boys, and whom you could not dismiss for gross incompetence, as you could hired hands. They had cattle that stepped on their own udders and died of the infections, sheep that drowned in a foot of water, turkeys so brainless Lewis wanted to ride them down on a charger himself, tobacco that killed the land, wheat that wouldn't grow in Eden, Hessian flies that would flourish in hell, plows and axles and tools that broke when you looked at them, and weather that broke you whether you looked at it or not. If those who labored in the earth were the chosen people of God, as it pleased his neighbor Mr. Jefferson to say, they had long ago transgressed some minor clause in the covenant, and were still paying for it.

Lewis labored for two and a half years, continually buying more wilderness as the slaves misfarmed and the tobacco killed what he already had, and he felt most of the time like Sisyphus with both hands on the boulder and a terrible itch. It would not be quite accurate to say he hated every minute. He hunted when he could. He reveled in the occasional company of Mr. J, both as Washington's Secretary of State down for the summer from Philadelphia, and later as a fellow farmer, *I have retired forever from public life, no, wild horses couldn't drag me* . . . Lewis could almost catch his enthusiasm for agricultural inventions: his plow, of course, with its moldboard rounded in what he liked to call a *mathematically perfect curve,* or the essence of dung, a pint of which, it was claimed, would manure an acre. Yes, that was promising, Lewis allowed, and kept to himself the observation that farming was never short of promises.

There was the chase; there was cardplaying. And there was botanizing. His mother could still teach him a vast deal about plants, and he listened for his own good, and struggled against gratitude, and lost. But he was damned if she was going to bury him, as she had buried William Lewis and John Marks. She would bury everybody, she would still be on her feet to greet Gabriel when he blew his horn, and she would tell him to pipe down, too.

Lewis was saved by his natural enemies. In the summer of 1794, Hamilton and his Federalist cronies had been howling for two years about the nonpayment in the frontier counties of the whiskey excise. The law was a dead letter everywhere but in western Pennsylvania, where the national government insisted on pressing the issue. In July, a rabble converged on the mansion of the government's tax man in Pittsburgh, and were fired on by his slaves, while the man himself absconded and cowered in a bush. Two weeks later a horde of yeomen and propertyless wretches marched through the town, crying havoc and defiance. In August, President Washington called out the state militias to suppress the revolt.

The debate in Albemarle society was lively. Good Republicanism dictated suspicion of the government's motives in acting so forcefully. Hamilton now had his excuse for a standing army. And Lewis knew from his years in Georgia that the scarcity of coin on the frontier made excise taxes burdensome. But he also knew the class of people on the frontier—the offscourings of more settled areas, they could be counted on to discredit any cause. Mr. J (in camera) said he judged the President's actions excessive. "Would it not be more consistent with Washington's own battlefield rhetoric," he rhetorically inquired, "to regard this rebellion as a salutary expression of that love of liberty that induced the colonies to throw off the British yoke?"

Lewis agreed.

A week later, he volunteered for the Virginia militia and marched off to war.

2

On his arrival in camp in Winchester, in September, Lewis was seized with an unfamiliar elation. A sun-fired leaf shivering orange on a maple fifty feet away had the brazen immediacy of a flag rippling in his hands. The water flowing in the nearby stream seemed distilled. The thought of a still caused him to laugh out loud. God bless the whiskey rebels!

Two regiments had been formed and drilled before Lewis's arrival, and he ardently envied the martial figure the men already cut. Provided at last with his own uniform, he was struck with a heightened sense of his body filling it, as though he were the stuff, and the handsome cloth his skin. Writing his mother, he made no effort to conceal his happiness, and when the first word that came to his mind for the training ground was *school* he wrote it down, adding *if I may term it so,* and left it to her to remember that other school she had forced him to relinquish for her convenience. *We have mountains of beef and oceans of whiskey, and I feel myself able to share it with the heartiest fellow in camp.* That was hardly avoidable, as the heartiest fellow in camp was he! *Remember me to all the girls and tell them that they must give me joy today, as I am to be married to the heaviest musket in the magazine.*

In this state of mind he continued for weeks. His regiment marched to the staging area at Cumberland, where the army was reviewed in the rain by President Washington himself, a large man with mighty Virginia hams who sat his horse like a statue, impervious to the freshet spilling from his hat down his back. This sight, Lewis said to himself, has my father seen: the same rain, the same line of soldiers, the same rock mountain on his steaming Bucephalus. The President returned to Philadelphia, and the march over the mountains began. The rain became continual, the mud diluvian. Braddock's narrow wagon road was frothed into a stew of stones. Yet Lewis found that nothing irked him. He saw a horse do a clog step with its front hooves and fall white-eyed backward into a ravine, its back breaking with a soggy crack on an unlucky rock. As the usual disorders spread, he watched men dodge out of line and dance to get their pants down before the black shit sprayed out their backsides. The boys called it camp coffee. He saw the drafted men, landless homunculi in the fight for the pay, or half-witted substitutes, in shirtsleeves, with bloody bare feet, shivering silently because they hadn't even a tin cup to rattle on their rope belts. They muttered feverishly in the languages of the Irish bogs and Scottish caves they were born in, unintelligible even to each other. He saw one blue-faced wretch panting by the side of the column, up to his neck in a bath of mud that was warmer than the air, until a lieutenant stepped on his forehead and pressed him open-mouthed under. He saw a drunken fool aim at a squirrel, then lose it in the trees, jam his pistol into his belt to climb over a log, and shoot himself, his breeches bursting open, the ruined leg kicking so that he tumbled over the log and landed face-up, speechless, the end of his tongue like a leech between his lips, half bitten off. In the two hours before each dawn, Lewis heard the leaf-whisper of deserters bleeding into the woods, and witnessed before most breakfasts the lashings administered to those caught. The food gave out, and men stole chickens and were whipped for it, and broke down fences for firewood and were whipped for that, but the whiskey kept up, and there was singing and shooting and tales around the fire. It all possessed a fierce gleam.

As the army approached Pittsburgh, it became obvious that no opposing army would meet it, not even a ragtag crew of farmers with pitchforks and matchlocks. Retributory zeal was directed instead at the liberty poles, or *whiskey poles,* as the soldiers dubbed them, since it was an outrage to associate them with the poles of their fathers' day. Some were so solidly built that destroying them made for a jolly joint effort. Lewis and some others took to going far afield in search of poles to knock down, and when they found 'em they swarmed 'em. They made a lot of noise, hoping for a challenge from the local folk, but got none.

In mid-November, when the army began its march home, Lewis stayed behind. He had been made an ensign in the militia, and he signed on for six months with the regiment charged with patrolling western Pennsylvania. He hadn't considered for a moment any alternative to staying in uniform, but now he had to explain his decision to his mother. *I am quite delighted with a soldier's life,* he wrote her, but knew that was neither here nor there. His role in her theater was the Planter, so he spoke his lines. When his enlistment was over in the spring, he wrote, he would be well positioned to head down the Ohio River to Kentucky to buy more land. He would also pay the taxes on warrant land his mother had inherited when John Marks had died. Most of his fellow officers seemed to consider patrolling primarily an opportunity to scout land for themselves, so his reasoning made sense. President Washington owned half the Ohio Valley.

By December, the weather was bad. Lewis had started his men building winter huts on the Monangahela, fifteen miles above Pittsburgh, but most of the men were still crowded eight to a tent, boots sticking out into the sleet all night, foot rot and fever setting in; the first cases of scurvy. Supplies came in rotten, or half purloined. Requisitioning from the locals had become impossible; the farmers had hidden everything. Even the whiskey was running low. One day, when Lewis buried a soldier and came down himself with a touch of the flux, he looked up from his damp squat by a tree and saw the gleam come off the world. It went that quickly. The moment it was gone, he doubted he had ever seen it.

Now it was just winter and work. He had begun to apprehend what a bunch of half-formed savages these westerners were. He met shuffling, doddering young men who had supported the rebellion because they had believed, because they still believed, that the excise tax was not only on whiskey, it was on all grain; no, it was on all agricultural production; no, it was on their own children too, fifteen cents for every boy, ten cents a girl. They spun out this rigmarole and believed it as they said it, as though they were hearing voices in their heads. They drank whiskey about as much as most men, but it knocked them flat. They lay in field ruts and froze in the night, or chopped fingers off cutting wood. On Sundays, when the men got together for fights, the most lauded feat was to gouge the other fellow's eye out, a practice that had been drummed out of Albemarle County in Lewis's father's day. In went the thumb, the attacker's elbow working like an auger, out popped the eye onto the cheek, and up went the crowd's roar, the backslapping. Lewis marveled that an army had been dispatched to deal with these people. What they needed was missionaries.

On a cold Christmas Eve, Lewis was alone in the hut he usually shared with three other officers. He could hear music and dancing in another hut nearby, but had no desire to join. Instead, he wrote to his mother, and complained weakly about the weather and the sickness and the incessant hut-building. *I can say little more than that I am here, and with propriety can vouch my being a more confined overseer than when at Ivy Creek.* He couldn't put it much stronger than that.

It was a mistake, of course. His mother saw her opening. This time she enlisted his younger brother, Reuben. A letter came in his handwriting, her voice: unease; a mother's concern; when would the prodigal come home? Lewis put off answering until April, when the spring sun had begun to burn off his fog; his letter helped him burn off a little more. He turned her tactics against her. She had fed Reuben the language of maternal anxiety, and he answered her as though that were really the issue: *I can assure you I shall not undertake any enterprise more dangerous than being on Ivy Creek.* (Sadly, this was likely accurate, though logically vulnerable.) As for his brother: *Encourage Reuben to be industrious and be attentive to business.* That is, his own damned business; which was (by the way) to learn enough at his studies so that by the end of the year he could replace Lewis as the happy farmer of Locust Hill. Lewis referred once more to the Kentucky lands. He would be discharged in mid-May, a matter of weeks. He would set off immediately to join the horde boating down the Ohio and crying *Eureka* at every bend. Both of his mother's boys, he thus implied, would be doing her bidding: Reuben working the land she already had, and Meriwether buying more, so that eventually they could have as many acres and squatters and lawsuits as George Washington. In his now irreverent mood, he signed off with a joke: *Remember me to all the girls, and tell them that I shall bring an insurgent girl to see them next fall bearing the title of Mrs. Lewis.* Let Mrs. Marks wonder about that! He pictured himself and the lucky homuncula riding together up to Locust Hill, the fleas hopping between them.

What really happened was, three weeks later he married the standing army. He enlisted as an ensign, and was posted to the Second Sub-Legion, under General Anthony Wayne. Therefore Lewis would, as promised, head down the Ohio; but alas, not to look for land. Now perhaps it was true, in a niggling, legal sense, that this was what he had intended all along. But was it his fault if his own letter had temporarily persuaded him otherwise? Or better to put it this way: he acknowledged what he owed his mother equally with what he was determined to have, and since she was a deserving woman, surely it would all come right in the end.

It took Lewis three more weeks to sit down and write the letter that could not be squared. In the meantime another missive arrived from Reuben. Lewis was irritated by the continued absence of direct communication from her, and doubly so by her refusal to accept the Kentucky lands as perfectly reasonable grounds for staying away. *So violently opposed is my governing passion for rambling to the wishes of all my friends that I am led intentionally to err and then have vanity enough to hope for forgiveness. I do not know how to account for this Quixotic disposition of mine in any other manner or its being effected by any other cause than that of having inherited it in right of the Meriwether family and it therefore more immediately calls on your charity to forgive those errors into which it may at any time lead me.* His mother's wandering eye had led her to a wandering man, and he and she had wandered on down to Georgia. Lewis supposed Georgia lands somehow counted, whereas Kentucky lands did not. Second husbands were obeyed, whereas first sons, even if customs of primogeniture called them proprietors, were mere sons.

He posted the letter and headed down the Ohio, making his best effort (which was really rather good) to forget it.

3

Lewis had high hopes for the army. He had not yet fired a shot at a single two-legged creature, nor been subjected to fire. He longed to hear the sound General Washington had famously called *charming,* the whistle of a bullet past his ear. Fallen comrades, rushing forward through a melee, surprising the enemy, saving a friend—all this had been denied him in the Virginia militia. For four years, the United States Army had been fighting the Indians of the Ohio territory. It had lost two major campaigns; the Indians had been emboldened; surely the fighting would continue for years.

At about the time Lewis was enlisting for the Whiskey Rebellion, General Anthony Wayne did rout an Indian force at the Battle of Fallen Timbers, on the Maumee River. However (Lewis reasoned), a single defeat, with the deaths of a mere few dozen of their warriors, could not so demoralize the Indians as to induce them to give up most of Ohio. Yet that is what they did, and Lewis arrived at Wayne's headquarters at Fort Greenville just in time to see them do it.

It was August. The heat was oppressive, the smell off the marshes a carrion reek. Lewis stood on the drilling ground outside the palisade, his once-proud Philadelphia-made epaulet a wilted flower on his left shoulder, and watched the chiefs of the confederation parade from their encampments in their rude pomp, with their subchiefs and demi-semi-chiefs and naked-bubbied women and suckling babes and feral children and snickering dogs slinking after them. They gathered under the marquee for the signing of the peace treaty: Ottawas, Miamis, Shawnees, Delawares. The men were veritable peacocks, in beaded buckskins and turbans and fluttering flaglets, their faces painted each in a different fashion: birds on foreheads, arrows on cheeks, extra eyes, spirals, chevrons. Most had shaved their hair on the sides, leaving a mane or ruff down the middle that stood up glistening with bear grease and twinkling with mica, chips of seashells, feathers, metal. Lewis saw in one brave's locks a score of hawk bells, clustered like foxglove; in another's, a half-dozen penny-nails and a brass key.

He could not decide whether the braves looked magnificent or ridiculous. They were creatures of impressive physique and bearing, and yet—or rather, because of that—he was disgusted with them. What were they doing here, suing for peace with the gouty, cautious Wayne? Could this frail bark of a fort, this nutshell of pointed sticks and callow recruits in their own wilderness, so awe them? Why did they not cut the supply lines, disperse, harry, exploit their knowledge of the terrain? All that Lewis had been told by hearths and campfires, with shadow-pointing fingers and eyes aglint to frighten the children, all that had been breathed to him as a lad of the cunning and endurance of the aboriginal warrior—all that, and yet here they were, their warpaint, their tomahawks, fusils, and stone clubs for show only. The analogy to birds, then, was apt. They strutted under the eyes of the plainer womenfolk, their thoughts more on wives than war.

Later, Lewis would look back and feel shame. At twenty-one, he should have had himself better in hand. But his disappointment was acute. An ensign in the United States Legion (as the Secretary of War had grandly dubbed it, casting the Indians as Gauls, Lewis supposed) with an unblooded saber at his belt, he spent his days drilling men, barking at sleepy sentries, convoying supplies across tracts of infuriating sylvan serenity, feeding Indians that showed up begging at the gates, and even grazing livestock out in the abandoned, sun-stilled Indian fields, a shepherd with a U.S. musket for a crook. Legionnaire Lewis had come out expecting to be surrounded, besieged. Perhaps (but he would credit this only later), robbed of his Indians, he fell into feeling besieged by Federalists.

Not that he was not, in fact, surrounded. The U.S. Army was a Federalist scheme to the core, and it would have been surprising if Republican officers had been less rare than hens' teeth. Lewis's messmates were sons of Philadelphia lawyers, New Haven merchants, Quincy ship captains; they no doubt dreamed of Washington on a throne with orb and scepter. Yet Lewis had thought he was adept at swallowing bile; he even knew that his predisposition to biliousness was a fault. Still, he entered into political arguments with his fellow officers. He championed France, and heaped contumely on Jay's treaty with England. A Lieutenant Eliott, a Boston tea scion, better educated than Lewis, with rhetoric enough at his command to make up for deficiency of reason, on more than one occasion overwhelmed Lewis's arguments with specious sophistries, to the applause of his coterie. On a black September day, Lewis, befuddled with drink, burst into Eliott's quarters and (according to witnesses) called him an ass and an onanist and a knot-headed nob. Other officers were present, deepening Lewis's humiliation when he was shown the door. Some minutes later, Lewis sent the puffed-up pup a challenge.

Once more, he was thwarted in his desire to get shot at. Perhaps when he had written to his mother that he would be in no more danger in uniform than at home, God had cursed him for the lie by making it true. Lieutenant Eliott, pusillanimous poltroon as he turned out to be, instead of taking up the challenge like a Virginia gentleman, charged Lewis with violating the Second

Article of War (a trifling dead letter prohibiting duels), and Lewis found himself in front of a court-martial. Thankfully, General Wayne, sitting in judgment, was of Lewis's opinion that it was a damned waste of his time to resolve his officers' disputes in this laborious fashion when a single morning's hour in a secluded spot would do it for him, so he found Lewis not guilty, and appended to the record the acid comment that this was the first trial of such a nature he had been forced to convene, and he fondly hoped it would be the last. Eliott lost, as well, in the eyes of his huzzah gallery, who, while not a whit approving Lewis's politics, applauded the ensign's pluck. That, however, was small satisfaction. Lewis knew he had dishonored himself. If previously he had thought it unfair he had never been tested in battle, now he saw that it was unjust. A sinner, he stood in need of a refiner's fire.

At this low ebb, he was transferred from the Second to the Fourth Sub-Legion. His new posting was to a Chosen Rifle Company, and here, over the course of the winter of '95–'96, he edged away from despair. When spring arrived, he even felt that it mirrored a budding, as it were, in his spirit. Partly, this relief was the familiar consequence of riding the storm head down until self-loathing grew tedious. But it was also due to a newfound acquaintance—or more accurately, what Lewis might call, with pride and no small amount of gratitude, a friend: the commander of the rifle company, Lieutenant William Clark.

Clark was another Virginian, and a Republican. His family had lived for a time, years ago, in Lewis's Albemarle County, but had moved east after Braddock's defeat in 1755. Clark had grown up in Caroline County, on the Rappahannock. In 1784, when he was fourteen (Lewis would have been ten, rambling in Georgia), his parents moved the family to Louisville, Kentucky, at the falls of the Ohio River. Clark's life had points in common with Lewis's own. He, too, had missed the War of Independence, but more narrowly, being eleven when the guns sounded at Yorktown, and thirteen when the peace was signed. He was the youngest son in the family, the ninth of ten children, and all five of his brothers had fought in the glorious cause. His second-eldest brother was the famous General George Rogers Clark, the savior of the northwest, eighteen years his senior. Thus Clark, like Lewis, walked in the shadows of giants. His shadows were longer, it might be judged, and Lewis judged also that Clark contended with them more manfully than Lewis did his own. Clark had experienced some of the fighting life that Lewis had so painfully missed—he had marched with both St. Clair and Wayne against the savages—but in the winter in which Lewis met him, he had his own reasons to be at low ebb. He was ill with intermittent fever, and a disorder afflicting his stomach and bowels; and his family was importuning him to resign his lieutenant's commission and return home to rescue the affairs of his brother George.

One evening, Clark explained it in a calm enough voice to the shocked Lewis. His brother was a hero, yes, the only revolutionary general who had never been defeated, the "Hannibal of the West," and yes, he had been given a standing ovation by the Continental Congress, and Benjamin Franklin had said, *Young man, you have given an empire to the Republic,* and Lafayette had ranked him alone with George Washington. But the state of Virginia had refused to honor his wartime expenses, because they had been incurred in the defense of territory that no longer belonged to Virginia, viz., Kentucky, and the national government would not assume the debt without the original vouchers, and the state commissioners in Richmond had lost the lot. George Rogers Clark had his hero's reward: his scars, his memories, his bills.

A bare six months after they had met, Clark did what Lewis could not find in himself to do. He gave up the army to serve his family. He returned to something far worse than the life of a planter—that of an itinerant haggler with creditors. Lewis could not contemplate the humiliation of it without horror, but Clark, on the day he left, was his stoical self. He was out of uniform, no longer Lewis's commanding officer, but the younger man saluted him for a last time as he rode out of the fort, his modest baggage on a single packhorse, and Clark returned the heartfelt gesture with a wry civilian's touch to the side of his hat, urged his horse across the open ground, and disappeared among the trees.

In the five years he remained in the army, Lewis took Clark's stoicism as his inspiration. He volunteered for as much wandering as came his way, and some of it was fine. Once, he got thoroughly lost delivering dispatches from Pittsburgh to Detroit and was starving when he stumbled on an old Indian cache of rotting bear meat. He devoured it, and in his hunger found the fetid tang *charming,* and thought with an inward smile that it would have laid Clark flat (or rather, Clark would have gone on without touching it) while Lewis merely burped up the vileness and rumbled a bit in his saddle. He took a furlough in November of '96 to return home at last and found his mother more tempered in her demeanor toward him. He did all her bidding for six months, then returned without apology to the army. In March of '99, he was promoted to lieutenant. Then in December 1800, he ordered a new coat made with a silver epaulet on the right shoulder, spent the day with fellows on a grand drunk, and in the morning tossed out of his bed a ripe tart on whom he had never before laid eyes. He was a captain.

He was also the regimental paymaster, an assignment he had requested, because it allowed him to travel to forts spread up and down the Ohio Valley. Unlike most officers, he never traveled with a slave, but with a hired freedman, whom he could treat like a proper, professional servant, rather than a clinging family appendage. He lived on his horse and slept in his tent. He observed the wenching and the drunkenness and the shady dealing by the officers in the forts of the quiescent frontier and rode out the gates in the morning, putting it behind him like the dust off his feet. He was contented enough. But he never regained that initial euphoria, when he had marched in the rain across the mountains of Pennsylvania, when he and his companions, all in a pack, had swarmed the whiskey poles and brought them crashing to the ground. In his long days on the trails, at night alone by the fire, those blissful memories recurred.

Those, and one other. A trifling occurrence, in the dark winter of '95, when he was still in the depths of unhappiness; but unaccountably, it had stayed with him:

Late evening in Clark's hut, Clark speaking of his brother's latest troubles. Stopping in mid-sentence, he walks out of the hut to retch in the bushes. His pale face reappears at the jamb. His red hair is a dull flame feeding off the waxy skin. Lewis exclaims, "My dear fellow, are you all right?"

4

"The Spanish may try to stop you, an unworthy suspicion had they not denied you a passport, and their minister spoken of 'certain umbrage' at your expedition, if I remember the phrase aright, but it is not, as you know, in that . . . what might I say . . . *senescent* quarter that our greatest concern lies, but with the more enterprising French. If it were not for their reversals in Santo Domingo, the French would have assumed the administration of Louisiana by now, making your prospects that much more precarious. As it is, the present status of Louisiana is, so to speak, hermaphroditic—like her name, now that I think of it, which might as easily have derived from Louise as Louis—or Lewis—my dear Lewis! you can say afterward that you claimed her for yourself!—doubly hermaphroditic, because although France has owned her these past five years, the Spanish still administer her, and yet, as you know, the inhabitants are predominantly French. The white inhabitants, I mean. The Spaniards' anticipation of imminent transfer into French hands will, I trust, benefit you, particularly as you have a French passport. For her part, France fears that if, as is likely, war breaks out again between herself and England, the English will seize Louisiana. Thus, the encouragement of American aspirations in that quarter seems, at the moment, a prudent counterbalance. And the English have given you a passport because the territory is French, and they would dearly love to see America and France come to blows over her. You therefore could be considered to be negotiating a stretch of Spanish rapids between the Scyllan English and Charybdan French, an apt riparian metaphor, ha ha!"

March light through the bluish window glass, making the green baize on the tables glow. Dust motes swirling in the light around Mr. J's gesturing hands. Geraniums on the windowsills. The mockingbird flitting to the President's shoulder and away again to perch on the top rung of a library ladder. Maps spread on the long table, a sextant in a chair, a tomahawk grabbed at some hour or day past as substitute for a missing trowel dribbling crumbs of soil across the notebook it has come to rest on. Lewis takes it in, standing by the table, lately bent over the Arrowsmith map he thought they were discussing, but having just now straightened to attend while Mr. J perambulates in his restless way, pausing to look at the freckles on his hands, touch a book, turn a globe, not really seeing any of these, lost in his words. No, not lost. Rather, navigating by words, directing their current down bifurcating channels to discover whither they carry him. Riparian metaphor, indeed. A river of words. Cul-de-sacs, slackwater. He eddies into them, spins awhile, poles his way out.

"One reads often of our red brethren being exemplars of Rousseau's noble savages, sans law, or of Montaigne's cannibals, or of their society, or lack of one, as a Hobbesian case of universal war, or of their being devils or Satan's spawn, in the Book-bound Puritan view, or of their lacking souls or the white man's intellect, a great deal of nonsense, and yet what appears to me the clearest parallel receives scant attention, I refer to the Iliadic heroes of Homer—" Lewis knows his mentor well enough to divine his course. It was that mention of Scylla and Charybdis that called Homer to mind. "—in both cases a social contract bottomed on reckless bravery and skill in warfare, ostentatious generosity to one's fellows, and developed, one might almost say hypertrophied, rhetorical powers. The loquacity of Homer's warriors may surprise some readers, especially if they take as their paragon our own Washington—who I often thought served his bevy of sculptors so well because he was already marmoreal!—but Washington had conscription, Washington had the lash. In Homer, as in Indian society, compulsion is forbidden. Their lash is the tongue, their prison disapprobation. Diomedes and Ajax, as Pontiac and Powhatan, must lead their men to duty by personal influence and persuasion. Hence eloquence in council forms a consequential foundation in both instances. The point is, Lewis, that the Indians are savage, of course, and must come up to our level if their survival is to be effected, but to move from that premise to the assertion that they are in some manner inherently deficient is as to say Achilles was a weakling, or Odysseus a dullard."

When Mr. J examines his hands, it is as though he hopes to see some alteration since his previous inspection; perhaps his lentigines have arranged themselves into an intelligible pattern, a code or map. Is his disquisition progressing in a satisfactory direction? He touches a thumb to a spot, then drops his hands and continues, either straight on, or crabwise, or abruptly to something new. He has arrived, via a quarter turn, a sidestep, and a moderate amble, back at the long table, where he pulls two maps out from beneath Arrowsmith and points between them to clusters of tribal designations, contradictory from sheet to sheet. "Why so many Indian nations?" he asks (Lewis assumes rhetorically). "Because in a society in which the individual is sovereign, his nation is little more than his family. Reputation accrues by name, which must not be forgotten. Consider the catalogue of the ships in the Iliad: *Say, immortal nine, say what heroes to Troy's destruction came,* and so on." He has shuffled off again, and rolls a ladder aside to search for a book, causing the bird to flit from the top rung to a Chinese vase on the mantelpiece as he plucks down the desired volume and turns back, palming pages. He lapses into the humming with which he fills silence when words fail him. Lewis sees the book is Pope, and wilts a little, not changing his stance nor allowing his shoulders to settle the breadth of a hair, but tapping once or twice lightly the Arrowsmith, perhaps to assure himself it is still there. The President stops, elevates the tome, inhales:

> "To count them all, demands a thousand tongues,
> A throat of brass, and adamantine lungs.
> Daughters of Jove, assist! inspired by you
> The mighty labour dauntless I pursue;
> What crowded armies, from what climes they bring,
> Their names, their numbers, and their chiefs I sing."

He glances up. "It suits, you see? One then could continue:

> "The hardy warriors whom *Ohio* bred,
> Blue Jacket, Pontiac, of something dread, or faces red
> Of Massac and Kaskaskia, muses tell,
> Missouri and Osage, their warriors fell,
> Of Mohawk, Onondaga, Sene*ca,*
> Of Huron, Winnebago, tra la *la*—

"And so on. This would be a worthy task for an American poet, I might pen a few lines myself, perhaps this evening." He sets the book on the table. "Worthy as an epitaph, I suppose. For their time is fleeting. Their names and *numbers,* Homer writes. Numbers, you see, are of the essence, the excellence of individual warriors notwithstanding, and we, Lewis, we *Homo sapiens Europæus* are going to supplant *H.s. Americus* because we outnumber them, not because our society is superior to theirs. Indeed, looked at through the lens of liberty"—the three kinds of society, Lewis prognosticates—"of the three basic kinds of society—that is, European: monarchical, the government of wolves over sheep, the laws an arbitrary tool of autocrats; American: republican, representative, laws equally applied; and Indian: a perfect democracy in which laws are not even necessary—the Indian is much the best, although inconsistent, I concede, with any degree of population. Which . . . which . . . returns me to my point, that these maps"—he sweeps a hand over them—"with their plethora of nations, their Stone Indians and Horse Indians, their Shawanees, Foxes and Sacs, Creeks and Crees, give an impression of plenitude, of multitudes, when in fact, the bare numbers of men, women, and children are exceedingly small. Having almost more names than people, is it to be

wondered at that their names acquire greater bulk than ever the people as-
pired to? Consider your artery to the west: the *Missouri* . . . a word to
quicken the pulse, if I may indulge, of every seeker of the Stony Mountains
and the all-water route across the continent. The rushing, the wide, the who-
knows-how-many-thousand-mile Missouri! What of the people who called
themselves 'Missouri'? What is remembered of them, what left, in feather
scraps and beads? Are they extinct, or does some pitiful remnant remain?
And how many were they in their heyday? Three hundred souls, perhaps. A
single street in Philadelphia houses more. Which is why smallpox is such a
scourge to them. A single epidemic suffices to wipe out a nation. We have discussed the kinepox matter you are to bring."

He pauses. The pause lengthens. He touches the corner of a map; he
curls it up between thumb and forefinger, pinching it, while an expression of
restless dissatisfaction comes into his eyes; a hum begins. Lewis knows: Mr. J
feels himself in an eddy. Some unfruitful turn has been taken. (Lewis blames
Pope.) If the President were at his writing desk, this is the juncture at which
he would strike out the preceding score of sentences and reach for a fresh
sheet of paper. This is why he dislikes speech, for all his ceaseless flow of talk.
The missive, as it were, has already been sent. But the recipient is only Lewis,
and Lewis understands. In a gesture expressive of this understanding, Lewis
has begun pinching with his own finger and thumb an opposite corner of the
map. Or perhaps, like his tapping, it is a mute appeal to return to Arrowsmith.
The Missouri, yes, the rushing, the wide, the so on, and as it happens, sir, a
line on this very sheet we were lately perusing.

Mr. J glances down. He breathes a snatch, it could be a strain of "High-
land Mary." "It is of some importance, Lewis"—his fingers hover, wander
toward Canada—"to ascertain, as far as circumstances allow, the northward
extent of the effluents of the Missouri. The French are not geographically situ-
ated to turn their treaty ownership into a true one through inhabitation of
their own people. Americans are crossing the Mississippi in ever greater
numbers, and the French might as effectively decree that the tide not rise.
Louisiana will be ours, and thus its extent, which by treaty is defined, as you
know, as the watershed of the Missouri, is of no small interest. I think it highly
likely that some of those effluents rise above the Lake of the Woods." Lewis
nods cheerfully. The Lake of the Woods marks the northwest boundary of the
United States according to the Treaty of 1783 with England. But if Louisiana

stretches above it, then the British fur companies in the west are (or will be!) operating illegally on American soil. Lewis and Mr. J are alike in relishing few things so much as the thought of taking territory, or trade, or both (plus honor, and happiness, and the merest possibility of the pursuit thereof) from the British. "And speaking of the north"—Mr. J is still touching the map, but Lewis can tell from the pitch of his voice, a lurch upward on "speaking," that he is veering off again—"remember that it is in those regions that science may yet, through you, my dear Lewis, discover living specimens of the mammoth. Genus?"

"*Mammuthus.*"

"Species?"

Lewis does not answer.

"My apologies. A trick question. The species is not yet named. We have spoken of this before. Do you remember the conundrum at issue?"

"Molars, I believe."

"Exactly. The mammoth remains of Siberia, as well as some of those in America, exhibit smooth, elephantlike molars, while those of the *incognitum,* as we have been calling it, or the *American incognitum,* as the Europeans call it, exhibit knobby molars. It would seem transparent to all but certain European natural philosophers who cannot bear to allow America another colossal animal all her own—perhaps they are still chafing over the bison and the megatherium!—that it is a separate species. It has occurred to me that instead of feebly conceding that the animal is *incognitus* we could boldly name it *Mammuthus incognitus* and quit ourselves of the problem. *Voilà!* The *incognitum* becomes *cognitus.* It is a marvelous creation, isn't it, Linnaeus's system? The most valuable contribution to natural history since Noah put saw to gopher wood. His binomial standard reminds me of terrestrial coordinates, the genus, say, representing latitude, and the species longitude, so that the two of them in conjunction enable you to pinpoint the one precise location, or the one recognized scintilla of Creation, that is here, *this one,* and no other. Alexander! Tch tch!" He turns, reaching into a pocket, and as the mockingbird flies to him, he places a sunflower seed between his teeth, which the bird, lighting on his shoulder, removes and eats. "*Turdus—?*"

"*Polyglottos.*"

"Very good." The bird flutters around his head, chattering, and he bites another seed to repeat the trick, something he often does for his female visitors, because it obviates the need for conversation. "And you could be a Russian writing to me on birch bark, or a Chinaman on rice paper, and if you said *Turdus polyglottos* I would know infallibly to what bird you referred. Although I suppose the Chinaman would use pictures . . . But my point is, you will be able, in your letters to me, to communicate all the known species you encounter in the west without a line of description or the merest scratch of a sketch, simply through two words that are universally recognized—that are themselves, if you will forgive me, polyglots, ha ha." He holds out his arm, elbow crooked upward, and the bird walks over the bridge from his shoulder to his wrist. He then brings his hands together, and as the bird hops from his right to his left, he drops his right to his pocket, then raises both hands, the left to his shoulder to deposit the bird, the right to his teeth to deposit the seed, and as he swivels his head the bird leans forward from the left shoulder and plucks the seed from his teeth as it rounds within reach. It could be a dance, or the gliding movement of an ingenious German clock.

He takes the bird back onto his hand and waves it gently toward its perch, whither it flies. "But to return to *Mammuthus incognitus,* which you and I, Lewis, in the comfort of this library, by this delightful fire, have just added to the roster of the Creator's achievements. It is deemed by most of my colleagues to be extinct, but I cling to my foolish doubts. There is the account of a Mr. Stanley, an Indian captive traded from one tribe to another until at length he was carried over, I quote, 'mountains west of the Missouri' to a 'river running westwardly' and there found bones in great numbers that he took to be those of elephants. The natives of that region informed him that the bones belonged to an animal that still existed in the northern parts of their country. I confess I fail to see why, in the absence of confuting evidence, we should discount the statements of those who, one presumes, are in a position to know what they are talking about. And in any case"—here he sinks into the closest chair, a gesture expressive of a certain weariness born of fending off contrary obstinacy—"I still balk at the very idea of extinction. It seems to me to violate a rule of economy that Nature otherwise observes, and in saying this, I do not naively impute to Nature human qualities, but base my argument on the sovereignty of Reason. You are familiar with Occam's Razor?"

"I have . . . heard the term."

"Good for you! That puts you in admirable company. Now I will induct you into the august circle of those who actually know what it means. Occam's

Razor is not a maxim, so much as a plea. It enjoins the fanciful mind of Man not to introduce assumptions that are not necessary to explain the observed particulars of a phenomenon. For example: the Hessian fly descends on my wheat field, and I subsequently note that my wheat crop has been devastated. It is wise—not necessarily correct, mind you, but given what I know, most *likely* to be correct—to conclude, 'The Hessian fly has destroyed my wheat crop.' It would be a violation of Occam's Razor, on the other hand, to say, 'The Hessian fly must attract malicious fairies, therefore, every time the fly gets near my wheat, the fairies come to consort with the flies, and while they are in the vicinity, they destroy my crop.' Do you follow me?"

"Closely."

"Good. The Economy of Nature, as I term it, amounts to no more than this reasonable Occamism: conditions are such—temperature, rainfall, and so on—in such-and-such a place, as to allow such-and-such a creature to thrive and produce offspring. Now if this is true at one time, why should it not be true at others? My colleagues at the Philosophical Society agree that our friend *M. incognitus* once existed. It should not surprise us that we no longer meet him alive near his bone fields along the Ohio River, just as it does not surprise me that, in three years of daily gazing out this window, I have not once seen a wolf walk by. But wolves still live, and will always live, in those areas undisturbed by man, and the wise man would hypothesize that the mammoth still lives in those vast northerly regions that remain undisturbed by us. And so, dear Lewis, especially as you reach the northern bend of the Missouri"—he pops out of his chair, presenting, as usual, the illusion that the furniture has *thrown* him out, and that his arrival at the table is by way of a landing—"here"—he indicates the villages of the Manders and the Tall Indians—"I remind you to question the natives closely about the mammoth. And I pray, if you happen to see a living specimen, that you not assume, as Monsieur de Buffon insisted on doing until his death, that it is merely a Russian elephant with false teeth."

"I will hail it 'Unknown!,' sir."

Mr. J emits a low, rich chuckle. "You know, the learned, late Monsieur de Buffon preferred to believe that Nature in America was *moins agissante, moins forte,* than it was in Europe, that the red man with his paucity of bodily hair was lacking in vigor, and that the white man in America degenerated. Occam's Razor, Lewis! What warrants his assumptions? It requires a different razor altogether to probe the vehemence with which Mr. Buffon accosted me with his theories in the years I resided in Paris. I will merely observe that I am nearly two meters tall, whereas Mr. Buffon, but for the color of his skin, would not have stood out in a crowd of pygmies." Whereas you, sir, would not stand out in a crowd of these here Tall Indians, on this here *map*, sir. Mr. J looks down. "But we were discussing the map, were we not?"

"I believe so."

"Then by all means, let us return to it. I have been examining more closely—where is Arrowsmith's other map, the earlier one? Ah, yes." He slides the 1795 map partially beneath the 1802 map, so that the two portions showing the far west lie side by side. "Note how in the 1795 map Arrowsmith shows the Stony Mountains—oh, by the way, I had a thought last night about these so-called Tall Indians, who share their villages with the Mandans, or the Montannes, or the Manders. Arrowsmith's map reminded me that they are also called Shoe Indians. We also know from Thompson that those selfsame Indians are called Big Bellies. My thought was this: what if the Shoe Indians are so called because they wear something unusual on their feet? As they are also called Tall Indians and Big Bellies, would it be unreasonable to conjecture that they wear a sort of shoe with an elevated heel, that makes them appear tall at the same time that it causes them to walk with their hips pitched forward? Now this sounds like a European shoe, does it not? And the Mandans, as we both know, are the tribe long rumored to be descendants of the Welsh followers of Medoc. Perhaps, along with the brass trumpets and blue eyes and Welsh cognates we have heard tell of in their possession, they brought along this shoe, and it was adopted by their neighbors, you see?"

"I will inquire into it when I am there."

"And of course, take down a vocabulary. Half an hour's studious inquiry should establish or discredit once and for all the Welsh theory. You will determine, I trust, whether or not *Mandan* is their word for themselves. I am woefully ignorant of the Welsh language, I merely note for your consideration that the Manx people, who live on the Isle of Man, speak a related tongue. Manx, Man, Mandan—you understand. But I digress. As I was saying, note how Arrowsmith treats the Stony Mountains on his 1795 map. He draws a single north-south ridge that terminates on the southern end at approximately forty-six degrees north. Then he writes this legend: 'Three thousand five hundred twenty feet high above the level of their base and according to the Indian account is five ridges in some parts.' Now compare his map of 1802. This time he styles them 'Rocky Mountains'—it is unfortunate no one has thought to dub them the Adamantine Mountains, and thus establish a pleasing alliteration with their sister range, the Appalachians—but to return to Arrowsmith—here is the crux—note that the mountain chain now continues below forty-six degrees, and at around forty-four degrees, Arrowsmith writes, 'Hereabout the mountains divide into several low ridges.' It appears that the five ridges the Indians speak of have been located, at about forty-four degrees. Thus, the *rest* of the range may, in fact, be a single line of peaks, signifying a single portage. Mackenzie tells us that he accomplished a portage of half a day at a mere three thousand feet at around fifty-six degrees north latitude from the Peace River to his Tacoutche-tesse river, which is assuredly a northern branch of the Columbia. So you see spread out before you, Lewis, my very good reasons for believing that a northwest water passage through the continent does exist."

He collapses again into a chair, throwing his right leg languidly over the arm, settling his back against the opposite corner, and hitching his right shoulder up nearly to his ear. He looks like a dropped marionette. "The Spanish minister Yrujo writes that it has by now become clear that no northwest passage can exist. As regards a sea passage, of course, your man Cook demonstrated that. But apropos a freshwater route, the minister's opinion could be termed political, as his government, of course, does not want us to go looking for one. But he is not alone. The faint-hearted are growing discouraged, Lewis. The Missouri is our last hope." His slippered right foot is bobbing in the sunlight, as though keeping time to some ghostly air. "I should say, *you* are our last hope. But just as I trust you absolutely—dear boy, don't scowl, I speak only what is in my mind—I trust, as well, Reason, and William of Occam. Yes, we are back to his razor, or to an as yet unnamed corollary, according to which, in the absence of contrary evidence, it is wise to assume symmetrical patterns in Nature. Why? Because equal forces shape equal events. I propose, for your consideration, the North American continent. On either coast, a relatively narrow plain rises toward north-south mountain ranges, and in the approximate middle of the continent a great river runs north-south. Ascending that river, we find its two largest effluents entering at roughly the same latitude, the Ohio flowing from out of the northeast, the Missouri from the northwest. Given this preponderance of evidence for a quite reasonable symmetry, surely it is wisest to assume that the Missouri, like the Ohio, heads in mountains approximately the height of the Appalachians, and that its various headwaters interpenetrate with those of the Columbia, as the Monangahela interpenetrates with the Potomac. Mr. Yrujo opines that if the northwest passage existed, it would have been discovered by now, to which I can only reply, after I have mastered my speechlessness, that his case is premature as long as the single most promising route of the interior has not been explored."

He is out of his chair again, grasping Lewis's shoulder in his emotion before backing up a step and crossing his arms. "That is your route, Lewis. On your return, *you* will give us the answer, yes or no. Like a Roman emperor above the gladiatorial combat, *you* will stand before us all, and turn your thumb up or down, and our hopes will live or die." He touches Lewis's shoulder again, at the same moment turning away and walking toward the west fireplace, his hands now gripping each other behind his back. The fire has been replenished in the magical way of Mr. J's households, one of his servants having gained silent entry via some secret door, and disappeared again by the same route. Gazing at the fire, he says, "I am a philosopher, Lewis. I care only for the truth. If there is no passage, you will determine that, and you will tell me. But if there is a passage"—he turns, no doubt conscious of the dramatic effect, the crackle of flames behind him—"then a prospect lies open before us that beggars description. With the Columbia and the ports of the Orient at one end, and the Mississippi, the Gulf, and our eastern mercantile centers at the other, we can capture the fur trade from the British, bind our red brothers to us, teach them the ways of industry and peace, and so tame the wilderness and make it our own. If Monsieur de Buffon is wrong, and he is, then the red man is our equal, as surely as *M. incognitus* is as terrible as the Siberian mammoth. Consider how white children, captivated by Indians, grow to be indistinguishable from their captors, or how Christianized Indians become industrious farmers and spinners, and even in some cases, I have heard, exhibit a lightening of their complexions. These are proofs of a permeability between the two races that would be inconceivable between, say, black and white. If the Indians are not to be exterminated, this is where their future lies: in instruction in the arts of civilization, in the adoption of Indian children, and in intermarriage, until we become one people, from sea to sea.

"But it will take some little time. You are to inquire everywhere in

Louisiana as to lands which the natives do not need, where we may resettle the tribes that must be removed from this side of the Mississippi, to make way for white settlement. At the same time, inquire among the white inhabitants of Louisiana as to what might induce them to remove themselves to the eastern side of the Mississippi. I envision for all of the lands west of that river a vast reserve for the Indians, free of whites, for perhaps a score of years—a precious interval during which, through trade, we can gradually make the Indians dependent on our goodwill. Trade will cultivate among them a desire for the necessaries that we alone can supply, and their increasing pursuit of those necessaries, which they will purchase with peltries, will accomplish the general destruction of their wild game, which in turn will leave them no choice but to abandon hunting, and become farmers. At the same time, trade will cause the chiefs among them to run into debt, and when those debts grow beyond what they can pay, they will become willing to settle them by ceding us land. At that point, as you may readily perceive, the coincidence of our interests will be complete. Having abandoned hunting, and thus no longer in need of the extensive tracts of land which hunting requires, they will be willing, nay eager, to exchange land, which they have to spare and we want, with necessaries, which we have to spare and they want. This is another kind of symmetry, Lewis, that a wise Creator has woven into the fabric of Nature for the happiness of man. The mutual dependencies of men interpenetrate like the headwaters of rivers, from which goods flow to all, or like two hands mingling fingers in fellowship." He demonstrates, interleaving right fingers with left, and shaking, as it were, his own hand.

He pauses. Not restlessly, as before, but with a smile and a rock back on his heels. He has reached a position that pleases him, a headwater (to borrow his metaphor) whence he gazes down, contemplating the river course that brought him here. Those phrases that, like compass headings, pointed him in the right direction will find their way into his writings. His speech is his workshop, in which he tinkers, returning again and again to locate the precise angle of penetration, the exact tension on the spring. Lewis's job is to listen, and not to disagree, since Mr. J will disagree with himself. Lewis once wondered whether his mere presence in the President's House was the thing desired, and agonized that his conversation was insufficiently bright. But he has latterly concluded that his *mere* presence is indeed the thing. Mr. J needs to speak his ideas aloud in order to judge how they sound, and thus he requires an auditor, because to talk at length in solitude would strike his servants (and perhaps himself, as well) as an alarming development.

"It is almost four, Lewis. We must dress for dinner. I have a keyword cipher for you to resolve, for practice. Some communications to me during your expedition will no doubt need to be in code. Bring it to dinner, we can discuss it over that pheasant you bagged this morning. By the way, Étienne tells me your sight must be going. His boy had to pick a deal of shot out of the bird's breast!"

"It flew over my shoulder—I lost my balance—clumsy—"

"My dear boy, I am merely making light. Alexander! Tch tch!"

Closing the door on the man and his mockingbird, Lewis feels a familiar, bruised exhaustion. He walks the halls wide enough for a carriage-and-four, hastens away from a chattering group of sightseers emerging from the north entry hall, gains his closet, sits at his desk. His Excellency and his auditor. The giant and the pygmy. Ah, well.

He must tackle the cipher. Following Mr. J's explanatory note, he constructs a 26×26 grid and writes in the alphabet, staggering it by one letter from column to column. The keyword is written end to end above the message to be encoded, pairing letter to letter. In Mr. J's example, the keyword is *antipodes,* and the text is *The man whose mind on virtue bent.* Each letter pair designates a row and a column in the grid, which one follows to their point of intersection to find the letter of the code. Decoding is a simple matter of reversing the process, using the same key. Thus, *The man whose mind on virtue bent* becomes *Uvy vqc amhts grds ss ojfndu qism,* which prompts Lewis to the philosophic reflection that too much thinking about virtue will drive a man insane.

Now for his practice: the keyword is *artichokes,* and Mr. J has run the coded words together to make it more difficult for an interceptor to break the code by divining words from their lengths: *jsgjwbwpmxbviowptxnltgoaliaw-bxmduwgbwpngeauwvadqfkgjcnqlaj*

Lewis sets to work. He begins to feel a rare swell of uncomplicated contentment as the letters slowly appear: *i . . . a . . . m . . .* This simple grid, by which Lewis transforms nonsense into sense, recalls what Mr. J said about Linnaeus's binomial standard, and the intersecting lines of latitude and longitude: the ruled lines, through which the unruly world is made known. Marvelous!

Antipodes and artichokes—Jerusalem artichokes are the President's favorite winter crop for cattle. We will tame the wilderness, he said; we will raise cattle from sea to sea; we will plant artichokes to the very antipodes! Lewis decodes the final letters, and rewrites the string, inserting spaces at the correct points:

I am at the head of the Missouri. All well, and the Indians so far friendly.

5

8 tents, 1 common tent, 15 three-point blankets, 15 watch coats, 15 woolen overalls, 30 pairs stockings, 45 flannel shirts, 193 pounds portable soup, 30 gallons rectified spirit, 6 brass kettles, 2 dozen iron spoons, 25 felling axes, 9 chisels, 6 augers, 4 tin trumpets, 6 brass inkstands, 100 quills . . .

There was too much of everything in life except time. Angelic, immaterial time absconded in proportion as material things multiplied and threatened to bury a man under his brute needs. It was mid-June in Washington City, and Lewis was supposed to be halfway down the Ohio by now, but he would not leave tomorrow, nor next week, and the keelboat he had thought would be built for him in Nashville had turned out to be an impossibility, so he would have to supervise the construction of a boat in Pittsburgh, and the thought of having to urge on in every way short of a sound thrashing a no doubt perpetually drunk and probably one-eyed boatbuilder in that capital of cretinism made him bone-weary. Meanwhile his provision lists grew extra limbs, his contingency plans propagated lustily. He had hoped to pass the first winter a thousand miles up the Missouri, then five hundred, then two hundred, and now he wondered in his worst moments if he would spend Christmas in sight of St. Louis.

1 collapsible iron-frame boat, 15 rifles, 15 powder horns, 15 gun slings, 30 brushes, 500 rifle flints, 125 musket flints, 176 pounds gunpowder, 52 lead canisters . . . The canisters weighed eight pounds apiece, and each held the amount of gunpowder sufficient to the balls obtained when the canister was melted down. This had been Lewis's idea, and he was proud of it. Symmetry, sir! That had been in March, when he was having the rifles made at the U.S. armory at Harpers Ferry. The collapsible iron-frame boat was a joint inspiration of his and the President's, a light, portable vessel for the shallow upper reaches of the Missouri and Columbia. Lewis's design involved two rounded sections for the stem and stern, plus a midsection (whose cross-sectional curve described a catenary, viz., the curve formed by a chain hanging between two posts, which struck Lewis, who had never before built a boat, as perfectly mathematical, verily *designed* by gravity, hence balanced, hence seaworthy). But unfortunately he was forced to tinker with the details, until the planned week at Harpers Ferry stretched into a month.

I have no doubt you have used every possible exertion to get off, Mr. J wrote, *and therefore we have only to lament what cannot be helped, as the delay of a month now may lose a year in the end.* Lewis read criticism into that, and chafed. By then, he was in Lancaster, to receive lessons in astronomical observations from Dr. Ellicott. Mr. J had hazarded that Lewis would need four or five days to become adept at the use of sextant and quadrant, but Ellicott had merely looked amused, and said a year would be about right. Nevertheless, he would try to cram what was absolutely necessary into Lewis within ten or twelve days. In the event, seventeen days were spent—only two less than the period it took Mr. J to learn Spanish on his first Atlantic crossing, as he was perhaps overfond of telling his dinner guests—and at the end of it, Lewis was still taking sets of readings which differed from each other, after conversion, by two degrees. "That would amount to 98 miles at 45 degrees latitude," Ellicott said. "It is a happy circumstance you do not have to worry about reefs and lee shores, is it not?" Lewis might have engraved a copper plate with that voice.

He arrived in Philadelphia on the 7th of May and went straight to the mathematician Mr. Patterson, who assured Lewis he had a formula for computing longitude from lunar distances that was, in his words, "extremely easy even for boys and common sailors to use." He then handed Lewis two closely written sheets of piled-up algebraic, trigonometric, and logarithmic contortions that looked like the sort of thing one of Lewis's mystically inclined Masonic brothers might dream up for the calculation of the weight, in Egyptian pounds and Chinese shillings, of King Solomon's Temple. Two weeks in Philadelphia turned into five as he bought provisions for his men, and trade goods for the Indians (*12 pipe tomahawks, 1 dozen ivory combs, 12 dozen pocket looking glasses, 8 dozen burning glasses, 8 ½ lbs. red beads . . .*) and ran various personal errands for the President, such as regulating his watch, paying his wine bills, buying him two pairs of fleecy socks, and searching for a vigogna robe and a tiger-skin saddle cover! (This irked Lewis just the smallest amount, given Mr. J's lament over the delays, which he had expressed in the very same letter that carried these requests.)

Lewis wrote letters to army posts for volunteers, and searched for interpreters, and consulted Wistar on anatomy and Barton on botany and Rush on medicine, and determined, through long afternoons and late at night, when he could not sleep, that Solomon's Temple had the miraculous ability to change its weight at every measurement. Dr. Rush, Lewis decided, had a better grasp of the average mathematical abilities of his fellow man when he avuncularly wrote in his instructions to Lewis that if he (Lewis) counted the beats of a patient's pulse in a *quarter* of a minute, then he should multiply by *four* to obtain the number of beats in a minute.

15 pounds Peruvian bark, ½ pound rhubarb, 4 oz. ipecacuan, 2 oz. gum camphor, ½ pound Turkish opium, 6 pounds glauber salts, 1 oz. tartar emetic, 4 oz. laudanum, 1 clyster syringe, 4 penis syringes, 600 Rush's bilious pills . . . Rush made and sold the pills himself, of calomel and jalap, thus rendering them both emetic and purgative, and felt, indeed, that they were sovereign against everything save, perhaps, bullet wounds and scalpings. "These will scour a man out like a chimney sweep's brush," he said, the metaphor likely a favorite one, as his name could be rendered B. Rush. "You'll have them spouting at both ends. I would recommend not having them in the canoe with you when you physick 'em."

Rush had a long list of queries about the Indians he wanted Lewis to pay particular attention to, such as:

What are their acute diseases?
Is goiter, apoplexy, palsy, epilepsy, madness, venereal disease known among them?
At what age do the women begin and cease to menstruate?
At what age do they marry?
How long do they suckle their children?
What are their vices?
Is suicide common among them, and does it ever issue from love?

Everyone wanted Lewis to provide answers to his own pet questions. Gallatin wanted information on the headwaters of the Rio del Norte. Lincoln wanted Lewis to concentrate on the morals and religion of the Indians (this to gain support from the President's opponents, the theory being that missionary tours were approbated even when they were disasters—often, especially then). The President wanted everything that everyone else wanted, plus Indian vocabularies, plus a vigogna robe and two pairs of fleecy socks.

Given the great diversity of the known Indian languages, it was unlikely Lewis would manage to find an interpreter for all of them, a *Homo polyglottos* who might, as it were, perch on his shoulder and whisper translations in his ear, but he was nonetheless on the lookout for someone who could speak several. During his service as army paymaster he had come to know a young man named John Conner, who lived on White River among the Delawares and spoke their language, along with Shawnee and Chipaway. Lewis had liked him extremely, for his unpretentious demeanor and his manly, frank honesty. As it happened, Conner had written to Lewis in Philadelphia offering his services (rumors of the secret expedition having traveled faster than the newspapers), and Lewis had responded warmly, offering him a place.

It was on the subject of the Indians that Lewis felt least prepared, and there was no renowned man of science in Philadelphia to help him. For a man who had spent five years on the frontier, Lewis had had, he was only too aware, fewer dealings with Indians than was to be desired for his expedition. He knew them as guides (excellent, boastful), guests (boisterous, wearisome, boastful), and beggars (wheedling, shameless, boastful). He had never fought against them, never parleyed with them, never witnessed them in their proud wildness, only in a cowed state. He found it impossible to respect them, yet he knew of Mr. J's respect; he assumed the revelation of the genuine article awaited him out west.

Lewis returned late to Washington City: June 17th, summer already. That was two days ago. A wagon was hauling his 3,500 pounds of brute needs down to Harpers Ferry and over the mountain tracks to Pittsburgh, where the Ohio would be slowing and lowering in the summer heat, and the presumed Cyclops of a boatwright still awaited a few hearty kicks before stirring from his crapulous slumber. Washington was hot and fetid, last needs kept appearing. Mr. J fretted, Lewis was irritable. Twelve men, Lewis had decided weeks before, was too small a party to move his brimming boats, but he could not bring himself to tell this to the President. Mr. J had once planned an expedition for a *single man* to cross Siberia, the Pacific, and the American continent from west to east, determining latitude by means of lines tattooed on his arms (thus acting as a human cross-staff) and inscribing his discoveries on his own skin (learning to write with both hands, Mr. J had explained, so that the right arm need not remain blank). Now *there* was an explorer like Adam, the world mirrored on his symmetrical body.

The War Department had authorized only twelve men, and Lewis knew the President needed to hide the true costs of the expedition from his Federalist enemies until Lewis was beyond their reach, so he assumed he had Mr. J's winking sanction to handle it in the way he had always preferred in such cases, which was to remove himself first, and send the bad news later by letter. He could find the extra provisions in Pittsburgh and St. Louis. Mr. J was sending him off with an unrestricted letter of credit drawing on the Treasury of the United States, and with this miraculous instrument, if Lewis desired and the objects were available, he could buy himself a frigate to sail up the Missouri, and a dozen French balloons to float over the Stony Mountains. So "twelve" men it was. But the need for a second officer had had to be raised. For Lewis, no choice was involved. He wanted Clark.

Oh, for a number of reasons, some less articulable, some more. On the less side, Lewis purely liked the man, and he trusted his rare, pure likes. More definably, he had seen Clark's maps from an intelligence operation he had conducted in Spanish territory before the two men met, and they were far superior to anything Lewis could produce. Also, Clark knew the Indians better than Lewis, not only because he had been among them longer, but (Lewis suspected) because he possessed a natural talent for divining the workings of the savage mind.

The President, of course, already knew the family of George Rogers Clark, and he had met William two years ago, when the younger brother was in Washington on one of his mendicant pilgrimages on behalf of the hero. "As it happens," Mr. J said, "I received a letter some months ago from George R., plumping young William for a post in the Ohio territory, or any other business I might see fit to engage him in. The general adverted rather crudely, I must say, to my certain desire to do him a favor, given his ill treatment, and so on. The treatment I acknowledge as disgraceful, and God knows I have labored like Hercules, all in vain, to correct it, but nonetheless I detect in the man's address the . . . how shall I say? . . . the coarsening that comes with too much devotion to drink."

"William, however," Lewis strove to redirect Mr. J's course, "William has his brother's virtues and, I verily believe, none of his flaws. I say with no false modesty that, regarding those talents relevant to the success of this venture, his are superior to my own."

Mr. J smiled. "My dear Lewis, if he is merely your equal in all things, I assure you that is sufficient."

Alone in his cell, Lewis began his letter:

Washington June 19th 1803

Dear Clark,

Herewith enclosed you will receive the papers belonging to your brother Genl. Clark, which sometime since you requested me to procure and forward to you. . . . .

From the long and uninterrupted friendship and confidence which has subsisted between us—

Curious that it should feel, to Lewis, uninterrupted, since it was, in a way, all interruption, with Clark in Washington perhaps three days out of a hundred. But so it felt.

—I feel no hesitation in making to you the following communication under the fullest impression that it will be held by you inviolably secret until I see you, or you shall hear again from me.

Here followed a lengthy excursus on the proposed tour and its goals, which Lewis, by this point, could write in his sleep.

Thus my friend you have so far as leisure will at this time permit me to give it you, a summary view of the plan, the means and the objects of this expedition. If therefore there is anything under those circumstances, in this enterprise, which would induce you to participate with me in its fatigues, its dangers and its honors, believe me there is no man on earth with whom I should feel equal pleasure in sharing them as with yourself.

This was so true, in a way it contained such an *excess* of truth, that its surplus remedied the slight deficit of truth in the following clause, into which Lewis rushed headlong—

I make this communication to you with the privity of the President, who expresses an anxious wish that you would consent to join me in this enterprise—

Privity, yes. And if the President knew Clark as Lewis did, he would wish it anxiously. Lewis wrote on, warming—

—he has authorized me to say that in the event of your accepting this proposition he will grant you a Captain's commission which of course will entitle you to the pay and emoluments attached to that office . . . ; your situation if joined with me in this mission will in all respects be precisely such as my own.

Clark had been Lewis's superior, in rank and ability. He had not attained his captaincy solely because he had quit the army to aid his family. *My dear Lewis, if he is merely your equal in all things, I assure you that is sufficient.*
he has authorized me to say

Pray write to me—

Two equal commanders on a military expedition, it was fantastic, it went against every particle of military sense. But they were friends.

Should you feel disposed not to attach yourself to this party in an official character, and at the same time feel a disposition to accompany me as a friend any part of the way up the Missouri—

A thirteenth member, listed on the manifest: *Friend.*

—I should be extremely happy in your company, and will furnish you with every aid for your return from any point you might wish it. With sincere and affectionate regard, your friend and Humble Sevt.

Meriwether Lewis

he has authorized me to say
It should have been true. And by God, Lewis would make it true.

First Clark

They called it cleaning out the settlements. They called it destroying the villages.

Sweeping. Rooting out. Teaching a lesson.

They didn't say: We shot women and children. We burned old half-blind men in their wigwams. We ran a hanger through a boy trying to get away up a tree.

William Clark was nineteen when he killed his first Indian. To scalp a man, you cut close around the crown; that was the important part, the proof; a man had only one crown to lose for his country. When you pulled the hair it sounded like a sneeze. Indians sometimes ripped scalps off with their teeth. They looked like ravening wolves. The blood was plentiful but the injury was not severe. A man could easily survive it, if you didn't kill him otherwise.

Shawonies, Dillaways, Mingoes, Maomis. They gobbled like turkeys to lure you into the woods. They crept close at night to hear you talk, to learn your name, then they called you by name come morning from the bushes. They left moccasins on the trail so you'd dismount. They offered the white flag, then brought out tomahawks on a signal.

Clark's impression was, an Indian wanted your scalp at least as much as he wanted you dead. He might get paid for it by the British, who carried on a hair trade to protect their fur one. There was superstition, too, about getting the power of the dead man. Some settlers shaved themselves bald to save their scalps, but the Indians never did. Even when they shaved back and around, they kept a scalplock. This was scorn for the enemy, and an agreement with him, too. Indians had more agreements in warfare than a white man could credit. They had more agreements with their enemies in warfare than they did with their kin in peace.

Clark was fourteen when he came down the Ohio in a flat-bottomed boat, with his boy York and his parents and sisters. Brother George waited at their new home in Louisville. Brothers Jonathan and Edmund would come later. Brother John was already dead from the tender care of the British. Brother Richard had just gone missing in Indian country. In the spring flood, you saw two or three boats along every reach, all going the same direction. Kentucky was a paradise. People said: Kentucky soil was so rich, if you sowed it and tended it, you'd get twenty bushels of corn an acre. Sowed but untended, you'd get ten bushels. If you didn't either sow it or tend it, you'd get seven bushels.

Clark was sixteen when he went out for the first time to fight Indians. That was up the Wabash River, with his brother George commanding. But the expedition was a failure. It was George's last campaign. He was thirty-four. Afterward they said he drank too much, but that was small men's lies. The drink came later.

When Clark had to mention his brother, he would say: he had his scars, his memories, his bills. For dignity's sake, he said it without bitterness. But his thoughts were bitter. And in his thoughts there was another word he never said: his scars, his memories, his bills, his bottle. George bathed in that fountain every day, and every day he aged a week.

George had killed too many Indians to count, he always said, but he remembered his first, and so did his little brother. William shot the man out of a tree. The ease of the scalp parting, the bloody sneeze: he remembered. Also the squaw maybe thirteen that jumped in a creek, and the shot that startled Clark, that broke her spine. They destroyed three villages, burned the fields. Captured twenty-two squaws and children. The others had nothing to return to but ashes and starvation. That was Colonel Hardin's campaign, August 1789. Later, Hardin was sent as a peace commissioner to the Dillaways and they butchered him.

The general idea was to spare squaws and children; trade them for white prisoners or hold them hostage for their braves' good behavior. Whereas they killed the men. That was called Indian Warfare. But it was unpredictable. Sometimes they caught friends. That was something people who didn't fight Indians didn't know: that they knew a lot of these braves. Indians made friends across lines. Friendship was a religion with them. If an Indian made friends with a captive, he would let him go, even though the man might tell where the villages were, how many warriors they had.

Sometimes they caught brothers. That was another thing people who didn't fight Indians didn't know: that a lot of the redskins were white. It was curious that Indian children raised by whites went back to their tribes if they had the chance, but white children captivated by Indians grew up Indian. Runaway boys turned Indian. The Shawonie chief, Blue Jacket, was a white man. He'd been wearing a blue shirt when he was captured during the war with England. He was seventeen, but still he turned Indian, and became one of the best. Did this mean the white man was more adaptable than the red? Did it mean the white man could beat the red at his own game? Clark didn't know.

The life was attractive. A boy's dream of woodcraft and warfare and women doing all the work.

If the Shawonies painted your face red, you were spared. If they painted it black, you were done for. They believed a death avenged by another death would lay a spirit to rest. They liked to burn you if they had the time.

The Kentucky militia scalped their dead, but in the army it was discouraged. Clark gave it up after the first time. But he had never resolved in his own mind whether scalping an Indian showed less respect for him or more.

Clark had heard his brother George's stories when he was thirteen, fourteen. George had killed more Indians than he could count, but he respected them. Whereas he didn't respect his countrymen. The Virginia Assembly voted him a sword of honor at the same time it was protesting his bills. He broke the sword and threw the hilt into the Ohio River. *We think you may safely confide in the justice and generosity of the Virginia Assembly.* That was what they told him when he rode out with his volunteers in 1778. The words were Mr. Jefferson's.

George said: When a captured brave knew you were going to kill him, he never begged for his life. He sat calmly. He sang his death song. George would imitate the sound, a beat like a heart and a tune like one loose fiddle string. It filled the firelit room of Clarks with something strange, and if George was drunk enough it made him cry.

There was the time one of George's men tomahawked a prisoner: the weapon stuck in the man's skull but otherwise did him no harm. The brave reached up and pried the blade out and handed it back to his executioner. That's how they beat you in death, George said.

They torture a captive, he said, to see if he can beat them. And if he beats them, they might let him go.

But not always. Nothing was predictable. One thing you heard a lot from escaped captives: Indians fought over how to treat them. Feed or disembowel. The captive tied to the stake and standing on kindling and listening to an argument that went on all day, that might end with one Indian tying up another and freeing the captive and making him a friend. People said they were fickle, but that wasn't it. It was just they had no rules.

The Clarks owned thousands of acres from land grants to George for his fighting in the war. They were the best family in Louisville, but they had to shuffle their holdings to keep George's creditors at bay. The Clarks had earned what they had; but absentee landlords owned some of the best acreage, and that was a shame. Squatters came over the mountains to claim land the old Virginia way. You saw what you liked and you made a blaze on a tree. That was a tomahawk claim. Then you girdled the trees and stepped corn into the ground and now you had corn title. You built a half-faced camp and you were a cabiner. Over every hill, along any stream that had enough gumption to trickle in March, Clark saw the dead standing timber, the mounds of speary corn shoots. George said: On the first day the land office opened in Harrodsburg, claims were filed on one and a half million acres. Kentucky was a paradise, and it was filling up. Across the river was the Ohio territory, another paradise. George had to close the land office to get the settler's minds off their claims long enough to go kill Indians. Clean them out. Teach them a lesson.

In return, the Indians butchered. They slaughtered. When they defeated Colonel Crawford in '82 they roasted him slow at the stake. They scalped him alive and piled embers on his skull. Maybe they were giving him his chance to beat them in death; but it was sickening all the same.

Clark was fighting under St. Clair nine years later, when the general was defeated and lost six hundred men. Two-thirds of his officers. There was hardly anyone left to lead the next campaign. Some of the dead men had dirt stuffed in their mouths. You want land, the Indians were saying.

The cabiners ran away from the hard fights, but when they caught Indians, that was when you saw things you didn't forget. Killing was one thing.

It was curious that men would cut the throats of wounded braves, but they'd slash open the stomachs of squaws. Clark has seen a white man's to-bacco pouch made from the scrotum of a dead Indian. He's seen bridle reins of Indian skin. He's seen a man holding a stick, and what he claimed was a squaw's privates on the stick.

This was not the general idea.

Indians always broke and ran from a bayonet charge. They didn't fight that way, massed. You could say it wasn't one of their agreements. They probably thought it wasn't brave. They had no idea what kind of bravery it took to stay in that line. Bayonets helped win Fallen Timbers. Clark remem-bered the nettles on that campaign. Waist-high and miles in length. His body aflame in an acid sea. He remembered the sweet blackberries of another cam-paign, when their supplies ran out.

The Shawonies called July *Blackberry Moon*. They called May *Straw-berry Moon*. The Ohio country was a fruitful paradise. Boys ran off to play Indian and live on berries, take three wives. Wouldn't you?

He remembered the campaign when the quartermaster sent saddles fit for elephants instead of horses. He remembered when they got the forges without any anvils. He remembered the routing of St. Clair, the cabiners flee-ing first and then the soldiers, and the camp women shrieking after them. Be-ware surprise, Washington had said to St. Clair. Maybe he knew he was dealing with a man not up to his duties, because he said it again: Beware, above all, surprise.

His brother George, in a long career, had not once been surprised. By the Indians, that is. Whiskey overran his defenses every day now. He sat by the fire and railed against his ungrateful country and talked about moving to Spanish Louisiana and cried like a girl, his own death song. His adventures were over. William rode thousands of miles, fighting lawsuits, settling claims, and every time he returned he found his big brother smaller. George was withering like an apple-john. They were the best family in Louisville, and they had this horror in the house.

Sometimes an old Indian foe visited, and George and the brave would hug and get drunk together and carry on. A weakness for whiskey was an af-femity George had with the red man. Whereas William sometimes thought his own affemity was sickliness. Ague and distemper for him were like the woman's curse, always coming back, while the Shawonie villages, the Dillaway, the Maomi, fell to the smallpox, the bilious fever, influenza. They didn't come back. Was the white man more durable?

One thing Clark knew. The red man east of the Mississippi was doomed.

Beware, above all, surprise. St. Clair was surprised on a cold November dawn. Clark was twenty-one, a lion, and late to flee the field. He remembered: he looked back and saw the ground covered with dead men, each marked by a white plume rising in the first light. Their scalped heads were steaming.

forest bear's second woman

This one woke before rising-time.

A fullness in her groin, a burn. Black inside the hut, but she knew where white beads lay from the stale heat off her, the dog breath of the ghost squatting there. Forest bear's hut robe was empty. That one was upriver on a hunt.

She ducked through the skin flap into a cool breeze. The wind had gone down during the night and shifted warmward. Above in the black a star appeared, winked out, appeared. Clouds breaking up. Only the white ends of shed-fur wood on a nearby corn scaffold were visible in the dark. She bottomed through the ditch and felt along the trunks of the village wall until she came to a gap wide enough to squeeze through. A few steps on, she squatted in the grass. She could have pissed into the buffalo heartskin in the hut, but white beads said the smell made her weak, and anyway this one had been too warm. The air on her forehead felt good. And the dewy grass blades licking her swollen sore asshole.

Always warm now, like work, like fatigue. Her palms and soles itching like the thought of running away. Warm and itching and shit-stuck and wakeful. The sharp sudden pains. This one wanted camas flower. To ask: is this right? To hear: yes. (To cry against her, unseen, unmocked.) She tried to remember what the tall grass women said when a child was coming. The jokes, the complaints. The quiet crying. A pregnant woman is foolish like Coyote, six baskets said. But inside this one was a sun-child, and maybe that was different.

She heard the spittle of foam on the ground, felt for it, licked it from her finger. Speak to me, water. The good bitter edge was dulled by a raw squash sweetness. There was a creamy scent of cunt, strong but fresh, no taste of sickness or death. But this one wondered. Her cunt oozed day and night a thin slippery milk, a salmon silt, sun-child piss. She put rootreed fur between her legs. She watched the pregnant undergrounders when they bathed, but saw nothing to help her know.

This one died.

In childbirth, among strangers? They would wrap the dead child with her and put them both up on a scaffold and the ravens would eat them. Hare would ask Raven *what have you been eating*? Raven would ask his shit, and his shit would say *a bird and her baby bird*.

Her own shit said that when the child came it would come hard.

White beads was no help. One or two winters older, but that one had been a child like water speaks when she was captured, and she was one of the dirt people from beyond the black rock plain. Those ones had no horses and knew little. They think babies come from eating pinenuts, blue crow used to say. Like this one, white beads had not been adopted by the undergrounders. She was part of none of their age groups, their sister families, their mystery bands with strange names and dances where knowledge was traded.

This one wiped herself with a handful of grass. Now she could make out the blades against her hand. *Rising-time,* the undergrounders called it. In two or three cornrows the sun would be born. She snaked back through the wall, recrossed the ditch. Undergrounders used the same word for sun and moon: *widi.* It seemed strange to her. And yet she thought of time in cornrows, how long it took to weed one. It was like seeing two worlds, like crossing your eyes, trying to walk between. She bent to enter the skin hut but straightened as a knife pain cut up from cunt to navel. She breathed once, bent again, went in.

White beads asked out of the dark for water. That one spoke we-people harshly. That was the dirt people way, ugly to a soft grass speaker. Water speaks filled a horn ladle and brought it to her. White beads sometimes gabbled in her fevers and asked afterward what she had said, to find out who the ghost was and what it wanted. She was angry when water speaks said she had not understood. White beads had never been pregnant, although forest bear had been fucking her three or four winters. She had gone to the undergrounders' baby hill with a small bow and arrow for a boy, but returned only with another ghost in her, or the same ghost back again. She had not been a good worker, and now she did nothing, as she thinned like a burning stick.

This one raked up an ember, laid on twigs, blew a flame. She stirred the mess in the pot, tipped in water, added corn, half-dried squash slices, a handful of beans. The strangeness of undergrounder food. This one had never learned how to cook it. Older sister thought she was too stupid to learn, and forest bear had his own strange way of cooking. He had a knife-metal pot with a low edge like an ant-roasting tray he used for frying cakes. The undergrounders said metal made the food taste bad, and maybe it did, but by the time forest bear took her to his hut, this one had long since pushed away the taste of food. She didn't know the Corn Mother songs, or the bean songs, so nothing she made of them could be good, but the mess did not make her sick and she offered Father a war-bird feather or a strip of jerked buffalo and turned her mind away from this food that was not we-people. It kept her alive. It filled her with its emptiness and she farted it out.

This one pulled aside the hut flap and looked out. Sunbirth. Or: *widi appears.* Or what forest bear called it: *lor-ror.* A triple world, like water and earth and sky and she between them all, dry and floating and in the dark. Blind bird. This one was born in a grass hut instead of a skin hut because the hardskins had stolen the skin huts. And now she lived in a skin hut among earth huts because forest bear was a sun-man and did not take undergrounder wives like other sun-men.

Lor-ror. Sun-men were not whole men. They were part woman and part animal, maybe bear-men, hairy and rank and comfort-greedy and full of power, yet cooking and carrying things like women, and howling and roaring like bears when they were in pain. They were not war-men. They only wanted to trade, and fuck women. They dressed like women, with few beads and no scalps on their skins, and some didn't even pluck out their face hair. And yet they had power. They had the strong, light robes of woven sinew that dried quickly, they had the knife-metal awls and axes, the bright beads, the black weapons. Without war, how did they get this power? Did they dig it out of the earth like their knife metal? Flip it shining out of water like fish?

Riders and runners had been coming to the village for days saying a large band of sun-men was coming up the muddy river. They had got past the headcutters.

—Are you hungry? this one asked white beads.

Low voice, facing the hut skin: —No.

—I heard yesterday the muddy river sun-men will reach mitutanka today. I want to see. After straight-sun.

Day-divide, undergrounders called it.

—I'll leave food by you when I go. And twoleaf.

This one had boiled the twoleaf many times. And bigroot, and whiteroot. She had not found good-sticky-tree, or she would have burned the needles, made white beads breathe the smoke. She had woven a sweat hut, and had poured the hot water on the stones and wrapped white beads in the buffalo robe. This one had no ghost-drawing power, no song, but she gave tobacco to spirit and had a weak dream that maybe meant something, so she tried, she sang *give me* from the dream, and ate the plant she thought she had seen, and sucked at white beads' dry stinking lips to draw out the ghost, as a man with ghost-drawing power had done when she was a girl. But nothing had come into her mouth, no bloody lump of slime or stone to be shown to sisters and cast away. She had waited for another dream, but nothing came. This one had thought forest bear would have a bear song, but he didn't. He had many gourds that he wore slung on him but none of them held his power. There was not one he opened with offerings or singing. She had never seen on him a bear claw, a bear tooth. Unless the teeth in his head were bear teeth.

The undergrounders called power *hopadi.* The sun-men called it *med-sanh.* But how did they get this med-sanh?

This one kneeled at white beads' hunched back and felt past her shoulder for her cheek. White beads shrugged her hand away.

—I'll hear if you call, this one said. She took a swallow of stew and went outside. Last knots of clouds were sinking coldward, leaving a sky silted whiteblue with early sunlight. One thumb said the sky was ice, which was why the air grew colder when you climbed a mountain. Storms broke the ice and that made thunder.

This one washed in the river and gathered wood while the sun climbed. She had no dog, so she pulled the sled with her forehead. Her neck throbbed. That was from being tied across bird rider's horse for two days. By midmorning the wind had risen again. Cornhusks on the scaffolds rattled; stretched skins boomed like drums. The tall grass valley and the salmon stream did not have wind like this, every day. She had pegged a skin to the ground in the lee of the hut. This wind would make her crazy if she could not get out of it. She thought that was why the undergrounders lived underground. It was a whole world in there, horses and tobacco and a sweat hut and a food cache and a sky of earth instead of ice and the sun always at the top of the sky. But this one lived in a skin hut with her sun-man, and the walls shivered all night.

Crazy woman had gone out of her earth hut into a snow wind and the wind blew her spirit away.

This one had two skins to work before she could walk downriver to mitutanka and maybe see the muddy-river sun-men. The skin on the ground was dry from its stretching and needed a second scraping. Another on a frame had had the brains worked in, and needed softening with the stick. She liked to do these chores together. Pulling the elkhorn scraper gave her an ache between her shoulder blades, and pushing with the softening stick worked the ache out. She could do the two chores all day, and by sun-entering hardly hurt anywhere. She fetched the scraper out of the hut and began on the first skin, pulling in short jerks. She moved across in rocking steps, keeping the scraper beneath her. After two passes she swept the scrapings to the side. They would go into a bag for boiling later into glue, or into soup if forest bear got too lazy, or a trade didn't go and they ran out of food.

Why did she think of time in cornrows weeded, and not hides scraped? She had used an elkhorn just like this one to scrape hides with the tall grass band. As long as she kept her eyes on the scraper and the hide, she could imagine looking up and seeing the mountains, the three rivers. She could imagine seeing one thumb. That one was not the man she was to be given to when she became a woman. Two bears had promised her to white feather, who never spoke to her. And was too old.

As this one squatted, knees apart, reaching between to sweep together the flakes like soft horn or thick toenail, she felt the slush of her cunt breathing between her legs. The lips were swollen, parted, a fullness. The undergrounders said if you saw an otter it would make the baby come easily. Forest bear must like the feeling of her cunt this way, he was climbing onto her every night he was in the village. That one thought the wetness meant she wanted him. It was better, he got in easily instead of the first dry forcing, a burning like a firedrill. Twice now she had even almost liked it by the end. Thinking she wanted him, he was gentler, and stroked her back and thighs afterward, and while he slept she coaxed out with her fingers the spirit that felt like a large good piss going backward, born from her like a baby or an otter rising out of the river, like twitching her salmon fingers and making the pronghorn run.

[67]

She lifted the scraper and started a new row. This was the tool Coyote used when he broke the teeth of the women's cunts. Coyote wanted to fuck all women, even his daughters, but his daughters threw him off. When he asked his wife to carry him home and started fucking her on the way, she let him, and she kept walking. Letting your man use you was a chore, and a good woman did her chores. You carried your man when he climbed on top of you. But like any other chore, it was good when it was done. Forest bear had been making her carry him every night and twice a night and this one was glad he was away.

On a hunt with undergrounders. Bringing along in his many gourds (or somewhere) his cache of sun-man power. Calling the buffalo.

The ache glowed. Like the glow of weeding in the field this one and white beads planted, because forest bear didn't want to trade for corn and beans and squash when his women could grow them for him. Her back would ache and she would look at those toothed cocks on the cornstalks. Last moon she was plucking them off and throwing them in the basket for the food cache, and she took the dry ones off the scaffold and wrung them, the teeth scattering, and that's what she wanted to do sometimes when he climbed on her, wring his cock and make him howl like a bear. The milky ooze wetting the rootreed fur in her crotch might be his semen, he had put so much into her.

He would not have gone on a hunt if he had known sun-men were coming up the muddy river. He tried to get to other sun-men first, speak between them and the undergrounders, get his trading between. He would hear upriver, and come down early.

They had got past the headcutters, the runners said. The biggest band of sun-men ever seen. They were taking two days to move a day. They had so many goods to trade, they were pulling a floating sled as big as a hill. They had a black weapon on the front of the sled as big as a log. They had a black bear that listened to them like a dog. There was a man painted all black. Sun-men did not paint themselves, unless they took undergrounder wives. No one knew what the black sun-man meant.

Ache. This one put down the scraper and walked around the hut to the other skin. The frame was tied to the corn scaffold. She cradled the butt of the big stick in her palms below her abdomen. Leaning along the stick, rocking forward, easing, she worked out the stiffness in the buffalo skin and her own back. This was a cow, easier to work than a bull. The wind banged on the frame from behind. She breathed thanks to the cow while she worked, for not being a bull, for softening, for massaging her back, for blocking the wind.

Crazy woman died in a snow wind, in the second winter. Her man beat her one night and his fists woke up a ghost and the ghost told her to go out. She lay without a robe in the snow wind and in the morning she was dead. A few days later, spirit sent this one a dream. She was standing alone on an ice floe on the big river. Black night and stars. No people anywhere. No animals. No trees. The ice floe was turning. Empty, snow-covered land appeared and disappeared. Everything was silent. Then there was a splash. She turned. A head was rising out of the black water. Dark eyes on her. At last! she thought. It is— Then she woke.

She moved back to the first skin, hefted the scraper. A double world. They called her a snake. A bird. Their word for horse was *strong dog*. The undergrounders had only had horses since their fathers' fathers' time. They had got them from we-people. They still had so few, some men did not own a single one, and those ones had to run like children. They called sun-men *skin hats*. They called them *robes*. The sun-men had so many bundles, and surely one was a power bundle, a hopadi bundle, a med-sanh bundle, but all of them contained nothing but robes. Buffalo, wolf, beaver, fox. It must be very cold where they lived. Sleeping sun-men, bundled sun-men, half women.

This one thought of the changed-men she had seen sometimes among the birds on the black rock plain. Men who dressed as women, who made baskets and scraped skins and cooked. There were changed-men among the undergrounders, too, like the one who adopted drops the robe and named him mountain child, and turned him into an undergrounder. The undergrounders said that Old Woman Above would choose a boy and send him a dream, and that was her sign for him to change. She wondered what sun-men had dreamed, and who had sent the dream.

This one returned to the other skin. She had seen something once. Her first spring here, her first sight of the ice breaking up on the muddy river. Her salmon stream broke into pieces like buffalo robes, but the muddy river ran thundering with white islands. She followed older sister and old mother and the rest, a stream of undergrounders leaving the village and heading toward the muddy river, the morning after the ice broke. Above the flooded, churning flats, the people lined the banks and looked upriver, and she did not understand. A call came down from a high bank and the first man shot out.

This one would never forget. Upriver from her, he jumped from a rock onto broken bank-ice and from there into shallow water, the spray flying from him like sparks. Other men followed, but he drew away. He leaped onto a passing floe bigger than twenty earth huts and he looked back and up at the high bank as he ran, a quick look like a silver fish flash to see where the look-out pointed, while he kept running across the floe that was turning slowly as it moved downriver. It turned like a cloud, and he curved across it and now she could see, floating in the water upriver, far out in the current, something black. He veered at the sight of a small floe riding fast and he leaped across the water to it and threw himself down, so he would not fall off the far side, and rose back up and rode it, balancing, then stepped, stepped, gentle steps, to other floes as they came rippling past. With each step he was moving faster downriver as he got farther into the current, and the floating black thing, which this one could see now was a drowned buffalo, probably good tangy eat-ing, was coming near, and he and it were both downriver from her now, and he stood at the ice edge, and one last small piece of ice was racing down, and as it passed, he jumped, hitting the chunk of ice that was so small it flipped under his foot, and jumped again, landing astride the buffalo. He rode it whooping, shouting his skill to the two banks and sky. He rode it until it ran far down-stream into a pack that drove into a bank and other men came running across the ice. Pronghorn! This one did not know what others called him.

She walked off to piss. She returned and picked up the softening stick. She remembered the love-boy songs of the undergrounder girls sitting on the scaffolds watching the corn, and she remembered the young women of the tall grass band talking about wanting it very much, the fucking with their young robe men. Why not her?

When this one was a child with her band, she had seen the captive girls being traded at the camas place. The birds came with metal and beads, and the mealyroot-eaters and the broken shoes had the long bow-horn bows, each worth at least a strong girl. And she had seen the big trading fairs here on the muddy river, the yellowlegs bringing black weapons, the birds bringing horses, the undergrounders trading their corn, the silent girls with bruised arms sitting on robes. The arrow contests, the foot races, the stick and ring game. Since she had not been adopted, she knew it would happen to her one day. To sit on a robe while two men called on their power and skill, throwing the marked stones or one of them balancing the stick to cast it while the other tried to unbalance him by saying something as he drew his arm back. *My loin-cloth is dirty.*

But this one had not been put on a robe. Too ugly, maybe, scar-ugly, small Coyote-washed ugly. Forest bear had come to the women of the hut and bought her for thirty round arrowheads and black powder, an ax, two sheh-feel knives, a red robe, and three pouches of vermilion. This one had often seen him in the village, with his swinging gourds (one of the things they called him was many gourds) and the strange way he spoke undergrounder. He was not like the other sun-men in the nearby villages. He did not take under-grounder wives and live in an earth hut, but in a skin hut by the wall with a snake woman. He came to the door of old mother's earth hut one day, and the deer hoofs rattled on the door as she opened it to him like the rattle of his gourds. The haggling was short, because the two woman thought he was of-fering a crazy forest bear price, too high. More than a good dog's price.

This one had heard many times that sun-men were hairy like animals, but he did not have the animal hair on his face, as traders who came with the yellowlegs sometimes did, so she was frightened when, after he brought her to his skin hut and he threw off his shirt and told her to wash him, she saw all the black hair and, for the first time, the white skin that he kept hidden out-side the hut. He cooked, but she ate nothing. A man who cooked when there were women to do it was either a healer or a ghost caller. Then he gripped her shoulders and smiled and pushed her down and climbed on her and forced her open and broke her cunt's teeth, though she was not yet a woman. Coy-ote's daughters threw off Coyote, but this one did not fight because he was bear-heavy, and he had bought her, and he was a strange sun-man who did strange things and she was floating in strangeness.

They called him forest bear and many gourds, but he called himself shah-bono.

Trader, skin hat, sun-man, robe.

Bird, snake, fam-de-shah-bono.

And white beads burned like a stick and this one was warm all the time with the sun-child and the undergrounders came close to shah-bono to pick up his power like warmth off a fire.

She put down the pole and ran her hands over the buffalo skin, pressing here and there. Enough.

—Are you hungry? she asked white beads in the hut.

No answer. She leaned over. Damp breath, lung whisper, glue stink. While twoleaf twigs boiled, she took another swallow of stew and put fresh redberries in a pouch. She left the hot twoleaf water next to white beads and went out. Few men except old ones in the village. The young men were hunting for meat and the first winter hides, or were away on last raids before snow came. This one had heard wolf bigman was out on a raid among we-people. She sang in her mouth every night for the tall grass band to be safe. *Wolf, Father, warn them. White elk skin, see. Camas flower, hide.*

This one passed between the earth huts and out the break in the wall, following the knife stream bank. Other women and children and old men were strung along the path heading in the same direction. Everyone going to see the muddy-river sun-men. Those ones had a big village down the river, it was said, but the headcutters usually stopped them coming. The headcutters and the big earrings called the muddy-river sun-men big knives. Maybe this band had killed some headcutters with that log-big black weapon. Or the black man had power. Maybe the big sled was filled with other log-big weapons and the undergrounders could trade for them and kill many headcutters.

The wind in the past days had stripped the last shed-fur trees bare, and now it flung grit and wet yellow leaves in her face. The sharpberries were gone from their trees, picked for pemmican and eaten by birds, but thousands of redberries still crowded in patches on the ashyleaf bushes beyond easy reach below and above the path. They grew more thickly here than in the land of the tall grass people. So many, the undergrounders ate them only fresh. In her mouth: first the bitter skin that made her tongue feel rubbed flat, then the red juice seeping, sweet now that a hard frost had come.

Shouts. One thumb galloped.

Neither the undergrounders nor forest bear ate ants. Snake, bird, anteater. She missed the taste of them, the muddy sting, like hunger on the back of your tongue, that breath of puke.

A boy and a girl ran past her on the path. Off to see the sun-men. Then a streak. A dog. Off to bark at them.

Seed-eater, root-eater. That was all women ate by the salmon stream when their blood flowed. If you ate meat during that time, the old women said, you would never stop bleeding. You sat alone in Coyote's blood hut and no man could come near you, or he would puke and die. This one had never bled that way. When her breasts began to grow, so did her abdomen.

The undergrounders called pregnancy *big abdomen*. The words also meant *big shit*. Her sun-child would come hard.

She had passed amahami, the small village of undergrounders where the knife stream flowed into the muddy river, and now there were more women and children and old men on the path. Two men had stopped ahead for a rest, one old, the other not, maybe he was protecting his village from headcutters or big earrings, or he had an old mother and no sisters to take care of her, or maybe he was crippled from the summer Sun dance, when the undergrounder men starved themselves and dragged buffalo skulls by thongs jabbed through their muscles and cut their fingers off, and none of it in mourning for a brother or parent (although they did that, too), as she had thought, so long ago, when she had seen bird rider's missing salmon finger. Too much to eat, and not enough to mourn. Easy life. She used to think.

The two men were testing their power on who came along the path next, betting woman or child, and neither probably won the knife or string of hair-beads as this one walked by, with her ugly scars and stupid look, and they gazing blankly back. Neither woman nor child. Bird, snake, she-bear, big shitter of a sun-child.

She had seen sometimes a good young man limping, or one who couldn't raise his arms over his head. They hung from trees, or off the edges of cliffs, the thongs through their chests above the nipples. They called on their Father to take them into his hands, to rip the muscles and let them fall and see how they stood it. To make them tough. Coyote made we-people tough when he washed them at birth. This one used to think. She still thought. But she also thought her people needed more power.

Wolf had wanted to make everything easy for people. He had wanted the animals kept in brush fences, so people could take what they wanted. But Coyote released the animals, so people had to go hunting. Wolf said, *People should not die.* Coyote said, *They must die, or there will be too many of them.* Coyote taught people to cut their hair when a person died. He taught them to cry. Wolf said, *People should be born out of fingers, without pain, without fucking.* Coyote said, *No, fucking is good. People should fuck, and they should be born with pain, through women's cunts.*

Pregnant women belonged to Coyote, and this foolish one was approaching mitutanka, the last undergrounder village. She saw a crowd along the bluff, and runners and riders hurrying downstream, and others coming up. She stopped, listening, leaning into her palms to relieve a backache. The wind was strong off the river, the sun three hands above the horizon, cooling and darkening to the color of piss. The walk had made her asshole itch again.

The undergrounders of mitutanka had skin as light as muddy river water and spoke strangely among themselves, honking like geese. There were a few families of them in her village and another big village across the muddy river. This one listened to the words she knew and the ones she didn't. She saw the children running and squealing, dogs snarling, spinning in tangles, the runners and riders coming up with news of which bend in the river the sun-men had reached, which bar they were stuck on, how big that big sled was, how many log-big black weapons it must carry, how many headcutters they would kill with them. Boys were below the bluff, tossing their arrow-wood rings in the water and trying to pierce them with their spears and pretending, when they hit them, that they were drowned buffalo, and closer by, men were betting knives and necklaces on how many robes, horses, or women it might take to get one of those log-big black weapons the big sled was full of.

The walk had made this one hungry. She reached into her berry pouch. Shouts.

The crowd was rippling, pressing to the edge of the bluff. This one rounded upriver and came to where a bush grew, gripping the soil so that a tongue stuck out over the lip. She looked, and at first saw only the undergrounders clambering up from the bottom of the bluff where they had been pushed by the crowd and beyond some boys racing across the hard mud flat, and beyond them the wind ruffling the river. Then she picked out a man, far off in the shadow of the sun-entering bank. That one was waist-deep in the water, looking down. Another man behind, and another coming into view, and although she could not make out the rope, they must be pulling the sled that slid into sight after the sixth man, and the crowd hushed, and she could feel uneasiness sweep through it and her. The sled kept sliding into view. It was enormous. An ice floe going the wrong way. A white cloud drifted above. The sled struck a bar and the cloud stopped. The men dropped the rope and others jumped out of the sled and now two smaller sleds appeared around the bend and men jumped out of them, and they gathered around the grounded floe and dug in the water and strung out more ropes and leaned into them and others stood on the big sled and pushed with poles. The sled looked so heavy, and the men looked heavy and tired, bear-heavy, sun-men mired in sand and water.

More strangeness, coming with a cloud.

This one was still gripping redberries in her pouch. She brought out her hand and put the berries in her mouth. Chewed slowly. The skin-bitterness passed and the frost-born sweetness rose on her tongue.

THE CAPTAIN
[1804]

1

The misery river, Lewis had privately dubbed it within a week of departing St. Louis. Between the muddy banks it came at you, in flood, in spate, in an ever-fresh freshet, ice-cold tea draining with a mocking, indifferent inexhaustibility out of Louisiana.

Well, it proved the vastness of the territory. And as Louisiana now belonged to the U' States, that was good news. Surely a tithe of a tithe of this superfluity rose above the Lake of the Woods. Lewis amused himself on his overland tramps with fancies of encountering at latitude 51° or 52° the composite redcoat dragoon who had raided his father's plantation in the war, and informing him that the Americans had contrived yet again to take the ground from under his feet. And leave the skins when you go, there's a good man.

Thus the very misery of the Missouri should have cheered Lewis. And it did, a little. But it was unpleasantly unlike the eastern rivers to which he was accustomed. It did not even flow in the usual way; strangely, it boiled. Lewis found something ever so slightly horrible about the upwelling, bubble-rich eructations, belches large as haywagons emitting vapors of vegetable slime, the fizzy rattling down the lengths of the boats like men's fingers scrabbling, the night-long mutters and muffled shrieks. It did not require a morbid fancy to conceive that some giant was stuck fast down in the mud, dying. No, Mother, he did not need rest and a course of lavender oil. Gentlemen, this singular phenomenon of ebullition was most likely attributable to the irregular motion of large masses of sand and mud constantly changing their positions in the riverbed.

But: there *was* something dead down there. A whole army, in fact—trees. The Missouri uprooted them from its friable banks by the tens of thousands. Some swam, and they bounded over the water at you like battering rams, or they swept down broadside like cannon-fired chain. But most were drowned by their rootballs, and the corpses, planted in the bottom, became gigantic submerged stakes, pointing downriver like an abatis. Worse, the current made them saw (the rivermen called them *sawyers*); their heads might be pressed beneath the surface for minutes at a time, until some incalculable shift in the liquid forces released them and they bounded upward with hull-splintering violence. This river goddess was protecting her virginity.

The Frenchmen that Captain Clark had engaged at St. Louis for the leg up to the Mandan villages had advised him, after two days of hourly hanging up on logs and almost losing the keelboat, to pack the boats heavy in the bows. In that way, they would strike and stop at a submerged obstacle, rather than ride up on it. So the little flotilla proceeded in ugly parade, noses down like the barges of the most lubberly settlers ever seen gesticulating in clownish panic down the Ohio, an orientation that exacerbated the effect of the adversary current.

Which was in spring flood, by God! Here they were, proposing to ascend the most rapid river of the North American continent at the worst possible time of year. The traders out of St. Louis went up to the Osage and Kanzas villages like rational creatures, in the autumn, at low water. After a winter spent with the Indians, they floated back down in the spring, the flood for them a boon, a highway. Every day or two they skimmed by the captains' laboring Corps of Discovery, shouting in galling Gallic *bonhomie,* waving hats and upraised oars (since to go so far as to actually touch oar to water was purely decorative, a coy allusion to the fact that they sat in canoes). This was one of the fifteen or sixteen reasons why Lewis had wanted to get as far up Miss Missouri as possible last fall. When his worst misgivings had been realized, and he was forced to winter near St. Louis, he and Clark spent all of March, it seemed, on the low bluff at their camp, opposite the mouth of the Missouri, staring rapt and cowed at the cyclopean vomiting of mud and shattered ice and continental debris skating across the Mississippi and smashing into the shore beneath their feet. Clark wrote out two schedules for the coming year, one assuming an average progress of a modest twelve miles per day, the other a miserable ten. In the event, it was *less* than ten. By Lewis's reckoning—as they hauled on the cordelle and rowed and poled, crossing and recrossing the river to creep up through the less cruel currents, where (of course) all the snags were, as the squalls heeled them over midriver and the gales trapped them on shore for days, as the sandbars built up before their eyes and shivered like curtains and slipped away all in a moment, catching the boats' bows and pushing them broadside and sinking the tow-men thigh-deep in quicksand, and as the riverbanks caved in, as much as a quarter-mile stretch of undermined forest collapsing all at once with a gargantuan roar, seeming to liquefy as it fell, the trees diving in every direction like ninepins, the wave of mud racing toward you threatening to carry away the oars or swallow the boats entire—by his reckoning, they were making about one mile in an hour. He thought he could attain that overland, with measurably less pain, on his bare knees.

But he was not in one of his black moods. Those unstrung him, whereas he found something bracing in his rage at the river and their delay. Were the task not near impossible, it were done already. Thank God it was so hard! Lewis was as tough in body as any man he had ever met, and Clark was long used to suffering. By God, they would endure to stand astride this river where it bubbled puling from its mountain source and there take up a palmful and swallow *it*. Or . . . piss into it!

2

The boatbuilder in Pittsburgh the previous summer had been an even sorrier specimen of bare, forked man than Lewis had imagined: otiose, mendacious, dissipated; and possessed of the infuriating imperturbability of a man whose nearest competitor lay in another watershed. On the day he fought with his workers, causing them all to quit, Lewis came within an inch of shooting him like a rabid dog, but mastered his vexation sufficiently to stalk off, later that day buying, to cheer himself, a different sort of dog altogether, a handsome, docile Newfoundland he had previously seen for sale, but had thought the price too high. Twenty dollars, a quite absurd sum. But he was in the mood for a hanging, so he hanged it all, and handed over the cash. Newfoundlands were good waterdogs, and this one was no exception; Lewis had made sure of that. He'd sent him into the Ohio, and when he came out, sluicing tail awag, Lewis dubbed him Waterman. Then he thought of a luckier name—as the dog, God willing, would live to swim in the western sea, he would be Seaman.

The keelboat, promised him by the 20th of July, was delivered punctually, Pittsburgh time, at seven in the morning sharp on August 31st. Lewis had the craft in the water and packed army fashion (lightest objects thrown in first) by ten. With the dropping of the last bundles, the men who had carried them— seven soldiers from the Carlisle post for the Ohio leg, and three young men on trial for the voyage out of St. Louis—sat at the oars, and Lewis whistled for Seaman and sent word for the pilot. He ran up the sail to make a festive show in the windless morning and they set off down a river that was lower (Lewis could have predicted this) than had ever been witnessed by the oldest settler in the country. To lighten the keelboat's load, Lewis had shifted some stores into a pirogue, and had sent still more overland to Wheeling, where he would buy a second pirogue. Nevertheless, within four miles he had grounded on a bar.

He scowled outwardly and grinned within. Blessed contrariness! He had his mother to thank for that. The harder he was hit, the less it hurt him. They had sworn in Pittsburgh he could not get down that river, and the pilot daily shook his head. But he had spades, hadn't he? He would dig a channel! He would engineer a canal all the way to Clark, waiting for him in Louisville.

As it turned out, digging through the bars was surprisingly quick work. The gravel dislodged easily, the current carrying it ten or fifteen feet before it subsided; one day the men cut a fifty-yard channel in the course of an hour. It was only when the gravel was intermixed with clay or driftwood that Lewis had to hire oxen to drag the boat across. The farmers from whom he got these animals were the familiar frontier medley of incivility, cupidity, and mental torpor. As soon as they cut down all their trees to fire their stills, and killed their soil (Lewis gave them five years), they would be heading farther west to squat on the land Lewis was presently off to discover. But any consideration of the service he was performing for them gratis did nothing to prevent them demanding outrageous sums for an hour's borrow of their beasts.

Bend followed bend; new clearings, new townlets. At times, for miles, there was no perceptible current between the bars. Mornings on the glassy river were foggy, the days mostly dry. In the mild drought, the first maples were early turning red on the hilly slopes, the hickory and beech butter-yellow. An enchanting scene. Squirrels were often discovered in the river, swimming from the north bank to the south. Lewis sent in Seaman, who brought them in his mouth to the boat. Fat with autumn, they made a pleasant supper when fried.

Mr. J had impressed on Lewis the importance of keeping records of the expedition up the Missouri, so Lewis practiced journalizing, an activity he had always deprecated as tedious and dispiriting. (What Lewis did, what Lewis thought—quotidian Lewis, daily quoted—who could care?) He had to remind himself that he just might make history. Or more important, that Mr. J cared. So he jotted in a memorandum book in the evenings, and surprised himself by feeling full of the moment. He longed to set himself a scientific task, to begin philosophizing.

On the second day, waiting for the fog to clear, he realized that the fog itself craved explanation. He knew from his army days that it was thickest on the Ohio on the brisk mornings of autumn, so he hypothesized the cause to be the difference in temperature between air and water. He busied himself the next morning with temperature readings: air, 63°; water, 75°. Calling on the mathematical ability with which Dr. Rush had credited him, he calculated the difference at 12°, and concluded *ipso facto* that that was sufficient to cause the water to steam. The following morning he went a step further, and after measuring the difference between air and water (63° and 73°, respectively) he waited until the fog began to dissipate, at which point he measured again, finding that the air temperature had risen to 68°. That night he wrote in his journal: *The difference therefore of 5° in temperature between the water and air is not sufficient to produce the appearance of fog.*

Confident of having discovered the mechanism, he cast about for other investigations. However, two mornings later, the air was considerably warmer, and yet the fog was impenetrable. He took out the thermometer again, and found the temperature of the air to be 71°, that of the water 73°. He measured once more on the following morning (a difference of 21°, foggy, but no more so than on the previous day), but his heart was no longer in it. He felt he had made a fool of himself. Obviously, the mechanism was more complex than he had supposed. Perhaps the depth of the water was implicated, or (and now that the thought came to him, surely this was so) the humidity of the air, which must vary for a number of reasons. He had no hygrometer. And in any case, he now became conscious of the sheer number of simple things that needed explaining, once one set about explaining simple things. Why was this maple turning red and not that one? Why had driftwood collected in masses on this bar, when the bar above it, identical in outward aspect, was unencumbered? Why were walnuts and hickory nuts abundant this season, whereas beechnuts were scarce? Lewis felt suddenly and forcefully that any edifice of scientific inquiry he attempted to build either would topple over on top of him or would require such a broad base that he would never reach the second story.

Writing to Mr. J from Wheeling, he adverted to none of this. But he had become aware of an uncomfortable fact, to wit: the most compelling evidence, to any casual observer, of Mr. J's scientism was his habit of daily recording the temperature. Now Lewis would prefer to believe that he modeled himself intentionally on Mr. J, as opposed to mindlessly mimicking his gestures like a monkey. Furthermore, once Mr. J had resolved to record the daily temperatures, he did so, and had not missed a day in twenty years. Whereas Lewis had lasted less than a week. The contemplation of this abyssal difference between them did nothing to inspire Lewis to return to his thermometer; on the contrary, it whispered to him to throw the instrument into the river.

Lewis felt the first blue tendrils tugging at his knees. Following the unhappy logic of such states, the mood became its own cause. The evening after he left Wheeling, he too sharply reprimanded his corporal for having failed to secure bread in the town. When he sent the man back the six miles to get it, and the damned fellow was late on his return, Lewis began to fear he had deserted out of pique. This provoked the usual self-reproaches about Lewis's limitations as a leader, his aloofness, etc. When the corporal did return, Lewis felt grateful to him, which grossly unmilitary sentiment provoked additional self-reproaches about his womanliness, his mercurial temperament, etc., etc.

Beyond a certain point, those etceteras would begin to breed like vermin. Lewis fought against it. He set himself the task of describing an artificial Indian mound, a few miles downriver from Wheeling. But while at the site, he hadn't enough time to do more than begin his description, so he left five pages blank in his notebook. Then he never filled them. He did write scientifically about the contrary wind; he noted the incidence of goiter in a certain neighborhood; but those five empty pages were a nightly rebuke. A journal, it seemed, was a record of what Lewis *didn't* think, what Lewis *didn't* do. Thus, one morning, journalizing became another thing that Lewis didn't do.

Another embarrassment awaited him in Cincinnati: a letter from Clark about John Conner, the interpreter among the Delawares to whom Lewis had offered a place on the expedition. Not having received any response from Conner to his invitation, Lewis had written in August to Clark, asking him to send someone up to the Delaware town and offer Conner a place as interpreter for three hundred dollars a year. Clark's letter to Lewis described the sequel of these efforts: Conner had replied he had too much business in hand to go, and even if he had had nothing to do at present, he would not have obliged himself for the sum Lewis had offered him, nor should he have considered five thousand dollars too much recompense! Hot chagrin rose in Lewis. Conner's insolence must have stunned Clark. But Lewis (chagrin rising further) thought he could guess what had happened. He had a fleeting, uneasy memory of writing the word *companion* somewhere in his invitation to Conner. This was before Clark had agreed to go. Of course Lewis had not offered Conner a share in the command, as he had never been in the army, but . . . What had he written? He had been warm, enthusiastic. Whyever not? He had liked Conner extremely. He'd seemed so honest, so . . .

Companion. It meant no more than friend. And Conner and Lewis had been friends. What should Lewis have written, *hireling*? Conner had grossly misunderstood. On receiving the embassy from Clark, he had felt himself supplanted. Ridiculous man!

Lewis winced. Something he had written to Clark, something about there being no man better qualified in every respect than Conner, something about sparing no pains to get him. And what Clark had written, absent any note of censure, after relaying Conner's uncivil answer: *As this man does not speak any of the languages to the West of the Mississippi, I do not think the failure in getting him is very material.*

What the whole sorry incident said about Lewis's faulty judgment, his untrustworthy feelings— He wrote to Clark from Cincinnati: *I do not much regret the loss of Mr. Conner for several reasons which I shall mention to you when we meet; he has deceived me very much.*

Chagrin. Was Lewis rash to hope that things would be better soon? Clark was in Louisville. Lewis wrote: *It is probable before the receipt of this letter that I shall be with you.* He wrote: *Adieu and believe me your very sincere friend and associate.*

3

Captain Clark. Only say it enough times, and it would become true.

In Pittsburgh, on July 28th, Lewis had received not one but two letters from Clark, accepting his invitation, and Lewis had written back, *I feel myself much gratified with your decision; for I could neither hope, wish, or expect from a union with any man on earth, more perfect support or further aid in the discharge of the several duties of my mission, than that, which I am confident I shall derive from being associated with yourself.*

Union: Clark's cartographic skills, Lewis's astronomical ones; Clark's ease with men, Lewis's facility with the pen; Clark's equable temperament, Lewis's indomitable constitution. Pound the two men to a powder, mix them in a crucible, cook out their impurities, and pour them in the mold: a single, perfect captain. Lieutenant Clark was unthinkable.

Yet when Lewis tied up his boat at the Louisville landing on October 14th, he had in his pocket a lieutenant's commission. With an uneasy heart, he walked into town to find Clark.

Or rather, to find *William* Clark. One hardly needed take a step in Louisville to bump into *a* Clark. Word of Lewis's arrival had gone ahead, and strolling Clarks veered toward him, purchasing Clarks popped out of stores. Distaff offspring had assumed disguising last names, but all of them were as conscious of their Clarkhood as if the clan totem were tattooed on the backs of their hands. Here came trotting a Gwathmey, son of Ann, née Clark. He called down the street, and up ran another son of Ann, and while the two escorted Lewis, they wondered about the whereabouts of a third. A Croghan (son of Lucy Clark) appeared with a ten-year-old Anderson in tow (Cecilia, daughter of Elizabeth). A strapping Clark in his teens (son of Jonathan—did he say his name was Isaac? Isaiah?) hopped off his horse at the corner and stretched his hand out, then gestured farther along the block to the Clark store, where Lewis met John Clark (son of Jonathan), who apologized for the absence of Edmund Clark, co-owner. Edmund was at the Clark townhouse, where Lewis might also find Jonathan Clark and perhaps Fanny as well, with her four children. As for Uncle William, John was not sure. He might be out in the woods putting recruits through their paces, or in town for supplies, or across the river in Clarksville with Uncle George. (William had recently moved in with George Rogers Clark, Lewis knew. No doubt little Billy had been designated the bachelor hero's companion and support in his old age. As though he were an unmarried sister! But Lewis would take him away from all this.) John was saying that now the family knew Lewis was here,

Uncle William would get the message directly, and Lewis should go to the townhouse.

Lewis did so, now surrounded by a little pond of Clarks, including younger children who ran ahead to scout hazards and play herald. At the door of the townhouse, a stiff old negro appeared and folded aside to make way for (Lewis was introduced) Captain Edmund and (coming forward from a back room) General Jonathan, and now this Roman turtle of Clarks invaded the drawing room, where sat sister Fanny and her brood, plus two or three more young Andersons. Lewis was swept out on the Clarktide to the garden in back, where half a dozen negroes were laying out a collation of ham, tongue, hardboiled eggs, and cider on a long table. Lewis was surrounded, and peppered with questions, congratulations, old army anecdotes, winks and nods, names of connections along the Ohio, promises to provide letters of introduction; plus several score suggestions, severally brilliant, irrelevant, cross-purposeful, and countermanded. Peripheral mutterings concerned William's whereabouts, and should they wait (a surreptitious ring of boys was tightening around the table), and didn't Billy say—? and wasn't John sent—? and then a horse was heard reining up on the street beyond, and a shout approaching through the house, and William appeared on the back step.

Lewis stepped forward. The two men clasped hands and elbows.

"My dear Lewis."

"Clark!"

Clark was laughing. "By God!" he said.

Lewis laughed.

"Do we have a week?" Clark asked.

"We do. We do!"

"We need it."

A wordless pause. Hands; elbows. Clark looked well. His delighted eyes— He began again, "By God, what we'll—" And broke off. And laughed again.

"*Two years.*" Lewis pronounced the words with infinite relish. He hardly knew if he was making sense.

Then the family came round. The table loomed; a chair was proffered; conversation roared, dogs barked; children all but swung from the trees.

Motionless at the center, Clark beamed. General Jonathan and Captain Edmund jointly proposed a toast, pronouncing their gratification at seeing little Billy make his rank, after long years in the purgatory they themselves had expressly designed for him. Lewis inwardly swore that the lieutenant's commission would never come out of his pocket.

He had a way he preferred to think of it. There had been some talk when Lewis was in Washington City about what to do if Clark declined the invitation, and Lewis had later written to the President about a Moses Hooke, who seemed a solid second choice. The blank lieutenant's commission in Lewis's pocket had been intended (therefore) for Hooke, in the eventuality that Clark could not go. Lewis had not learned that Clark *could* go until he (Lewis) had already left Washington, and thus Clark's captain's commission had still to be worked out. Lewis would write to the War Department and demand Clark's due.

Clark would be debating when to inquire about it. In his letters accepting the invitation, he had asked Lewis to have his commission forwarded to Clarksville. After the luncheon, as soon as the two friends were alone in the closet Clark was using for his office, Lewis brought it up himself. "Your commission has not arrived yet?"

"In fact, no."

Lewis spoke with quiet force: "Damn me, but they are a pack of half-wits and time-servers." If Lewis's letter of credit enabled him to buy Cleopatra's barge and the wrapped lady herself in the bargain, surely he could obtain— "I expect it will be waiting for us at Kaskaskia. Of course you have the rank already, it is merely a question of some ink-stained functionary getting the scrap of paper out to us."

And so the curtain went up on the comedy of captains. Clark had his manservant, York, rip out the epaulet on his dress coat's left shoulder and resew it on his right. General George R. hosted another celebration a day later at his modest log home in Clarksville, and even more Clarks showed up. George R. drank until he collapsed in a corner of the porch, which was perfectly regular frontier manners, but Lewis had noted his wandering mind and cracked-china eyes, even when nominally sober. As a lad during the war, Lewis and his playfellows had been burstingly proud of their two Virginian Georges who were showing the other George the door, and this ruin before him was a shock, and the lieutenant's commission crinkled in his pocket, and he drank heavily himself and the next day could only hazily remember gliding as though under an enchantment through the doorway to his bed, a black hand swimming near his face. It must have been York carrying him.

Lewis vetted the men Clark had provisionally chosen, but it was a formality. Clark had had his choice among dozens. Once word of the expedition had got around, every enterprising young man within a hundred miles had shown up at Louisville, and Clark had had them swimming the river and running races and bringing in game in relays. The seven men, plus two Lewis had approved out of the three who had joined him in Pittsburgh, were apprised of their good fortune. Three days were allowed them to get their affairs in order, after which they were enlisted into the army on the grounds before the Clark plantation at Mulberry Hill, General George presiding and vertical for the occasion. Expedition supplies were replenished; the keelboat was repacked more heavily (the water below the falls being at last sufficient) so that the lightened pirogues would be more manageable. Throughout, Lewis had many occasions to say, You will report to Captain Clark, or Ask Captain Clark, or Captain Clark and I have agreed.

Lastly, there followed two or three days of the clamored-after captains making social rounds in the thin annulus of Louisville society that lay outside the Clark circle. While "Billy" gathered more congratulations, Lewis told and retold the story of his construction of the Pittsburgh–Louisville Grand Canal. He also danced with the ladies. It was what he liked to do best with them. He was not particularly graceful (God knew), but he was punctilious and inexhaustible, and as he swam in the music there was little call to speak; he merely held the lovely lady in her ribbons and flounces like a wrapped gift and smiled down at her and murmured a word, *exquisite, charming*. The fair sex seemed to favor taciturnity in a dancer as much as it frowned at it in a diner. Holding the ladies, admiring their intricate fabrics and inhaling their complicated scents, a mix of artifice and animal, Lewis did think they were lovely, lovely. He told himself: This is what I am leaving. And this is what I am going in the service of. Taffeta, crinoline, civet, lace. Together, known as civilization. Two years! And he swung his lady and looked down into her eyes and laughed, and she blushed, charmingly charmed. Oh, the dashing captain!

Then there was a last continental congress of Clarks, a final century of toasts, a parting gross of suggestions, and with heads of damp cotton, Lewis and Clark climbed in their boats (having first thrown in three of the men, the lightest first) and proceeded downriver.

Progress was now easy; consequently, Lewis had leisure to worry again. He daily thanked God for Clark's uncomplicated nature. It was not in his friend to probe for hidden meanings behind his commission's delay. At the same time, this unreflective trust made Lewis feel the more oppressed by his quandary. How had a single well-intentioned line in a letter months ago come to haunt him like this?

At Fort Massac the two captains hired a half-Shawnee interpreter, a George Drewyer or Droullier—it was one of those French names that slid across a pool of spit in their mouths—who was an incomparably better acquisition than the deceitful John Conner. He had grown up in the Cape Girardeau region of Missouri and was proficient in the Indian language of signs. Why Lewis had not thought of this before, he could not imagine (a consequence of his inexperience, he supposed, but really, he preferred on the whole not to imagine that), but here was an approximation of *Homo polyglottos,* since it was said that the language of signs was common to many of the plains tribes. Drewyer accepted without the smallest protest the pay of three hundred dollars per annum, and Lewis felt so gratified at thus effacing the Conner fiasco that he opened up his memorandum book for the first time in weeks and noted the hiring down. The log jam having been broken, he wrote a brief note the next day, and another the next, and Lewis the journalist stuttered back into life.

On November 13th he came down with an ague and fever. He dosed himself with Rush's pills and spouted volcanically, after which he felt much improved. By the 15th he was recovered. When Clark came down with the same illness the following day, it laid him far lower; but he bore up with his usual fortitude. Engaged in a survey of the confluence of the Ohio and the Mississippi, he counted chains along the shores with a face like oiled linen, pausing now and then to hug himself or crouch, at times shaking so violently he had to hand the circumferentor to York, who held it for his master to peer at while steadying him with his other hand. In the evenings in the captains' tent, he lay crumpled on his cot, talking lucidly about men and maps, occasionally apologizing for his indisposition, while York tended him. One day after they'd turned up the Mississippi, Lewis saw some heath hens on the shore and sent a man to shoot one, to make chicken soup for his friend, as his mother would have done. When the pirogue came aside the keelboat, it was York who reached down to take the bird and moved to the stern to pluck it. That night the big negro made the soup, adding herbs he appeared to have secreted in his bag. It was apparent he had done this often for his master.

York's presence on the expedition had been an unpleasant surprise to Lewis—a personal luxury that Clark, all unexpected, was allowing himself. But now Lewis saw that York was more in the way of a necessity. It went without saying that an expedition of this nature required men with healthy constitutions, and both Lewis and Clark had known that Clark did not meet that requirement. But Lewis had wanted Clark regardless, and Clark apparently had realized that only by bringing York could he confer benefit on the party without adding too heavily to its burdens. York, in a way, *was* Clark's constitution.

Yet Lewis was still not happy with this development. For one thing, he doubted the ability of a negro, even one as strong as York appeared to be, to exhibit the fortitude required by their journey. There would be extremities of discomfort and exertion, and all Lewis's experience with slaves had taught him that they were quick to wail and wilt in the face of adversity. For another thing, he could not judge how the Indians of Louisiana might react to a black man in their party, as many of them doubtless had never seen one.

Through the rest of November and into December the party labored up the Mississippi, its dumb onslaught a foretaste of what awaited them the following spring on the Missouri. A multitude of tasks remained: more men to enlist from the posts at Kaskaskia and Cahokia; relations to establish with Spanish officials in St. Louis, who would continue to administer Louisiana until the formal handover in March; maps and traders' accounts of the Missouri to gather; supplies to replenish; a location to determine for winter camp. The captains barely needed to trade a word to divide their labors. Clark (who was still too weak to sit a horse) would handle the men and the building of the winter camp. Lewis would tackle officialdom at the army posts and in St. Louis. On November 28th, a dozen miles short of Kaskaskia, he went ahead overland.

The following weeks were busy, and during them, Lewis half succeeded in believing that the matter of Clark's rank would resolve itself in the unofficial way of the frontier. In Louisiana, a man took a squaw into his house, and if he neglected to throw her out in the morning, she was his wife. Clark called himself captain, the men called him captain, Lewis called him captain. He was commander of the winter camp, which he was constructing at River Dubois, opposite the mouth of the Missouri. And he already had a right to the *title*, as he had once been a captain of a militia in Kentucky. Against all this, what mattered a slip of paper in Lewis's pocket, from a city a thousand miles away, where people knew nothing of local circumstances?

But in mid-December a letter arrived from the President regarding a number of territorial legal matters, which served to remind Lewis that the officials of Washington City might not understand Louisiana, but their word, nonetheless, would be law. Mr. J underscored the point, however unintentionally, by twice referring in his letter to *Mr. Clark*.

Lewis would be damned. He'd be damned! Not *Mr. Clark!* Not *Lieutenant Clark!*

In his reply, Lewis found the opportunity to insert three references to *Capt. Clark*. The Missouri and Mississippi daily deposited uncounted tons of Louisiana in the Gulf of Mexico, with no one's permission—could not Lewis's ink carve out of paper the ant's track needed to hold *Captain Clark*? He was outraged, and his outrage felt as strong as action.

Besides, he had other things to occupy him, as he waded into the political and mercantile waters of St. Louis. The town was not to his taste, a stew of wily French greed and fossilized Spanish rule. The peltry merchants held the real power, and such a cabal of unscrupulous bastards Lewis had never seen. Soliciting their aid in outfitting an expedition they feared would undercut their monopoly was like trying to teach *beg* to a wolf with his teeth deep in your leg. And in seeking information about upper Louisiana, Lewis found himself confronted by the paralysis of officials who feared the arbitrary lash of despotic power. They whispered to him from corners; they begged him not to reveal; they promised, then later retracted in a panic, having been apprised of the commandant's displeasure.

Oh, he detested the place!

And as if his real duties were not sufficiently onerous, he had another of Mr. J's fanciful tasks to perform, viz., inquiring into whether the white inhabitants of Louisiana might be induced to relinquish their lands and remove themselves to the east side of the Mississippi, so that the Indians on the east could be removed to the west. Lewis knew only too well that a reasonable answer to this question required no more than one word and three punctuation marks, all of them exclamation points. Yet he doggedly looked into the matter. To arrive at a valuation of the white-held land, he asked after Louisiana census figures, trade totals, land holdings, land improvements—all of which made him seem a left-footed agent for appropriationists in Washington, since naturally the officials to whom he spoke did not believe for a moment his stated reason for the queries.

The wealth of the French of Louisiana was entirely bound up with the Indian fur trade. To ask them to remove to the east was not unlike proposing to Boston whalers that they pursue their livelihood on the Great Lakes. Furthermore: Americans were coming. They were clearing and building and fencing, and more were coming after them. And they were like frontiersmen everywhere; you could tell them what to do until your teeth squeaked, and they would turn their backs and do what they wanted. A scant few weeks before, Lewis had observed a horse race at Cape Girardeau, and it had reminded him of the years he'd spent having to deal with the backwoodsmen along the Ohio. They bet like thieves, drank like sand, fought like dogs. When a man lost, he swore he'd won, and tried to make off with his own mount and the other fellow's. Thus the race was only a preliminary to the real contest, which was the fistfight that followed it. The only way to remove these people from Louisiana was to shoot them and throw them in the river.

But these were not the sorts of obstacles Mr. J would measure at their true size. To him, it would seem like a purely material problem, like separating red grains of sand from white, an experiment in which he would posit, no doubt, that the red grains were ferrous, and so use a magnet: *voilà!* Thus, in his report to Mr. J, having mildly laid out the facts militating against the President's scheme, Lewis concluded with a polite reference to the only magnetic force humans feel: *I am fully persuaded, that your wishes to withdraw the inhabitants of Louisiana, may in every necessary degree be effected in the course of a few years, provided the government of the U. States is justly liberal in its donations.* Was it merely craven of him that Lewis did not go on to suggest the scope of liberality required? *For example, we might offer the Louisianans the states of Kentucky and Tennessee, and remove the people presently inhabiting those regions to Iceland.*

Lewis's report crossed somewhere on the post road with another letter from Mr. J, in which he again referred to *Mr. Clark*. This letter was dated January 13th; the President had apparently not yet received Lewis's letter of December 16th. It was now February 8th.

Suddenly, the light poured in: Lewis saw that he had to act immediately. He and Clark planned to start up the Missouri in April. Clark needed his commission. What practical good, in God's name, had Lewis imagined could come of whispering *Captain Clark* in the President's ear?

Mr. J's letter had reached Lewis at Camp River Dubois, where Clark had finished the huts some weeks previously, and was keeping the men busy with footraces and shooting contests to prevent them falling into drunkenness and disorder. Along with the letter came invitations to two balls in St. Louis, and thus on the 10th of February Clark and Lewis took a pirogue down to the town. Lewis pleaded an engagement (he hinted at a lady's involvement, hoping it might explain the agitation Clark had no doubt noticed in him) and departed from his friend to retire to the room reserved for him in the large house of Pierre Chouteau, one of the principal traders of the town. There, perched on a typically meretricious and undersized French chair, by a smoking bear-oil lamp, he wrote the letter that he had feared all along, behind the shut doors of his heart, would be fruitless. Not merely fruitless, but inane: *Dear Sir,* he wrote to Dearborn, the Secretary of War, *I must write to you on a matter of some urgency . . . unaccountably left unattended . . . the press of preparations necessitated by a venture of this scope . . . a lieutenant's commission intended, as I understood the matter, solely in the event that Mr. Clark was unable to accompany me . . . his long service in the army . . . resigning on the verge of promotion in filial duty to his illustrious family . . . seniority to myself . . . perfect understanding between us . . .*

He stopped. Two captains! It was ridiculous!

But no more ridiculous than Mr. J's idea of a white east and a red west. Why was only the President allowed to indulge his absurd fancies with no one to stand on his hind legs and say him nay? For two months now, Lewis had dealt with St. Louis, while Clark had handled Camp Dubois across the river. Why not a captain for the east and a captain for the west? Yes? Was there anything there, any scrap, any crack? Lewis and Clark had captained entirely different projects over the winter. They had divided their labors. Clark had built the camp. Captain of—

Square the circle. Try. Buck up, for God's sake!

Lewis forced himself to write the words: . . . *cognizant of the inadvisability of two leaders of identical rank in the same regiment . . . a proven need for the construction of quarters, palisades, breastworks, etc., to be replicated next winter . . . the due owed many times over to Mr. Clark, and the requirements of the expedition, may be said to converge happily on the expedient of commissioning him as a Captain in the Corps of Engineers, which commission could be transferred to the regular army with retention of seniority at our return to St. Louis, if Mr. Clark so desired.* He dashed off the final line, . . . *at your earliest convenience . . . most obt. Servant . . .* , stuffed the odious thing in a cover, sealed it with a curse, slipped it into his pocket, and delivered it up to the Cahokia boat ten minutes before its departure.

When he went to the ball that evening, he could hardly speak to Clark. Instead, he bowed to the ladies, and danced, and danced.

And in the following weeks, waited. Clark was to remain in St. Louis for a fortnight, so Lewis crossed to Camp Dubois and found reasons to stay there. Had boat lockers built. Made sugar. Took lunars several times and sweated through the math, laboring to produce the exact degree and second of where he stood, so that lightning could find him if it wanted. Then back to St. Louis. Bribed some bastards. Tried to quash a malicious rumor that under American rule slavery would be abolished. Intrigued with a coquette; at the crux, fled her coils; self-disgust.

Waited.

On the 9th and 10th of March, hermaphroditic Louisiana lost her monstrous ambiguity. At the first day's ceremony, the Spanish flag came down, the French went up; the sun was allowed to set and rise once on the tricolor; then it, too, came down, and up went the stars and stripes. The captains suddenly had official duties. Their first task was to ride off and stop a party of Kickapoos from attacking a village of Osages. This was the other face of Mr. J's improbable scheme. The Kickapoos, along with several other Ohio tribes, had moved across the Mississippi in recent years to get away from white settlers. The arriving Indians did one of two things; they either maintained themselves as a nation, in which case they attacked another nation to appropriate their fields and hunting grounds, or they dissolved into wandering bands of beggars and drunkards, like the tatters of Delawares that eddied about the River Dubois camp.

The captains had intended to depart in the latter half of April, but May came, with still no word on the commission. The Missouri was long free of ice. Everything was in readiness. Lewis had told Clark he had written in February to remind the War Department of its duty. Clark was stoical. Lewis was in agony.

Finally, on the 6th of May, it arrived express; from Secretary Dearborn, addressed to Lewis:

War Department 26th March 1804

Sir,

The peculiar situation, circumstances and organisation of the Corps of Engineers is such as would render the appointment of Mr. Clark a Captain in that Corps improper—and consequently no appointment above that of a Lieutenant in the Corps of Artillerists could with propriety be given him which appointment he has recd. and his Commission is herewith enclosed. His Military Grade will have no effect on his compensation for the service in which he is engaged. I hope by the time this reaches you, all obstructions to your ascending the River will be removed & that you will be able to progress with facility and safety. I am &c.

What you are, thought Lewis, is a fucking *idiot*. Perfect official nonsense! *His Military Grade will have no effect on his compensation for the service in which he is engaged*—what in God's private acre of hell did that mean? Clark's engagement *was* his military grade! Lewis retired to his room, his cramped chair, his smoking lamp. He sat for close on an hour with a blank sheet in front of him.

So then: was a bureaucrat's word mightier than the pen?

He took up the quill. Instead of gripping it in his right fist and driving it through his left palm into the table, he breathed deeply, muttered, "Clark," dipped it in the inkhorn, touched the point to the rim to draw off the excess, carried the pregnant tip to the page:

St. Louis May 6th 1804

My dear friend,

I send you herewith inclosed your commission accompanied by the Secretary of War's letter; it is not such as I wished, or had reason to expect; but so it is.

He stared for another long period. Then added: *A further explanation when I join you.*

Yes, what, pray? Lewis longed to hear. Say, The world is what it is? Say, Clark's friend is a fool for thinking friendship can change it?

I think it will be best to let none of our party or any other persons know any thing about the grade, you will observe that the grade has no effect upon your compensation, which by G–d, shall be equal to my own.

Sealed it; sent it.

Mercifully, he had reasons not to see Clark for two more weeks. His friend was busy at Camp Dubois packing the boats, getting them in the water, starting up the Missouri. Lewis would cross overland to meet him at St. Charles, twenty-one miles from the river's mouth. In the meantime Lewis had to deal with a last flurry of business. There was the Osage party to see off to Washington. There was another parley to hold with the fractious Kickapoos. And now a roving band of Saukes, newly pushed out of Illinois by the energetic Governor Harrison, had got in line to make war on the Osages.

On May 20th, Lewis rode out of St. Louis; a number of luminaries accompanied him. He arrived on the bank of the Missouri opposite St. Charles in a downpour. Clark came across in the white pirogue. Lewis took his friend by the hand, but could say nothing with the others present. The company was determined to fête the Corps' departure, so it was not until the next evening, after they had left St. Charles and made three and a half miles up the Missouri under a gentle breeze, that a private moment was found in which the two men could lament the perfidious ways of officialdom; and in which they agreed to keep the matter secret.

By then, Lewis had opened his journal again for the first time in months, and recorded for posterity the beginning of the Lewis and Clark expedition:

The morning was fair, and the weather pleasant; at 10 oCk AM agreeably to an appointment of the preceding day, I was joined by Capt. Stoddard, Lieuts. Milford & Worrell together with Messrs. A. Chouteau, C. Gratiot, and many other respectable inhabitants of St. Louis, who had engaged to accompany me to the Village of St. Charles; accordingly at 12 Oclk after bidding an affectionate adieu to my Hostess, that excellent

woman the spouse of Mr. Peter Chouteau, and some of my fair friends of
St. Louis, we set forward to that village in order to join my friend companion and fellow labourer Capt. William Clark . . .

Only say it enough.

Lewis's relief was double. He was out of St. Louis. And although he had
not raised Clark to his rank, at least he had brought him in on his plot. The
lieutenant's commission now rustled in *Clark's* pocket. What had been a
comedy of captains had become something less bitter, something even, in a
curious way, sweet: a conspiracy of them.

4

It had only been in St. Louis that Lewis had come to realize how thoroughly
the lower Missouri was known. In 1796 Mackay and Evans had mapped
the entire stretch to the Mandan villages, and the sole reason there was not
a continual traffic of cheery *voyageurs* to the Mandans and back was that
the Teton Siouxs would not allow it. That powerful nation traded on the
St. Peter River with the Canadians of the North West Company, who had
no doubt seduced them into regarding traffic along the Missouri as a threat
to their lucrative position as intermediaries between the Canadians and the
tribes farther west. Thus the trick of reaching the Mandans was not an explorer's problem at all, but a diplomat's: weaning the Tetons from Canadian
influence, or failing that, cowing them. Lewis was confident he and Clark
could do one or the other, but as a task . . . as a task (if the truth be silently
breathed), it did not greatly interest him. Yes, yes: developing trade was necessary and beneficial to the spread of civilization. So was tilling the soil. So
was digging privies.

Furthermore, the Indian tribes the captains would be passing were
hardly the wraiths of legend, the Herodotan monsters, that an explorer's
fancy might still deem (if only for his own amusement) the Blue Muds, the
Snakes, the Blackfeet. The French and British had been trading for decades
with the Osages, Ottoes, Missouris, Mahas, Ayouways, Panias, Yanktons,
Tetons. A sentence in Evans's journal that Lewis had got hold of accorded entirely with his expectations: *The nations who have but an imperfect knowledge*

of the whites (being yet in a state of nature) are of a softer and better character, whilst those who have frequent communications with the whites appear to have contracted their vices without having taken any of their virtues.

As the captains ascended the river, Lewis mostly busied himself tramping through the bottoms for botany or along the prairie bench for topology, while Clark brought up the boats. Thus, it only made sense for Clark to keep the journal, a responsibility he accomplished faithfully each evening, without fuss, even when ill. Perhaps it was owing to Lewis's not having kept his own journal (and possibly, too, to a mild malaise, a sense of the vast happiness of which he knew he was capable deferred once more) that later, during the winter among the Mandans, he remembered this first leg less as a steady progression up the river than as an anthology of discrete incidents, unfurling their translucent petals before his mind's eye, now one, now another, as he lay on his camp bed in the night in the sturdy fort his good captain of engineering had built, waiting for shy sleep to come.

Throwing a stick into the Missouri. Clark by his side. The two of them on an island. Clark has the chronometer, Lewis the unrheumatical arm. Lewis throws. It drops in the exact spot on his first try; where the current is fastest. "Mark." Clark's eyes on the chronometer, Lewis's gaze through the glass, at Private Shields on the jutting willow bar at the island's tail.

Bright blue light, breeze of cool spray. Shields signals. "Mark." Clark holds the spot on the watch with his thumb. "Twenty-three seconds."

"A distance of forty-eight poles, six feet . . ." Lewis says.

"Sixteen and a half feet a pole, or twenty-four times forty-three."

"Thirty-three, I believe."

Clark takes out his pencil, jots on a length of cottonwood. "Two, shift the one . . . seven . . . seven hundred ninety-two."

"And six."

"Seven ninety-eight."

"Divided—"

"—by twenty-three." Clark labors. Lewis tries it in his head, gets lost somewhere in the conversion to Chinese shillings. Clark examines his result in near disbelief. "Close on thirty-five feet in a second."

"We made a mistake somewhere."

"My friend, we did not."

York swimming the river. Cress he's spotted on an island. Powerful strokes, bargelike jet back. Negroes always good swimmers. The cress prepared for the captains' dinner that night. One of Captain Cook's antiscorbutics. The hero swore by it. Clark, unwell, nods as York serves, "My dose of greens, eh?"

York murmuring, "My mother used to say—"

"Yours too?" Lewis says.

Reading Clark's journal at night, delighting in his friend's artless neologisms: *atmispeer* for atmosphere; *ball hill* for bald hill. Here and there, mistakes of genius. Lewis would love to eat one of Clark's watermelons—he writes them *watermillions.*

In the tent. Moderate rain on the oiled linen, hissing outside in the guard fires. Clark journalizing at his portable desk. The lantern between them, a shared light, Lewis reading Du Pratz's *History of Louisiana*, bootless right foot propped on the medicine box, an infected tick bite on the instep. A slap, a Ha! from Clark. "I was just writing of these devil musquetors, and now I've got three smashed and bloody on the very word."

"Pressed like flowers on an herbarium sheet," Lewis observes.

Clark smiles, "We ought to send it down the river with your specimens to show the President how greatly we suffer."

"I doubt he would believe it."

"No one would believe these musquetors."

A happy line occurs to Lewis: "We few, we happy few, we band of brothers!"

Independence Day. An early camp, an idyll, a grand stretch of countryside, a golden afternoon at the mouth of new-minted Independence Creek. Clark and Lewis on a rise above the camp, the river valley spread before them, Clark on his camp stool adding to his notes and Lewis prowling for new plants, grasshoppers ticking away from him like mechanical toys flashing orange underwings. Moving into an area of short grass where a spring Indian burn came partway up the slope, he approaches a waist-high branching plant. Narrow leaves three to a stem, each branch terminating in a flower of pale purple, a conic button. A stranger to him. He digs around the root and unearths it, heads upslope to show Clark, a prairie candelabra, and nearing, hears Clark scratch out a line with an impatient grunt. Curious, he stands behind and looks over his friend's shoulder:

—interspersed with Cops of trees, Spreding ther lofty branchs over Pools Springs or Brooks of fine water. Groops of Shrubs covered with the most delicious froot is to be seen in every direction, and nature appears to have exerted herself to butify the Senery by the variety of flours ~~raiseing~~ Delicately and highly flavered raised above the Grass, which Strikes & profumes the Sensation, and amuses the mind throws it into Conjecterng the cause of So magnificent a Senery—

"My dear Clark," Lewis says, intending the most affectionate, gentlest raillery, "a literary effort!"

A chuckle, a covering hand. "Doomed to failure."

"Not at all!" Lewis is charmed by this facet of his friend he has not previously glimpsed. Filled, he flows: "It perfumes the sensation!" And instantly knows his mistake—Clark has sometimes copied Lewis's very words in his letters back to him—

Clark stiffens—

—by way of a literary mentor—perhaps all unaware—oh! he only meant to join Clark on his island of words, to pluck with him the strange flowers—

—a quick movement of Clark's hand; the edge of the sheet tears—

Lewis bites back contrite words. To apologize would make it worse.

The day ends with a discharge of the bow gun, an extra gill of whiskey, one-eyed Pierre Cruzatte sawing the fiddle. The men dance, Clark smokes by the fire, Lewis pleads fatigue. Alone in the tent, he opens the marbled book in which Clark writes his final drafts:

as we approached this place the Praree had a most butifull appearance Hills & Valies interspsd with Coops of Timber gave a pleasing deversity to the Senery

There is nothing more.

Oxbow lakes iced over with goslings—bears feasting on bottom fields of rasp-berries, shitting purple paint—deer crowding the bars, browsing the willow shoots—a black mass of turkeys avalanching up a hill—enormous catfish bloated white, quarts of oil with whiskers—blue grass eight feet tall, evergreen timothy, sand rush and red haw, wild roses in profusion, cherries, apples, plums, whole honeysuckle cities—and yet, along the river, one after the other, abandoned Indian towns. The captains discussing the mystery while peram-bulating the sunken mounds of a Kanzas settlement. "War with their neigh-bors must have compelled them to retire to a better situation for defense," Clark is saying.

Lewis is looking down the valley, the mantling of oak and ash on the sec-ond bottoms. If Washington had made this tour, he would have ended up own-ing the whole Missouri. "Universal war," he says meditatively. "All against all."

"The only way for them to prove valor."

They pass along a midden. Bones, hoe blades, rotting buffalo skins, a travois with its legs in the air; grass rising to drown all. "I suppose we must not rule out smallpox as a contributory factor," Lewis says.

Why does that universal scourge fall disproportionately on the savages? Mr. J would not accept the view that it shows God's displeasure with them. What then? Lewis brought kinepox matter, but it got wet on the Ohio and lost its virtue. He wrote to the President from Cincinnati, requesting that he send more. "Du Pratz writes," Lewis goes on, "that the Indians die in such great numbers from the smallpox because they abhor the blotches on their skin, and so destroy themselves. He remarks that the Choctaws are naturally ugly, consequently do not regret their loss, and are more numerous than the other nations." The savage male's love of his own beauty, then? And if beauty is a mark of divine favor, then their own belief that the Great Spirit is dis-pleased might eventuate in a loss of vital spirit. Mr. J never sent more kinepox matter. Must have forgotten; more pressing matters. "Clark, you have been vaccinated, have you not?"

Clark pulls back his sleeve, shows the pitted scar on his forearm.

The first sight: pursuing an elk across a bottom, up a draw, bursting through the last cover, gaining the ridge—stopping, wind in his mouth.

Grass. Grass for miles, in every direction, to the horizon. And on beyond, to Ultima Thule. Of course, he's heard. But . . . there is something strange . . . His self streams out of him, blowing across that green sea. Not a tree, not a tree. No ax will ever touch . . . Sky and sky and grass and grass. Before the Garden, before all. Wordless.

Then he wakes; looks around. Elkless, too.

York shaving Clark. Helping him out of his sweat-soaked shirt. Holding him up at the edge of the bed, the jug angled just so, while he takes a puke. Wiping the froth from his mouth. Wetting the cloth, fussing over the pillow. His voice: a grainy hollowness, that edge of barrel-growl big negroes have. Otherwise, he talks like a white man. Like most valets. Then why is it a surprise, every time he speaks? Perhaps because he's large and dark, the picture of a field hand. Planters like their house slaves light; and they lighten through the generations, like the farming Indians Mr. J spoke of, but with nothing mysterious about the cause. With the admixture of white blood, presumably more intelligence, thus better English. Mr. J's servants are the cream, so light they're almost white, as contemptuous of the field slaves as the foremen. So different from ebony York with his peaspod lips and nose like a smashed pear, his ape brow. And yet that unperturbed voice (with less Kentucky in it than Clark's), fit for the dinner table: "Another spoonful . . . One more."

The court-martial of Willard for falling asleep at his sentinel post. Pleading as every soldier has done since Adam, viz., guilty of lying down, as I am an honest man, but not guilty of sleeping. His expression when Lewis reads out *punishable by death.* Mercy: a hundred lashes on his bare back instead. Try lying on that. Divided over four days, so he can still work an oar. Written in the proceedings: *The Commanding Officers Capt. M. Lewis & W. Clark.* Lewis smiles at that: Captain William Meriwether Lewis Clark.

At the mouth of the Platte. A shallow racing sea, so impregnated with sand it glitters like snow. Above it, the Missouri slower, no longer boiling. Better progress. But adversity (this side the grave) doing its duty with characteristic zeal: the mosquitoes much worse. Impossible to stand still. Some circle of hell. The men smearing on the tallow and hogs' lard they otherwise eat with their corn mush. Dancing like Indians, hopping and stamping, leaping into the yellow smoke from the punkwood fire. Blood: the only magnet mosquitoes know. Clark holding a snowberry branch in one hand and flailing himself in the eyes, mosquitoes resettling after each stroke like long lashes, like blue spectacles.

Clark's birthday, August 1st. York cooking him a saddle of venison, elk steaks, a beavertail. The table is planking across lockers, a cover of red flannel nipped from an Indian gift bundle, Barton's *Botany* and Kirwan's *Minerology* holding it down in the northwest breeze. York appears from the cookfire behind the tent with successive dishes, silent, the presentations voicing his domestic boasts for him: steaks girt by faerie rings of roasted Indian potatoes, sprigs of greens scalloping the platter edges. "May your appetite and opportunity ever coincide," Lewis says, raising his glass. York bending with the dessert platter. Wheels within wheels: cherries, plums, currants, grapes.

For long wearisome days, the river coiled in folds. Stopping to dine at the narrow point of an isthmus and sending drunkard Hall to pace off the distance across to where they had dinner the day before. "Nine hundred seventy-four yards, sir."

Clark consulting his notes. "And from there to here by water is eighteen and three-quarters miles."

" 'The most direct and practicable water communication across this continent,' " Lewis says archly.

"Eh?"

"From the President's instructions. What we are directed to find."

"Oh. I thought you were quoting Shakespeare again."

A council with the Ottoes and Missouris. Hot. Chiefs and brave men in the Indian circle, attitudes of impassive curiosity. The resident trader interpreting. Lewis gives his speech under the sailcloth awning. He informs them of their new American father. He speaks of great things: of the advantages of peace along the river, of undisrupted trade, of the indissoluble bonds of prosperity.

The Ottoes and Missouris answer: The French and Spanish never gave us so much as a knife for nothing.

They answer: You have more than you need in that boat.

They answer: We also want peace, but you must give us goods to keep our young men at home.

They answer: We do not want French guns, we want Mackinaw guns.

They answer: We are poor, we are naked.

They answer: To quiet us, give us a drop of milk.

By which they mean whiskey. Land to whites, blood to mosquitoes, whiskey to Indians.

Lewis's birthday, August 18th. His thirtieth. He and Clark both Leos: lions, leaders. Mr. J would scoff. Three decades! And to show for it? He has started more journals than most men. He has learned how to divide by four. He has confirmed for posterity that the Ottoes and Missouris still crave whiskey.

A search party brings back Private Reed, who deserted to run off with the Indians. Instead of feasting on elk and cherries, Lewis presides over another court-martial. By all rights he should have Reed shot. God is laughing at him. His birthday present: a terrified man. And the eyes of the Ottoes and Missouris, who have come for another council. Reed is a poor specimen. But man enough to acknowledge the captains must act consistent with their oaths.

They spare him. He is removed from the permanent party, and must only run the gauntlet four times. Even to this, the Indians object. "The idea is foreign to them," Clark asides.

"What?" Lewis snaps. "The gauntlet? I seem to remember it's a favorite blood sport with them."

"Only for their enemies. A man's always allowed to leave his nation. It's how they settle many of their disputes."

"Universal license is the other face of universal war," Lewis rejoins. "I learned when I was five years old that I could not always have what I wanted. If it upsets them, let them ask for more milk."

Reed runs the gauntlet and, to no one's surprise, survives. To desert again some other day. Fiddling and dancing at night, for Lewis. God laughing in the ha ha of the handclaps. Clark toasts him a long life and leads the men in a huzzah, and Lewis thanks them, so moved and ashamed he turns his face out of the firelight.

Cutting new oars on the shore. Gass throwing sand in York's eyes. In fun, but York carrying on as though dying. Clark leading him to the water and bathing his eyes. Telling Lewis later in some irritation, "He was very near losing one."

Lewis writing orders, signing his name, *Meriwether Lewis, Capt. 1st U'S. Regt. Infty.* Clark signing below him, *Wm Clark, Cpt. &.*

On an evening walk to find a wild goat, fail of the goat but kill three buffalo that cross your path—dressing the buffalo, shoot two deer that come to see—quartering the deer, bag the turkeys drawn by the noise—plucking the turkeys, throttle the squirrel that jumps in your lap—

September. At the Grand Détour of the Missouri, more than thirty miles of river around, and the portage across the neck two thousand yards. Clark in his notes attempting the French: *What is Called & Known by the <u>Grand de Tortu</u> or Big Bend of the Missourie.* Tortoise; torture; tortuousness. How does he do it? But no conceivable way for Lewis to share his delight with his friend.

Approaching the Teton Siouxs. A bad beginning: Colter is ahead hunting, and his horse is stolen. So that is how it will be. On this nation, Mr. J particularly wants to make a friendly impression; but he has not met them. Four anxious days in their company. The banks lined with their brave men, every morning more, as they see the signal fires and come in from the hunt. Staring sullenly, gripping their bows and arrows, their trade muskets.

In St. Louis, Lewis heard about the Teton chiefs: Black Buffalo, head of the largest band, a man of good character, but prone to fits of anger. The second chief, the Partisan, a dangerous rapscallion.

The flag raised, the awning, the peace pipe, the chiefs disposed in attitudes of impassive etc. Lewis: *My children: peace, trade*— But the fiddler, Cruzatte, half-Maha, who said he spoke some Sioux, stands there leaking disjointed words, his one myopic eye flashing panic. "Good God, man," Lewis mutters to him, "don't you know the word for peace?" No. "Prosperity?" Apparently not. "The firm ties of mutual advantage?" An apologetic squeak. "Well damn you, then!"

The captains distribute gifts instead. They take the chiefs and several of their soldiers, short, Herculean men, on board the keelboat to show them curiosities. Each brave is given a quarter glass of whiskey. Then, as though passing a peace pipe, they suck in turn the neck of the empty bottle, a glass teat yielding its last drop of kindness. Avidity, a rapture almost religious. Now the Partisan begins to feign drunkenness, staggering into Lewis's men, making to steady himself by pulling open lockers to discover what he may steal, casting mocking glances at his supporters on shore.

Lewis is revolted deep in his bowels. He and Clark endeavor to get the Indians off the boat. Hand gestures, smiles, would you be so kind as to step this way, we might more profitably continue our parley ashore— Now other braves clutching this or that, fingering brass buttons on the chests of their owners: Give us. Gestures indicating: You have many things, you have not shown us respect. Lewis smiles the more: Yes, you are poor, you are naked, we can discuss this curious paucity of clothing on shore— Prying rope out of red hands, appealing to the wavering Black Buffalo, the men tensing all down the boat and the second pirogue maneuvering nearer, thumbs rising to the flanges of the flintlocks. What's this? You give? More milk? The Partisan remonstrating, thumping his breast and pointing downriver, Cruzatte sweating, "We must go, he says . . . back down." Gestures toward the pirogue waiting to return the Indians to shore, Lewis grinning like a lockjawed horse, get off my boat you bitches' bastards before I toss you off. "Talk on shore!" Cruzatte groaning in fright, forgetting everything save his role as translator, mimicking Lewis's gestures as though by performing them at shorter stature he might convert them to Sioux.

At last Black Buffalo coaxes the Partisan and the others into the pirogue, and Clark and Cruzatte and four other men paddle them across. Lewis watches from the keelboat. The moment they touch the shore, three of their young men seize the bow cable, a fourth hugs the mast. There is a confusion of bodies, shoving. Lewis sees Clark step back and draw his sword. "Prepare for action!" Lewis barks. Cook died this way, a fight over a miserable cutter. Rifles shouldered, the bow cannon trained, the mounted blunderbusses swiveled. Fifty arrows pointed blank at Clark's body, he will die instantly, his body flung backward like an empty suit of cloth, porcupined. The cannon packed with sixteen musket balls, thirty rifles at the ready, the savages will be mown down, and their women and children, they will not dare—

They do not. Black Buffalo steps forward and takes the towrope, orders the young men roughly away. Clark is in a passion, speaking high, and Lewis catches a phrase on the wind: "—more medicine on board my boat than would kill twenty nations such as you in one day." Cruzatte gesturing, bleating God knows what. The Indians withdraw to counsel among themselves. A test, of course. Which the captains have passed. It seems they have more mettle than the common trader who paddles up here with whiskey in his boat and greed in his uncomplicated heart.

Now follows the infinitely more tedious part. Having failed to cow the captains, the Siouxs attempt to seduce them. You must stay! You are our guests. Let us smoke, let us feast. Lewis is carried like a pasha in all pomp to their lodge camp in a buffalo robe. He and Clark are treated to a scalp dance. They are offered squat dark women. Kiss our toads. This grinds on for three wearisome days, and the finale proceeds precisely as Lewis expects. At the moment the Corps makes ready to continue upriver— No, you cannot go yet! We love you too much! You have not given us enough!

The final moments are tawdry. A wrestle back and forth over the bow cable, demands for more tobacco. Clark throws a carrot ashore but they howl for more, and Lewis, two days past patience, refuses in fury, and Cruzatte says of Black Buffalo's haughty words and deprecating gestures, "He is scorning us for caring so much about a little tobacco." We caring so much! *We!* Lewis grabs up a fistful of carrots and flings them to the ground, coins in the mud for urchins to fight over, the Indians let go the rope, the Corpsmen pole and row with a will and they are away.

If this is Indian diplomacy, Lewis would prefer the quick boyhood kind, bloodying noses with some other brat over who killed the sparrow they both shot at. If even the uncorrupted ones are like this—the Blue Muds, the Snakes, the Blackfeet—he fears he will hate them all.

Reading Clark's journal entry on the Teton encounter: *They again offered me a young woman and wish me to take her & not Dispise them, I wavered the Subject.*

October. Running low on whiskey; daily rations suspended. Still some ninety leagues short of the Mandan villages. The river shoaly now, several channels to choose from and the chosen one seeming always to grow too shallow after a league, forcing a retreat. A constant wind in their teeth, flinging cold rain. Brant and geese streaming south. It is obvious they must winter with the Mandans. Clark's most conservative estimate in Dubois had them at the Mandans in September, in the Rockies by winter. Immaterial time. Thirty years gone by like (divide by four) seven and a half. A life swallowed.

The Ricaras are the last nation they must pass. They are not nomads like the Siouxs, but agriculturalists. The Corps comes first upon abandoned villages: clustered earth lodges raised for the living but with the air of burial mounds, collapsing palisades, shaggy fields lumpy with volunteer squash. "The scarcity of wood in these bottoms forces them to move as they exhaust it," Lewis observes to Clark. The Indians are found at last in a rare stretch of good timber, three villages near the mouth of the Grand River. The resident trader, Mr. Gravelines, informs the captains they are the survivors of nine villages devastated by war with the Siouxs.

"We shouldn't rule out smallpox as a contributory factor," Clark says.

"Yes," Lewis says. "That was said in St. Louis, wasn't it?"

Beautifully maintained fields, now harvested; small-eared corn; three different kinds of squash; two varieties of tobacco. And the people, mercifully, not beggars, taking what is given them with unstudied gratitude. They even abjure ardent spirits, which Lewis would attribute (taking his cue from Mr. J) to the spiritual benefit conferred by their honest toil in the earth, had he not the example of the two-legged fish who call themselves Kentucky farmers. "I'm sure it has been noted previously," he notes to Clark, "that plagues such as the smallpox fall disproportionately upon the villagers. Logically so, as contagion spreads more easily in their crowded conditions than among the far-flung nomads. Still, it is ironic that this sickness we have visited upon them punishes most those whom we most wish to encourage, I mean the settled farmers. While the lawless Tetons grow ever more powerful."

The flag, the awning, *My children*— Gratifyingly, they listen. A chief agrees to accompany the captains to the Mandans to make peace. The captains will isolate the Tetons, who have preyed so brutally upon these people. Good feelings, hospitality. The Ricaras living up to their reputation for compulsory licentiousness. That is, compelling others: if you do not lie with our women, you despise us. *Quite the contrary, my good people.* Lewis does not say this. But neither does he lie with their women. Still, they have little reason to feel despised. The men conferring *sotto voce* with the resident traders, bleeding into the village to show their respect. In three weeks' time, some will need a course of mercury, but that is preferable to the *sub rosa* abominations of garrison life. And it is not impossible that the unpleasantness with the Tetons was exacerbated by the captains' refusal to bed their unappetizing Dulcineas.

And York! Here beyond the Teton pale, the Ricaras have never seen a negro. Crowding to touch like papists at a saint's statue, fingering the wool on his head, grabbing his groin to see if he is like a man in that respect. Pronouncing him the big medicine. Of course it goes to his head. Lifting the largest gift bale like a carnival strong man. Growling and chasing the children, who scatter shrieking, word getting back to the captains he's telling them he was a wild bear before Clark caught him, and lived on people, and children made good eating. "Good God, just what we need," Lewis ejaculates.

Clark reins him in. But is indulgent toward his animal needs. Big medicine in big demand. A Yorkist dynasty in the making. For three days he keeps going missing. Clark sending men after him who must only point to skin and black metal to get whoops and grins and a thicket of pointing fingers. Private Gibson finding a man guarding the door of his lodge while York attends to his wife within. The closest the Corps gets to a confrontation with the Ricaras: almost a fistfight between Gibson, armed with his orders, and the husband determined to gain his horns. The husband prevails.

After making the acquaintance of such as Ricaras, there is another thing as sure as mercury: mutiny. John Newman this time, for repeatedly answering

Sergeant Pryor that he would not return to the boat, no, not if Pryor and the two captains lined up in the rain to kiss his ass. Pleads: Not Guilty. Found: Guilty. Sentence: Seventy-five lashes on his bare back, and banishment from the permanent party. Some restiveness among the men. There, but for the grace of God. The Corps leaves the villages and proceeds a stretch upriver before punishment is inflicted, on a sandbar. In the rain.

At least the Indians are not there to set up a wailing Greek chorus. But the Ricara chief accompanying the Corps remonstrates and affects to cry, as they do when their rhetoric demands it. Later, he explains he understands the necessity of making examples, he has done it himself, but his nation never whips, not even children, because it breaks the spirit. What does he do then? Clark asks through Gravelines. He kills the offender, comes the answer.

Clark signing the court-martial: *Wm Clark Capt. E N W D.* Captain on an Expedition of North West Discovery, probably. But who knows? It might mean Captain of Engineers Not Withstanding Department!

The Ricara chief is named Piaheto. He is also named Ah-ke-tah-nah-shah. And after he imitates for Lewis the call of a certain goatsucker (*attah-tonah, tonah*), he answers to the name Tonah, too. Whatever his name is, he tells the captains what his nation calls the tributaries they pass. One is Wah-rika-anee, meaning Elk Shed Horns. *Wah* means elk, he explains. *Rica* means horn.

"I do believe we have discovered the origin of their tribal name," Lewis asides to Clark.

Last leaves falling. Timber increasing in the bottoms. Ice rimming the clay at the river's edge. Passing abandoned Mandan villages. Low mounds of collapsed earth lodges. The ground cobbled with human skulls. Siouxs and smallpox.

On October 24th, they reach a hunting camp of the Mandans. One of the grand chiefs is there, and he and the Ricara chief meet in cordiality and smoke. Then the boats *proceed on,* as Clark always writes it. Indians watching from both sides of the river, running or riding ahead with the news, calling to the boats to come near so they might satisfy their curiosity. Shoals, sandbars. Even were a freeze not imminent, the captains would be forced to stop by the low water. They pick up two chiefs for the last two leagues. Around the ten thousandth bend since St. Louis—1,605 miles of river, 166 days of *going on on*—the first Mandan village heaves into sight: a palisade such as the Ricaras make, but open along the edge of the bluff, a cluster of lodges like overturned bowls. Smoke from dinner fires and the ululating of the native dogs.

Towing the last mile through shoals, while the braves splash down, gape at the towrope, at the boat, go back, call out, the water so cold, several of the privates inflicted with rheumatism, Clark so bad a few nights ago he woke and could not move, called out in the dark, Lewis waking for once before York and rising to wrap a hot stone in flannel and cradle it against his friend's paralyzed neck.

Beaching half a mile below the village, a fallowed cornfield. Lewis steps ashore. Men, women, and children pour down from the bluff and rush at him, in flood, in spate.

5

Lewis sat on the grass in the council circle under the awning, his speech on his knees. A southwest gale was blowing. Sergeant Gass had rigged up sail-cloth breaks, but airborne sand still invaded Lewis's mouth, and a whitish patina was forming on the painted skin of the chiefs, turning them into the Welshmen of legend before his eyes. Perhaps it was just this—wind and sand and grease—that had given rise to the story in the first place. It continually astonished Lewis how these fanciful tales arose and endured. There was also supposed to be a lost tribe of Israel somewhere in the vicinity.

Clark sat on his right, with the Ricara chief next to him. On Lewis's left was René Jessome, a resident French trader whom the captains had hired as interpreter and informant. Lewis worked his lower lip, trying to dislodge a bar of sludge at the base of his front teeth. He signaled to Pryor, who stood in the wind just outside the shelter; Pryor signaled to the river; the bow gun of the keelboat boomed over the water. Several of the chiefs had witnessed its operation yesterday, and Lewis felt rather than saw a ripple of professional interest travel through his guests.

He stood to speak. He was more or less used to this by now: the circle of chiefs and considered men, the smell of buffalo grease and pot meals coming off them, the sweetgrass they burned for luck, the reek of the kinnikinnick

they smoked, tobacco mixed with various shrub barks, plus powdered buffalo dung, which contributed a not unpleasant murky tang. They looked up
at him with the impassivity they cultivated, and attained to such impressive
degree. You had to remind yourself that they were listening; that they had, in
fact, remarkable powers of recall. The sail walls shook. "To the chiefs of
the two Mandan villages and those of Mahawha and those of the big and
little Minetare villages." Lewis followed Indian custom, extending his hand
open-palmed toward each man and looking him in the eye as he pronounced
his name: "To chief Ka-go-ha-me of Ma-too-tonka; chiefs Pos-cop-sa-he
and Cah-gah-no-mok-she of Roop-ta-he; chief Ta-tuck-co-pin-re-has of the
Mahawha village; chiefs Omp-se-ha-ra and Oh-hah of Minetare Metaharta;
chief Cal-tar-co-ta of the big Minetare village; additionally to She-he-ke and
O-hee-nah of Ma-too-tonka, who we regret have been delayed and are not
present; also chief Le Borgne, who is away on a hunt; and to the other chiefs
and brave men of the Mandan, Ahwahharway, and Minetare nations, those assembled here and those to whom we request that this greeting and our gifts
be conveyed."

Lewis had already met some of the chiefs; Jessome had supplied the
names of others. He had worked hard to memorize the welter of syllables, fix-
ing them in a map in his head as an aid to memory. Ma-too-tonka was the first
Mandan village the Corps had come to, on the west bank of the Missouri, and
Sheheke was the first chief there. He was called Big White by the traders, because he was light-skinned and somewhat obese. The second village, going
upriver, was Roop-ta-he (also Mandan), on the east bank. The principal chief
there, Pos-cop-sa-he, or Black Cat, was intelligent, honest, and well disposed
to whites. Across the river from Roop-ta-he, near the mouth of the Knife
River, was Mahawha, the village of the Ahwahharways. These were the so-
called Shoe Indians. Alas, the President's ingenious sartorial conjecture had
proved incorrect: they wore moccasins. They were also called Wa-ta-su-nari
by the Ricaras and the Mandans, so some traders called them Wattasoons.
(Perhaps they were a lost Dutch tribe.) The Ahwahharways apparently spoke
the Minetare language, whose precise relationship to Mandan—sister or
cousin or familiarized stranger—Lewis had not yet determined. The two
Minetare villages were one and three miles up the Knife River, so named because the Indians obtained flint from quarries along its course. The second
Minetare village was the largest of the five, and its powerful chief, Le Borgne,

was said to be a great warrior, but also a rogue and tyrant. His village was represented in today's council by the old chief Cal-tar-co-ta. The Minetares were also called Gros Ventres by the French, or Big Bellies, although they appeared to be neither more corpulent nor (on average) more pregnant than the Mandans. No one appeared to know what *Mandan* meant. Jessome had said they called themselves Nu-mang-ka-ke. Lewis had asked him what the word meant, thinking it might provide a clue to their origin. Jessome had replied, "It mean *people.*"

"*Children,*" Lewis began his speech. "Commissioned and sent by the great Chief of the seventeen great nations of America, we have come to inform you that a great council was lately held between this great Chief of the seventeen great nations of America and your old fathers, the French and Spaniards; and that in this great council it was agreed that all the white men inhabiting the waters of the Missouri should obey the commands of this great Chief. Your old traders are of this description, and are bound to obey the commands of their great Chief, the President, who is now your only great father.

"*Children.* This council being concluded between your old fathers—" For the most part, it was the same speech he had given to the Ottoes, Missouris, and Yanktons. He had modeled his rhetoric on Mr. J's, when he welcomed Indian delegations to Washington. "—the French and Spaniards have surrendered to our great Chief all their fortifications and lands in this country, together with the mouths of all the rivers through which the traders bring goods to the red men on the troubled waters. These arrangements being made, your old fathers the French and Spaniards have gone beyond the great lake toward the rising sun, whence they never intend returning to visit their former red-children in this quarter." Mr. J admired Indian oratory extremely, combining, as it did, nobility of expression with a Greek-like simplicity, a concreteness of image (*toward the rising sun,* for example), which his own formulations, soaring on alliterative wings into the upper atmosphere, often lacked. He adopted their tropes with such relish that Lewis imagined him imagining himself an Indian like them, a red heart beating in his Virginian breast: *Great water. As many as the leaves of the forest. I take you by the hand. White brother and red brother.* We are not European, but American; which is to say, half Indian: *We understand each other.*

"*Children,*" Lewis continued, turning the page. A devious gust pulled the sheet out of his hand and he was forced to make an undignified snatch at it.

"The great Chief of the seventeen great nations of America, impelled by his parental regard for his newly adopted children on the troubled waters, has sent us out to clear the road, remove every obstruction, and to make it the road of peace—" *Troubled waters* was the Indians' own term for the Missouri. They signified it by a roiling motion of their fingers. "—to inquire into the nature of their wants, and on our return to inform him of them, in order that he may make the necessary arrangements for their relief. He has sent by us flags, medals, and clothes such as he dresses his war chiefs with, which he directed should be given to the chiefs of the Mandan, Minetare, and Ahwahharway nations, as a pledge of the sincerity with which he now offers you the hand of friendship." Chief Lewis and Chief Clark. There would be no troublesome paper crinkling in a pocket. Clark would be fully a chief from the moment he was treated like one.

"*Children*. Know that the great Chief who has thus offered you the hand of unalterable friendship is the great Chief of the seventeen great nations of America, whose cities are as numerous as the stars of the heavens, and whose people cover with their cultivated fields and wigwams the wide country reaching from the western borders of the Mississippi to the great lakes of the east, where the land ends and the sun rises from the face of the great waters." Lewis glanced down at the expressionless faces (smallpox-scarred) before him like a ring of pupils under a tree drifting open-eyed into sleep as their teacher droned on. He wondered what they made of his reading. They had seen it before, as many traders were literate. Still, the efficacy of haranguing, for them, was bottomed on personal intimacy, on direct appeal and the play of the eye. *I open my heart to you.* Perhaps, to them, Lewis opened only his sheaf. Did they believe these words were not his, since he could not speak them without prompting? But if so, wasn't that only proper, as Lewis spoke for the President? In fact, wasn't it true that the first thing they must learn in order to become Americans was that not every last male with the power to climb to his feet could always speak for himself, but must bow to the voice of commonality? To become, in other words, good Republicans? "—to give you his good advice; to point out to you the road in which you must walk to obtain happiness—" Or perhaps this reading from marks on paper struck them as prophecy? Piaheto had said that the Mandans and Minetares each spring visited a sacred rock upon which figures had been carved in some aeon past, and a tribal haruspex claimed to discern in the scratchings omens of the year to come. Perhaps Lewis's words, then, by virtue of their being read, had *more* power to persuade, rather than less. Might it not be analogous to the superstitious dread in which many of the Indian chiefs who visited Washington seemed to regard the painting of their portraits? That was all part of the routine: the tour of Washington City, the stop at the "Great Council" (Congress), the audience with the great Chief—then the official portrait, in full regalia, for Mr. J's ethnographical collection. Unaccustomed to realistic representation, the chiefs saw actual life in their likenesses, and reasoned that whatever vital principle was there must have been taken from them, thus lessening their stock. Which, Lewis had to concede, was not completely ridiculous, once one accepted their premises.

"*Children.* The road in which your great father commands that you must walk is that you are to live in peace with all the white men, for they are his children; neither wage war against the red men your neighbors, for they are equally his children and he is bound to protect them." While Jessome translated these words, Lewis regarded the faces in the circle. (The sand had collected in the pox scars, making them piebald.) He was entering on the portion of his speech most likely to provoke complaint, and he hoped the Frenchman was up to the task of conveying his sentiments undistorted. Jessome seemed tolerably well informed about the chiefs of the various villages, but he was hardly prepossessing. Bandy-legged, with blackened teeth, he dressed in all respects like a native (he had a Mandan wife and children) and shaved his beard, or perhaps plucked it, as many traders did, since the one solitary thing the warring tribes of the plains could agree on was their abhorrence of facial hair. A curious taboo. "Injure not the persons of any traders who may come among you, neither destroy nor take their property from them by force. Do not obstruct the passage of any boat, pirogue, or other vessel, which may be ascending or descending the Missouri River—" Jessome had claimed he could translate both the Mandan and Minetare languages, but in the ceaseless coming and going of visitors to the captains' camp in these first three days, Lewis had noted this was not true. Jessome relied on Indians to translate Minetare for him. Lewis's impression was that many of the Mandans could speak Minetare, while few if any of the Minetares could converse in the nasal Mandan tongue.

Yes: a look of dissatisfaction breaking across a face as Jessome spoke: Cal-tar-co-ta, the old Minetare chief. One of the Mandans was relaying Jessome's words to him. Lewis knew well this was a sticking point. *What, no highway robbery?*

"*Children.* Do these things which your great father advises and be happy. Avoid the councils of bad birds, turn on your heel from them as you would from the precipice of a high rock, whose summit reached the clouds, and whose base was washed by the gulf of human woes, lest by one false step you should bring upon your nation the displeasure of your great father, the great Chief of the seventeen great nations of America, who could consume you as the fire consumes the grass of the plains. The mouths of all the rivers through which the traders bring goods to you are in his possession, and if you displease him, he could shut them up and prevent his traders from coming among you, and this would bring all the calamities of want upon you." Jessome spoke in Mandan. The Mandan chief, his expression unaltered, relayed the words in Minetare. Cal-tar-co-ta listened, his scowl deepening. Perhaps a privilege of age among them was the license to betray one's emotions. "But it is not the wish"—Cal-tar-co-ta was shaking his head, the feathers on it bobbing like admonitory fingers—"of your great father to injure you"—he was shifting on his haunches—"on the contrary he is now pursuing the measures best calculated to ensure your happiness—"

Cal-tar-co-ta rose to his feet. With his mangled hands (like many of the men, he was missing fingers) he pushed away what he was hearing with such an expressive gesture that Lewis could almost see the words striking his palms and falling like deflected darts to the ground. He made another gesture, of gathering his robe, and it was as though age and wisdom were precipitating out of the air to plate him in armor, and he spoke, not to Lewis, but to the seated chiefs, in a tone of patience sorely tried. Black Cat rejoined, in apparent rebuke. Appeals to the other chiefs, nods to Black Cat. Jessome was stumbling through a translation, "Cal-tar-co-ta say his village . . . enemy . . ."

Lewis's heart sank. He leaned down to Jessome: "He is saying we are enemies?"

"*Non, je*— No, I do not . . ." Jessome consulted with a Mandan chief next to him, and Lewis knew he and Clark must find an interpreter who spoke Minetare. Cal-tar-co-ta had sat again, but with the demeanor of a host who, from a civilized determination to play his role, hears out the impertinences of a foolish guest. (Really, the histrionic talents of these people were remarkable.) "He say he cannot rest *ici* long while his village is exposed to the enemy," Jessome said to Lewis. "The other chief reprimand him for so a petite cause of inquietude in council."

A poor enough ruse. Why could he not express his real objection, and thus avoid opening himself to the charge of captiousness? Perhaps their oratory was most impressive when least understood. *Give us guns, give us milk.* Begging with the greatest dignity. It was fortunate these three nations appeared to be like the Ricaras in abjuring great spirits. *"Children,"* Lewis continued, staring at Cal-tar-co-ta to show he was not intimidated, "if you open your ears"—not great spirits, of course he meant ardent spirits—"to the counsels of your great father, the great Chief of the seventeen great nations of America, he will as soon as possible after our return send a store of goods, to trade with you for your peltries and furs. These goods will be furnished you annually in a regular manner, and in such quantities as will be equal to your necessities. You will then obtain goods on much better terms than you have ever received them heretofore." Give us, give us— Your boat full of— You do not respect— Always the French give— Why do not—? *"Children.* We are now on a long journey to the head of the Missouri; the length of this journey compelled us to load our boat and pirogues with provisions; we have therefore brought but very few goods as presents for yourselves, or for *any other nations* which we may meet on our way. We are *no traders,* but have come to consult you on the subject of your trade in order that your nation may hereafter receive a regular and plentiful supply of goods." While Jessome translated, Lewis wondered whether some of the other chiefs shared Cal-tar-co-ta's impatience. The Minetares, Jessome had said, preyed on other nations more than the Mandans did. At this very moment, they had a raiding party out against the Snakes. The conclusion of peace treaties would naturally deprive them of the revenue from their depredations. Perhaps it was not to be marveled at that, being unable to conceive of the number of goods that would flow to them once a chain of American forts was constructed along the Missouri, they took a message of peace ill.

"Children. If one or two of your chiefs wish to see your great father and speak with him, they can readily do so. When the snows of winter depart with the return of the sun, our boat will go back down the Missouri River, and those among our men that go with it can take those chiefs with them to St. Louis. The commandant at St. Louis will furnish them with all the means

necessary to make their journey thence to the great father's town comfortable and safe." *To make them acquainted with our power,* as one of Mr. J's pet locutions ran. And God send you don't sicken and die there. That, too, a part of the routine, or nearly: the east coast tour, the presidential audience *(I give you my hand),* the portrait, the precipitous decline, the pitiable end, the regrets carried back to the tribe by some unlucky messenger.

Last page— "*Children.* We hope that the Great Spirit will open your ears to our counsels. Follow them, and you will have nothing to fear, because the Great Spirit will smile upon your nation, and in future ages will make you to outnumber the trees of the forest." Jessome interpreted; the sailcloth boomed; Lewis folded his speech. Cal-tar-co-ta stared at him unwaveringly, once more expressionless. When Jessome had finished, Lewis continued without notes. "We know that you must retire and counsel among yourselves; therefore, we do not expect a reply until tomorrow or the day after. However, on the subject of peace, we are providing today an opportunity to take a step that would, I trust, be welcomed by any nation subject to the insults and injuries of the Siouxs, as we know you to be, and no less your neighbors to the south, the Ricaras." Lewis dilated: the ravages of war—security of women in the fields—children at their innocent games—mutuality of interest of the provident villagers as against the thieving nomad— As he spoke, Clark was filling the pipe that he had prepared "very flashy" the night before, holding it up for Lewis's appreciation: the tail feather of a calumet eagle, white wampum, blue beads, a lock of porcupine quills. When Lewis finished speaking, he lit it, offered it to the four directions, and handed it to Piaheto. The pipe went around the circle; Cal-tar-co-ta did not refuse. Good. An effective and eloquent custom, the peace pipe. Not that much different from the oval dining table: breaking bread together; drinking from the same cup. Lewis wondered if the two native varieties of tobacco he had seen killed their land as effectively as the kind he'd grown in Virginia.

Time to make chiefs. Lewis stood again and nodded to Pryor. He beckoned to the Fields brothers, who approached the marquee in their brass-buttoned and top-hatted finery, bearing between them on a litter one of the 150-pound gift bales Clark had packed at Camp Dubois, festooned with ribbons and tinkling with hawk bells. They set it down next to Lewis, who removed from it, with all due solemnity, the mahogany case that usually carried the chronometer. Lewis intoned, "The great Chief of the seventeen great nations of America has sent these medals and certificates, which he directed should be given to the chiefs of the Mandan, Ahwahharway, and Minetare nations, to be kept by them, as a pledge of the sincerity with which he now offers you the hand of friendship." He opened the box, noting with approval how well York had waxed it the night before, and lifted out the medals one by one, raising each above his head, not unlike a Host, before distributing them in their gradated sizes to the different chiefs. The largest bore a portrait of Mr. Jefferson in profile. *(Take, wear; this is my body.)* On the obverse, a white hand shook a red. *(I am at the midpoint of the Missouri; the Indians so far friendly.)* To the second and third chiefs of each village, Lewis gave smaller "season" medals: a woman weaving on a loom; a man sowing wheat; cattle and sheep. The demi-semi-chiefs received certificates of friendship, which were supposed to function like passports along the river: *Know ye that so-and-so is a friend of the United States,* etc. Lewis felt like a damned mountebank. Step up, my friends! But that was nothing new to him. He had burned with a sense of fraudulence often enough at the President's table, uttering some urbane pleasantry to this or that guest, or proferring his worthless view on a pending piece of legislation. Nor was this ritual anything particularly significant to the chiefs. These medals were all over the frontier, embossed with portraits of Jefferson or Washington or George III. You could no doubt find Good Queen Bess, if you dug far enough into middens on the Virginia coast. But you handed them out anyway, and you said the words, for the same reason you kept up chitter-chatter at table, and did not let go of your pretty dance partner mid-swing to watch her crash into the wall: it was expected of you, and human society crossed the abyss every day on a cobweb bridge of mutual expectations. Not only Mr. J expected it, but the chiefs, and precisely *because* they already had a medal of George III hanging in their lodges. The Indian chiefs were chiefs only on sufferance. They gained their people's respect through the respect shown them by others. Black Cat, the Mandan chief of Roop-ta-he village, was the man the captains could most profitably deal with, and by giving him the largest medal, the captains made him, in the eyes of his people, the Grand Chief of the Mandans.

Lewis nodded to the Fields brothers, who delved farther into the bag and brought out American flags, lace coats, feathered hats. One flag, coat, and hat went to the first chief of each town. Also for them, and for the second and third chiefs, white calico shirts, scarlet leggings, scarlet breechclouts, copper and silver wrist- and armbands, three-point blue blankets. Lewis knew very well that it was not much. What he could no longer remember was, had he already known this when he had bought the gifts, or had he deduced it from the disgruntled reactions of the Indians he had encountered along the river?

Because of the bad weather, there were fewer Indians outside the awning than usual, perhaps a hundred. They now crowded close, and the distribution became a general hubbub, items borne from hand to hand, braves running off to gamble away what they'd just received, a certain amount of unseemly wrangling, but no out-and-out fights, the accepted decorum of gift-giving enforcing a certain level of self-control. The goods had been chosen for brightness and lightness: ribbons, none-so-pretties, Jew's harps, fishhooks, fire steels, skeins of silk, looking glasses, mock garnets, cards of Venetian glass beads. Always too few blue beads. Lewis had already known in Philadelphia (this he did remember), from ship captains back from the mouth of the Columbia, that western Indians coveted blue beads more than any other, but the stores of that city (and later, those of St. Louis) had been maddeningly short of them. Supplies, no doubt, had been exhausted by whatever transcontinental explorer had been in the week before!

And the knives, Christ! Lewis watched a brave at the edge of the melee examining the knife he had received, hefting it in his hand and looking along the edge, scoring his forearm as though it were a length of wood. No studied impassivity here, but a frank look of disparagement. Yes, they were of poor quality—Lewis knew that! He had bought them in Philadelphia by the dozen, brittle blades indifferently attached to poplar handles; he'd thought any steel edge would be coveted on the plains. They were sold as "Indian Trade Knives." Those damned cunning merchants! Lewis had had no idea of the variety of manufactured goods available this far west. *Sheffeel,* the Ottoes had kept saying to him in a badgering tone, and Lewis had looked a question to the interpreter. "They want to know if you have any Sheffield knives," he had explained. "From Sheffield, England. They consider them the best."

Clark had probably known all along. Too tactful to say anything. "Sergeant Pryor, bring me the air gun." A show of white man medicine to take the taste of embarrassment out of Lewis's mouth. Pryor brought the gun and Lewis pumped up the chamber, while Clark joined him and the chiefs gathered around. Clark gestured for each man to come near and see that there was

[*119*]

no flintlock, no priming pan. Lewis took a bullet from his pouch, but ostentatiously set aside his horn. "No powder!" he said. Nor nothing up my sleeve, neither. He wadded the bullet, rammed it home, pointed out a cottonwood about fifty yards off. In this wind, he didn't trust the gun's accuracy much beyond that. He lifted it to his shoulder and pulled the trigger. The strange sound it made—a sharp *puhh*—increased the impression of supernatural agency. Without replenishing the air in the chamber, Lewis loaded another bullet and fired; a third. Three shots in twenty seconds. He and Clark led the chiefs to the tree so that they could inspect the marks. True, the ball did not penetrate so deep as from a powder charge, but enough to kill a man at this range if you hit him in the neck or eye, or opened up an artery in his leg. Satisfactory amazement. Practical interest, too. Flintlocks took too long to reload in the face of bows and arrows. And the relative silence of the weapon was suited to stealth. Furthermore, Indians were always short of powder, and most of what they had was of inferior quality. No point in telling them that the gun was a tinkerer's curiosity, rather than an item produced in quantity for trade.

That evening there was the usual complement of visitors in the camp, many of them female, and far more handsome than the Sioux doxies. The Corpsmen had been in high spirits from the first night, when the braves had shown up at their tents, urging their women before them like farmers herding swine to market. White brothers and red sisters, engendering a company of pink cousins. At this rate, Mr. J's vision of one race from coast to coast would be realized in twenty years. Lewis envied his men the simplicity of their desires. Perhaps they had not suspected until now that their paradise existed on earth, but at least they had always known of what it would consist.

Lewis was standing at the open flap of the captains' tent, listening to the fiddle and the laughter, when he heard the roar. "A fire," he said, as Clark came to his side. Together, the captains moved to the edge of camp to observe. Plains fires were common occurrences, since the natives set them as signals, and to create fresh pasturage for the buffalo. But this one, fueled by two days of gale, was unusually large, and coming on with great rapidity. In fact, it was tremendous. The rolling front was lofting sparks and flaming grass tendrils hundreds of feet in the air. Smoke, screams. Indians were out there, in the high grass between the captains' camp and the village half a mile downriver. Husbands bringing wives. Children coming to gape. The Corps never camped in high grass, out of respect for this danger. The inferno roared past. It was like a raging battle (well, Lewis could only guess, having missed them all), but one that stopped short after a few seconds, as though the aim of all its fury were a single murder. Darkness redescended; the Corpsmen swatted out the grass glowworms that had fallen on the tents. Where the field had been, there was a black void, a fallen sky of red stars. Wailing. The natives in the camp ran out into it. The captains sent Jessome after. He returned half an hour later with the news. A man and woman had burned to death. Several others half roasted. There was also a boy—

"Dead?" Clark asked.

"No. He live. They say Great Spirit sauved him." Jessome explained: the boy's mother, despairing of carrying him to safety, had thrown him to the ground and covered him in a green buffalo skin. Then she herself had fled. Returning after the fire had passed, she had found the boy unhurt, the grass in a circle around him untouched. "They are say Great Spirit sauved him because he have white father. They think white flesh is medicine."

After Jessome left, the captains traded a look. "The usual superstitions," Clark observed.

"But . . . good God!" Lewis expostulated. "The woman had known what she was doing when she threw the buffalo skin over her son—an intelligent and intelligible act! I confess I do not understand how their thinking runs; the other Indians, I mean. They acknowledge the mother's act, and yet count it as immaterial. How else could they conclude that only the boy's white flesh mattered?"

"They are ignorant," Clark said.

"Yes, of course, but— Does it not strike you as ignorance of a particular sort? There's a maddening perversity to it."

"Perhaps," Clark said contemplatively.

Lewis had the impression, not for the first time, that Clark was musing less on the substance of what Lewis had said than on the fact that he had said it. Clark sometimes looked at Lewis with an expression Lewis could not quite read: an expression of interest in *him*. But whether colored with approbation, love, amusement, or mere puzzlement, Lewis could not tell. Clark could be as impassive as any Indian. "I'm going to make a round of the camp," Lewis said, and walked out.

Past the fiddle playing and firelight, to the dark perimeter where the sentries kept their lonely vigil. Lewis walked the circumference, waiting for the challenges, calling out the countersign, surprising no one asleep or sitting down. He paused as he drew near again to his and Clark's tent, and looked out over the stretch of burned grass. The glow in the north where the fire had run would remain visible for hours. He could not see the village of Roop-ta-he a half mile south, but presumed the families of the dead were engaged in whatever obsequies their beliefs dictated. He and Clark would have the whole winter to satisfy their curiosity on that and many other subjects.

The displeasure of your great father, who would consume you as the fire consumes the grass of the plains. He regretted that phrase exceedingly. It had been negligent of him not to have read through his speech again before delivering it; irresponsible not to have changed the wording months ago, when he had become aware of how immediate to these tribes was the danger of plains fires. The boy protected by his white flesh, good God! It was not Lewis's fault that these unfathomable people insisted on seeing divine favor in happenstance. But not to have foreseen the possibility—unpardonable negligence. After all, he had long known that the imp assigned to him by a practical-joking Deity reveled in making him look ridiculous through trivial ill luck. For example, that air gun, which on the first day out of Pittsburgh had accidentally discharged during a demonstration for local citizens and had almost killed a woman. She'd fallen in a faint, blood pouring from her hair. Only a grazing, but imagine: the expedition over the day it began. Now Lewis never shot the thing, the toy, without remembering that mortification.

They think white flesh is medicine. The Mandans had already suffered grievously from the smallpox, which killed more of them than it did white men. Well, that was not Lewis's fault, either! Curious that the savages themselves ascribed to a belief held by so many of his countrymen, viz., that the white race enjoyed God's favor. *Children,* they called themselves. Was that ignorance, then, or wisdom? Lewis was not blind to the utility of their believing white men to bask in the sun of God's love; but for him to have given the appearance of invoking this fire to consume the red man and spare the white! If they crossed that line, they would all be consumed. Unpardonable!

Second Clark

He was engaged in building the fort through December and had the rheumatism very bad from the raw weather. He'd fixed on a sandy point of land two miles below the first Mandan village; there were ash trees for ax handles and some elm, but mostly cotton timber, a junk wood like Lombardy poplar, spongy and riddled with windshakes. But Sergeant Gass was an able carpenter, Clark was pleased. The fort was going up snug. It was triangular, huts on two sides, a bastion at the point, the third side a picket eighteen feet high with a double gate. The Indians were passing in great numbers to the hunt, they stopped to watch and found it all interesting. Their own lodges looked like beehives.

Big White came with a hundredweight of meat on the back of his squaw, she grinning up past the load that bowed her, her fat husband puffed up in his new chief's coat. Clark gave her a small ax, which pleased her much. The chiefs came visiting on the fine days, when there was work to be done on the fort, and although Gass was able and the men in good spirits, Clark was impatient. Gangs of brant and ducks were passing south, which meant ice was coming, and Windsor, Thompson, and Shannon were laid up with the venereal, so Clark was shorthanded, but there he was, sitting on a buffalo robe smoking with a chief. They stayed all day, and sometimes all night and the next day, too. They wanted particular attention, so Clark gave them paint and handkerchiefs and showed them curiosities. They were taken with the glass matches, the flame starting by itself when Lewis broke the vial, it being phosphorus inside. They could sit for hours and tell Indian anecdotes, their traditions about animals and superstitions, most of it not worthwhile recording.

The Mandans believed in a Great Spirit or *great medicine,* which was the same thing. It also referred to anything they didn't understand—mystery, medicine, spirit: all the same. Clark wondered if Indians didn't advance, despite their intelligence, because of this attitude toward mystery. They didn't try to explain what they failed to understand, instead they fell down before it. A Mandan warrior passing south on foot to hunt one morning told Clark he'd turned all of his horses loose on the plain as an offering to his medicine. His medicine would take care of them, he said. Clark nodded and looked grave and thought to himself that the horses, not being so religious, were out taking care of themselves.

The Menetarrees were not visiting, and after a while Clark and Lewis found out the reason. The Mandans had been telling them the Americans were planning to join the Soues and attack them; the strength of Clark's fort gave force to the lie. And these Indians were allies. It showed the difficulties of making peace.

A few years ago the Mandans came upriver to live with the Menetarrees, after the smallpox reduced them. Before that, they lived in eight villages, and they said all the nations including the Soues were afraid of them. That was usual in Indian tales: in the good old days, every tribe was feared by every other tribe.

The Soues attacked a Mandan hunting party at the end of November and killed a man, wounded two, stole nine horses, and the men who came back said there were Rickerries with the Soues. Which was disheartening. At the council when Clark and Lewis first arrived, Piaheto the Rickerrie chief had smoked with the Mandan and Menetarree and Wetersoon chiefs, and the second chief of Rooptarhee had gone with some of his considerate men down to the Rickerrie villages to confirm the peace.

Clark remembered the night after the council when Piaheto showed up in camp and told him and Lewis he wanted to go back to his own village; he felt uneasy in the presence of his former enemies. Weeks later, Clark learned a Mandan chief named Big Man had told Piaheto after the council that the Rickerries were liars and bad men, and the Mandans had made peace with them many times, and they (the Rickerries) always started war and the Mandans always beat them. He said they killed Rickerries like the buffalo when they pleased. Big White said a similar thing, when he came visiting: We're tired of killing them; we kill them like the birds. It sounded like a man with his arm sore from swatting mosquitoes.

It showed the difficulties of making peace. The nations hardly looked on each other as human beings: Snakes, Crows, Wolves. But on the other hand, Big Man had been born a Chyanne. He'd been taken prisoner and adopted, and now he was a Mandan chief. Another chief, Sho-to-rar-ra, was born a Rickerrie.

Captured boys were adopted, whereas girls taken captive were enslaved. Which for Indian girls wasn't much different from getting married. Like the Frenchman Shabounar's two Snake squaws; slaves first for the Menetarrees, and now slaves to their husband. Doing all the drudgery for him, when one was sick and the other pregnant. You'd think a man would be ashamed.

Clark was figuring out the trade relations for his report to the President. The Mandans and Menetarrees traded corn to their neighbors. Tribes to the west, like the Chyannes and Ravens, brought in horses and leather, and the Mandans passed them to the Ossinaboins and Cristanoes, who in return supplied arms and ball, kettles, etc. from the British posts on the Ossinaboin River. The Ossinaboins were descendants of the Soues; they spoke the same language corrupted. They presumed on the Mandans, as the Soues did on the Rickerries, stealing their horses and such, and since the Mandans depended on them for manufactured goods they had to suffer their insults in silence.

The American plan would put an end to this. A sure Missouri River trade from St. Louis would make the Mandans, Menetarrees, and Rickerries independent of the Soues and Ossinaboins. If the Soues refused to open their ears, they'd be reduced to order by force. The Ossinaboins would be pushed back into Canada.

The Ossinaboins plundered and sometimes even murdered their own traders from the British companies, which was an indication of their character. The North West and Hudson's Bay Company men came down from their posts about 150 miles to trade with the Mandans and Menetarrees, and Ossinaboins who encountered them on the way demanded payment, or if they were strong enough, stripped them of every article they possessed. A few weeks ago a party of Ossinaboins murdered the old Frenchman Menar, who'd resided in the little Menetarree village for thirty years. Leaving Shabounar the only Menetarree interpreter.

It was a piece of luck he had those Snake squaws. Just when Clark and Lewis were learning they needed horses from the Snakes to cross the divide, Shabounar shows up where Clark is raising the huts and says he wishes to hire as interpreter and mentions his two janeys in the next breath. Crafty old bird. He knew what the Corps needed, and he knew he had it: an interpreting chain—the captains, Labeeche, himself, his women. English, French, Menetarree, Snake. Do you have horses? *Avay-voo chevalles? Ooka-booka,* etc. Twenty-five dollars a month. Same as Drewyer, and five times what the privates got. The old rascal probably never saw so much.

Not so old. He said about forty-five. But not so young either, for a man crossing the continent. He had that Indian look of jerked meat, ageless. Middling size, and the big shoulders and bad knees of a canoeman. Unlike an Indian, a complainer, wagging shoulders and eyebrows, but that was just the Frenchman in him. They didn't suffer in silence. Probably stronger than he looked.

What Lewis said when Clark mentioned the matter to him: "A woman along, good God! What next?" What next came clear when the women visited the camp a week later. Clark almost enjoyed watching Lewis perform. "A Hobson's choice!" You could see him thinking about the way to put it. "Between the one needing a sick nurse and the one nursing." He clattered around the tent, working his hands behind his back. "An infant!" It always struck Clark how awkwardly Lewis moved; stiff, straight-backed. He leaned away from people, turned with a jerk. Thin upper lip that looked curled even when it wasn't; bird's eyes sharp with thinking of disasters. Punctuous about his dress. He could count the stitches on a lace cuff from forty yards. "Squalling when we wish to remain unobserved. The baby dies, our interpretress declines. Or *she* dies and . . . you and I, Clark, are up all night squeezing buffalo milk out of a handkerchief."

Clark was more used to this regular-irregular, as they called it in the army. With Indians, if you could get what you wanted without wrapping a rattlesnake around your neck, sticking your pecker in a tree hole, and singing "Billy Boy," you should count yourself lucky. They were a traveling menagerie as it was: Americans and Frenchmen and a half-Mahar and a half-Shawonie, and the big dog some Indians thought was a bear and the performing York *other* Indians thought was a bear, and the barking squirrel Lewis had caught by pouring barrels of water down its den, and the four pied corvus birds and the short-tailed grouse they were sending back to the President in the spring. The animals were in cages in the captains' hut, and Clark wrote at night with the squirrel or ground rat or *prairie du chen* as the French called it snoring and twitching in its winter sleep, and the grouse chirring and rattling her bars with her beak, and the dog in the corner passing gas, and Lewis trying to teach one of the birds to take a seed out of his mouth. Who'd notice an infant?

Clark knew the feeling of luck. You felt it in your back teeth, and when you ran out, your mouth went dry. So far, they had it in spades. When you had luck you were saved from yourself. For example, the delay going down the Ohio, which forced them to winter at River Dubois, where they trained and added to the stores, instead of getting snowed in with the Mahars, who turned out not to be there, or the Tetons, who would have provoked a fight. And the delay coming up the Missouri: if they'd kept to the schedule, they'd be perishing in the Rocky Mountains about now.

Clark had never seen cold like this, it was 43° below zero one morning, porter and taffia frozen in the mugs, York stupidly taking a piss in the wind and his penis, like that, nipped tolerably bad. Wolves were plenteous around the buffalo gangs, you killed ten buffalos and lost six to the wolves and most of the buffalo so meager they weren't worth hauling back. The Snakes of the Rockies (if they'd found them), from what Clark heard from the pregnant squaw, those Snakes didn't have extra corn to barter like the Mandans, they were only a notch above perishing each winter themselves.

She seemed reluctant to speak. An Indian never asked his wife for her opinion, and Shabounar was probably the same. But she was more capable than his other janey; who you couldn't blame, being sickly. Her mind on her mortality. York had been taking care of that one off and on since the squaws moved into the fort, stewing fruit for her, tea, etc.

The Snakes didn't eat dogs, the pregnant one said. Clark could sympathize. When the Tetons served them up roast pup, the whole Corps partook, but the idea turned Clark's stomach. Lie down, Rover.

She said her people were well disposed, but most of the nearby nations made war on them. They had a few Spanish goods like horse bits, but the Spaniards wouldn't trade them guns. They lived on both sides of the Rocky Mountains, and were divided into three tribes. Hers was called *So-so-na,* the other two were *So-so bu-bar* and *I-a-kar*. She was so small her belly was as big as the rest of her. Maybe fifteen, but hard to tell because Indian girls ripened earlier than white girls. The other was small, too. Black Cat said Snake women were all that way.

Clark figured Shabounar had his fingers in a little bit of everything. The

North West Company party down this winter for peltries needed him because none of them spoke Menetarree, whereas the Hudson's Bay man did. The jealousy between these two companies was greater than anything Clark had seen. They cared more for undercutting each other than securing trade for themselves. They called each other liars and cheats, giving the Indians an unfavorable impression of all whites. And in their zeal to steal trade from the other, they gave the Indians an exaggerated idea of the worth of their peltries.

The American plan would put an end to this, too. The government trading post would undersell individual traders when they pursued bad policies. There would be a uniform price for peltries. With the situation more secure, traders wouldn't feel obliged to tolerate any vicious acts the Indians might be bent upon. Trade would be diverted from buffalo robes to beaver. The best location for the American trading fort was the mouth of the Yellowstone River, about 250 miles upstream. The Mandans, Menetarrees, and Wetersoons would move their villages up there.

It would take time to set up; Black Cat was concerned about that. He said the Mandans had decided to put up with the insults of the Ossinaboins and Cristanoes until they could be confident of what the Americans promised. He said Evans promised to return to them with guns and ammunition, but he'd deceived them, he never came back. (He had a pretty good excuse, being dead of drink.) Red Hair and Big Knife might do the same. Clark agreed it would take time, but he assured Black Cat he could depend on it.

Red Hair was Clark; Big Knife was Lewis.

Time and tide will not abide; and neither will luck. You get on her, or watch her gallop away. His brothers had told him that, when they were all soldiers and Clark was a boy stuck at home with his sisters. The Clarks had luck, and the Clarks with red hair had the most luck. Clark was afraid his brothers said it to consult him: maybe you didn't fight in the war, maybe you missed everything of importance, *but you have luck!* Then where was she, Clark wanted to ask, when he became a man. Instead of waiting for a redcoat charge, he was watching squaws and papooses fleeing burning fields. And he was sickly; every time he puked, the noise out of his gorge sounded like *luck*. Then he had to come home to help that other lucky redhead in the family, the one ruined by drink and debt.

So when the letter from Lewis came, his brothers nodded: *Get on her, boy.* Clark had to write his reply over twice, and he sent another after, he couldn't contain himself. Little Billy.

He and Lewis were lucky in their men. Clark knew how low army soldiers could go: thieves, perverts, men who couldn't tell you the truth about how many fingers they had. He remembered the Hellfire Club in the Ohio country, men who prided themselves on willingly taking one hundred lashes for the theft of a quart of whiskey. There wasn't much to do with wretches like that but keep them out of responsibility until they succumbed to their vices. Some of the Corpsmen were drinkers, of course—Hall and Collins, who stole from the whiskey barrel when they were supposed to be guarding it, and Howard, who as far as Clark could tell never drank water. But none were as hopeless as those Hellfire sots.

Drewyer was the best hunter Clark had ever seen; Colter and Gibson not far behind. The Fields brothers were all-around woodsmen, Gass a skilled carpenter, Ordway a dependable New Englander, Labeeche and Crusat experienced boatmen. Goodrich could catch fish in water running off a roof. Bratton and Willard were competent blacksmiths. Shields was so good at rigging repairs to guns and everything else Lewis called him an artist. Clark liked to think of them as his Band of Brothers.

Like luck (maybe it was the same thing) you could feel a group of men coming together. In Dubois they'd had the usual divisions. That time the Kentucky boys rebelled under Ordway because no damn Yankee would tell them what to do. They'd had the whiskey stealing, the sneaking out. That was high spirits. If you didn't have to beat that out of them, you'd worry. Then came the river. Luck saves you from yourself. The worst time of year to ascend it, which meant it was the best time. The men had no time for a Hellfire Club, they had to band against that devil of a river. The way they jumped to it, to keep a boat from turning against a reef, five seconds that decided everything. Pulling each other out of collapsing banks. And the bilious colic and death of Sergeant Floyd: all the men tending him (Clark purging, warm bath prepared, Floyd's bowels emptying in a green flood, Clark dull and heavy from being up all night, Floyd's eyes on him, composed, "I'm going away—write a letter for me," but that was the last, the pulse indiscernible, that helplessness you felt when a man died on you), the burial on the hill, Floyd's River flowing below. You could sense them coming together. Now, in the way they took an order. There was a world of difference in the ways a soldier could say *Yes, sir*, and what Clark heard, he heard in the back of his teeth. A happy family.

Except Lewis.

The Spaniards in St. Louis kept calling him Captain Merry, which was pretty funny. From Merry de Weather de Lewis, Clark supposed. Ponce de Leon de Caballo de los Dios Virginos de Guadalupe de Fuck-all. Clark remembered first setting eyes on Lewis at Greenville, almost ten years ago. He'd heard about a court-martial of a young hothead, but he'd been on furlough; five minutes after his return, Lewis stood in front of him, transferred to his command. Clark thought for a hothead he seemed pretty quenched, and concluded the man was a bully. Which was about as wrong as it could be. He attached himself to Clark, as young men sometimes do to their commanders.

Strange man. That *good God* he always said, throwing his shoulders up, pressing his arms against his sides; like he'd been thrown into icy water. A man of imposing mind, great physical endurance. And fearless; really fearless—an absence, not what people usually meant by the word. Hot and cold. Taking notes on one of his bird specimens: Clark saw him once spend an hour tilting a black tailfeather against the light, writing down the reflected colors, dipping it in different solutions to compare, teasing out strands, peering at them for minutes through a magnifying glass. And the North West Company man, La Rock, mentioning on a visit that his compass was damaged, and Lewis spending five hours the next day cleaning it, oiling, hammering out the case, balancing, reassembling. This for a man he didn't like or trust.

But other days: a look in his eye sometimes like a man who'd fallen into a river in winter and was drifting away. That dull look that didn't say *save me*, but *let me go*. Clark, Gass, Whitehouse, Ordway, Pryor, and Frazier all scribbling in their journals, per the President's orders (but they ignored his suggestion to write on birch bark; the idea was it was more durable; an absence of birch trees was a problem, though): sometimes the camp at night looked like a law firm burned out of its offices. It was Lewis who brought along the fancy morocco notebooks; he'd thought up the tin boxes Ordway and Gass made for the completed books; he'd thought up sealing enough air in to make them float. All his doing. Yet weeks on end when he wrote nothing.

Clark remembered the letter from Lewis: *Thus my friend . . . If there is*

anything in this enterprise which would induce you to participate with me . . .
Believe me . . . He remembered where he stood reading it, at the first turn in
the track above his brother's house. He remembered the sun on the page, and
the sound of York nearby chopping wood. *The President has authorized me
to say that he will grant you a Captain's commission; your situation will in all
respects be precisely such as my own.* And Clark's fevered reply: *I will cheerfully join you in an "official character" on equal footing &c.* He struck that,
substituted: *in an "official character" as mentioned in your letter.*

The first wording betrayed him. It showed an anxiety to pin Lewis to his
promise. Because Clark was a military man, and he might be beginning to believe in his luck, but he couldn't believe in this captain's commission until he
saw it. Even then, he doubted he would believe it. Maybe a man like the President, who dreamed of writing journals on birch bark, or imagined a man
might safely confide in the justice and generosity of the Virginia Assembly,
could conceive of two captains leading a party across the continent. But the
War Department would know better.

Clark's brothers scratched their heads. They'd been through a war; they
didn't want absolutely to rule out any official inanity you might think of, and
a deal of others you might not. So maybe a small part of Clark believed. He
supposed it did, or he wouldn't have felt bitter later. More fool he.

When Lewis arrived without any commission, Clark's brother Jonathan
(whose advice he much depended on) winked: "If you come back, you'll be
made a colonel regardless. And if you don't come back, you're not leaving a
widow on a pension, so what does it matter?" And then the winter in Dubois
and the delay waiting for the papers, and finally the only conceivable outcome. And the words that jumped out at Clark from the Secretary of War's
letter: *Corps of Engineers.* What in hell had been going on?

Afterward, Lewis came to him in a hard rain, and Clark could see too
clearly how afflicted he was, how downcast. "It is of little importance," Clark
said. He didn't say, *I knew all along.* One reason he didn't say it: he could see
that Lewis, strange man, had not known.

In the rain and wind, he held Lewis's hand. He longed for Jonathan's advice. Second Lieutenant Clark.

He remembered.

THE EXPECTANT

[1805]

1

Lewis woke at dawn to the same ghostly keen of young pain to which he had fallen asleep five hours before. Seaman's head rose by the side of the bed. He put out his hand. "Not yet." He dressed and quit the hut for the cold of the triangular yard, where Sergeant Ordway reported all well.

Fair sky, the sentry on the bastion a motionless black figure against azure. In the half-light, Lewis saw off the men he'd deputed to fetch meat left by Clark's hunting party a score of miles downriver. When the top of the bluff across the Missouri ice turned orange, Ordway ordered the gates of Fort Mandan opened for the day. Lewis consulted the thermometer hung in the shadow of the log stockade. Eight degrees below zero; positively balmy. The wind less ferocious, what in Albemarle he'd designate a gale, but here was a tonic breeze. From the west, as usual. *Zephyr* would never mean the same to him. Back at his hut, he let out Seaman, who loped, spruce-tail wagging at the new day, through the gate (he understood he was not to defecate in the yard).

Lewis wrote the date, February 11th, 1805, and the temperature in his weather notebook, adding *f* for fair, and *NW* for wind direction. He would record again at 4 P.M. *S* meant *snow; c, cloudy; cas, cloudy after snow.* It was entirely Mr. J's system. Lewis had been following it religiously since September 19th of the previous year; nearly five months in which he had not missed a day, all in his notebook. Pray ask: What was the weather at sunrise on October 22nd, 1804? Why, it was 35°, cloudy after snow, with a NE wind. And by 4 P.M., by God, the temperature had risen to 42°. And where was that on the river, exactly? Unfortunately, for that, you would have to refer to Clark's journal, as Lewis was still failing to keep one. A step at a time—Lewis *had* been writing the entries in Clark's journal for the past week, while his friend was hunting downriver.

The buffalo bulls and cows so fleshless now that two out of three shot were not worth butchering. Rich winter robes on skeletons. And any lucked-upon meat more than you could carry or scaffold was gone the moment your back was turned, carried off by other skeletons of the prairie dressed in wolves' clothing. This astonishing cold and wind, burning up flesh. Lewis had imagined his men well set up for the winter. But the Indians had not had meat in weeks, and were it not for the services of its blacksmiths, the Corps would be destitute of both meat and corn.

A Mandan brave had been forced a fortnight back to spend a night on the prairie without fire, with nothing but a buffalo robe and leggings to protect him. The temperature fell to 72° below the freezing point, yet he suffered no ill effects. Indian flesh, Lewis was tempted to conclude, was medicine. In a curious way, he was comforted when an Indian boy had had his toes frozen. Lewis had been forced to saw them off. The boy's father (who'd fairly shrieked in distress when the boy went missing; their impassivity flew out the window when it came to their children) had deferred to Lewis for the operation: his gleaming surgical saw, his snowy gauze. White medicine, in any case, was medicine. And no wonder, since the native treatment appeared to consist of blowing on necrotic tissue and singing songs to it.

Lewis stepped out again and moved down the range of huts. Muffled drumming. He stopped outside the second door, listened. For more than a minute, silence. Then came the low groan, wandering, as though feeling its way around the contours of distress. Rising gradually, it traversed two octaves and culminated in a high cry not unlike the howl of a prairie wolf. A sound quite distinct from that of the gray wolf; the prairie wolf began with a terrier-like bark, two or three notes evaporating into a scream with an eerie, carressing quality. A lovelorn song in the night, if Lewis might indulge. Or a wail of starvation. The natives' dogs made a similar noise. One presumed they were close relatives. Both traders and Mandans had regaled Lewis with tales of the prairie wolf's wonderful intelligence. It was said they were nearly impossible to trap, never approaching the bait via the intended route, rather digging under or snatching from above or, if they were forced to, leaving the food behind, no matter how starving, their tracks in the morning round and round the undropped box. Mr. Larocque had passed on the anecdote of a certain scientific trapper who had suspended a dozen baits from several trees. He disturbed the ground equally beneath each, but buried only one trap. In the morning, all the meat was eaten except for the morsel above the trap. (The possibility that the tale had been embroidered could not, of course, be discounted.) The natives' respect for the sagacity of this animal was such that it occupied an important position in their superstitions. There was even an indication, if Lewis had understood the tale correctly (it had seemed purposeless to the point of being stupefacient), that their Lord of Creation was partly, or at times, or with the correct stage lighting, a prairie wolf.

He knocked on the door. Jessome's woman opened it. Behind her, he glimpsed Charbono's sickly squaw, crouched and stroking something, a split mound. The confused sight snapped into intelligibility: the laboring girl—kneeling facedown on a buffalo robe—her naked hindparts open—

Lewis stepped back as Jessome's woman stepped forward and shut the door at her back, shaking her head. Lewis made a gesture indicative of his desire to know how things stood. She kept shaking her head, No, no. No birth yet? (Of course he knew that.) No, no. The woman was not even looking at him. No progress? No chance of survival? Nothing to worry about? No use asking? She held the door square behind her as though he might try to force his way past, and she kept pushing her eyes to his right, toward his own door, presumably whither she wanted him to retreat. He took another step back to reassure her regarding his infinite patience and cast about in his mind how to ask if the girl was holding up all right, how to dance out that particular question. But the stupid woman must have interpreted his falling back as a cessation of their interview, because she retreated into the room and shut the door on him.

He stood for a moment regarding the door. *Dear Mr. President: I wish to inform you that our hopes for negotiating the northwest passage are bottomed on the fortunes of a fifteen-year-old slave girl who is currently dying in childbirth. Your ridcls. servant, M. Lewis, Capt., 1st Ragtag.* "Sergeant Ordway!"

The man came running. "Captain?"

"Tell Charbono and Jessome to come to my hut at once."

Charbono arrived looking as though he had fallen from his bed the moment before, Jessome as though he had never been to bed at all. Lewis spoke through Jessome, since Charbono had no English, and at some point during the exchange the captain saw that Charbono must have been fearing a reprimand, presumably for having left the meat downriver (he had been with Clark on the hunting expedition, and had arrived at the fort last night, saying the horses could not bring the meat farther up without sleighs), because he noted the relief that came across the old rogue's face when the subject turned out to be nothing more important than his distressed wife. Lewis charged the two of them with following the progress of the labor and reporting to him every three hours. And naturally, with informing him immediately if there was either a crisis or a happy event.

He watched them go. He disliked both of them. Jessome was a classic mongrel of the frontier. You might say he had become a Mandan, except that your average Mandan was far superior to him. Something about losing your own ways and taking up others; you fell between two pieces of firm ground into quicksand. The Mandans had their ideas of right and wrong, Lewis had his; but Jessome, Lewis felt sure, had long since forgotten there were two such categories. Evans had claimed in his journal that Jessome had tried to murder him. And although, judging from his writing, Evans had been a typical blustering choleric Welshman addicted to overstatement, whenever Lewis caught Jessome in one of his averted sniggers, or saw calculation march in a detectable ripple across his face, he was inclined to believe the worst.

Charbono was not of that type. At least he looked you in the vicinity of your eye. And he had faithfully kept Lewis and Clark informed of the political maneuverings in the Minetare villages. (For example, that the Hudson's Bay Company man was spreading lies about the Americans.) And he was a hardy old soul. In January he had journeyed in extreme cold near a hundred miles up the Knife River to trade with some Minetares at Turtle Hill, and he'd returned with his thick rubbery buffoon's face frozen, but he smeared on bear grease and picked off the bad bits and cooked himself a welcome-home dinner, to which he invited the captains. And it was damned good. But Lewis detested the man's proclivities. How old had that girl been when he first took her? Kneeling on the robe, her nakedness open— Of course you saw their breasts from time to time, young muffins (no, that wasn't right, what was the word . . . pippins!), or pendulous wrinkled flaps, thoroughly disgusting, like parfleche covers. But that huge belly slung under her like a cauldron on the boil, the slender back and defenseless buttocks, the other girl-woman rubbing something slimy in the cleft. The sight had wrenched him.

Bird Woman. Presumably because she was so small. Or because she communicated with signs. Birdlike gestures, thin arms. The top of her head didn't reach Lewis's chest, so what he generally saw when he looked at her was the center part in her hair, the vermilion line the squaws invariably drew there. She was nearly as dark as a negro, with a straight nose descending from a straight brow, the two eyebrows nearly touching. The impression was of a capital T superimposed on her face. The nasal base flared out to the cheekbones; the nostrils were small but extremely well defined. The effect, purely a trick of physiognomy, was one of anger. The lips were thin, almost nonexistent, the mouth another straight line. (He intended to note this down, when he had a moment; the Rocky Mountain races were as yet unknown to science.) The face would perhaps have been austerely handsome—certainly not pretty—were it not for the mottled scars below her cheekbones. Lewis wondered if she had taken an arrow through both cheeks when she was captured.

He breakfasted alone on coffee and a mush of corn. Parched in the native manner and reconstituted in a stew, the corn tasted somewhat like ham. He received Ordway's report at the end of the sergeant's tour and then walked out for an informal inspection. The blacksmiths were at work at the forge, the usual half-score braves looking on, the one whose weapon was under the hammer offering smoke to the four winds. Three other men were tending the coal pit. Pryor had a wood-cutting crew out, and Colter was back with an antelope that perhaps had just enough meat on it for Seaman's breakfast. In the infirmary, Lewis changed the dressing on the Indian boy's trimmed foot (it looked like the conjurer had been sucking on it again), and nodded on his way out to whichever three relatives it was today, crouched in the corner, drumming and howling.

He paused again outside the girl's door. The infirmary chanting was a distracting pulse; he put his ear to the door. Much the same; though the height of each cry sounded more ragged than previously. Exhaustion? Weeping? Perhaps both. Suddenly, pity stirred in Lewis. He tried to ward it off, but it rose so quickly it filled his lungs with damp melancholy. A woman before her time, among strangers. How old had she been at her capture? Nine, ten? Sleeping in her skin lodge, perhaps, or splashing innocently in a mountain brook, making chains of wildflowers. The arrow striking her. Well, if she survived this, she would see her nation again. A thing she could not have hoped for.

A low jibbering. She was falling asleep between the crests of her labors. Good God, what if he was called upon to—? Trudging back toward his hut, he veered off for the gate. He stood in it, squinting against the blinding expanse of snow-drifted bottom and frozen river and robin's-egg sky. On his left, the low sun had sundogs at heel. No sign of Seaman.

He found him waiting by his door; "There you are!" They went in. Lewis set out jerked meat and a buffalo fibula in the corner. Seaman squeezed past him to get at it; Lewis stood for a moment, allowing the tail to thump him solidly in the thigh. Doctoring them was one thing, but delivering, perhaps piecemeal— Childbirth was supposed to be easy for them! How many times had he read it in explorers' accounts? The squaw heading off alone to drop her babe by some stream, returning with it cleaned and strapped to her back, ready for the day's work. Was this birth difficult because the child was half white? Had Dr. Rush included this in his list of queries?

The thought of the list made Lewis wince. Clark had a compilation somewhere of all the questions Rush, Wistar, Barton, and the President had desired answered. He remembered the query about pulse; Rush had wanted Lewis to record it among the Indians in both sexes, in children, adults, and the aged, at morning, noon, and night. He'd wanted information on Indians' longevity, their age of marrying. Questions about suckling and weaning and pleurisy and goiter and madness. And sudatories and bleeding and evacuation. Spousal relations and murder and punishment and possible affinities with the religion of the ancient Jews. *What is their mode of treating the Small pox particularly?* That one was easy. They had none, except the habit of anticipating its end. See: *suicide.* Lewis thought with chagrin of the kinepox matter he didn't have. The Mandans probably would not have allowed him to administer it to them in any case. To be doctored by a white man when they were not sick? Probably as likely as the Siouxs agreeing to become farmers. Civilization: first the cow matter, then the cow.

He went to the door. "Sergeant Pryor!"

The man came running. It never ceased to surprise him. "Sir?"

"I do not wish to be disturbed, unless one of the first or second chiefs comes visiting. The interpreters are to be allowed in only if it concerns the girl in labor."

He set about arranging his writing desk. Somehow it was already eleven o'clock. *This may be especially done wherever you winter.* Mr. J's words. And in fact Lewis knew the answers to many of the questions: Sudatories? He had seen them in operation; wild sage was employed. Agricultural implements?

He had examined the Mandans' scapular hoes, and the elkhorn scrapers with the flint blades they quarried upriver. The flint was of such high quality they traded it to all the nations around them. (Thank God Clark was writing the treatise on trade.) Games: the women stood in a circle and passed a small leather ball to each other by means of their feet and knees. Children sledded on pan-pipes of buffalo ribs. Men rolled rings along a stretch of ground and tried to toss spears through them. Ritual self-mutilation: some of the warriors had so many raised concentric scars on their chests they looked like practice targets. Lewis wondered if this was the next logical step, after painting red stripes on their bodies, to signify the wounds they had suffered in battle. Deviancy: the astonishing berdaches (as the French called them), men who dressed as women and performed women's chores, and were suffered to do so openly.

The rub was, he had not written anything down. Not on paper, nor on birch bark, nor on a single square inch of his own skin. And how long would it stay in his head? He could no longer remember, for example, where he was standing at 4 P.M. on October 22nd, 1804, when it was 42°, with a northeast wind. The rub was, he was so far behind. His boxes were full of scribbled notes from months ago, on minerals, plants, mammals, birds, medicines, that he had yet to put into legible form. He was forty pages into a treatise on the tributaries of the Missouri River that he'd thought might require ten, and the end was nowhere in sight. The rub was, he was constantly interrupted. Howard climbs over the stockade at night after the gate is closed and an Indian who observes it imitates him, and the following day they have to hold a God damned court-martial with witnesses and statements and due deliberation, when all Howard need manfully say is "I did it" and Lewis can hand the switch to Gass and go back to his desk. The boats freeze in the God damned river and are in danger of being crushed, and day after day has to be spent hacking at the ice with axes and building fires, the water between the ice sheets welling up as soon as you break the upper one so that you cannot get to the lower. And so many cases of venereal to attend to, and thank God the Corps will be at the mouth of the Columbia when half the Mandan squaws are howling ass-up on buffalo robes trying to push out their oversized white babies. And the God damned visits from the God damned chiefs who, once they are admitted to your apartment, drop like turnip sacks next to the fire and pull out pipes and tell stories, or admire your bootjack or the second coat button from the bottom and wait for you to offer it to them, or compare your goods to the other white traders', or recite obscene jokes, or wonder aloud why it was you sat with Big White the other day for five hours whereas you're looking impatient with them after a mere four and a half.

Lewis retrieved from its box his sheaf of scribbled natural history notes. From another box, the pressed cuttings they referred to. From a third, the book into which he had begun transcribing the notes. Cut a quill. Mixed a paper of ink powder in water. Seeing these operations, Seaman ambled over, turned twice, and settled with a bellows-groan next to his master's chair. Lewis set the inkhorn just so, a spare quill lined up beneath, the penknife on the right side. The air on these plains was so dry, two spoonfuls of water in a saucer evaporated within thirty-six hours; he'd measured it once—when? Had he written it down somewhere?

No. 3, he wrote. He glanced at the cutting, which had faded considerably since he had pressed it. "Have you ever seen this specimen before, Captain Lewis? I remind you that you are under oath." He peered closely. "No, sir, I have not." He wrote, *Was taken on the 23rd of May 1804, near the mouth of the Osage Woman's creek, it is a shrub and resembles much in growth the <u>bladder scenna,</u> it rises to a height of eight or ten feet and is an inhabitant of a moist rich soil.* The 23rd of May; he had reached the third day out of St. Louis.

Was his impression correct that the chiefs were not remaining at the fort as long during Clark's absence? Lewis was perfectly aware he was called Big Knife, which meant nothing more than *the American.* Whereas Clark had been honored with a name peculiar to himself, Red Hair.

No. 4. A cottonwood seed. *Was taken at a small village north side of the Missouri—* Through the two walls, he heard the girl topping the crest again. For example: he had yet to write a line descriptive of the prairie wolf, even though Drewyer had shot their first specimen sometime in September.

That story he had heard from two or three different informants, the one about the origin of the world. How had it gone? There was a first man, whom they called Alone Man. The world was all water. When Alone Man *came to himself*—that had been Jessome's attempt at the phrase—he had been walking across the water for a long time. He asked himself, *Who am I? Where did I come from?* He arrived at a place where a duck was diving. He asked the duck to bring up earth from beneath the water. He threw the earth in several directions, creating land. In one version (one of the exasperating things about these tales was that no two chiefs told them alike; did they really believe what they were saying, or were they amusing themselves at Lewis's expense?)—in one version, after Alone Man *came to himself,* he retraced his steps and saw that they ended at a red flower. So Alone Man decided the flower was his mother! There was also a frog, Lewis thought he remembered, and a buffalo. When Alone Man encountered each of these animals, he asked them, *Where did you come from?* And they each answered, *I came to myself here.* At some point, Alone Man met the Lord of Creation. But they seemed more in the nature of brothers; when they argued about who was older, instead of speaking to Alone Man out of the whirlwind (viz., *behold now behemoth, which I made*—but this Lord could hardly say that, as behemoth presumably *came to himself*), the Lord established his precedence through a wager; something to do with both of them sitting down, and who stood up first. Ridiculous. And then the two of them divided the world, Alone Man shaping the land east of the Missouri River, the Lord the land west. Like brothers.

In sum, there seemed to be no conception of a first cause. No absolute, either of goodness or power. No *let there be,* no breathing life into. No attempt to posit a motive (let alone a moral) force. In short, no *God.* It was quite hopeless as a religion. Questions without answers: *Who am I? Where did I come from?*

However, perhaps it was worthy of recording, for what it revealed about the incurious minds of these people. (And yet—for example—Lewis had not recorded it.)

No. 5. Was taken on the 27th of May 1804 near the mouth of the Gasconade; it is a species of cress—

Lewis labored on into the afternoon. He got up to let Seaman out and back in. Twice he received Jessome, who reported little progress. "Is the girl holding up all right?" Lewis asked.

"Yes, yes!"

Lewis waited. Jessome's grin faded. "Euhh . . . holding up—what?"

"Is. She. Doing. All right? Still strong?"

"Oh, strong." He made a grubby fist. "Squaw, they are tough."

For his dinner, Lewis champed jerked meat and corn mush, thinking *tough bird.* It made sense that the one who could speak at least a form of English would report. Still, it left Lewis with the impression that Charbono was not concerned. Well, really, why should he be? If he lost this one, there were other slave girls to be had for a song. Lewis scraped together a last mouthful from the bottom of his bowl. His men had danced for some of the corn he was eating. They'd learned among the Siouxs that it was proper to toss gifts to native dancers, but the reverse was a touch uncomfortable; particularly when you sent the men with fiddle and tambourine to the village with the express expectation that they return with a few ears on a string. Lewis hadn't written anything about the native dances, either. (For example.) He set the bowl on the floor by his feet and Seaman licked it clean.

When he and Clark decided in mid-September not to send the keelboat back until the spring, Lewis had felt reprieved. All winter, in which to keep a journal! He would send hundreds of pages to the President, who would forgive the late start. Lewis had begun his journal the very next day.

And had stopped—when was it?—two days after? He pushed his bowl aside, went out for a piss. "York, clear my table." Returned, sharpened his quill. *No. 13. The <u>narrow leaf willow</u> taken on the 14th of June—*

At least he had got down a few lines and a sketch of the war hatchet the natives preferred. When Shields set up the forge they stood ten deep the first day. They had probably never seen a blacksmith at work before. There was that brave who got his hands on the bellows, then dozens who wanted to take turns, Shields gesturing *Go* and *Stop;* another fellow lunging to catch a spark that flew off the anvil; he hurried off as though he'd trapped a firefly. They brought all their broken metal implements, trading corn for repairs. But inevitably, the day arrived when Shields and Willard had fixed every ax, gig, awl, hoe, knife, pot, and horse bit in the five villages; and it was still January. Then came the requests that they make war hatchets. The Corps needed the corn; the Indians showed them the weapons they wanted duplicated. And so here was Lewis, haranguing the natives about peace, and all the while manufacturing war hatchets for them. When Mr. J extolled trade as the firm foundation of amicable tribal relations, Lewis doubted the arms trade occurred to him.

—its leaves are numerous narrow, slightly indented, of a yellowish green on the upper side, and whiteish green underneath, pointed— He was still on the willow, still in June. Number thirteen out of one hundred and eight. Good Christ. *—this tree is invariably the first which makes its appearance on the newly made lands on the borders of the Mississippi and Missouri, and seems to contribute much towards facilitating the operation of raising this ground still*

higher . . . puts forth an innumerable quantity of small fibrous roots from every part of its trunk near the surface of the water which further serve to collect the mud . . . the weaker plants decline and die and give place to the cotton-wood . . . these willow bars form a pleasant beacon to the navigator at that season when the banks of the river are tumbling in, as they rarely fall in but on the contrary are most usually increasing—

Lewis laid the pen down to rest his fingers for a moment. He lowered his hand and Seaman's head rose to intercept it. He stroked the dog's skull and rubbed between his fingers the thick silky ears. Thump thump. After a minute, Lewis rose. He circumnavigated the small room, offered a seed to the corvus birds. No interest. Listened through his own door. Men's voices in the yard. No one disturbing him.

What o'clock was it? He glanced at the chronometer. She read nearly two o'clock, which translated (this being mid-February) to approximately three-thirty. He had last set her to the local noon on October 30th, and she was a trifle under a minute slow in every twenty-four hours. He'd always conceived of the chronometer as female. Why? Perhaps because she was expensive and unreliable! Her inaccuracy was one of the things confounding his astronomical calculations. That, and the error of 8' 45" in his sextant and 2° in his octant (or 2° 11' in the back observation, a divergence whose cause he could not fathom). Plus the fact that he was not absolutely certain he had correctly determined the precise rate of going of the chronometer by means of his faulty sextant and octant. Moreover there were the calculations he still erred in: corrections for refraction; an angular shift from the moon's edge (which one sighted for convenience) to her center (which the tables presumed); proportional logarithms to conform his time of observation to one of the eight-daily times printed in the *Ephemeris;* and parallax: because the figures in the lunar tables presumed the observer to be at the center of the earth: God's standpoint, as it were, where the math (like His sight) was clear. Whereas instead, of course, you were a mere confused creature on the surface of a spinning ball, corkscrewing through space in a complex curve.

Nothing was as it appeared. A star shining above the horizon might in fact be below it. The apparent distance between the moon and a reference star was not the actual distance. Clock time, even on a perfect instrument, was not the same as solar time, because the sun did not move uniformly across the sky. No, not even the sun! Yea, Phoebus Apollo, proverbial for his constancy (in contrast to the fickle moon), was not, it turned out, so very different from the chronometer, which not merely lagged, but lagged unevenly, her average daily error varying from week to week (owing to temperature?) and her slowness increasing (perhaps at an uneven rate!) over the twenty-four hours between each winding. There was, no doubt, an algorithm for calculating the mysterium of her movements, and perhaps God would tell Lewis what it was when he stood before Him with a hangman's noose around his neck on the Day of Judgment.

Clark held the chronometer and Lewis held the sextant, and they stood on the plain, a pair of Lunarians in the moonlight, when all was quiet but the prairie wolves, and they worked together seamlessly for an hour at a stretch, Lewis reading out the angles and Clark writing down the times. But the answers were still wrong. As ardently as he wished otherwise, Lewis knew they were wrong: he had recently sweated out a longitude for Fort Mandan and it was 2° off of Thompson's figure, which (Clark had eventually convinced him) was assuredly correct, because Thompson was a trained astronomer.

A question without an answer: *Where am I?*

He stopped at his desk and cast his eye over his notes, but did not sit down. The sense of futility with which he had been wrestling all day was rising in him.

He needed a wife.

A pleasant beacon to the navigator. That was an understatement. What Lewis had felt for those slender willows, holding on against the Missouri, had been something like a fierce love. (No, Mother . . .)

He had never so clearly apprehended why poets were fond of equating time and rivers. The Missouri was a clock, ticking out the centuries. You could read the time on its face by the destruction it had wreaked on Louisiana. From the river's side, beyond smiling meadows where venerable oaks held sway, you saw the hills—but those were not hills at all, they were the banks of a drainage ditch cut through the plain above. But that was nothing. When you climbed to that plain, you saw the thing that unstrung your knees. Ten, twenty miles away, alone in all the space to the four horizons: a hill, six hundred feet high, with a top as flat as a threshing floor: evidence of a former plain as vast as this one that, but for this forlorn remnant (which one might dub, with a nod to its incomprehensibility, Alone Man), was entirely washed away. Contemplating—trying to contemplate—that unimaginable stretch of time, all else—say, the forty-mile bend that pinched each year a foot tighter until it was left behind as an oxbow, that filled an inch each year to become a marsh, that dried through twenty decades to meadow, that grew an oak forest, that was pitched entire into the water to drown when the river shrugged its shoulders and undermined it all in a matter of minutes—all that seemed as nothing, as the blink of an eye.

He was thirty years old. He needed a wife, children. Yet he could not imagine it. Curtains and a bed canopy and domestic intercourse at the dinner table. Clark already had a couple of girls in his sights. A Miss Martha, whom Lewis had met in Louisville; a coquetting, designing creature. And a Miss Judith, whom Lewis had never seen, but he'd heard his friend wax poetic. A tender bud in Fincastle, Virginia. A Hancock; her older sister had already ensnared an old army friend of Lewis's.

Two-fifteen, now, by the clock. That is, three forty-five. Time kept passing, whether you accomplished anything or not. Of course he had known since the cradle that if he did nothing from morning till night, he had lost the day. What oppressed him, upon looking up in the evening after sixteen hours of a horse's labor, was the realization, ever new, ever surprising, that he had lost the day anyway.

He sat. *No. 14. The wide leaf willow or that species which I believe to be common to most parts of the Atlantic States—* Whose Linnaean name he should have known, but did not. Perhaps it was in Miller's *Termini Botanici,* a book he had paid good money for and lugged upriver, but had not yet opened. *—the leaf is smooth, ovate, pointed, finely indented—* And Barton's *Elements of Botany:* six dollars, paid direct to the author, and Lewis had been pleased, at the time, at the thought of poring over its five hundred pages, learning the true language of science, instead of this patois he spoke. Because it was not only the Latin names of genus and species that made up this universal language, but a host of descriptive terms that, once learned, allowed you to convey with utmost clarity and exactness the appearance of a root, a stem, a leaf, a seed, a calyx, a corolla. Lewis got up again, opened his book chest, found his Barton beneath Maskelyn's *Tables Requisite.* He flipped through the first pages, past categories and subcategories of roots. *Host* was indeed the word . . . Here, page 30: Leaves. Three headings: *Simple Leaves; Compound Leaves; Leaves According to their Determination.* Let us begin simply, and consider only the simple leaves. Barton enumerates eighty-eight descriptive terms, which are merely a selection from Linnaeus's fuller list in his *Philosophia Botanica.*

1. *folium orbiculatum,* an orbicular, or circular leaf. 2. *folium subrotundum,* a leaf nearly round. 3. *folium ovatum,* an ovate, or egg-shaped leaf—

Ah! Note, my attentive students, that the patois-mumbling amateur whom I have invited to our classroom today, as a cautionary example, has sadly botched his description of the leaf of the wide-leaf willow. He calls it *ovate,* when it is not egg-shaped at all, rather— Yes, Mr. Eliott?

A lanceolate leaf, sir. Your number nine: *folium lanceolatum.*

Excellent, Mr. Eliott! Your Boston breeding carries the day. Whereas this Virginia barbarian, this backwoods son of an herb-woman who presumes—

I would put forward that he is an ass, sir. Not to mention an onanist and a knothead.

Precisely, Mr. Eliott! My dear students, this person whom you see before you, this *Homo ludicrens*—

A tap on the door, a faint voice through the wood. "Beg pardon, sir. It's four o'clock."

"Very good."

Lewis laid the Barton on his notes, checked in his pocket for slate and pencil. As he went out the door (Seaman bounding ahead), he saw Jessome hurrying toward him. He did not break stride nor turn. "Yes, Mr. Jessome."

Jessome fell in behind him. "The squaw, she is weak."

"That is hardly surprising, she has been laboring like Sisyphus for twenty-six hours now."

"The baby is not come. I fear—"

Lewis had reached the thermometer. "One moment, Mr. Jessome."

He brought out his slate. Two degrees below zero; fair, the wind remaining northwest. He turned back toward his hut. "You fear—"

Jessome trotted after him. "She—the squaw—she cannot—*quelque chose*—something, something must—"

"Pray step in." Lewis closed the door, moved behind his desk. "Is she in danger? What does your woman think?"

"The baby is not come."

"I believe I have grasped that point. The question is—"

"Has *monsieur capitaine* a rattle?"

"Excuse me?"

"From snake. A rattle."

Lewis looked at him. Shake, shake. Quicksand.

"I do before. One, two ring. Break up, little piece. She drink. Baby come soon."

Lewis glanced down. 18. *folium reniforme,* a kidney-shaped leaf. 19. *folium cordatum,* a heart-shaped leaf. Herb-woman's son. "As it happens, I do." Lewis went to a corner, displaced a bow, a box, a horn, a bag, opened a small chest, rummaged. Loosened the drawstring on a leather pouch. "I see I have three. Enough to bring forth a whole clan, by your calculations."

"Yes, yes. You have one?"

"I said I have three."

"Yes, yes." Jessome stuck out his hand. Lewis placed one of the rattles in it. Jessome broke off two rings, handed the remainder back. He turned toward the door.

"Mr. Jessome."

He turned back.

"In alcohol?"

"Eh? Euhh . . . *non.* In little water. I break, little piece. She drink."

"Baby come soon."

"I hope." Jessome hurried out.

Lewis stood for a moment, abstracted. Then he remembered the slate in his pocket. He transcribed the figures into his weather notebook. He closed the book and remained standing by his desk for several minutes. A nearby ticking, a distant shout of pain.

The chronometer, she ticked. The woman, she died.

23. *folium panduræforme,* a guitar-shaped leaf. 28. *folium lyratrum,* a lyre-shaped leaf. 33. *folium truncatum,* a truncate leaf. The Prince of Naturalists, Barton called Linnaeus. The Great Architect. The Swedish Sage. God's Registrar. The young men Linnaeus sent around the world to catalogue Nature were called his apostles. One of them, Daniel Solander, sailed with Captain Cook. Several died in the service of science, of exotic diseases that perhaps, too, had not yet been named. Lewis was not of their caliber; but he, too, had a life to give.

He shifted the Barton off his botanical notes, leaving it open to the side, aligned just so. Quill below the inkhorn. Penknife beside it. He remembered an evening from the previous summer. He had been examining a specimen in the tent at night, a branch from a bush that resembled the privet. Trying to remember the Linnaean name for the privet, or at least recall whether he had ever known it, he'd murmured, "Swedish Sage." Clark had glanced over. "Are you certain? It bears no resemblance to common sage at all."

80. *folium ensiforme,* a sword-shaped leaf. 81. *folium acinaciforme,* a saber-shaped leaf. 82. *folium dolabriforme,* a hatchet-shaped leaf.

Through the wall the cries had changed, deepened. A grinding shout: *Yaahhh!*

Silence.

Yaahhh!

Lewis returned the Barton and his notes to their boxes. He left his hut and stopped outside the second door. He did not lean to listen, but stood a pace away, facing out into the yard, hands clasped behind his back.

Yaahhh!

The lone sentry on the bastion. The distant bang of the forge. February 11th, 1805. A fair day.

Yaahhh!

From the far side of the door, an urgent, whispered word: *pompey.* Then the girl's voice, a stream of words, exhausted and so high-pitched it sounded barely human: *pompey pompey pompey pompey pompey* . . . Fading to silence; gathering strength.

Yaahhh! from the mother-to-be.

Pompey pompey pompey pompey pompey . . . *Yaahhh!*

A liquid sound; an exclamation; a hubbub.

Waahhh!

He exhaled.

Waahhh! He unclasped his hands. What was it called, that cry? The vagitus. This vale of tears; they know.

Sounds of movement, murmurs. The outraged wail quieting. The breast, presumably. And rushing on and over everything else, still high-pitched, quivering now from sobbing or laughter or both, *pompey pompey pompey pompey pompey*

Life.

Lewis left them to it. He ambled back to his hut and waited, busying himself examining the construction of a bow he had requested Black Cat to make for him. Pompey, pompey. He rather doubted the girl was thinking of Pompey the Great. A good Republican name, which was probably the reason it was a common slave name in Virginia. Didn't Jefferson have a little yellow Pompey running around somewhere at Monticello?

Nearly an hour passed before Jessome saw fit to inform him of the birth; as though the outcome mattered to him not in the least. "A boy!" the Frenchman announced at the door. "Ten minute after I give her—"

"Damn you!" Lewis barked. "You were supposed to report to me immediately."

"*Pardon*, but—"

"I have heard you, a boy. Very good. Now leave me."

Late that evening, Lewis wrote the day's entry in Clark's journal.

11th February Monday 1805

The party that were ordered last evening set out early this morning. The weather was fair and cold, wind N.W. About five oclock this evening one of the wives of Charbono was delivered of a fine boy. It is worthy of remark that this was the first child which this woman had born and as is common in such cases her labor was tedious and the pain violent; Mr. Jessome informed me that he had frequently administered a small portion of the rattle of the rattle-snake, which he assured me had never failed to produce the desired effect, that of hastening the birth of the child; having the rattle of a snake by me I gave it to him and he administered two rings of it to the woman broken in small pieces with the fingers and added to a small quantity of water. Whether this medicine was truly the cause or not I shall not undertake to determine, but I was informed that she had not taken it more than ten minutes before she brought forth. Perhaps this remedy may be worthy of future experiments, but I must confess that I want faith as to its efficacy.

Nearly midnight. Seaman asleep by his chair. Lewis cleaned his pen.

2

The last days of winter fell one by one into the past, and at night Lewis unrolled the penultimate draft of Clark's map, the final having been packed away for the trip downriver (and in any case he preferred the crossouts and corrections of this copy, the other falsely implying all was known), and with the cries of geese dropping out of the darkness through the wind-scoured chinks of his hut, he lowered himself into it, going away, to the great falls, how high, the three forks, how far, the Snakes, how many, climbing the eastern slope of the divide to stand between the waters, the first white man.

Near.

He'd had another chance to get shot at, pursuing a Sioux party that had robbed his men of two horses, but the Mandans accompanying him had seemed reluctant to press the chase, arguing the Siouxs were well away, and as it proved, they were right: nothing but the empty expanse of plain before him, his frustration a red haze in his eyes. But he would turn away from that, he would put the Siouxs behind him like dust off his feet. Ahead were Blackfeet, Blue Muds, Flatheads.

On the 1st of March at 4 P.M. the temperature was 38°, and on the 3rd it was 39°, and on the 5th it was 40°, and then an east wind brought cold again, but on the 14th it was back to 40°, and on the 16th it was 42°, and on the 17th it was 46°.

In the final days, the grand sachem of the Minetares, Le Borgne, "One-Eye," at last came to the fort, after standing aloof all winter and letting disparaging remarks be known, and his excuse for coming was to see whether it was true, what he had heard, that there was a black man with the Americans. The curiosity was duly displayed; Le Borgne spit on his hand to rub the skin, York with a flourish pulled the handkerchief from his head to reveal the woolly hair, and Le Borgne, a satisfied customer, declared him a different species entirely. Only then did he perform the rest of his visit, for performance it was, no British minister in his sash and orders could be more pregnant with hauteur. The men presented, Lewis ordered two guns fired, he smoked with Le Borgne and offered sesquipedalian compliments that Charbono passed on as grunts of awe, took him on a tour of the fort and loaded him with presents, the more numerous as Le Borgne claimed not to have received the gifts sent him in November, a thing Lewis did not believe for a moment, but neither was he put out at the deception; despots took pleasure in deceiving, and Lewis was there to please. Orders were given, minions stepped forward: another medal for Polyphemus, another flag, a shirt, a scarlet cloth, a gorget, an armband.

A giant, he stood four inches taller than Lewis, swung huge limbs, shook bushy hair, and glared monocularly along the enormous hatchet-blade nose *(nasus dolabriformus)* on which Indians put so high a valuation that one of their gestures denominating Beauty was a hooked finger jutting out from the face. Lewis had no doubt that he was every bit the warrior he was reputed to be, that beneath his beaded and quilled shirt his torso was a mass of scars, where he had cut out strips of his muscles like meat for jerking, or thrust arrows through them to show his indifference to pain. Lewis could believe the stories he'd heard of the man's murderous rages, the killing of associates over trivial disagreements, the tomahawking of a runaway wife before the horrified eyes of her family, with whom he had just smoked the pipe of forgiveness. Would-be avengers, his custom was to announce, could find him at his lodge; they never came looking. Lewis watched the idol roll offstage with his flock of supernumeraries, and remarked to himself that as the Minetares' distrust of the Americans was owing to this orgulous ogre, they must continue to find ways to appease his superhuman vanity. But Lewis was turning blessedly away from Le Borgne, who was damned welcome to perch here enthroned on his hairy buffalo robe, half buried in his cadged gifts—Lewis was going up-river. He unrolled the map at night and lowered himself into it, and half hoped it was all wrong, not three forks but ten, and five great falls, and mountains such as no American had ever seen, and blue trees shading the Blue Muds, squatting around a village pot in which fresh mammoth seethed.

Soon.

In the final days, Charbono was corrupted by Mr. Chaboillez of the North West Company, who gave him three braces of cloth and a corduroy coat and two hundred balls, and, his pockets full of his importance, he told the captains he would not accompany them unless he was exempt from guard duty and camp work, and had the right to return if any man displeased him. Lewis stood over the presuming ferret and brought his face down to his ravaged nose and told him to pack up and move out of the fort by sundown, they would do without him and his wives and his squalling brat, and if he thought the North West Company could employ him to the equal of twenty-five dollars a month, he was a damned fool, and if hearing that displeased him, why, Lewis was pleased to hear it. It took the Frenchman three days to think it over (or perhaps it took him that long to multiply twenty-five by twelve), after which he sent word, begging the captains to excuse his simplicity, he would agree to all their conditions.

On the 25th of March a gang of swans lighted on the river and the last snow disappeared from the ground, and on the 26th the ice gave way with a thunderous roar, and on the 27th a southwest wind sprang up and it was 60° and the first gnat appeared, and on the 28th it was 64°, and on the 29th there were clouds of flies, and on the 31st ducks and geese flew overhead in thousands.

And and.

The sky was a haze of smoke, as the Indians fired the plains to promote new grass, to induce the buffalo to draw near, and the Minetares were venturing out on their first spring sallies, riding west to raid the Snakes, carrying war hatchets that Shields and Willard had made for them. And buffalo that had broken through the ice above were floating down the river, and for once the fort was free of visiting Indians, because they were lining the banks, peering after carcasses, and Lewis paused one afternoon in his packing to watch braves jump from ice cake to ice cake, with a dexterity scarcely credible, and all for rotten flesh that fell apart at the touch, and was cooked into a green soup that filled the air with an infernal stench.

In the final days, Lewis took down a Minetare vocabulary, from a brother of Le Borgne, to add to the Mandan he'd recorded months before. The chief composed himself on the floor of Lewis's hut, Jessome and Charbono flanking him, and Labiche next to Lewis, who unrolled one of Mr. J's commodious printed blanks. With 280 pet words in four columns, it was, like so many of the President's projects, eminently reasonable in its principles and exasperatingly impractical in its demands.

"Fire," Lewis read out, pointing to the hearth, and Labiche said something in French and pointed to the fire. Before Charbono could speak, the chief pointed to the fire and said something in Minetare. Jessome nodded and repeated the word, pointing to the fire and trying to catch Lewis's eye. Charbono shook his head and said something different in Minetare. He commenced arguing with the chief. Jessome said something to Labiche in French, who turned to speak to Lewis, but Jessome tried to say it in English himself so that the two spoke over each other. "He says—" "Charbono no know, he *pas*—"

"Stop!" Lewis said. "Labiche." But now Charbono was speaking heatedly to Labiche, gesturing dismissively toward Jessome and with vehemence toward the fire. Indian sign language, perhaps: *throw Jessome into the fire.* "Perhaps we should have Drewyer in here," Lewis said, and Labiche said, "Charbono says the chief thinks you say hot, not fire, and he says Jessome is completementally an idiot." Lewis wondered if Mr. J had any conception how long it took to inquire thus into 280 words; he wondered if he should tell Labiche to tell Charbono to tell the chief that *heat* came later, and *hot* about a hundred words after that. He decided to trust Charbono (a sure sign of desperation) and wrote down the word the old Frenchman was now chanting with deliberate provocation in Jessome's face: *mi-da-ha! mi-da-ha!* He wondered how far they might get before Jessome and Charbono came to blows. Jessome had been increasingly discontented in the last days, as the Minetare chiefs had begun visiting frequently and Charbono's services had come to the fore. "Water, gentlemen, water," Lewis said.

Then *earth,* then *air.* Characteristic, that Mr. J would begin with the four classical elements. Characteristic, too, that he included so many species of bird and tree, which required drawing dolabriform or lanceolate leaves in the dirt, or attempting honks, roars, and howls, to the amusement of the multitude. And uniquely characteristic that the first animal listed, before buffalo or elk or bear or wolf, was the mammoth.

Behind him!

In the final days, Lewis packed his specimens for the keelboat going down: male and female antelope skins, with their skeletons, which he had boiled clean; a Mandan bow and quiver, an earthen pot, Ricara tobacco seeds; an ear of corn, a red fox skin; a martin, a hare, horns of the mountain ram. In strong cages, the living animals: the barking squirrel, the four magpies, the prairie hen.

He dutifully wrote a letter to his mother that (breathe it silently) was mostly a verbatim copy of a letter he'd written the day before to the President— *The difficulties which oppose themselves to the navigation of this immense river . . . The country as high up as the mouth of the river Platte, a distance of 630 miles, is generally well timbered . . . from thence to the Kansas river, the deer were more abundant . . .* The only personal note was a yoke of two flagrant untruths: *I request that you will give yourself no uneasiness with respect to my fate, for I assure you that I feel myself perfectly as safe as I should do in Albemarle; and the only difference between 3 or 4 thousand miles and 130, is that I can not have the pleasure of seeing you as often as I did while at Washington.*

An unfilial thing; and unfortunate, should it turn out to be his last. But he sealed it and packed it, along with a second letter to Jefferson that included a paragraph so dismal and devious it had made him swallow. He was sending down Clark's journal, he wrote, and *I shall dispatch a canoe with three, perhaps four persons, from the extreme navigable point of the Missouri; by the return of this canoe, I shall send you my journal.*

Which, in its multiple volumes, lay stacked at this very moment by his elbow, but which could not be sent down, at this very moment, because because.

And which, when he did send it from the divide, with the four strong men required to portage it in its gilded palanquin, would say (God send) more than *I am at the head of the Missouri, the Indians so far friendly.*

And he spread out the map and lowered himself into it and before going away he unhappily recalled the day when Clark was writing out the fair copy, and Lewis, on that day (remembering an *earlier* day, when he had offended Clark on the subject of his writing, while striving to do the opposite), was trying to make it right, coming to the table and looking over Clark's shoulder and saying *superb* and *tour de force,* and he managed to blunder again, adding *marvelous,* and Clark responded pointedly that marvelous was exactly what a good map should not be.

And April 4th became April 5th, and the buds of the elms were swollen and red, and the keelboat was packed and the canoes were ready and the ice was gone, and the chiefs had come for the last smokes and the braves had come for the last war hatchets and the forge was packed and then two days of wind of astonishing violence came howling out of the vast expanse of the treeless northwest, rendering embarkation impossible, the voice of God speaking out of the whirlwind to Lewis, *Who are you to enter paradise?,* but Lewis kept his head down until He ran out of breath, and on April 7th, at four o'clock in the evening, the temperature 64°, the weather fair, the wind southwest, the Mandans and Minetares and Ahwahharways thronging the shores, the keelboat turned downriver and the two pirogues and the six canoes pushed off upriver, and Lewis proceeded along the shore, something of a private ceremony, and an internal vow, that he would walk as many of the two thousand miles to the Pacific as (consistent with his duties) he could do, his footsteps a dotted line across the blank spaces, his legs a two-pole chain measuring the continent.

That night, after an early supper, Lewis retired to the conical tent of dressed skins he and Clark had bought from Charbono, opened one of the pristine red morocco notebooks, and wrote, *Fort Mandan April 7th 1805, Having on this day at 4 P.M. completed every arrangement necessary for our departure—* and he persevered for some eight hundred words, describing the party, and the boats, and even the lodge he was sitting in, and somewhere in there he wrote—recalling it as he closed the book and blew out the candle, acknowledging it as no more than the truth, yet at the same time praying (or was he vowing?) that it *was* true—*I could but esteem this moment of my departure as among the most happy of my life.*

Third Clark

He was inking in the Missouri. Above the Platte, around the bends, past the Yankton Soues and heading for the Tetons.

"Excellent," Lewis said, looking over his shoulder.

March 2nd. The river cracking. Soon they must proceed on. The men were hewing dugouts to replace the keelboat going down, making ropes, jerking meat; Clark had his report to finish on the Indian nations, his chart of trade forts, this fair copy of his map. Lewis had his own work, but he was restless. Tapped his teeth for minutes on end. Like rain on a tent. Paced. This was the third time in half an hour he'd stood behind to watch Clark's progress.

"My dear Clark, it is a *tour de force*! Marvelous!"

This pleased Clark more than—more than what? He didn't know. Lewis did not often— He chuckled, not looking up. "I suppose *marvelous* is just what it shouldn't be. Though too many maps are." Clark straightened to view it: St. Louis a dot on the right, the Pacific Ocean vast on the left; the Missouri like an absentminded doodle twisting and looping west and north toward the Mandans; the tributaries still to be filled in from the last draft. He'd already put in some of the river courses above the Mandans to the Rocky Mountains. They'd been faster to execute, being conjectural. Just push the pen in the right direction and wiggle the line, so they don't look like you laid them down with a ruler and a prayer.

The thought crossed his mind that posteriority would not attribute this map to him, but to Lewis, as commander of the expedition; which vexed him a little. But he set it aside as fruitless. Not to mention ungenerous. With Lewis beside him, generously praising. Clark knew praise came hard to his friend. He'd never suspected criticism of himself in all these months; but he sometimes wondered, when Lewis was snappish, what the cause might be.

Lewis had gone back to pulverizing a root the North West Company man, Heney, had sent down a couple of days ago. Said by the Indians to be sovereign against the bites of snakes and mad dogs. Clark bent again to the map. The work required care, but not much thought, so he allowed his mind to wander.

He thought about the marvelous in maps. He'd been reading and making maps all his adult life. He knew how much desire bled into the drawing of them. Give a man a pen. For example, maps of the west—he'd had occasion to smile. He'd seen, on Spanish maps, the rivers Spain wanted for commerce—River Colorado, Rio Bravo, River des Los Apostolos—stretching so straight and so far north through Louisiana they almost touched Canada. But on American maps, those same rivers were miserable, shriveled things, sagging off to the northwest. Well, hell, they had to get out of the way of the big American rivers, the Arkansas and the Platte, barging straight west.

There never was a course ran smooth. The course of something never did run straight. Something from Lewis's man, Shakespeare.

One of the maps Clark had picked up somewhere was Evans's, showing the course of the Missouri upriver from the Mandans. Evans had it heading northwest; he said he got that from the Indians. That was in 1797, when the Spanish owned the Missouri, and Evans was working for them. Northwest was a fine and dandy direction for the Spanish, because it gave them more territory.

Clark had another map: Thompson's; same area, a year or so later. Thompson was working for the English. And maybe you wouldn't be surprised to hear he had the Missouri heading *south*west.

And then there was the map made especially for Clark and Lewis. The draftsman, Mr. King, must have figured he had to follow Thompson, who was a trained surveyor; but Thompson showed an un-American direction upstream from the Mandans. Fortunately, his map only covered fifty miles; so King's map had the Missouri head southwest from the Mandans, but at the exact place where it reached the end of Thompson's detail, it wheeled 90° like a good soldier and marched northwest, heading at 50° latitude; Canada no more.

"If wishes were rivers," Clark said, inking a tiny triangle on the north bank of a bend and writing *The Wintering post of the Exploring Party of the U.S., an. 1804–5.*

Lewis looked over. "Yes?"

"I don't know. I'm trying to construct a witticism."

"Ah." Lewis added a spoonful of water to his root fibers, compacted the mash with the back of the spoon. "If wishes were rivers, they would flow both ways?"

"That's good."

In Clark's experience, even when a man went so far as to actually travel up the river he meant to learn about, the map he brought back was not as accurate as the one he'd have made overland. The reason was, you couldn't get lost on a river; your life didn't depend on the map you were making. Look at Mackay and Evans. They'd thought they were at 110° W by the time they reached the Mandans, 450 miles too far west. If they'd been that wrong overland, when they tried to return to St. Louis they would have wandered into the worst of Soue country—on their way to Illinois! Instead, all they had to do was turn the pirogue around and float home. A jackass's landfall, perfect every time. As ignorant of the location of the Mandans when they got back as when they'd left.

"If wishes were rivers," Lewis said, smelling the mash, dipping a finger in to touch to tongue, "explorers would . . . Hm."

Clark was pretty sure both Thompson and Evans were wrong. From the Indian reports he'd gathered, the Missouri headed roughly west from here, not southwest or northwest. Evans wrote that the Indians told him the main course reached 49°, about 125 miles farther north; but Clark had to wonder how he got a latitude out of the Indians, when they didn't know the earth was round. That was one of the difficulties, Indian geography. For example, they talked about going toward the sunset. But which sunset did they mean, the one on the day they were telling you, or the hypothical one, straight west? He wondered if that was Thompson's mistake. Thompson visited these villages in the winter; maybe the Indians told him the river went toward the sunset, meaning west, and Thompson watched the sun go down that day in the southwest and drew his map accordingly.

For his own map, the best Clark could do was forge a middle course between the arguments. You were going to be wrong, that was certain; the goal was to be only half wrong.

Note to Mr. Jefferson: *You may safely confide in the accuracy and fidelity of this map.*

Lewis turned from his desk and made an expansive gesture. "If wishes were rivers, Clark, they would go on forever."

Desire was a danger. It could wear away mountains and change the course of rivers. Still and all, what the Menetarrees had told Clark was cheering: ten days to the mouth of the Yellowstone, twenty-four to the Great Falls. They seemed to reckon a day at about twenty-five miles, therefore the mouth of the Yellowstone was 250 miles upstream, the Great Falls 600.

Clark had first heard rumors of a falls on the Missouri when they were in St. Louis. Before that, every last report paddled it as gospel that the Missouri had no obstructions anywhere. Desire could smooth out a little cataract of two or three hundred feet without breaking a sweat. Fortunately, the Menetarrees said there was an open plain on the north side of the falls, and the portage was about half a mile. So the Corps could manage it in a couple of days. And they said the river above continued navigable to the three forks and beyond.

"If wishes were rivers," Lewis said, "they would not boil, I can assure you of that." He was scoring his forearm, preparatory to applying a poultice of the root mash. Probably to ascertain its drawing power, or whether it killed sensation. Clark was a little surprised he hadn't first gone out and got a mad dog to bite him.

Clark dipped his quill, inked in black across the middle Yellowstone River: *Kee hat sa (the friend to all) or Raven Indians. 300 tents. 900 men.* The Yellowstone, they said, was also navigable at all seasons, to the foot of the Rocky Mountains. The valley was fertile and well timbered, according to Big White, and abounded in beaver. All that beaver could be floated down to the fort Clark wanted to build at the mouth of the Yellowstone.

The Ravens were cousins to the Menetarrees, whose language they spoke. Also called Corboes, Crows; they called themselves Arp-sar-co-gah. Maybe the Menetarrees called them *the friend to all* because their outlaws found asylum there. If a brave killed another brave of his own nation, the dead man's family was bound to avenge it; so he hightailed it to the Crows, who spoke the same language, took him in, rolled up their skin tents, roved into the mountains. Even a frontier needed a frontier. His poor brother George had wanted to get lost in Spanish Louisiana after the U' States ruined him; now with Louisiana part of the U' States, and settlers streaming across the Mississippi, George would have had to move on, up the Missouri, maybe taking Daniel Boone with him. (Clark had met the lion last spring, where he was living in ill health and poverty on the farthest extremity of white settlement on the Missouri, and no more fond of his ungrateful country than George.) The two of them backing up the Missouri, rifles trained downriver, past the Yanktons and Tetons, maybe pausing awhile with the Mandans, but cursing Little Billy because he was going to build a trade fort for the U' States at the mouth of the Yellowstone, bring soldiers in, so proceeding on, up the Yellowstone, putting out a white flag for the Ravens, *Take us in.* Disappearing into the hills. Best thing for George. For one thing, the Ravens didn't have whiskey.

300 tents, 900 men. Clark's eye roved over his legends: Nimousin, Dotame, Chyanne: so many lodges or tents, so many men. Always men; because the thing the white man wanted to know was: how much of a fight are you going to put up? As if there were no women or children. *Root them out. Teach them a lesson.*

Well, if trade was established, maybe that could be avoided. Teach the Ravens and Snakes how to trap; float all that beaver down.

Clark thought of little Pompy. Pumping his lungs, a lusty bawl. Giving away their position, Lewis worried. But the janey would quiet him with a breast. Sah-kah-gar-we-a. Full young pretty breasts, and she not coy with them. It raised in Clark thoughts of little Judy Hancock. Just a girl when he met her, ten years old, perched on a big gelding that wouldn't do what she wanted, no matter how she scolded and thumped. Clark led the brute, brought the girl and her cousin home. She'd be about thirteen now, maybe getting breasts of her own. Which Clark could see in three dimensions, and smell their powder, too.

No, he didn't wish rivers went on forever.

Clark envied his men this one liberty. But as captain he felt he oughtn't undermine— Or should he say, as a *mock* captain he felt he oughn't make a *mockery* of—

He sensed, in any case, in Lewis, adamant opposition. And quite right, you couldn't have the leaders disabled with the pox, all for a momentary indulgence.

That medicine dance the Mandans had put on in the first village in January, when they'd wanted the buffalo to come near; all for the benefit of the old men, who'd probably invented it. The young men bringing their wives, stark naked under buffalo robes, begging the old men to lie with them. Imagine. Some of the ancients scarcely able to walk, led out by the hand by a pretty young naked girl to do the business in a convenient place, on top of the robe the girl was wearing. Or make the motions, if the relic couldn't perform the substantial service, save face all around. And receive presents besides. Imagine. Pryor sent on over to observe, they gave him four girls. Looking for a consideration from him, which he willingly gave. Less hair on their privates, straighter, the men said.

Clark's chance. *Get on her, boy!* He wouldn't have another, no, not when *he* was a doddering old fool in his lawn chair leering after the girls picnicking in their pinafores, he could be sure of that.

He forced his thoughts back to the map. Wishes, rivers. The passage west he'd drawn looked invitingly easy. Maybe the Rocky or Shining Mountains were more formidable than they had supposed. But Clark, on the whole, didn't believe it. Where Mackenzie had crossed them, at 56° N, they were such a low ridge his account didn't even talk about climbing. His portage was 817 paces. And the Indians told him the mountains were lower farther south. The Menetarrees said there were five ranges, which agreed with Evans and Arrowsmith, but they also said the Missouri cut through four of them. As for the fifth, the Menetarrees said they could pass it in half a day to a river flowing west, without shoals. From the divide, they said, it was open and level plains, descending gradually to the Pacific.

Leave the Mandans on the 1st of April, pass the Great Falls by the end of May. Cross the divide at the end of June, reach the sea by August 1st, Clark's birthday. Recross the divide by mid-September, float at their ease down the Missouri, reach the Mandans again by the end of October. And since you were half wrong, make it the end of November: riding in, blowing trumpets, on the first ice cakes.

First Charbonneau

He want tell these stupid captain, Indian say what you want hear. You say, this right word for that? they say, exact so. You say, that mountain easy go over? they say, easy as fuck. You say, my ass on backward? they kiss finger, they so happy you notice. So Captain Big Knife, Monsieur Frown, he say, this river good for boat? and old Charbonneau say to Fear Snake or Black Moccasin or who, river good for boat? and Fear Snake or who say, river good! yes! best goddamn river you ever see! But what he know? Minitadi don't got canoe. They only got bull boat women paddle, little washtub. Minitadi go upriver, they ride horse. River big enough wash face in, drink for horse, is good river. So he want tell these stupid captain, you don't say, river good? no Indian ever say, no, you wrong, you stupid, river not good. You say, how wide river? you say, how deep river? They say, ten foot wide, one foot deep. Then you know it not good for boat, you know it not river, it little stinking creek. All his year work engagé, many year, he know what he talk about, from Grand Portage, Lac des Bois, and so, or up on Athabasca, fat bourgeois always jump like rabbit out of canoe moment tree give out, Indian camp at edge forest, they know, they got horse, they ready. Tree give out, river turn into wandering stinking creek, bourgeois trade for broken nag he pay too much for, but better than stinking canoe he leave behind with old Charbonneau paddle big pile of gun, ball, kettle, what-all. Monsieur Frown or Red Hair never wonder why Minitadi use horse, not canoe?

And while they at it, never wonder why Mandan friendly, Minitadi not? They think Mandan good, Minitadi bad. Old Charbonneau want say, look at fucking map. Minitadi own upriver, Mandan own downriver. Minitadi get first look at trader from Canadian fort, take best good, tell lie about Mandan, sell good higher price to Mandan. Mandan want same, trade from St. Louis, they see first, Minitadi come beg Mandan for American good. Captain think Mandan and Minitadi good friend. What. They make deal, like everybody. I give you this, you give me that. You don't give me, I smile, you turn around, I stick canoe awl up your ass.

Old Charbonneau speak French perfect, Minitadi pretty good, little Cree, little Saulteaux, little Mandan, little English, little sign. French mother tongue, he Montreal boy, get out when maman drop dead, he fifteen, sixteen, no way he take care nine, ten brother, sister, that boat going to bottom, put X on paper, climb in canoe. Trap in muskrat country, five, six stinking year, then up north Athabasca, watch all Indian drop dead. That twenty year ago, smallpox, one year stay in hut all year, no Indian, no one make canoe. Then old Charbonneau stupid engagé for North West Company, paddle like donkey, bring up trap to Cree, carry in canoe fat company man, bourgeois, with pillow and parasol and whore, oops, he mean lady, set up tent for his majesty, cook meal, listen him fuck all night, in morning lift him back in canoe, dip ass in cold water, pardon monsieur, spend winter freeze ball off in tent, food run out, you ever wipe wolf spit off buffalo bone, suck out marrow, thank God best thing you ever tasted?, collect debt from Cree, float fur down in spring, company take most profit, pat on flank, good donkey! Later at Fort des Pins, Fort Espérance, still stupid engagé, running errand to Indian camp, like boss want horse you promised, you know, but he come down to Minitadi and Mandan village and see Ménard and Jusseaume free trader, live like pasha, and he know, if idiot Jusseaume can do, old Charbonneau do better. So he quit company, become free trader, residenter. Now he middleman, lucky Pierre. This for that. That is device of plain. This for that, then that for double this. All you have need is more brain than stupid green idiot you trade with. Say Minitadi got ten wolf pelt. Old Charbonneau trade for red blanket. Then trade wolf pelt to North West Company trader for thirty ball, knife, pouch vermilion. Trade twenty ball and knife to Crow for twenty kitt pelt, trade kitt pelt to Hudson Bay man for red blanket, trade ten ball for fathom tobacco, wait until big dance when Minitadi all want tobacco, vermilion, trade tobacco for three beaver skin, vermilion for fifteen ball. Now old Charbonneau got red blanket, three beaver skin, fifteen ball. At dance, gambler lose shirt, legging, loincloth, naked stinking beggar, red blanket worth more, trade for three fathom tobacco. If winter, old Charbonneau now trade tobacco and ball with Mandan for dog, when free trader come from Canadian fort and trade and feel rich and need dog for sled to pull pile of good, he trade dog for forty ball, two red blanket, pouch vermilion, then trade same man three beaver skin pile on sled pull by damn expensive dog for twenty more ball, fathom tobacco. Now Charbonneau got two red blanket, sixty ball, pouch vermilion, fathom tobacco, and he not spend one stinking night freezing ball off on hunting trip. Add ax, he got enough to buy slave girl after Minitadi raid, and now we talk, slave girl worth take week trip to some stinking Canadian fort out nowhere, fuck her whole way, trade to poor stupid engagé with tired hand and sore asshole for two mackinaw gun and one hundred ball. Then trade one gun for healthy strong horse from Corbeaux, got yellow hoof, white hair on feet. Trade horse to green North West or Hudson Bay man for gun, plus four hundred ball, plus three red blanket, plus two ax, plus dozen knife, plus six string bead, plus vermilion. Green man from east know horseflesh, he check strong leg, back, teeth, he happy, he not know yellow hoof wear out on hard plain, he not know white hair on feet rub off in crust snow, horse go lame, that why Corbeaux trade horse cheap. Green man think he smart, but old Charbonneau smarter, he turn around, old Forest Bear give him little poke in ass with canoe awl, he feel so good, and this not even count what old Charbonneau get paid for interpret, for say, river good? and turn around and say yessir, river so incredible good your eyeball fall out.

Jusseaume think he speak Minitadi, he want get paid every talk, but he get all confused. Minitadi hard language, not like Mandan, easy as fuck, old Charbonneau learn enough Mandan for this for that in one, two visit, but Minitadi little stinking crazy, every word say twenty different way by same person, Minitadi, Miditadi, Minitari, Miditari, Binitari, Binitadi, Binitali, Winitadi, Widitadi, Widitali, Winitali, old Charbonneau love do that to Jusseaume, manakoeh, balakoeh, warakoeh, wanakoeh till he ready scream, manakoeh mean my friend, but old Charbonneau mean, Jusseaume, you stupid. Like when Jusseaume get all confused when captain ask Fear Snake about little stinking creek upriver, Fear Snake talk about place Minitadi call river fork, amaati adushashash, Jusseaume think he say amati, earth lodge. Amaati, amati, sound same if you got ear like earthworm, so old Charbonneau tell him shut up, let old Charbonneau do job and Captain Big Knife say, wait wait, that frown like he papa and you boy about get belt across ass, he say, wait wait, *what* it mean? and old Charbonneau say, it mean if I river and Jusseaume river, I say to him, you are fucking idiot. Labiche interpret to Big Knife in English, probably not say fucking idiot, probably ignorant fellow or like that, put in Big Knife language, and Big Knife stare for second and say, river scold other river? and old Charbonneau say, that close, but better, you all fucking idiot. Big Knife say, name is River Scold All Other River? and Charbonneau say, exact! Big Knife, you not ignorant fellow! And there on Red Hair map, old Charbonneau river, come out of Canada and say to all American river, you all stupid stinking American creek!

Old Charbonneau come out of Canada nine, ten winter ago, canoe awl hole in ass and sore back from carry fat bourgeois, and say suis arrivé!, Minitadi, Mandan, old Charbonneau got red blanket, who got ten wolf pelt? Settle in Ménard village, ask Ménard what this, what that, learn quick. Ménard get old, not mind new residenter, anything bother Jusseaume, Ménard know he idiot and criminal, madakoeh, manakoeh, badakoeh, my friend, priend, pliend, not like Jusseaume, Ménard beau vieux, damn too bad Assiniboin kill him. What he want tell these stupid captain, every Indian middleman, like old Charbonneau. Big Knife and Red Hair like other green men, think Indian care only about war. That because young red man need war, only way get power, become chief, young man stand up in council, you might as well take nap, wake up hour later, he still talk about war. But that just young men, they pain in ass like everywhere. What Indian really care about is trade. Even war kind of trade because war give power, red man trade power. Minitadi-Mandan trader par excellence, they eat, shit this for that, they make white trader look like Jesus Christ, give away loincloth, turn other cheek. Minitadi see dance he like, he not copy, he buy. Dance not work if he not buy. Minitadi have dream of wolf, get wolf power, he not need wolf power, he trade. He sell dream! Old Charbonneau like these people. Sell dream. Sweet crazy. He like trick they play. He remember in Athabasca, Cree want take white trade from Saulteaux, bunch Cree ask bunch Saulteaux, how much you pay for gun, how much for pot, Saulteaux say how much, Cree say, that too much! you stupid, we tell trader price we pay, they say no, we beat shit out, we get good price. Stupid Saulteaux beat next trader, lose all trade to Cree. Sweet. So Assiniboin kill Ménard, Assiniboin rob trader on Mandan plain between Canadian fort and Missouri, and Big Knife make papa frown and say Assiniboin bad children. Old Charbonneau want tell him, look at fucking map,

Assiniboin middlemen, they lucky Pierre between Canadian fort and Minitadi-Mandan, they trade for horse, corn, slave girl at Minitadi, take to fort, trade for twice price, normal. How you think they like trader go direct from fort to Minitadi-Mandan? They meet trader, they demand price. Trader say no, they kill. What else they do? Stupid trader not give price. Old Charbonneau, he give up slave girl once, kiss goodbye two gun, what-all, but leave old Charbonneau one red blanket, he start over, he still got scalp. Red Hair and Big Knife say Minitadi-Mandan not trade with Canadian, not trade with Assiniboin, trade with St. Louis. They notice maybe Minitadi-Mandan got horse, got corn, got buffalo robe, they notice maybe St. Louis not want any that? Maybe old Charbonneau miss something, but St. Louis want beaver, Minitadi-Mandan not got beaver. Last time Charbonneau look, beaver live where tree. Captain maybe notice hardly no stinking tree in Minitadi-Mandan country? Maybe old Charbonneau take Big Knife up on plain and say, all surprise, I say, mon capitaine grand-couteau, where-all got those stinking tree to? Old Charbonneau little worried. He like these people. He come out of Canada nine, ten winter ago, he Jesus Christ, they tricky Jew, they turn old Jesus Christ Toussaint Charbonneau into tricky Jew like them, he happy. This for that. When they beg good lord, Itsikamahidish, mean First Made, he not frown, say pull down pant, he smile, say, yessir! this for that! you give me tobacco, I give you horse you want steal, I keep old canoe awl in pocket for now.

Minitadi call old Charbonneau Forest Bear, why? Because bear big powerful medicine hopini animal and old Charbonneau got white man power, red women fuck white men get power, then fuck husband, husband get white man power. Power like syphilis that way. Like he say, residenter middleman, lucky Pierre. But old Charbonneau too smart for that, he see free trader come from Canadian fort with debt thirty beaver skin, lay out gun, ball, pot, you know, trade for wolf, buffalo, kitt worth fifty beaver. Profit sixty percent, not so stinking bad. You think he take back to fort, get more gun, ball? No, you forget, he stupid, he spend week in village fuck red women, whole reason he come, fuck fuck fuck, and he pay, Minitadi don't take crap in grass without trade, like old Charbonneau say, you give for free, thing lose power. Trader go back with no profit, stupid smile on face, little present. Trader say syphilis here mild. That like, what, like opposite of fox and grape. Old Charbonneau say, you think mild, you stay, you see red men old Charbonneau age totter, spotted, crazy old sick, scream, lie on robe in corner and die. That not Charbonneau plan. Old Forest Bear outlive everybody, reach hundred, last day fry up boudin blanc, lie down buffalo robe under best red blanket with young girl warm, get kiss all over, little happy hundred-year-old cock with skin like little baby ass, die with big smile on toothless face. Old Charbonneau learn quick, it take only one mercury cure at Grand Portage, one canoe awl up ass at Lac Manitou-à-Banc. Young Saulteaux girl at Manitou-à-Banc, old Charbonneau see her when he fetch winter trade for boss at McKay post, she like new copper ring, just get first little bud breast like lip pout, almost sure first fuck, safe, and she happy, old Charbonneau give her card bead, ven-iss, she say, Indian always know, they trader from moment they born, Charbonneau say, exact, Venice, best glass, you smart girl, he pull up shift, see legging up to little knee, above naked, all up sweet thigh to young cunt wait, he take out happy cock, he just get in there, she look at card bead, happy, he just that first tight like strong hand, when stinking bitch mother, old warpath mother come down path, stinking luck, she come behind, jam canoe awl in old Charbonneau ass, complete through right cheek, he not walk right two month, he still feel sometime, he ask his ass, we going get rain, ass? his ass say, yessir, rain like you never believe! Unlike Indian, his ass never lie. So old Charbonneau learn. Start with red blanket, end up own slave girl, fuck first, middle, last, no mercury, no stinking mother. Ménard have Minitadi wife, Jusseaume have Mandan wife, it help in trade, you fuck Minitadi woman, like fucking whole clan, clan give you trade, but stinking problem is, you got give wife over drooling old men at winter buffalo calling dance, she come home give you old man power all right, little present. Slave girl not part of clan, no power, she just lie on back, get good fuck like good lord First Made plan, old Itsikamahidish tell red women paint red in hair, old Charbonneau come along like First Made right hand, he trade vermilion, women put in middle part, black hair either side, red line in middle, they like walking cunt, that whole idea, Charbonneau like these people, no stinking Mother Church black robe idea, no Monsieur Frown hold hand behind back, Indian notice nose on face, notice cock between leg, like notice no tree, no stinking beaver. Plenty slave girl. Serpent girl best, short, dark, Minitadi think they ugly, they less try fuck while old Charbonneau away on trip. He first see little Bird, sit alone in cornfield, no talk, he think, perfect, scar on face, when Minitadi woman fuck behind husband back he punish with scar on face, they think worst, maybe remind smallpox, old Charbonneau not know, but last time he look, you fuck cunt. He like Serpent cunt, they little tight, little lip pout, and Bird ugly, so she cheap, Bird slave whole crew of bitch sister Bird Rider, so she grateful old Charbonneau, he take her away, he give her man, she work, she quiet, she wash old Charbonneau, she warm, she give him strong boy, Jean-Baptiste, she good woman.

out of water

Ohwa! Ohwa!

Weak cries in the night, hunger and blind hands, blind mouth smacking after bursting nipple. This one sang a song:

> *ice*
> *floating on water*
> *not a good land*
> *you came*
> *out of water*
> *you came*

Her dream, her song. His song. His blind mouth, his hands, her ohwa. This one sang.

This one made a we-people holder for ohwa, not the buffalo-calf skin sack the undergrounders made. Before he came, she gathered arrow-tree sticks. Before she gathered, she gave tobacco. On the sandbars below the wooden hill the sun-men made, she chose the sticks carefully. She made a hoop of green arrow-tree. This one knew the good shape. In forest bear's wooden hut inside the big sun-man hill made of whole shed-fur trees, she lashed the sticks across, drawing in the sides of the arrow-tree hoop. She bound the sticks together with thongs she wove lengthwise. Her fingers wove with a snakelike motion. On the back down the middle she lashed a stick to stiffen it. She climbed to the second bottom and searched among the mishpa trees, and found a good stick for the hoop that would protect his head if the holder fell.

Mishpa was an undergrounder word; they used this hard wood instead of stone for their corn-pounding. Mishpa gave them bows and spear shafts. There were no mishpa trees by her salmon stream or on the plain of three rivers. A we-people ohwa-holder with a mishpa hoop. Ohwa would know early he lived between worlds.

This one covered the frame in a buckskin she had smoked with dry arrow-tree sticks and rubbed with chalk, as the birds did, to make it white as teeth. She lined the pouch that would hold him with the soft groin skin. She sewed red veniss beads in spearheads pointing out around the circle behind his head, to make the sun come up for him. She cut a small square of buckskin and sewed the bag that would hold his birthcord. She tied thongs pinching four corners of the birthcord bag to make legs and another for the head, and it was a turtle, to give him long life. She covered it in blue and white veniss beads, in a we-people sun pattern, with red lines curving out from the center, a hard pattern she had never been good at, and spirit guided her, and it was well done. Forest bear usually told her to use porcupine thorns, because beads were too good for trade, but this time he let this one use all the beads she wanted, because after years of fucking white beads, he was going to have an ohwa.

This one filled a buffalo stomach with rootreed heads and hung it in the wooden hut. She made his shift of pronghorn skin, which let air through to cool and comfort moist hot ohwas. She made a toy of elk teeth that clattered like hail. She made a doll of cornhusks, as the undergrounders did. She braided sweetgrass around the mishpa hoop. She made two ropes of buffalo hair and tied them to a buffalo-skin sack and hung them from the flat hut top: a swing.

For days, in the cold moon, she searched, on the second bottoms and up ravines and near the undergrounders' baby hill, for good-sticky-tree, to powder its needles and fill a buckskin pouch, to hang around ohwa's neck to ward off ghosts that want to squat in small bodies. In her tall grass band this was done. But she had never seen good-sticky-tree in undergrounder country, and although she gave her best thorned pouch to Porcupine, who goes to good-sticky-tree in winter, she did not find any.

Ohwa came hard, as this one had known he would. She gripped the posts and pain filled her. There was no Coyote's blood hut for her, no sisters to sit outside and talk to her through the brush. When the dream came that ohwa was near she told forest bear to leave. He wrapped his bundles and filled his gourds and went downriver on a hunt with red hair. This one did not know if a sun-man would bleed from the nose and die if he stayed, as a tall grass man would, but he was gone, and she was glad. She put up with his strangeness, but not that for ohwa, not yet, not a strange beginning to his between-life, her small half-bear.

He came hard, clawing. White beads dug the pit for her and laid the buffalo robe and placed the wooden sun-man sleep platform so that this one could hold the posts and she kneeled across the pit and pain squatted in her and day turned to night and there was no camas flower, no small frog, no smells good, only a pinenut-eater and an undergrounder, whispering words, arguing, what herbs, what songs, what spirits, bear or snake or otter or mink. Her sun-child was a burning stone. Camas flower! Kneeling, crying, this one heard no thaw-water speaking in the voice of her mother, hard ice was outside the hut and blocked inside her, her child pounding against it.

The undergrounder, corn hair, was calling for a snake rattle, an under-grounder cure for a stuck child, snake slither, snake slip through rock crack, and this one did not want strangeness at ohwa's beginning, but the under-grounders called her snake, and when corn hair held the bighorn ladle to her lips, snake drank, and the pain climbed and the shudders clamped down and the fire shot through her and she was in a dream of cracking ice battering her between her legs. White beads said, the head is out. Head, this one said dreaming. Head. And her dream of ice returned. The black water, the empti-ness, the turning floe, the head rising out of water. She cried, head, head, or maybe she whispered, or maybe it was spirit whispering, and her body drained into the earth and she was lying on her side and holding him, her blood-smeared ohwa, his dark eyes on her.

Forest bear named him zhaw-bop-teest and peh-ti-too-sanh and moh-graw-fiss. Red hair and big knife named him pahm-pi, an onglay word. How did they know what name to give him, when he was still an ohwa and nothing had happened? Was it part of their sun-man power?

This one put his birthcord in the turtle pouch and hung it from the mishpa hoop. She burned sweetgrass for him. She slipped her bursting nipple gratefully into his hungry mouth and flowed like a long good piss into him until his eyes turned milky. She removed the balls of wet rootreed fur and sniffed them with delight before throwing them away. Sour milk ohwa, speak. She rubbed his skin with grease and red dirt. He gripped her salmon fingers in hot hands. His eyes followed her everywhere. He slept hot and moist on her neck.

Red hair had asked about names, before ohwa came. Why did that one want to know? It was bad luck to say your name. When this one first saw him close up, in his wood hut, she was afraid. Was he a people-eater, like the red hairs of the caves? She did not give we-people to red hair. Instead she gave him tall grass, shoshonii.

—So-so-na? he said.

—He ask what mean, forest bear said.

This one held her hand high. —Tall grass. She put her hand low. —Short grass, buibeh.

—So-so bu-ba? red hair said. That one was decorating a piece of white wood. Was this one giving him med-sanh, a war song?

—He want know about other, forest bear said.

—No others, this one said.

—What about diba-rika? forest bear said. —You call white bead band. Pinenut-eater. This one looked at forest bear. —Maybe he is people-eater! she said, nodding toward red hair. —Nimi-rika!

Forest bear shrugged. —What-all you say, diba-rika, nima-rika.

—Ika? red hair said, adding a spear point or sun circle to his med-sanh board. —Iaka?

—Iaka, forest bear nodded. —Egzakt!

When the day came, this one tied ohwa in his holder and slung him on her back. White beads was not going. The fever ghost was back in her. Big knife spoke to forest bear. She die soon anyway, forest bear said to this one. That one was left with corn hair. She lay on the buffalo robe. A whisper, maybe out of a dream, but this one did not understand.

This one picked up her digging stick and the buffalo stomach full of root-reed heads and her bundle with the shoe awl and fire drill and sinew and scraper and the second pronghorn shift. She walked behind forest bear out of the wooden sun-man hill to the river. She climbed in the big flat-wood boat and took off the holder and sat in the bottom of the boat with ohwa in her lap and gave his hungry mouth her nipple and looked in his eyes. Camas flower? Doesn't walk? One thumb? No spirit spoke. The tall grass valley, her salmon stream. Snow on the mountains. Good-sticky-tree. Mountainfish. The sun-men pushed the boat away from the bank. They pulled it forward with their flat sticks. The sun-man in the back sang a med-sanh travel song:

wan-too
wan-too

Red hair was in the other flat-wood boat. Big knife walked on the shore with his black weapon and pronghorn spear. Other sun-men rode in hollow shed-fur trees. The very big boat went the other way. The big black weapon cracked, making ohwa cry, the sun-men swung their skin hats above their heads, ohwa chewed on her nipple hiccuping, eyes shut. She put him in his holder and held the holder in her lap and rattled the elk teeth for him. She looked at the beaded turtle pouch that would give him long life. His birthcord would keep him from growing into a foolish man. Her digging stick would find roots for her to eat. Her breasts would feed him. The root-reed fur would keep him dry.

She looked at the sky. She looked at the banks crowded with under-grounders. She looked at the sun yellowing toward sun-entering. The sun stood over the spot this one would head toward if she was walking to her tall grass valley. This one breathed thanks to spirit for speaking. The sun-men, she thought, would reach her band. Would ohwa?

Silence.

Would this one?

This one died.

When? How?

Shouts.

How?

Ohwa! Ohwa!

At night in the skin hut the wind shivered the skins and she slipped her nipple into his hungry mouth and looked in his eyes and removed the ball of rootreed fur. She sniffed him all over and tasted him everywhere. He sat up in her arms and looked around, his head wobbling like a seed-heavy yellowflower. Red hair said something and smiled. That one was not a people-eater. And big knife did speak sometimes. And maybe they would trade black weapons to her band.

In the skin hut at night, there was this one and ohwa and forest bear and red hair and big knife and his dog and the sun-man droor and the black sun-man york. Droor knew signing. York was not a burned man, or if burned, maybe by the sun, he had not died, maybe because he was a sun-man. This one knew see-men was a dog and not a small bear because she had seen him fucking the undergrounder dogs. She tied up the swing and swung ohwa. Red hair and big knife were decorating the thin white skins they kept bundled. The black marks looked like a grass pattern this one might press with a sharp stick in a clay pot. Maybe they knew nothing of red or yellow dirt or redberry juice or blue clay. York was sewing a new pair of shoes for red hair, like a changed-man. No beads, no thorns. Like beggars. Yet they had many beads.

Red hair and big knife called a shoe *maw-k'sin,* an onglay word. Forest bear called it *sool-yay.* The undergrounders said *hupa.* A four-way world, the number of spirit, of the winds, of coldward and warmward and sun-birth and sun-entering. She swung ohwa. She was getting used to their smell, that unwashed stink that forest bear had until this one or white beads got him to sit for a wash. They piled up big wood fires, they made white smoke fires and stood in the smoke like their kind of washing and it mixed with their smell and made it better, like dried meat. Only york washed every morning like a not-sun-man, like a poh-roozh.

When they blew out their small-sun sticks she lay in the dark with the rich sun-man stink and forest bear snoring until red hair spoke and york reached out and rolled him over and big knife still and silent at the edge and she felt and sniffed her sweet-grease naked ohwa all over and slipped her nipple in his hungry mouth and his fingers dug into her breast and she sang in her mouth, so all those ones would not hear, her song, his song,

ice
you came
ohwa
you came

In the mornings on the river, ice collected on the flat sticks and on the legs of the sun-men hauling on elk-skin ropes in the water. They came ashore stumbling. Why this way in water, like crawling on bellies? They could trade black weapons for horses. An undergrounder had agreed to come with them and make peace with we-people, but after two days he turned back, he said the sun-men were crazy, he would miss the summer hunt if he was foolish enough to go with them. It was a half-morning walk back to his village.

Big knife showed this one a big clear bead that made a small sun that made fire. Red hair gave her a brown lump that was the best thing she ever tasted, like the sweetest squash or frost-bitten or sun-burnt berry, like surprise and laughter in her mouth. They had a fish net so fine it looked like smoke and caught insects, so lying in the skin hut at night was like being underwater or covered with mud. It was big knife's power that had given ohwa to her, it had been his snake rattle. He had broken it in water for her with his own hands and had sung the healing song. They were sun-men, yet they were not traders. They had black weapons, yet they were not a war band. They were—?

Spirit sent this one a dream of her salmon stream. She was there among the brush huts. Camas flower and small frog and two bears were sitting. Camas flower was feeding her salmon. When she woke, she thought the dream was saying she would reach her valley. She would crawl back on her belly like a snake. But two bears and small frog were dead, and maybe camas flower was dead. Maybe the dream was saying the other thing—that this one, too, would die.

Ohwa was nowhere in that dream.

She held him tight to her and he squirmed and she slipped her nipple in his mouth and sniffed and tasted him all over and shook the elk teeth and he laughed, the first time, and it was as sweet as that brown lump in her mouth, and he laughed again and red hair in the front of the boat looked over his shoulder and smiled.

She did not like to sit in the boat slopped by cold water so she walked along the river when the bank was not cut by ravines. Especially when red hair walked, she walked behind with ohwa on her back and with forest bear. Forest bear did not like the boats because some witch had cursed him and made him heavy in water like a stone, he could not float.

—Red hair and big knife has much big many grand hopini power, forest bear told her. —More bad-smelling power than little serpent wife and no-help no-fire-stick serpent people in shiny mountain ever see. Little serpent wife do what-all robe chief want, quick good bird, they make forest bear big man. Do what-all except fuck, they not ask anyway.

This one walked by the muddy river with ohwa on her back and her digging stick in her hand and jammed the stick into the ground among the piles of driftwood searching for mouse winter-hoards of groundbean. When she had filled a bag, she brought it to big knife, who brought the beans to his nose and whispered to them for a long time like med-sanh and york cooked the beans and red hair told forest bear to tell this one how good they were. She waded along the shore pulling rootreeds, snapping off the heads to refill the buffalo stomach and cutting the roots into another bag for york or forest bear to cook. Going back to her salmon stream with two sun-men cooking for her like women. Bird that flies far, maybe. She had not had to push that foolish thought away for a long time.

It was the sweet root moon, and she dug up whiteroot and goodbreath root to chew on as she walked above the river and soaproot to wash herself in the river in the morning and she showed the roots to red hair, and the whiteroot she held up to his mouth signing eat, eat, and he ate. She did not know this river or these hills, because when bird rider carried her to the undergrounders five or six winters ago they followed a path warmward from here. But she walked and looked back along the river and looked at the sun and counted every day as half a day with the crawling boats and when they passed a big river flowing into the muddy river from warmward she thought it must be the buffalo trail river that led to the buffalo pass and the plain of three rivers. That was the shortest way to we-people, but the omens were bad. Red hair and big knife asked Sun with their ring-metal bent pipe, and Sun told them to go the other way.

Three mornings after, this one was walking with ohwa on her back behind red hair and she saw a yellowberry bush in flower. The flowers were longer than those on the undergrounder yellowberry bushes. They were like the yellowberry bush flowers in the tall grass valley. She had not seen that little brother since she was a child. She ran forward to red hair, holding a flower in her hand. She signed to him, this flower, this, I know! until forest bear and droor came up and she told red hair about the good-tasting yellowberries, better than the undergrounders', maybe because mountain frosts came earlier, and how many there were on the slopes around her tall grass valley, and red hair took the flower from her hand and looked at it closely and then twirled it in front of ohwa and smiled, and forest bear looked pleased.

This one was learning onglay words. Hut was *laawdzh*. Dugout was *k'noo*. River was *m'zoor*. Woman was *skwaaw*. The brown lump was *shoo-ga*. Power was *mehda-sin*. The onglay Father was *Grayees-peert*.

When the blackwater wind slammed into the boat forest bear said shit and the front swung around and the wind robe pulled the boat over with a clap. This one saw the water coming up toward her as she fell sideways. She tried to turn underneath ohwa who was in her child arm but her shift caught against something at her back and as she pitched half out of the boat the snagged shift dragged her around so her child arm holding ohwa swung beneath and she hit the water with ohwa under her. Shouts. She jammed her toes under some ledge or crack to keep her legs in the boat. The waves were washing over her face and she was clawing with her free hand. She could not turn or lift herself and ohwa was beneath her under the water. The water was ice-cold. She felt something with her free hand and pulled on it but it fell into the water next to her and she pushed it down under the water to push herself up but it rolled away from her and she sank again, her face half under water. She flailed upward again, for anything, but her arm touched nothing. Forest bear was shouting and the sun-men were shouting and ohwa was still beneath her under the water. She let go with her toes to slide out of the boat and bring her legs beneath her but her shift was still caught and as her legs began to slide the shift turned her facedown and her head sank under the water. She arched her back and barely lifted her eyes out, and ohwa was still beneath her. She could not see anything in the muddy water. She could not feel her arm. She had dropped him. She howled and her upper arm flailed and she writhed in horror and fury against the place where her shift was caught, and it tore free. She twisted around and grabbed the boat and pulled herself up. The water poured off her and the child arm that had dropped ohwa came out of the water clutched against her side and ohwa was still held there, ohwa came out of the water locked in her arm with his face a blue fist spurting drops of water in spasms from his nose and the fist opened and he puked water in this one's face and screamed. She hugged him to her shoulder as the boat righted and forest bear and the sun-men were still shouting, and the boat was half full of water. Clutching him and whispering thanks and vows and *clawth* and tobacco and beads to Father and Sun and First Made and Grayees-peert she clutched him and rocked and thanking everything, she thanked with her free hand, she grabbed the sinking bags and baskets within reach, piling them between her legs and in her lap around ohwa, screaming.

In the skin hut at night, big knife was saying this one's undergrounder name and showing her what he had painted on one of his white skins. It was strange for him to speak to her, and his smile was strange. He'd made the same pattern, the black grass pattern. Maybe sun-men, like undergrounders, had to buy their patterns, and this was the only one big knife owned. He pointed and waved her closer and kept saying sakakamia, sakakamia, and pointed at a snake shape half hidden in the grass scratches. She said good, she looked for forest bear but he was not in the hut, she signed good, she groped for an onglay word and said *yessa* and that seemed to satisfy him.

Every day the crack of black weapons. More black powder and round arrowheads in the flat-wood boats and k'noos than her band could use in a year raiding hardskins or cheekpainters. Make enemies fly again. Dance the scalps. Eat the buffalo. Crack of black weapons and fresh meat every day, until this one was hot in the face and shit-stuck. She dug up whiteroot, and camas when she found it. She ate threadleaf. She chewed arrow-tree bark. Milk leaked from her nipples when ohwa called from his holder. Her milk smelled like meat.

More and more, the land was speaking we-people. The dry turtle hills, the small feather-trees clinging to rock cracks, the slopes and plains covered in twoleaf and thorn and harebush. This one walked slow, pulling up a moist harebush root to chew on, to taste its water after many winters, stopping to give ohwa her nipple, watching red hair or big knife go on ahead, looking downriver to see if the boats and k'noos had appeared around the last bend. In the dry warm wind, with the we-people smell of twoleaf singing in her nose, she sat and watched the sun-men come toward her, calling to each other, pulling the ropes or flashing the flat water sticks all at the same time, like the finger feathers of a hawk high on the air. But they were bears, not hawks, heavy, mired in mud and water. Sometimes now, with the m'zoor current faster, those ones were in the water all day, hauling the k'noos that were supposed to carry them, like horsemen crossing plains with their horses on their backs.

Red hair and big knife were on a search for a spirit, for power, for a song. The boats the sun-men hauled with elk-skin ropes against the current and across bars were like the buffalo skulls the undergrounders dragged with thongs through their flesh during the power dances. The bends in the m'zoor like a bunched rope they worked around, bend after bend, when any morning if they allowed themselves to be weak they could stand up and walk straight across the plain next to the valley—this was a vow, like the one tree a tall grass man might always pass on the making side, never the child side, or the way another might always walk backward to the meeting place for a raid. She had not understood at first, because these ones did not carry out the vow each alone, as a we-people or undergrounder man would do. And their search was not for a few days. This one knew now that there were sun-women and sun-children, forest bear had told her that winters ago, there were sisters and mothers waiting in sun-villages far away, giving tobacco to Grayees-peert for the safe return of sons and brothers, and it was not a few days they were gone, missing their hut fires, up in a mountain you could see from the band-place, but moons, and under different skies, and maybe that was why the sun-men did not fast, because their vow was too long. Big knife had had a dream, or red hair. Or maybe sun-men dreamed together, as they went together to search for spirit and power. Red hair and big knife had had a dream of the muddy river and of the mountains where we-people lived and of the bad-tasting water at the end of the salmon rivers. There was a spirit there. That was where Coyote went when he followed water girl and fucked the women with the toothed cunts and made people. Maybe sun-men had first been made there, too, and it was a mehda-sin place for them. In their dream, big knife and red hair were told not to wear beads or thorns, or paint their faces. They were given the wooden bird the one-eyed man perched on his shoulder and made sing for the mehda-sin dances they held every night. Bears, she had thought. But maybe that was forest bear's sun-men, the traders from ka-na-da. Maybe these onglays were more like wolves, hungry, in a pack, with a leader, a speaker. And gathering power with every dance and every day they kept to the vow.

The k'noos filling with water.

The ropes breaking.

The sun-men falling among the sharp rocks.

Hot in the face, she stumbled. Later, they put her in the boat. Ohwa chewed on her nipple. She shivered. A fever ghost. The cold rain for three days. Sitting, giving her nipple to ohwa, her shift open, in the rain. A ghost had caught her. *This one died.* And now the hot sun, and this one burning like a stick in the bottom of the boat until red hair moved her under the shade skin.

—Mehda-sin, red hair said. But he sang no song. The wooden bird did not sing, the onglay drum with the metal pieces did not jangle. Only bitter water, a boiled plant. Where was big knife? He had the rattle, the healing song.

Pain in her belly. She crouched on the shore shuddering. Her shit spattered. Where was ohwa? Someone was holding her. York.

A bite in her arm. She looked. She was lying in the skin tent. Where was ohwa? Red hair was holding a knife, and her arm. Her blood flowed into a bowl. Mehda-sin. No song. Where was ohwa? Where was big knife? This one drank bitter water. Sweated. Pain in her abdomen. York was holding a spoon.

Night. Hot on her buffalo robe. *This one died.* Where was ohwa? Here. Hot. Her salmon stream. Weir runner was running, laughing. Camas flower was crying. Water speaks reached her hands up. Mama! She ran. Mama! Ohwa was crying. Where was he? She slipped her nipple in his mouth.

Red hair was holding the knife again. Her blood was flowing into the bowl. Whose ghost was it? She was thirsty.

She lay in the boat while the sun-men pulled it. The boat tossed. Cold water splashed her. Ohwa was crying. Where? Another night. Whose ghost was it? Small frog sat up and the arrow burrowed, white bits flew. Crazy woman lay in the snow wind. White beads lay on the buffalo robe whispering, but this one walked down to the river.

Morning. Pain between her belly and her cunt. More bitter water. This one turned away from the spoon red hair was holding. It followed. She turned. It pressed against her lips. No, no. Forest bear's voice, shouting. Ohwa was crying. Where? Someone was pushing up her shift. Gripping her knees, pulling her legs apart. She looked. Red hair was between her legs. He lifted her ass. Where was forest bear? Red hair eased her back down. He wrapped the cool clawth around her thighs and cunt. No song, no drum. Red hair had no healing power. The ghost was near her cunt, thrashing, jamming an arrow in her guts. Where was a healer to suck the ghost out? Where was big knife? He had drawn ohwa out. The spoon pressing against her lips. No. She turned. No.

Then forest bear. He was holding ohwa. *Da'dits,* he was saying. Drink. Good small bird. Please drink. He was holding a spoon. Please. She drank.

She opened her eyes. Big knife was holding her hand. She sang thanks. Where was ohwa? Big knife leaned close. One bright eye loomed. Strange gray eye, a blind old one's, but clear, like a clear sky. But cloud-colored. A wolf's eye. Where was big knife's rattle? He opened his mehda-sin basket, his power bundle. He curled his upper lip, baring his teeth, a wolf face. He drummed his fingernails against his teeth. Da-da TAH. He chose something from the bundle. He held the spoon. She drank. So stinging she gasped. Closed her eyes. Opened them. Big knife held a bowl. Blood-smell water. She drank. He held the spoon again. Bitter. She drank. She dozed. Where was ohwa?

da da TAH.

She woke. Big knife was holding her hand. She closed her eyes.

da-da TAH
da-da TAH
da-da TAH

His wolf song, his healing song. Her salmon stream. Mama! Camas flower turned. She smiled, and pointed. Look, she said. Water speaks could not turn her head. She heard shouts.

She woke.

She sat up. Clear light. The ghost had fled. She was in the skin tent. There was a sound of distant roaring. —Where is ohwa?

—Here, forest bear said.

Ohwa gripped her breast hard and sucked hungrily. She flowed into him. Forest bear had not washed or greased him. —What's that sound?

—Fall of m'zoor. We close. You bad sick, six day. I thought you die.

She slept. She was running. Blood on her legs. She woke. York was holding a hunk of buffalo meat. Roasted meat smell, blood-smell, good.

—*Da'dut,* york said. Come, eat.

When red hair saw the black cloud coming he hurried forward, waving this one and forest bear with him. They turned up a draw and ducked into shelter under a rock ledge.

The wind hit hard, howling. Ohwa cried. This one shrugged off the holder and took him out to hold him. After the wind came the hail, fist chunks battering the rocks, and she was glad red hair had found this place. After the hail came the hard rain. Now they must leave. She looked at red hair. He was leaning against the rock wall, his black weapon and bundle at his feet. She waited for him to speak. The rain came down like a waterfall. Red hair did not move.

—This is not a good place, this one said to forest bear.

—Unh? that one said.

—*Skwaawl*, red hair said.

Was he telling her not to speak? She stood silently for a few heartbeats, holding ohwa. Maybe he had some power. Or maybe this was a vow. —This is not a good place, she said again.

—Some bad-smelling spirit speak to bird? forest bear said, smiling.

—*Dam!* red hair said, grabbing his gun.

Here came Water-Giant down the draw toward them, chewing rocks. —*Goh!* Red hair pushed her in front of him. She climbed the slope. Forest bear was above, pulling. Red hair pushed from below. She could not use her hands. She crouched over ohwa. Water-Giant climbed after them. She slipped and looked back and red hair was in water to his chest. He pushed her and clambered. She skidded, gripped with toes. Up. Water-Giant leaped. Roar of stones and mud.

At the top, she sat, ohwa in her arms. Both of his pronghorn skins, his buffalo-calf sleeping robe, his holder, his turtle pouch, his birthcord—all gone. He was naked. This one sat in the rain and stared at the torrent of brown water. If a child lost his birthcord, he would have no tether. He would grow up to run around as a foolish person.

But he was alive! Three times he'd come out of water. Red hair was gesturing for her to get up. He was pointing in the direction of the camp. Ohwa was turning blue. This one huddled around him and ran toward the camp.

THE DISCOVERER, I
[April-June 1805]

1

Out of darkness, light. Lewis rises. He ducks through the flap into freshness, silence. The miracle recurs. Light fills the world.

One by one, the cookfires are lit. Seaman at his heel, Lewis walks among his men. He holds out his hand. Don't rise.

"Good morning, Captain."

Sergeant Ordway's mess: Bratton, Colter, Willard, Werner, Goodrich, Potts, Hall, Frazier. Cookpot hanging from the tripod, torn tissue of steam. A breakfast of meager venison and parched corn, buffalo having been scarce the past three days. Wild onions.

Lewis walks on to Gass's mess: McNeal, the Fields brothers, Howard, La Page, Thompson, Windsor. Or is it Windsor, Thompson? No, he was right the first time: Thompson taller, Windsor wider.

"Good morning, sir."

"Captain Clark and I intend an early start today, boys."

"Yes, sir."

"A beautiful day!"

"Yes, sir."

Pryor's mess: Gibson, Shannon, Shields, Collins, Whitehouse, Weiser, Cruzatte, Labiche. Lewis knows them all. Good men, or good enough, some dullards, some born reprobates, but all willing now, formed and molded. Army life is good for them. They are happier now than they have ever been in their lives.

Tents are struck, camp cleared. The hunters off. The smell of morning, that dusty scent like rain that never comes, and camphor, from the bushes resembling wormwood that dot the slopes, and a prickle of sulfur, from the smoldering seam of carbonated wood running like a pen-stroke across the face of a bluff opposite. A southeast wind. The river fell half an inch during the night. Lewis steps into the white pirogue at the point; Bratton and Windsor push off and climb in. Lewis turns to watch the sun break above the bluffs behind, as white and penetrating as midday in Virginia, this dry air, there has not been a dew since Council Bluffs. The sun rises in the east and sets in the west, Lewis tells himself, not knowing why he should articulate such a banality, nor why the contemplation of it fills him with something near bliss. Or perhaps it is precisely bliss. The west, the sunset country, the golden land, Lewis heading there, I am at the headwaters of the Missouri, the Indians so far—invisible. Remains of recent camps have been spotted, the smashed rum kegs marking them as Assiniboin, but neither hide nor hair of brave or squaw.

On an April day, Lewis lies on a patch of ground between the prickly pears and the dwarf cedar and the aromatic herb with the agreeable smell (new to him), of which the antelopes are so fond. He is studying one of the little hillocks of loose earth that appear everywhere on these plains. No hole is ever visible, yet here are ten pounds of excavated soil; perhaps they were poured during the night from some faerie vessel. He gently scoops the mound away and probes the ground beneath with the point of his pocket knife, discovering a circle of softer earth an inch and a half in diameter. Loose soil fills it as deeply as he can dig. What an industrious and retiring little creature!, whatever it is, mouse-cousin or prairie periwinkle. I name thee *Minimum incognitum.* Hidden under its midden. Lewis is reminded of similar hillocks made by salamanders he investigated when he was a boy, among the sandy hills of Georgia, during his mother's venture there with Citizen Marks. Out on one of his long hunting treks. Half hunting, half sulking; poking his knife in the earth a bit harder than a man of science should.

He gets up, brushes the dirt off, continues his hike along the edge of the bluff. To the rhythm of his steps, a word-scrap sets up a tattoo: *hidden in its midden; hidden in its midden.* This has been happening to him lately. For example, *rises in the east and sets in the west.* Or *artichokes and antipodes,* which danced a hornpipe in his head the other night, to the diddle-daddle of Cruzatte's fiddle. Thoughts press on him, fecundate. He is up late at night writing in his journal, or reading Barton, or Miller's *Linnaeus,* or browsing in his dictionary of arts and sciences, up early, still dark, ducking through the flap, smelling the air, counting the stars, walking through the camp to test the guards.

In his journal, Lewis writes of the wild onion, *the bulb grows single, is of an oval form, white, and about the size of a small bullet; the leaf resembles that of the chive.* Tramping among the broken hills and up on the plain, he stops now and then to cut a square of turf with his espontoon, and digs down through three feet of rich black loam. In the bottoms, he measures the cut-banks, and finds as much as twenty feet. *A soil fertile in the extreme,* he writes. Curling in a chocolate wave from the mathematically perfect curve of the President's plow. He surveys the plain on which, as far as the eye can reach, not a solitary tree or shrub can be discovered, except in the declivities. The traditional rule of thumb decrees that oak forests indicate the best soil, followed by beech, and then pine. Land barren of trees is thought to be the most sterile. "But of course," he says to Clark, "the Indians burn the plains year round, and thus trees are never permitted to establish themselves."

One morning Drewyer shoots a beaver swimming in the river, and Lewis writes, *the beaver being seen in the day, is a proof that they have been but little hunted, as they always keep themselves closely concealed during the day where they are so.* Hidden in their midden. But where man has not yet blundered and despoiled, animals know no fear. The hidden is seen clear. The pellucid light of the plains, the far vistas. To a forest-dweller like Lewis, the treeless-ness is a perpetual amazement. The blank space on the map. If Lewis could ascend a mile into the air, he could gaze down and watch himself cross it.

Climbing the hills, looking ahead and behind, Lewis hopes to meet and kill the white or yellow bear of which the Indians speak, whose tracks (three times the size of men's) he has studied around the carcasses of drowned buffalo. Only Cruzatte has seen one. The Indians are frankly afraid of this bear; they hunt it as the supreme test of their courage, first performing all the superstitious ceremonies common to their war-making. It is a terrible god they go out to kill. They attack in groups of eight or ten, and often lose some of their party to the wrath of the deity. But they employ only bows and arrows, and the indifferent muskets with which the traders supply them; this god has not yet met a rifle, nor a white man's skill in using it. (After Cruzatte shot at his, he ran in a panic, leaving his gun and tomahawk behind; but Cruzatte is equipped with only half the usual complement of eyes.) As Lewis turns a corner up a draw or crests a rise, rifle in one hand, espontoon in the other, he awaits the revelation of the beast.

Crouching in the wave-tossed white pirogue, his pen jittering jagged lines, Lewis writes, *Captain Clark brought me a flower in full bloom. It is a stranger to me.* He rises before dawn and ducks through the flap into starlight, speaks softly to the guards and walks away, miles up the silver river bottom, young grass and tongues of sand and budding bracken, quiet and cool. He sips from a rivulet coursing down, and sits by its edge dandling a reed like a country swain in a sentimental engraving.

The two captains divide the tramping more evenly now; Clark's health is good, and moreover Lewis acknowledges the desideratum of being more among his men, who seem to like him. Lewis writes, *I met with great numbers of grouse, or* prairie hens, *as they are called by the English traders of the N.W. These birds appeared to be mating; the note of the male is kuck, kuck, kuck, coo, coo, coo.*

He observes to Clark, "Trees are to be found in every slight declivity in the plain. Such declivities, being shielded from the wind, enjoy an advantage in the retention of moisture, which mitigates the destructive action of fire. Clearly even the smallest protection suffices to allow the growth of trees, such is the fertility of the soil."

The bends in the river blend and blur. The captains hand back and forth a ruled sheet, six miles to an inch, eighty miles from edge to edge, becoming crumpled and soiled, across which the Missouri agonizingly grows, oscillating between hatch-marked bluffs. Every seven or eight days the scribble-blackened sheet is packed away, a fresh one ruled. Clark or Lewis ascends a bluff with the circumferentor and spyglass, measuring the angle back along a laborious stretch, estimating the distance from the time it took to traverse, adding a pinch of log-and-reel, occasionally checking with the two-pole chain and trigonometry, throwing in a handful of adjustments (for river current, wind speed, moon phase) that Clark collectively calls *physicking*: "You keep dosing the figures," he explains to Lewis, "until they feel right in your gut." At night in the tent they pore over the map together, crossing out here, squeezing a notation in there. Lewis scans the tangent tables, Clark checks his figures; Clark adds up the mileage, Lewis finds a mistake. Their Missouri grows.

Lewis is granted a glimpse of the yellow bear; then a second and a third; always at a distance, running hell-to-split away from the Corps. It would seem that the bear-god, like Jehovah, when Moses beseeched Him to show His glory, chooses to reveal only his hindparts. Lewis writes in his journal, *I there-*

fore presume that they are extremely wary and shy; the Indian account of them does not correspond with our experience so far. Watching a pair of them run, Clark says to Lewis, "For such a large animal, they ascend those steep hills with surprising ease and velocity."

The buffalo are still so poor as to be scarce worth eating, except for the tongue. The beaver are better; Lewis consumes them with gusto, relishing the liver and oily tail. Charbono gesticulates to York concerning the proper cooking of the latter, shouting for Labiche to come translate. Lewis writes, *the Beaver of this part of the Missouri are larger, fatter, more abundant and better clad with fur than those of any other part of this country that I have yet seen.* At night in the skin lodge, he proposes to Clark, "Might a philosopher not adduce a lesson from the beaver's fatal attraction to the castoreum with which hunters bait their traps? I refer to the remarkable fact that a beaver that has already been caught once, and gnawed himself free, is readily caught again. The mere odor of the sex gland appears to induce in him a state of excitement so reckless one may fairly term it dementia."

Day after day, the country appears unchanging. Even along straight stretches of river, the men must paddle or pull the canoes back and forth around the sand bars that interleave like the fingers of hands mingling in the spirit of obstruction. Bends within bends; too many days in which the Corps manages only thirteen or fourteen miles. But the provisions are improving. The buffalo are calving, and their plump, lowing young are easy to shoot as they lope awkwardly after their mothers, and Lewis, delectating a toothsome morsel, decides it is equal if not superior to any veal he has ever tasted. Louisiana Felix! He writes, *I saw several parcels of buffalo's hair hanging on the rose bushes, which had been bleached by exposure to the weather and became perfectly white. It has every appearance of the wool of the sheep, tho' much finer and more silky and soft. I am confident that an excellent cloth may be made of the wool of the buffalo.*

Lewis rises early and ducks through the flap and smells the sand-laden wind, and encounters the Snake woman washing naked in the river, splashing water up under arms, milk-swollen breasts pendulous, Pompey the Small in his cradleboard hanging from a willow. He veers off, uttering not a word. Outside camp, he whistles for Seaman and hikes up the river bottom, which is well timbered with cottonwood, box elder, ash, red elm. He picks through underbrush of wild rose and honeysuckle, red willow, gooseberry, currant, serviceberry. He crosses meadows thick with hyssop. Shoots a deer and hangs it from a tree by the shore with his coat arrayed on a stick to attract Clark's attention when he comes up with the boats. Walking on in his shirtsleeves, sweat cooling pleasurably, Lewis thinks about the Bird Woman. By keeping her and her husband in the same tent as themselves, he and Clark have circumscribed the opportunities for mischief. After a winter of extreme licentiousness, what the men might have come to expect as their due—fighting over her favors— tomcats in a bag—how fortunate that the other squaw was too ill to take along; imagine if Charbono had two dusky squiresses at his disposal. In a private interview, Lewis forbade Charbono on pain of immediate dismissal from the party (yea, even in the middle of a howling wilderness), from pimping his wife—fortunate, too, that she is a young mother, a fact which appears to mitigate the male predatory instinct. Lewis crawls through a thorny brake, smiling grimly: *As you will readily conceive, Mr. President, it was imperative we bring the infant along, so that we would not be forced to deliver another one en route.* Emerging on the far side, he sees he has come upon the remains of an Indian camp: stone circles, where their lodges stood; dead fires. Beyond, a funerary scaffold.

Lewis investigates. Seven feet high, cottonwood. The body has fallen to the ground. It is wrapped in buffalo bull skins, one of the few uses the natives have hit upon for this exceedingly thick and cumbersome material. Shrouds and war shields: a bull's protection in both worlds, *in terris* against arrows, and *in aeternum* against the beaks of crows or (when you fall down) the teeth of wolves. Two dog sleighs on the scaffold indicate that this was once a woman. Lewis kneels. No odor. No seepage. He wonders whether the body mummifies, if wrapped with sufficient expertise. Do they enclose some preservative vegetable matter? But in this case, the corpse must be recent; an undecayed dog lies near. Lewis opens the bag of grave offerings: a plait of sweetgrass, tobacco, hide-scraping tools, some dried roots of medicinal or superstitious value. A pair of moccasins, presumably for the journey to the land of the dead. Red and blue clay for painting herself once she got there.

The savages' opinions regarding the afterlife appear to be as unimaginative as their accounts of their origins. The dead live much as the living do, only there is more buffalo. It is unclear to Lewis whether punishment of the wicked is an element. He thinks not. This woman, paragon or termagant, will don her moccasins and arrive at that other place and make herself pretty, if that lies within her power, and return to the endless round of work, scraping hides, cooking, carrying her husband's packs (is she paired with the same man?), loading her dog when the camp moves. And there the poor brute lies, his throat cut. This his reward for performing the friendly office of transporting his mistress's body to the place of deposit.

Lewis pauses before turning away. This native belief that all of a man's life, here on earth, this groping and blindness, is nothing more than preparation for more of the same—he finds this an appalling conception, a recipe for despair. And would it be cause or consequence of the Indians' seeming inability to progress, while the white man, taking it for granted that the path leads upward, expecting (to continue the metaphor) to eventually arrive at the Shining Mountains, the white man forges iron and builds great ships and cleaves the seas and mounts the rivers and . . . supplants the Indian. Lewis gazes on the silent parcel at his feet. He tries to conceive of the unexpectant and unrewarded life of the woman wrapped in it. He fails. Could she but speak to him.

The wind cutting through his shirt is chill. He looks up. And warfare, which they so love? Does their heaven offer it up daily? And whither go the fallen, to a second shadowland identical to the first, another bend in the river? He turns; heads downstream. This wind will prevent the boats coming up. "Seaman, come away from there!" He was sniffing around the corpse of his cousin; now bounding down, he smacks past Lewis's held-out hand and runs on ahead, his hindquarters tracing a circle in the air, an insouciant motion Lewis finds cheering. One thing to say for their beliefs, at least the dog also lives again. Whereas the Christian teaching that dogs die forever strikes him as cruel and implausible. Mr. J's natural religion (which on some doctrinal questions used to shock Lewis) is here preferable. Mr. J would say that a man's divine Reason should be his guide, in preference to either the Bible or the pulpit. Well, Lewis's reasoning faculty reveals to him that if doubting, mercurial Man can be granted an immortal soul, then surely constant Dog, to whom faith comes as naturally as breath, has an undying spark to match.

For several days, the contrary wind is violent; the Corps makes little progress. Lewis ascends a bluff and gazes west upon immense herds of buffalo, elk, deer, and antelope, feeding on one common and boundless pasture. In other words, not a single tree. He says to Clark, "The President has postulated that the soil of the upper Missouri might be *too* rich for trees. Perhaps by some previously unobserved mechanism, a soil of superabundant fertility so promotes the growth of luxuriant grasses that their matted root systems starve the less dense roots of tree seedlings."

The wind lifts the fine sand off the bars and scours it from the cutbanks, and it flies for miles, obscuring the sun and the opposite riverbank, sifting into eyes and clothes, under fingernails, through mosquito netting. The men's eyes are sore. Lewis's pocket watch stops, and when he opens its tight double case to check whether the spring has broken, he finds the works impregnated with sand. When the view clears momentarily, he sees in the distance a whirling column. "And the Lord went before them by day in a pillar of a cloud," he remarks to Clark. Mr. J has made of Lewis enough of a Deist that he extracts from this an exegetical hypothesis rather than an epiphany: not that the Creator is so abysmally trivial-minded as personally to conduct Meriwether Lewis on his merry way, but that the Israelites in Exodus, crossing a sandy wilderness, witnessed the identical natural phenomenon, and interpreted it in their own God-struck, self-obsessed way.

"I was thinking just that," chuckles Clark.

Yes. This sharing of thoughts between them occurs with increasing frequency. Lewis has acquired Clark's easy way with the men; Clark has taken on Lewis's bodily health. Lewis contributes to Clark's map; Clark brings Lewis an unknown flower. Pound the two men and cook them in a crucible, pour out William Meriwether Lewis Clark.

On a clear day, he and Clark stand together on the larboard shore of the Missouri, Clark holding the chronometer (which, triply packed, still runs, *mirabile dictu*) and Lewis the sextant (error, 8' 45"). Lewis views the waning moon through the unsilvered half of the horizon glass and swivels the index arm until the sun appears in the silvered half, then nudges the arm in tiny increments until the sun bestows a tangent's kiss on the near limb of the moon. He tightens the screw and says to Clark, "Mark," and as Clark notes down the time, Lewis reads out the number on the vernier scale. They can record one reading in a minute, and on the clear day by the river they take sixteen readings as the minutes pass, as a cloud tendril floats into view and attaches itself to the sun like a warrior's feather, as a curlew flits overhead, as the clock creeps up on noon and as the leonine sun, arc-second by second, creeps up on the pale moon. *The sun is in the east, the moon is in the west.* A pair of Lunarians by the shore.

At night in the tent, Lewis opens the red morocco notebook and dips his pen in thick ink (this dry air) and observes to Clark, "And the paucity of rainfall, of course, is due to the lack of trees. The action of sunlight is unimpeded in open land, evaporation is consequently the greater, and the winds that carry moisture away more violent. With a reintroduction of forests in these regions, the humid vapors of the soil will be retained, the winds abated, clouds permitted to form, and rainfall will return to its previous level." When he has completed his entry, he hands it to Clark, who reads it before writing his, and when Clark is done, he hands his entry to Lewis, who often finds his own words transmuted. (They doth suffer a Clark-change / into something rich and strange.) As tonight—Lewis wrote, *So penetrating is this sand that we cannot keep any article free from it; in short we are compelled to eat, drink, and breathe it very freely.* Back it flies to him in Clark-Lewese: *I may Say that during those winds we eat Drink & breath a prepotion of Sand.* Marvelous! Might that be *preparation* crossbred with *potion?* Or shorthand for *significant proportion?* Or a coinage (long overdue!) meaning *prepotent potion?* "Of my bones are coral made, dear Clark," says Lewis.

Clark's eyes ask a good-natured question.

"Shakespeare, I'm afraid."

"You've made me desirous of reading him again," Clark says. "I don't remember much beyond 'To be or not to be.' "

"Well," Lewis reassures him, "after all, that *is* the question."

Clark breaks out in a full, surprised laugh.

Bends in the river. The Corps no longer kills most of the animals that offer themselves to the guns; there are far more than needed for provisions, and it wastes ammunition. Lewis writes, *the buffalo, elk and antelope are so gentle that we pass near them while feeding, without appearing to excite any alarm among them, and when we attract their attention, they frequently approach us more nearly to discover what we are.* Where man has not blundered.

On the 25th of April, Lewis forges ahead overland with four of his men to scout the country, and that afternoon he has the inexpressible satisfaction of gazing down from a bluff on a handsome plain in which the broad, timbered valleys of the Yellowstone River and the Missouri join. At noon on the 26th, a discharge of guns signals that Clark and the boats have reached the junction, and in the evening Lewis hikes down from a hunting excursion along the Yellowstone to find the Corps camped at the point of land formed where the two rivers commingle. The men approach from their cookpots to congratulate him, and Lewis peruses their shining faces, every jack awash in pleasure at having arrived at this long-wished-for spot. "A dram!" Lewis cries. "A dram for all!" And before a man can say "Roll up the carpet," Cruzatte has his fiddle out, and men are buckdancing, clapping, and cat-calling. Clark unfolds two camp chairs and sits, gestures to the other; Lewis settles by his friend to luxuriate in a smoke and observe the merriment. What frightful extremes of labor have been required to reach this spot rumored in Indian lore, where the foot of civilized man has never trod; and here they are, in the thickening dusk, banishing cares past and those to come.

Clark looks around. "York! Get on up there, you can do better than those women!" And York leaves his chores to leap and slap his heels. York was the Corps' star performer for the Mandans, it always surprised them that a large man could be so agile. Their trinkets fairly rained down on him, the corn ears piled up at the side. "Do a Ree-vay!" Clark calls out, and York kicks his legs up to dance on his hands, as one of their engagés at Fort Mandan, François Rivet, used to do. He manages three steps before toppling over backward. "For shame!" Clark mocks. "I can do better," York throws back, grinning out of his perspiring jet face, and tries again, and does worse. Other men join in, and soon they are crashing into each other and falling in heaps.

"Let us have a contra dance," Lewis says. "Potts! Call us a dance."

Ordway beats the tambourine. "What's this tune?" Lewis asks Clark. "I know this tune."

"We always called it 'Whiskey Before Breakfast.' "

"Cast off back," Potts calls, "and up again!" The top couple turns out, joins hands at the bottom, comes up the middle. These contra dances particularly impressed the Mandans. Presumably they looked on them as they did their own, that is, as medicine, ensuring crops and calling buffalo, which would explain their extreme attentiveness. Lewis wonders how an Indian might interpret what he is now seeing. Forward and back: lines of battle? The right-hand star might be the sun, the left-hand star the moon. The men turn, the day turns, the dusk falls, the stars come out, summer approaches. The sun rises in the east and sets in the west.

"Cruzatte!" Clark calls. "What's the name of this one?"

" 'La Jolie Blonde,' sir."

"Bravo!" Clark leans into Lewis, his frank, broad face crinkled in good humor, and says *sotto voce*, "I tell you, Lewis, I could stand a jolly blonde about now."

"Yes," Lewis laughs. "The fair ones! How I miss them!"

Soldier's Joy. Devil's Dream. Cruzatte saws on. A mere dram for each man. Less than half a keg remaining. There was not nearly enough whiskey for sale in St. Louis; the fur traders snap it all up, to sell to the Indians, turn them into worthless sots. Lewis was a little worried about what would happen when the Corps suspended daily rations. But at this point, where would a disgruntled would-be drunkard desert to? And the body grows accustomed; even a dram now has a noticeable effect on the men's spirits. Lewis's, too. Probably add years to their lives.

"Only one more, Cruzatte." Clark stands, taking a brand from the fire to light his pipe. "We're proceeding on tomorrow." The captains move through the moonless dark toward their skin lodge. Clark rests a hand on Lewis's arm a few feet short of the flap; he touches a finger to the side of his nose. "Ten minutes. I saw Charbono pulling Janey in just as we left the fire."

Lewis feels himself flush. "Good God! The woman is barely two months out of childbed. The incontinent dog!"

Clark makes a small shrug. "She seems healthy. Full of life."

Lewis says no more. He regards Clark's profile against the circumambient glow of the campfire. His handsome nose with its Roman bump, his somewhat heavy jaw; Clark family features. Everything comes so easily to him; so naturally. What any man would do.

Lewis turns, so that he and his friend are facing in the same direction. He gazes into the darkness of the plain, the distant bluffs outlined against the stars. A minute passes. Silence from the lodge. "I should like to walk on shore tomorrow morning," Lewis says. "To scout for a location for the U.S. trading fort."

"Very good," Clark says. He puffs quietly on his pipe.

With an internal grunt of self-exasperation, Lewis throws off his peevishness. "I do believe this is one of the handsomest plains I ever beheld," he says.

"Mm. Yes."

"There is more timber in this neighborhood than we have seen on any part of the Missouri above the entrance of the Chyenne River." The last dance is over. Lewis watches the men fetch their bedrolls. He'll walk the camp perimeter before he turns in, test the guards. "And so much game that a regiment would need no more than two good hunters to supply it with provisions."

artichokes and antipodes and artichokes and antipodes and

"Although that would cease to be the case, of course," he adds, "once the Mandans and Minetares settle here."

"A fine place for them," Clark agrees. He knocks out his pipe, looks back at the skin lodge. "They should be well satisfied."

2

Rifle in one hand, espontoon in the other, Colter behind him, Lewis crests a rise to discover two yellow bears, twenty paces distant. They swivel their cubic heads to regard him. "I've got the right one," Lewis says, dropping his espontoon and throwing his rifle to his shoulder, and he notes as he pulls the trigger that the bear in his sights is not fully grown, perhaps three hundred pounds. The two rifles crack as one, and through the wind-snatched smoke Lewis sees the impact of his bullet, the shiver and spurt of hair, precisely where he wanted it, through the lung, a bloody wound for tracking. Both bears sit back with grunts; Colter's turns and runs. But the other, to Lewis's astonishment, lumbers to its feet and charges. He and Colter turn tail, Lewis veering right, Colter left, and without a moment's hesitation the monster chases Lewis, who, while sprinting—the Mandans warned him of this behavior but he assumed they spoke of light wounds—blows down his rifle barrel to clear the touchhole. He gets his hand on his powder horn, thank God the bear is lagging, and pulls the plug with his teeth, stops for a moment to pour an approximate charge into the barrel—and Cruzatte claimed the same thing, but he even ran from a buffalo cow—the bear is lumbering forward, snorting blood in spurts. Lewis runs again, aware of Colter off to the side, loading, but Colter is hindered by the need to keep moving so that the bear will not get between him and Lewis. Lewis fetches a patched ball from his shot pouch, inserts it in the muzzle, wrestles with the rod, these operations slow him, the animal is gaining, almost at his heels. Colter's gun sounds, and Lewis hears the slam of the bullet, the snap of a bone breaking. He runs on ten paces and turns to see the bear on its side. A broken shoulder. He seats the head of his rod on the ball and starts to force it down the barrel, but the bear, incredibly, rises again and comes forward on three legs. Colter is reloading. Lewis skips backward, by God, he is doing the Cruzatte two-step, dancing with a bear, his ramrod half out, he turns, runs ten more paces, turns back, the bear is unsteady, stumbling, slower, but still coming on, coughing blood. Lewis rams the bullet home, drops the rod, sprints back a final few yards, now fumbling for his priming horn, pulls the stopper, thumbs forward the frizzen, turns and fills the priming pan as the approaching monster fills his vision, and shoots the beast through the head from ten feet, steps back a last time as it collapses toward him like an upended wagonload of turf, sudden silence, only internal creaks and wheezes as the great bulk settles and air whistles bubbling from the nostrils.

That night Lewis writes, *it is a much more furious and formidable animal,* he is thinking of the retiring black bear of the eastern forests, and he puts his hand down, Seaman's head rises to intercept it, he strokes the dog's brow, *and will frequently pursue the hunter when wounded. It is astonishing to see the wounds they will bear before they can be put to death.* Lewis twirls the quill. The headshot from close range; but that sharp projection in the center of the frontal bone, the thick muscle tissue on either side, make the shot uncertain. He writes, *The Indians may well fear this animal equipped as they generally are with their bows and arrows or indifferent fusils, but in the hands of skillful riflemen they are by no means as formidable or dangerous as they have been represented.*

A few days later the Corps is setting up camp, and another specimen ambles into view on a sand beach some hundred yards distant. This one is brown rather than yellow, but otherwise identical: a higher forehead than the black bear's, smaller ears, lending a more human appearance. A shambling walk, like a man wearing slippers that might come off. This one is Clark's. "I suggest you take along a second," Lewis says, and he and the other men watch from the elevation of the camp as Clark and Drewyer creep up. The bear takes no notice, but points his nose upriver and down, with an absentminded air, as though he suddenly had no idea why he was standing here, at this moment, by this river. He shuffles backward, waddling massive hams, and sits, hind legs stuck out, front paws lifted. The resemblance to a man is remarkable.

When the two bullets hit, he lets out a roar. He makes no attempt to attack, but runs up the beach, turns at a stand of trees, and runs back down, where Clark and Drewyer shoot him a second time. This accomplishes little that can be discerned, other than to make him stop in confusion, so that he is standing there, shaking his head, when the third volley strikes him. Now he plunges into the river, where the seventh and eighth bullets hit him in the shallows, and the ninth and tenth some thirty yards out, and he keeps swimming, making all the while the most tremendous noise Lewis has ever heard from an animal, a hoarse thunder. He swims some four hundred yards before emerging on a sandbar, where he paces, head down, massive shoulders bunched, sits, walks again, kneels—roars and roars—lies. It is twenty minutes before he expires, blood streaming out from him into the sand in several directions.

When Lewis and Clark paddle across to examine him, they find that five of the bullets passed through his lungs. Lewis writes that evening, *We had no means of weighing this monster; Capt. Clark thought he would weigh 500 lbs. For my own part I think the estimate too small by 100 lbs. He measured 8 feet 7½ inches from the nose to the extremity of the hind feet, 5 feet 10½ inches around the breast, 1 foot 11 inches around the middle of the arm, and 3 feet 11 inches around the neck.* "Shall we call it yellow bear? Brown bear?" Lewis asks Clark. "I'm beginning to think they are the same species."

They proceed on. Lewis now finds the Corps divided between those who declare their curiosity has been pretty well satisfied with respect to this animal and those whose appetites have been rendered keener for an opportunity to engage so redoubtable an enemy. Private Bratton must belong to the latter party, because one evening he fires on a bear when he is alone on shore, a mile from the rest of the Corps, and with a sore hand, no less, that renders him slow to reload. The shot is perfection, the ball (Lewis determines later) passing through the center of both lungs, and the excellent hunter now reaps his reward, viz., he flees in terror through woods and brush with death roaring at his heels, until he arrives at the boats mewling piteously and so out of breath he cannot speak for minutes. Lewis picks four men to accompany him. He then rethinks the matter and adds three more. They go out in quest of the dragon, which, they discover, pursued Bratton for half a mile before doubling back, and then, leaving a copious trail of blood, excavated a tunnel more than a mile long through thick brush and willow brakes. At last, feeling somewhat weary, he dug for himself a bed in the earth five feet long and two feet deep, where Lewis finds him, severely put out, but perfectly alive, fully two hours since Bratton shot him. Lewis opts for two headshots simultaneously, in case his dispatch of the first bear by only one bullet straight through the brain was the purest luck.

Lewis writes, *These bear being so hard to die rather intimidates us all; I must confess that I do not like the gentlemen and had rather fight two Indians than one bear.*

A few days later, Clark puts a bullet through a bear's heart, destroying two chambers. The animal runs a quarter of a mile before collapsing.

3

Lewis rises and ducks through the flap, and it is the transparency of the air that always thrills him, as though he swam in some electric ether that engraved distant objects directly upon the eye, the orange bluffs, the black slashes of coal seams, the ash foam of pumice, the near violet of the sky at the meridian, the sight of Venus impossibly high, a companion of the sun at noon. The chokecherries are in bloom and the bald eaglets are hatching and Lewis hears the voice of the turtledove.

> 'Twas in the merry month of May
> When green buds all were swelling.

Captain Merry, the Spaniards called him, so wrong then, so right now, he walks among his merry men,

> Bratton, Colter, Shannon, Shields
> Windsor, Weiser, Werner, Fields

don't rise, eat my good fellows, eat hearty, another day is upon us, the sun will rise in the east and set in the west and another twenty river miles will be behind us, or a dozen miles as the crow flies, or fifteen minutes of longitude, and the Rocky Mountains one day will appear, I know not when, but they must, as I trust absolutely in Occam's Razor, I trust the maps and Indians who agree that these mountains exist, one day they will rise shining. Venus is visible at midday and it feels as though, if you jumped hard enough, you would break free of the atmosphere and gravity altogether and float away like a French balloon.

O Mother dear, go make my bed,
Go make it long and narrow

And then lie in it yourself!

He pores over the map sheets, adding the miles, and he notes that the Corps covered 261 river miles from the Minetare villages to the mouth of the Yellowstone, and he recalls that the Minetares told them it took ten days to accomplish that journey, and he and Clark figured that a day, for them, equaled about twenty-five miles. Thus, one might conclude that the ingenious captains had it almost exactly right—but no! He and Clark assumed the Minetares meant 250 miles *in a direct line.* After all, the Minetares travel by horse. Yet the direct-line distance from the Knife to the Yellowstone (Lewis measures once more with the ruler, taps the paper, measures again) is only 138 miles. "How could that possibly take them ten days?" he asks Clark. "Even on foot, that's a poor showing."

"Maybe," Clark ruminates, "they were estimating what they thought *we* could accomplish, going by boat."

"Well, it shows how little they know us. Since it took us, in fact, nineteen days."

"This contrary wind—"

"Which we have no cause to think will not continue."

"At this rate, it will be July or August before we cross the mountains."

"And our map of the west—?"

"—may still be correct in every particular," Clark smiles, "except the one portion we've experienced, which turns out to be badly wrong."

Scurfs of salts lie on the land in pans, and sparkle in the morning light like snow. Lewis samples the brackish creeks and compares their purgative effects. He sets out water again in a saucer to measure the rate of evaporation, and he watches, week after week, the joints open in his sextant's case of well-seasoned wood. He stands on a high bluff looking up the Missouri Valley and knows from simple mathematics that he can only be seeing some thirty miles to the horizon, but it seems like sixty or seventy, the river diminishing forever under the purple sky, or perhaps it seems like only ten, the air so clear, distant objects so close. But neither mountains nor Indians, near nor far.

A goatskin, part-worked, is found on the shore. A scarlet cloth tied to a tree in supplication of a deity. A camp of a hundred lodge fires, a week old.

In the white pirogue, Lewis looks up and catches his first glimpse of the big-horned animal the Indians speak of, from whose horns they make their ladles and bows, running with apparent ease across the face of a perpendicular cliff. Two of the party fire on it, but it takes no more notice of their earthly bullets than it does of gravity; it skips on through air and disappears. Shannon kills a bird of the plover kind, new to Lewis and perhaps to science, and Lewis opens another packet of ink powder and mixes it with Missouri water and flexes his writing hand and writes 540 words: . . . *the legs are flat, thin, slightly imbricated and of a pale sky blue color . . . the nails are black and short, that of the middle toe is extremely singular . . .* He dubs it Missouri Plover. And now that they are in virgin land, all the little tributaries need names as well, and Clark walks three miles up a stream in whose broad valley he sees but a single tree, and perhaps (who knows?) that lone tree suggests the one good man a popular girl might recognize among her many suitors, because on his return Clark proposes they name it Martha's River, after that practicing tyrant of Louisville society whom Lewis witnessed toying with his friend. "Martha's River it is," Lewis says. "The bed is principally of mud, I see, and the water has a brownish-yellow tint."

Lewis rises early in the dark and hears Clark's breathing and Charbono's snoring and smells Drewyer's feet and the grease and milk of the squaw and her baby, and he ducks through the flap into starlight, the glint of river and cold dry air, and he never catches the sentinels asleep, those good men who work hard and cheerfully, and without their daily ration of spirits, either. The sun rises in the east and the men man the boats and Venus is visible at midday and twenty river miles slide to the rear and the sun sinks in the west and Lewis, at the edge of camp, notebook in hand, watches Charbono prepare his famous white pudding, his *boudin blanc,* one of the great delicacies of the forest, or rather of the nonforest—isn't it strange that when Lewis dreams in the night of discovering the Rockies, he *still* descries their summits through a scrim of tree boughs?—Lewis enjoys even Charbono (that shirker, that bumbler), enjoys, in spite of himself, the man's histrionics.

Pas bon pour manger; non, non! the Frenchman waggles his finger, grimacing, as he takes hold of the last six feet of the large intestine of a buffalo cow, and with a lover's passion, making nursing moues with his mouth, he grips it at one end and compresses it along its length with his other hand. *Pas bon, non non!* he repeats as the shit extrudes, and Lewis's role is that of the child (or, what is the same, in this particular *mise-en-scène,* the foreigner) who just might forget and eat that fecal matter, so he cheerfully echoes, *Non non!* Now Charbono selects the muscle underneath the shoulder blade and chops it fine with kidney suet, flour, pepper, and salt. Then he takes up once more the intestine, indicating with raised eyebrows the remaining particles of soil, and gestures toward the river and waggles his finger and says, *Pas bon!* and Lewis repeats, *Pas bon!* and understands him to mean that one does not wash the intestine, *non,* that would spoil the entire procedure, it would be grossly un-French, after all, to stoop to clean what you are to eat. Charbono ties the end and inverts it, and commences stuffing the tube with the ground meat, *Bon pour manger!* (he kisses his fingers, leaving a circlet of suet and flour on his thick lips), exchanging the outer wall for the inner as he goes, so that the thick coat of fat on the outside turns inward and the soil is left exposed. Now! ah now (or *maintenant,* as we say), it is time to baptize the whole in the Missouri with two ceremonial dips and a shake, followed by a toss in the kettle for a boil, and when it is judged done, the chef fries foot-long lengths in bear oil in one of his glistening coke-caked skillets. *Bon?* he asks archly, *Bon?,* pure boastfulness, knowing perfectly the answer as Lewis punctures with his fork, the sausage splitting, the dappled fat pooling and the salt and the pepper and the perfume— *Bon!* Lewis exclaims, you malingerer, you old cheat, you shameless child-fornicator, *Bon!*

And the bends in the Missouri blend and blur, and the captains come upon a river disemboguing on the starboard side, 150 yards wide, a gentle current, its water the color of milky tea, and they conclude from its location and size that it must be that which the Minetares call the River That Scolds at All Other Rivers, "Although its placid current belies its name," Lewis observes, and in consequence of that (plus the unwieldiness of the native denomination), they rename it Milk River. And from its size and location Lewis feels justified in believing it might (surely!) reach near to the Saskatchewan River and thus give the U' States land above the 49th parallel, and provide easy access to the Athabasca country, thus affording a means of acquiring (that is, sneaking, or stealing, or, properly viewed, redressing, or revenging, earlier depredations) beaver from land even farther north that must remain, alas, British.

And there is no dew in the mornings and it never rains more than a sprinkle that barely wets the clothes, and they pass a dry creek, its bed twenty-five yards wide, which they name Little Dry Creek. Then they pass another, and name it Lackwater Creek, and one farther on, fifty yards wide, which they call Big Dry Creek. Then another, with a bed two hundred yards wide: Little Dry River. And finally, one of the most extraordinary sights Lewis has ever beheld, coming into view on the larboard side: a riverbed half a mile wide, without a drop of water running in it.

"Obviously, Big Dry River," Clark says.

"But then, whatever will we call the next one?" Lewis asks dryly. "Extraordinarily Big Dry River?"

That night, in the skin lodge: "Can we with propriety denominate them rivers at all, when they don't run?"

"Spring runoff—"

"How about Big Runoff Channel?"

"They must drain level and dry plains," Clark muses.

"The spring rains must melt the accumulated snow across a great expanse of plain, all the snow melting at the same time, causing a vast quantity of water to run for just a few days."

Lewis, in the dark, the others asleep, realizes he must recalibrate his conception of the Missouri River. He was counting on a certain rate of diminution of the Missouri's volume as he ascended it, passing tributaries that he assumed added water to the main stream. He thought he had a good feeling for the approximate length of a river, given its size. But it is an eastern feeling, a forest-dweller's feeling.

In the dark, he acknowledges, he accepts: the Missouri diminishes at a slower rate than he anticipated.

He admits: therefore, it is farther to its headwaters than he thought.

He writes: *I begin to feel extremely anxious to get in view of the Rocky Mountains.*

4

Rifle in one hand, espontoon in the other, Lewis prefers to take his walks alone, the brown bears be damned, he has never in his life, even as a boy, hesitated to go wherever he pleases. Encountering one of the monsters in an open wood, he could shoot while keeping trees between him and his quarry (his one concession—he will not take Seaman with him), and even climb a tree if he had to. Encountering one near the water, he could retreat into it, where the bear would be encumbered. But he is forced to concede inwardly, silently, that to meet one on the open plains, only Lewis and the bear, would be a serious matter. And just as he has grown accustomed to the strange fact that he no longer shoots most of the buffalo he sees, but instead must throw rocks to drive them out of his way, he must acquaint himself with leaving the bear alone. Lewis awaited the revelation of the bear-god, and it has turned out to be *Touch me not*.

5

In the merry middle month of May, when wild roses all are blooming, Captain Merry recalibrates his easterner's idea of what it means for a country to be wooded. At the mouth of the Musselshell River, he writes

> from the circumstance of the Indians informing us that we should find a well timbered country in the neighborhood of this mouth, I am induced to believe that the timbered country of which they speak consists of nothing more than a few scatterings of small scrubby pine and dwarf cedar on the summits of some of the highest hills, nine tenths of the country being wholly destitute of timber of any kind.

He is seeing with new eyes. The source of that little stream is not thirty miles distant, but at least a hundred. That jungle of pine on that sandy summit there—why, a bird could flit from one tree to another and hardly have to rest once on the ground between! The land is changing him, turning him into *Homo louisianensis*.

Lewis rises early and ducks through the flap and walks alone and experiences visions. He sees perfect, placid lakes in the bone-dry hollows. He sees distant river bluffs hanging above the horizon, clear as clear, a strip of sky between them and the earth. He raises his gun to shoot a buffalo two hundred paces off and it turns its head and gobbles at him; it is a wild turkey, fifty feet away. That horse loping across the treeless expanse stops and tucks its tail and lets out a wolf howl. And he descries the mammoth, alive! oh, Mr. Jefferson! shuffling its elephantine bulk in silhouette along a ridge, swinging its head. But there are no tusks; Lewis tips his hat to the bear and walks on.

He flexes his right hand, writes 750 words, adding the western variety of deer to the roster of Creation, *the ear and the tail of this animal, when compared with those of the common deer, so well comports with those of the mule when compared with the horse, that we have by way of distinction adopted the appellation of the mule deer* . . .

Day by day, the waters of the Missouri grow more transparent. The current strengthens, the bottoms narrow. Mountains must be near. But when Lewis ascends the broken hills, he sees nothing but plains. The sun sets in the flat west, and the campfires are lit, and there is beavertail and Charbono's *boudin blanc,* which is so good, Lewis forgets what a bad waterman he is, and fails to order him never again to man the white pirogue's helm after he almost overturned it in April, and the incompetent ass does it again, only worse. When the squall strikes the boat and turns it broadside, Charbono, instead of putting her before the wind, tries to luff up into it, and the brace of the square-sail is torn out of Goodrich's hand and in an instant the boat is slapped on its side, articles floating down the Missouri, instruments! medicine! God in heaven! the journals! (Lewis has no trouble recognizing, from the opposite shore three hundred yards away, those bobbing tin cases.) He fires his gun and shouts, but they cannot hear him, and while the boat continues to drift on its side and Charbono cries to his French-Minetare godling for mercy and the bowman, Cruzatte, threatens to shoot him on the instant if he doesn't recollect his duty and take hold of the rudder, Lewis can only think of the journals being lost, all evidence of his goodness swept away, and he realizes he has thrown away his gun and half unbuttoned his coat to plunge into the river and swim those three hundred yards of wind-tossed ice-cold water, which would kill him; but if the journals are lost, what will he have to live for?

Cruzatte is the hero. He gets the boat righted. He directs some men to bail like demons, while the others row with him toward the shore. They reach the bank scarcely above water. Lewis crosses in the red pirogue, leaps out and pumps the one-eyed man's hand and claps him on the shoulder and wonders aloud if poor sight improves balance, or strengthens character, or augments pluck, or somehow or other makes a man *the finest waterman by God on the Missouri!* Then he turns on Charbono—but the man is wet and miserable, and (as it has turned out) not much has been lost, he is only an old Frenchman with rheumatism and corns, they didn't take him along for his river skills, and his *boudin blanc* is an unlooked-for bonus, and there is a ragout that he makes—Lewis says nothing, only that a fire should be lit at once, and a gill of spirits distributed to all. Later Clark mentions, what Lewis in his vexation at the time failed to notice, that it was the Indian woman, sitting in the stern, who rescued most of the floating articles, including the journals (God in heaven!), and for the next night or two, in the lodge, Lewis looks at her with new eyes as she performs those tedious and intricate tasks that an infant entails. Her uncomplaining demeanor, her downcast eyes. Those scars. Days go by during which, as far as Lewis can tell, she says not a word. He wonders how intelligent she is. Perhaps naturally quick, but stunted by circumstance. Living entirely in the present, as is the natural aptitude of her people.

One evening, he says her name: "Sah-ca-gar-me-ah." She looks at him shyly. He beckons her toward him, come, that's a good girl. She leaves the baby in its swing and approaches him more hesitantly than do the wild animals of the plains these days. He shows her the sheet on which he and Clark are collecting courses and distances, the Missouri growing inch by inch up the side. He points to the tributary stream he and Clark have named after her. And well deserved, he assures her. Look! Sah-ca-gar-me-ah Fork. Her little piece of immortality. One day, a settler family will sit among the wildflowers by its banks, and the parents will tell their children the story of its name. *Here the Indian girl, with fortitude and resolution equal to any man on board—* You! Lewis says, wondering if he needs Drewyer or Charbono to make her understand. But she looks at the map, and at Lewis, and exhibits clear marks of gratification. She touches her heart with the palm of her hand and stretches the hand toward him, an eloquent gesture, and says, "Yes."

And the river bottoms continue to narrow and the last bluffs yield entirely to broken rounded hills of barely indurated sand and clay, rich black loam lower down, barren and sandy and "well timbered" with pine above, and the banks firm up and the current strengthens and the water is too deep for poling, so towing the boats from the banks is often the only way to proceed. The mountains must be near, although Lewis cannot see them in the scrubbed, bright air, and he and Clark plot the river course at night and count the miles and wonder where the mountains are, and could it be that they are so low they will remain invisible until the Corps is upon them?

One night he and Clark are awakened by Pryor. A cottonwood tree directly over their lodge has caught fire from cooking embers blown in the high wind—"And He shall lead them by night in a pillar of fire," Lewis says to

Clark—and five minutes after they move the lodge, the top half of the tree crashes onto the very spot. There lies *Lewis orientalis*.

The mountains must be near, and therefore the falls are near, and *Lewis louisianensis* begins to collect elk skins for the covering of the iron-frame boat he designed so long ago at Harpers Ferry, and has lugged these two thousand miles and more up the Missouri: designed by gravity, hence balanced, hence seaworthy, competent to a burden of something remarkable, Lewis cannot for the life of him remember what. When he walks in the hills, he examines the pines, which resemble eastern pitch pine except that the needles are longer, and the cones are covered with resin, which is an excellent sign, as he will need the pitch to pay the seams of the elk skins. Some of the skins are cut into new towropes, and the men brace themselves against roots and rocks, and the ropes rise out of the water and snap taut, flinging out a halo of droplets that catch the light. A pair of moccasins wears out in three days, and the hunters kill mule deer and Whitehouse and York make more moccasins, and the elk-skin towropes break and more ropes are cut and braided. The men work so hard and so willingly, and the captains name pieces of the west after them, Werner's Run, Gibson's Creek, Bratton's River, Weiser's Creek, Goodrich's Island, Windsor's Creek, Thompson's Creek. Instead of spirits, they drink water, which will extend their lives, out of creeks that will bear their names forever.

One day Clark climbs a hill and sees an isolated tuft of mountains in the west, about fifty miles off. An outrider of the Rockies? Or is it part of the Black Hills chain of which the Indians spoke, which would mean the Rockies are still far, far beyond? Lewis unfolds the map sheets at night and counts days and miles, and determines that Clark's conjectural map is now off by more than two hundred miles, and he says, "Be careful what you wish for."

"Hm?" says Clark.

"I wished for a river that would never end."

And the men brace their feet against rocks and haul on the towropes and the current grows stronger and the soil more sterile, so that even in the bottoms only hyssop and a fleshy-leaved thornbush grow. Beavers disappear; then elk; then buffalo. Clark's tuft of mountains draws nearer on the north, and another isolated group becomes visible in the south, and the captains name them North Mountains and South Mountains, and the Corps slowly creeps between, hauling the boats, and only the bighorn animals are left. At last a hunter bags one, and Lewis writes eight hundred words, paying especial attention to the hoof, *black & large in proportion, is divided, very open and roundly pointed at the toe, like the sheep; is much hollowed and sharp on the under edge like the Scotch goat, has two small hoofs behind each foot below the ankles as the goat, sheep and deer have,* endeavoring to determine (but far from satisfying his mind on the matter) how this unusual but far from arcane instrument enables the animal, alone in the great kingdom, to ignore the laws of physics and mortality.

The hills of indurated sand and clay give way to jutting cliffs of a soft sandstone that the rivulets break up, carrying boulders down to the Missouri, where they block the narrow shore and constrict the river so that the current is fiercest just at the points where the men must clamber with the towropes. One morning, late in May, it is Lewis's turn to stay with the boats while Clark goes walking, and the towropes twang and snap, and the haloes of droplets fly, and Clark returns at midday and says, "I have seen the Rockies," and that evening Lewis runs like a boy up the eight hundred feet to the highest point in the neighborhood, arriving gasping like an old man, but (he writes) *I thought myself well repaid for any labor, as from this point I beheld the Rocky Mountains for the first time*—the points of four summits poking like volcanic islands above the horizon in the west-southwest, bright with snow. The first white men! An especial literary effort is called for. Lewis dips his pen, taps the page.

> While I viewed those mountains I felt a secret pleasure in finding myself so near the head of the heretofore conceived boundless Missouri; but when I reflected on the difficulties which this snowy barrier would most probably throw in my way to the Pacific, and the sufferings and hardships of myself and party in them, it in some measure counterbalanced the joy I had felt in the first moments in which I gazed on them; but as I have always held it a crime to anticipate evils I will believe it a good comfortable road until I am compelled to believe differently.

Still no Indians. A lodgepole floats down the river. A small leathern ball. The hoop of a drum.

The Corps passes another abandoned camp. The Indian woman examines moccasins found there and says they do not belong to her people, but to a tribe living north of the Missouri. Lewis observes to Clark, "It seems that each tribe has its distinctive method of making and decorating moccasins. Perhaps one might develop a useful taxonomy of the western Indians according to moccasin design."

He climbs the highest hill. Summits of snow rising in the west, pink in the sunset. But no sign, anywhere, of a lodgefire.

6

A bold river discharging itself on the larboard side, the water clear. Though larger than the Musselshell, it was not mentioned by the Minetares; thus unnamed; thus the argument.

Clark wants Judith. After that twelve-year-old in Virginia. Because of the purity of its water, no doubt; or its wooded little valley, the most fertile stretch for miles around, an oasis for the weary traveler, etc. "I had thought Big Horn," Lewis says mildly. "You mentioned the abundance of those animals in the country through which the river passes." Lewis ascended the valley only half a mile, whereas Clark penetrated it three times as far. Which would give him precedence in naming it.

"Except there's the tributary of the Yellowstone that the Menetarrees call Big Horn," Clark says.

"But we needn't follow them. We renamed the River That Scolds."

"We already have it down on our map as Big Horn."

"So have we the River That Scolds; and yet we changed it."

Clark says nothing. Lewis tries to explain. "I'm not entirely convinced of the propriety of naming major rivers of the west after young women who have not set foot in Louisiana, nor eyes on the rivers in question."

"Lewis, we already did it with Martha's River."

"Well, perhaps that is my point. Are we going to—" cover the map with the names of every little chit, slip, and twit in a dress you've ever felt yourself drawn to? Lewis stops short.

Clark is looking at him. Lewis looks away. Weary traveler—

"Clark. Forgive me, I must be tired. She is your river; Judith is a fine name." He raises his pen to cross out *Big Horn*.

"No," Clark says. "I quite see your reasoning. I think we should keep Big Horn."

"No, friend, it was a quibble; beneath me—"

"There are men in the Corps we have yet to honor. You are correct and generous to remember them. To honor someone not of the party—"

"But dear Clark—" Lewis risks a glance at his friend, and is dismayed to see his chin tucked against his neck, a carriage he assumes (all unaware, ingenuous man) when he feels affronted. "Clark, she *is* of the party. She is your muse, let us say, who perches on your right shoulder—but that makes her sound like a bird—who hovers, then, behind your right shoulder—or in any case, in your general vicinity!—and inspires you to *proceed on,* as you say. Toward what other purpose do men penetrate the wilderness than the furtherance of civilization, whose flame is tended by the gentle sex? Or what's more, whose radiance finds its best reflection in their fair forms?" Better. "No, I insist on Judith. Though my fortune has been never to have laid eyes on her—my misfortune, rather!—I can believe her to be the most enchanting creature in Virginia."

7

Lewis cannot sleep, so he rises and ducks through the flap into silence and solitude, speaks softly to the sentinels, stokes the fire. Light returns with a sprinkle of rain. There is now a perceptible fall in the river's course from bend to bend, and the cliffs often jut to the banks. The rain has made the ground so slippery that the men must go barefoot, and they set their shoulders against the ropes, grunting, and they are often up to their armpits in icy water, working around the rocky points and through the riffles, the towropes breaking at the worst moments. The men must clamber over sharp rocks for hundreds of yards, their feet torn and bleeding, yet they bear it without a murmur, O faithful fellows! and when they rest at noon, Lewis distributes whiskey, and he goes among them, don't rise, laying his hand on slumped shoulders wet with spray and sweat, and he loves them all and thanks his God for them. Every Jack shall have his gill, except that it is a mere two thimbles, and half-and-half grog at that, and yet the men are cheered by it, they are returning to the innocence of boyhood, when a drop brought color to their cheeks.

They labor on, and a new stretch of river opens, revealing cliffs of soft white sandstone, rank on rank, mile after mile, rising perpendicular two and three hundred feet, carved into fantastic shapes by rain and wind. An especial literary effort is called for. Lewis taps the page; his duty to posterity—

a thousand grotesque figures, which with the help of a little imagination and an oblique view at a distance, are made to represent elegant ranges of lofty freestone buildings, having their parapets well stocked with statuary; columns of various sculpture both grooved and plain are also seen supporting long galleries in front of those buildings; in other places on a much nearer approach and with the help of less imagination we see the remains or ruins of elegant buildings; some columns standing and almost entire with their pedestals and capitals; others retaining their pedestals but deprived by time or accident of their capitals, some lying prostrate and broken, others in the form of vast pyramids of conic structure bearing a series of other pyramids on their tops becoming less as they ascend and finally terminating in a sharp point; niches and alcoves of various forms—

—he is not pitching it high enough; bogged down in details, how many capitals? how many pedestals? He taps; how did the first white man *feel*?

As we passed on it seemed as if those scenes of visionary enchantment would never have an end; . . . so perfect indeed are those walls that I should have thought that nature had attempted here to rival the human art of masonry had I not recollected that she had first begun her work.

Lewis rereads, dissatisfied. *Scenes of visionary enchantment.* A hackneyed phrase! Clark could express it better purely by accident. Visiolunary encanticles. Lewis rises restlessly and walks out of the lodge. Gass and Shields are crouched over an enclosed fire, making bullets. Some of the men are asleep in a line. Whitehouse is seated sideways to the open fire, writing in his journal. A falseness creeps in. Like that palaver on seeing the Rockies, *but when I reflected on the difficulties which this snowy barrier,* etc. Hypocrite! He had no such thoughts at the time. The only alloy to his gulping joy was a contemptible twinge of regret that Clark had seen them first. Or: *I have always held it a crime to anticipate evils.* A sentiment cribbed from some other explorer's journal; Lewis is a perfect artist of pessimism.

Following a turn around the camp, he fetches up at the tent again. He pauses by the flap. In the firelight, he examines the scorchmarks caused by embers blown from that burning cottonwood tree some nights ago. All cottonwoods assume a tortured shape; penitential pilgrims ascending the Missouri to some frightful shrine. Aflame, the species finally looked right: a spirit writhing magnificently in the torments of hell.

Lewis circles the tent. An Indian would paint his story on his lodge: arrows feathering buffalo, stick men pointing muskets one-handed toward enemies, from whose bodies blood showers like rain. What would Lewis paint? Any figures at all? Perhaps nothing but a brown line, snaking coils within coils from base to apex of the cone and back again, encircling the lodge to join its tail to its mouth, river without end.

But these chance scars from that midnight burnt offering evoke more of the adventure than anything Lewis might ever paint or write. These, and the sight of Gass (this instant) pouring lead with his ass in the air. And the men asleep in the line. And the blackness above that must be clouds, because there are no stars, and the purl and hiss of the invisible river, and the smell of grease and milk, and Drewyer's feet, and Charbono's snore, and the way Clark sleeps with his hands between his drawn-up knees, and that species of fox Lewis saw this evening, a beautiful creature, orange-yellow and white and black like a tortoiseshell cat, that he shot at but missed, and it disappeared in a twinkling.

Why is it all so lovely? This.

Why so precious? Is it merely to mock man? *Yes, you love this,* God says; *however, I regret to inform you—*

Be careful what you wish for, Lewis said to Clark, but that was merely a clumsy attempt at fellow feeling, in truth he still does not want the river to end; yet he so much wants to discover its end. And he loves this night, and at the same time he feels he will die from waiting for the sun to rise.

He touches the skin of the lodge. *This, now.*

Tomorrow is June. He goes in.

And June dawns, and the scenes of visionary enchantment (viz., the cliffs) come to an end, and he and Clark reach a major fork in the river that the Minetares never mentioned. The north branch is muddy and rolling, like the Missouri, whereas the south runs clear. The north is 200 yards wide, the south 372. The north is deeper; the south faster. The Corps believes, to a man, that the north branch is the Missouri—because (sirs, please you) it *looks* like the Missouri. But Lewis, examining with the eyes of *Homo louisianensis,* is convinced that the true Missouri is the south branch. All these weeks, ascending this river, he has watched it grow more transparent, like the air, and now, as is fitting, it becomes perfectly so. Clark agrees. Fast, clear rivers flow from mountains, whither the captains wish to go, whereas the muddy north branch must wind through a great expanse of the northern plains between this point and the Saskatchewan River. Moreover, the Minetares said the water of the Missouri was nearly transparent at the Great Falls, and the falls must be near.

But the men believe to a man—and thus, to ease their minds, and to grant those with the worst-bruised and -lacerated feet a respite, the captains form two parties, and one morning before sunrise, under a pale sky of breaking yellow clouds, Clark heads up the south fork and Lewis the north, for two days of reconnoitering. Lewis has another reason to go: if the north branch flows through a great expanse of plains, then perhaps it rises above 49° 37' N. Or rather, surely it does! Urged on by this hope, he ascends the river farther than necessity strictly demands, and then is delayed on his return by heavy rains that make the bluffs treacherous, and so finds Clark anxious for his safety by the time he arrives back at the main camp two days late.

The captains confer on what they observed, and agree that their original supposition was correct. Not being the Missouri, the northern branch must have a name, and since Lewis ascended it, he has the right to name it. Until now, he has been naming rivers like an Indian; that is, from circumstance. If he sees a porcupine, it is Porcupine River. If a suffering cottonwood-spirit showers embers on his lodge, it is Burnt Lodge Creek. By that rule, this might be Bad Bed River, as he spent one of the worst nights of his life on it, huddled in the mud and rain. Or Slippery Bluff River, since he nearly sledded off a ninety-foot cliff.

But he really ought to civilize himself, like Clark. Pick a name purely for the pretty sound of it. The most enchanting girl in Virginia—and Clark looking at him. Well? Who, then? He runs his mind over all the chits, slips, and twits in dresses he's ever danced with. Eyes shining up at the dashing captain; wondering what his pay is. He can barely remember a one of them.

Maria, then. His cousin. Handsome enough. And she did play a trick on him once in company, when they were both children, that discomfited him about as much, all in all, as falling off a ninety-foot cliff. Lewis dips his pen, writes

> I determined to give it a name and in honour of Miss Maria W—d called it Maria's River. It is true that the hue of the waters of this turbulent and troubled stream but illy comport with the pure celestial virtues and amiable qualifications of that lovely fair one; but on the other hand it is a noble river, in addition to which it passes through a rich, fertile and one of the most beautifully picturesque countries that I ever beheld, through the wide expanse of which innumerable herds of living animals are seen, its borders garnished with one continued garden of roses, while its lofty and open forests are the habitation of myriads of the feathered tribes who salute the ear of the passing traveler with their wild and simple, yet sweet and cheerful melody.

In the morning, Lewis endeavors to convince the men that the south fork is the true one. By this point, nothing could be more obvious to him, yet the fellows continue to shake their heads. They solicit a word from Cruzatte, whom they respect for his many years' experience on the Missouri, and Cruzatte gets up on his hind legs and scratches the bristles on his chin and pronounces, "In my opinion, the north fork is the true genuine Missouri, and can be no other!" If the blind lead the blind, Lewis wants to say, smiling at them; but instead he asks, do they think the Missouri springs muddy from its mountain source? Oh no, says they, they are not so simple as that; but mightn't this clear branch end too soon in the mountains and leave them still far from the Columbia? To which Lewis replies, the branch in question is 372 yards wide, a suggestive fact, of which they might remind themselves by turning their heads to the left. But they merely continue to nod to each other and point to Cruzatte and waggle their ears. Obstinate fellows!

But also excellent fellows. They declare with all cheerfulness that they are ready to follow the captains wherever they think proper to direct, right branch, wrong branch, or up a tree. Which does go without saying (the Articles of War dealing with mutiny and capital punishment being what they are), still, it is gratifying to hear them say it, and without the smallest amount of grumbling, neither, indeed with what could almost be called shining countenances. Lewis wants to comfort them, and hits on the idea of another small party, this time to ascend the south fork in advance of the boats until it finds the falls, which news, sent downriver, will prove, even to Cruzatte, that the south fork is the true one.

Clark agrees to the idea. "As you are the better waterman," Lewis says, "I thought it best that I lead the advance party."

"Of course," Clark says.

Preparations are made. With the current growing ever stronger, the red pirogue is drawn up and concealed on an island, its crew distributed to the other boats to increase hands on the towropes. In order to lighten the loads, inessential heavier articles and some of the provisions are cached—the bellows, hammers, and tongs; felling axes; beaver traps; bear skins; kegs of pork, salt, and parched corn; extra powder and lead. Watching it all go into the hole, Lewis marvels that they carried it so far; and wonders the more at the great mound of trinkets the men have picked up: knives and pots and souvenir arrows, necklaces from Indian girls, lucky stones, pumice chunks, Indian drums, hoof rattles, horn ladles, a goodly number of human skulls (no doubt plucked from Mandan funerary rings), *seven* buffalo headdresses various men have amused themselves making, packs of precious beaver skins, and all manner of unclassifiable objects found and saved for some future day on which their gravely obscure utility would become clear. Even in the wilderness, it would appear, material things multiply and threaten to bury a man.

So a man must bury *them* instead! In the morning, lightened, Lewis rises and crows like a cock and the sun vaults into a cloudless sky and he swings a pack with his blanket on his back and sets out up the Missouri—or should he say, the *putative* Missouri—with his little band, Drewyer, Joseph Fields, Gibson, Goodrich, to discover the Great Falls. Oh Lord! Thanks be! Lewis regrets to inform his God: he is happy!

However, he's had a touch of dysentery for the past two days, and God gets a message back to him by noon. The band has hiked nine miles and shot elk for dinner, and the feast of the marrowbones is about to begin, when Lewis is struck with such severe intestinal pain that he cannot stand. The agony increases through the afternoon, and toward evening a high fever comes on. Lewis has a bed of willow boughs made, in which he curls and rocks. He has neglected to bring along any medicines (holding it a crime, as he does, to anticipate evils), so he experiments with a simple. Chokecherries being abundant about the place, he recalls the anti-irritants his mother used to make from wild cherry bark; he directs Gibson to gather and strip twigs, cut them into two-inch pieces, and boil them for an hour. The decoction thus produced is black in color, bitter and astringent. Lewis drinks a pint of it at sunset; another after an hour. Thirty minutes later, the pain lifts like a blanket drawn away; the fever abates; he breaks out in a gentle sweat. Lying on the willow boughs, under a chokecherry tree, Lewis swims in profound peace. Good Goodrich steals up quietly, bringing baked fish; Fields lays a strip of roast elk liver on a plate. With these offerings at hand, the homely sight of Drewyer and Gibson stretching their feet to the fire, Fields standing the first watch, Lewis slips into sleep.

He wakes renewed, drinks another pint of Missouri and chokecherry, sets out at sunrise. He leads his men north up onto the plain to skirt the ravines that branch out laterally from the main valley, then turns southwest. In the afternoon he climbs a ridge, and from the top is granted his best view thus far of the Rocky Mountains: stretching from the southeast to the northwest, a succession of formidable lofty ranges, entirely covered with snow. *But when I reflected on the difficulties which this snowy barrier—* God has once again cursed him for a lie by making it true. But cursed? No, rather blessed. When Lewis, in his dreams, first descried the Rockies through a forest canopy, what he always saw were the mountains of Virginia. The meager fancy of man! It is Lewis's great honor to discover a range incomparably more majestic than the Appalachians, a different geographical species entirely. And now that he gazes on these august peaks, which he has before seen only as a line of pimples on a map with a name attached, he laughs, because the truth was staring him in the face all the while: their *names.* Shining Mountains! Rocky Mountains! No one would use those terms for the rounded, wood-clad Appalachians, whose snows are melted by the first of April. These are *mountains,* by God! Those of his boyhood were hillocks. Let them rise out of the atmosphere altogether, Lewis *will* pass them, and he'll tip his hat to God as he passes by His throne: Forgive me, Lord, I mistook You for a bear.

He and the others make about twenty-seven miles that day, before he begins to feel a bit weary, no doubt a consequence of his recent illness. He orders an early camp, eats heartily, writes in his journal while it is still light, and amuses himself through the evening sitting on a sandbar, catching two new species of fish.

On the third day, Lewis rises and sets out at dawn and ascends to the plain and strikes southwest, and from the top of a hill he gazes fifty miles over a level stretch of garden country on which more buffalo graze than he has ever seen in a single view, perhaps ten thousand. Is it because of this sight that he sends Fields to the right and Drewyer and Gibson to the left with orders to procure meat while he, Lewis, walks on, south across the plain, to meet the river valley five miles distant? And is it merely because he feels strong again, and is pleased to feel strong, that he quickens his pace, so that the only other man with him, Goodrich, falls farther and farther behind? Or does *Homo louisianensis* somehow foreknow, in his marrowbones, where the Great Falls are, and in his selfish heart of hearts does he want to reach them not only first, but alone?

How else account for the fact that when he catches the sound of falling water on the wind, he realizes he has been straining to hear exactly that for the past hour? A column of spray rises above the plain in front of him.

Gun in one hand, espontoon in the other, companions far behind, and all the world before—Lewis runs.

8

How to describe it?

I hurried down the hill which was about 200 feet high and difficult of access, to gaze on this sublimely grand spectacle.

No, not that way. The looming mist, the shout in his breast, the wordless awe. But that is just it: wordless. A crash of white filling his ears and I! I! I! as he flew down the cliff. (Not a hill.) Later, looking up, he could not make out how he came. Or rather, the *way*. The *how* was: like a bighorn, scorning gravity.

The crash and roar: *Who are you, are you, are you?*

I took my position on the top of some rocks about 20 feet high opposite the center of the falls. Arms wide, taking the mist in his face, down his front, wetting him more than the last two months' rain, I! I! But he cannot write that; he can't write that his real thought on discovering the Great Falls of the Missouri was, *I* have discovered them. That is no kind of sublimity. And in any case, *was* that his real thought? Or was it *Here!*? Was it *Roar!*? Was it all a tumult, and did thought only begin when he thought, *How to describe it?*

Which came all too soon. His duty to posterity, a literary effort. And with that thought, the falls were cruelly reduced to a scene before him; a subject for his pen.

> Immediately at the cascade the river is about 300 yds. wide; about ninety or a hundred yards of this next to the lard. bluff is a smooth even sheet of water falling over a precipice of at least eighty feet, the remaining part of about 200 yards on my right forms the grandest sight I ever beheld—

—but the shock has faded, the doubt intruded: is it grander than—?

> —the height of the fall is the same as the other but the irregular and somewhat projecting rocks below receive the water in its passage down and break it into a perfect white foam which assumes a thousand forms in a moment, sometimes flying up in jets of sparkling foam to the height of fifteen or twenty feet and are scarcely formed before large rolling bodies of the same beaten and foaming water is thrown over and conceals them. In short, the rocks seem to be most happily fixed to present a sheet of the whitest beaten froth for 200 yards in length and about 80 feet perpendicular.

He is in camp, damp, alone (Goodrich is fishing, the hunters have not yet arrived), below the falls on a little bottom that is shielded from the violence of the river by a ridge of rocks. —*this abutment of rock defends a handsome little bottom of about three acres*— Mist drifts above and around him. Sunlight makes it glow. He flew down the cliff, Oh! Oh! (*Not* I! I!) Then he spent his time pacing off sublimity—*about 300 yards below me there is another abutment . . . about 60 feet high . . . at right angles . . . distance of 134 yds.* He flew down the cliff—here! roar!—he stood with arms flung wide! *From the reflection of the sun on the spray or mist which arises from these falls there is a beautiful rainbow produced which adds not a little to the beauty of this majestically grand scenery.* "Not a little"! False and coy! Lewis rises from the tree root he was sitting on (a rock his writing desk) and climbs to a vantage point to view the falls again. *After writing this imperfect description I again viewed the falls, and was so much disgusted with the imperfect idea which it conveyed of the scene that I determined to draw my pen across it and begin again*—save that that, too, is a hackneyed rhetorical gambit, that impatient striking out of one's words—*I wished for the pencil of Salvator Rosa or the pen of Thomson, that I might be enabled to give to the enlightened world some just idea of this truly magnificent and sublimely grand object, which has from the commencement of time been concealed from the view of civilized man—*

Lines in Thomson's *Seasons* that struck Lewis as a schoolboy:

> Wide o'er the brim, with many a torrent swelled,
> something something something
> At last the roused-up river pours along:
> Resistless, roaring, dreadful, down it comes.

Which recalled to him Rivanna; the long word for river. And then a line or two later in the poem: *Nature! Great parent!* And he thought of his father, swept away.

> How mighty, how majestic are thy works!
> With what a pleasing dread they swell the soul!

At which point he decided the poem, after all, was no more than a pretty lie. There was nothing majestic about a river flicking its little finger to knock a father off a horse, holding him under, chuckling. *I hope still to give to the world some faint idea of an object which at this moment fills me with such pleasure and astonishment, and which of its kind I will venture to assert is second to but one in the known world.*

Viz., Niagara Falls. And Lewis wonders: a hundred years hence will there be viewing platforms here, as tourists have proposed for Niagara? Will there be pavilions and carriages, and enthusiastic ladies, who will write about sublimity, and strike out their words with impatience?

9

The next morning, Lewis sends Fields downriver with a letter to Captain Clark. He sets Goodrich, Gibson, and Drewyer to scaffolding and drying buffalo meat. This leaves (as it happens) only himself for the exploration party upriver. For of course they need to know where the rapids end, if they are going to plan their portage. Consequently, at ten o'clock, Lewis climbs out of the gorge (taking the sensible Indian path discovered by his men, rather than the vertical wall down which he floated yesterday) and proceeds upriver alone along the rim of the bluffs.

He has told the others he will be back for dinner in two or three hours. But Fortune has other plans for him. Or is it not that inconstant Lady, but the river-god and the buffalo-god and the bear-god, conspiring?

It is the river, first, that leads him on. He is merely looking for placid water, a portage-end; the Minetares said it would be about half a mile. They also spoke of the falls as a single entity, and as Mr. J would say, they are eminently positioned to know what they are talking about.

Why, then, does Lewis discover a second falls? It lies five miles above the first. About twenty feet high; the usual tea party of drowned buffalo churning in the foam at its base. Did the Missouri throw up this barrier, just as Lewis was telling his men he would return for dinner, for the simple pleasure of belying him?

He almost doubles back; his men will worry. He does turn. But as he turns, his upriver ear catches the whisper of another roar. *Come! Come away!* Lewis crosses the point of a hill where the river bends, the roar growing louder—and so discovers the third falls. Nearly as grand as the first, fifty feet high (more dead buffalo, piled on the banks), a quarter of a mile from side to side, pitching over a shelving rock with an edge as straight as art might make it. How to describe? (Alas, he must.) Perhaps: whereas the first falls, in its tumult and impetuosity, was an expression of sublimity and the ineffable, this one, falling in a single, even sheet, is a vision of ordered beauty. (Did he crib that from Burke?)

Lewis lifts his eyes upriver. More? *Proceed on!* He sees the mist. He walks toward it. All thought of return has left him.

The fourth cascade is fifteen feet. Lewis is firmly in the grip of the river's spell, he hurries farther upward, past riffles and foaming bends, along the bluff edge, expecting—foreknowing—a roar ahead—

The fifth falls! Six hundred yards wide, thirty feet high, a fulsome rounded curve to the drop, a tower of mist in the air. Lewis is now the discoverer of the second-, third-, and fourth-greatest falls in America. He sees a sixth a short way above, five feet, a last pert lifting of a Missouri eyebrow, and beyond—*come away, explorer!*—the water seems (but he must be sure) to lose its velocity, and is that a plain he glimpses, and over there is a hill, and his duty is clear. He climbs, and at the summit, he gazes across a thousand square miles of country shading into blue, the snow-clad mountains in the west, the Missouri meandering full to its grassy brim a great distance to the south, huge herds of buffalo feeding, and their attendant wolves, and on the placid bosom of the mile-wide Missouri vast flocks of geese riding like mottled clouds, and Venus riding down the purple sky.

Lewis is lost to his men. They are beginning to worry. He sees, four miles farther on, a large tributary, edged with woods, descending from the west. Might it be the Medicine River, of which the Minetares spoke? His duty is clear. He descends, and walks on.

His dinner is eaten; he might as well kill a buffalo. If he hasn't time to get back to his men by evening, he will camp here for the night, alone, with drift-wood for his fire and buffalo hump and tongue and marrowbone for his feast. He turns toward the herd. A fat specimen detaches itself for him; it presents its chest to receive the shot.

And now the trap is sprung. The river has led him to this spot, the buffalo has stepped forward to empty his gun. Does Lewis foreknow the encounter, and act his part?

Why else does he not reload, but instead gaze with a strange fascination, as though he had never seen its like before, at the blood streaming from the buffalo's mouth? Why does he linger, waiting for the animal to fall?

A whisper in the grass.

Lewis turns. And there is the bear. It has been creeping up on him. Thirty paces away, advancing with a purpose. It is by far the whitest bear Lewis has seen. He raises his gun, and just as the bear comes into his sights, he remembers it is not loaded. The bear comes on, unhesitating. It knew that the river and the buffalo would deliver the man. In the space of an instant, Lewis recollects that he is on a level plain, without a bush in miles, nor a tree within three hundred yards. Lewis is in the middle of the blank space on the map, and this is Death, whom Lewis cannot outrun.

He turns with an air of unhurry, he takes one step, but at that moment the white beast pitches at him full speed, open-mouthed. Lewis runs. For the river; where else? Empty gun in one hand, toothpick espontoon in the other, he runs with no thought but that the river is different from Death's plain. He reaches the water's edge with the bear's breath on him and a thought bubbles up, feeble, absurdly so, but at least it's a thought, if he can get to a depth where the bear is obliged to swim while he can stand, he might hold him off with his espontoon. Lewis plunges into the water to his waist and spins about, he brings the point of the espontoon down, and he sees—it is a vision, twinkling with clarity—the blade of the espontoon driving into the open mouth of the bear, spitting him as he runs up onto it.

A vision—which perhaps the bear shares. Because at the edge of the water, at the sight of Lewis facing him, he abruptly stops. He gives one inscrutable snort and wheels. He flees, disappearing over the low riverbank. Lewis splashes to the shore and mounts the bank, and he sees the bear on the plain, pelting away, glancing once, twice over his shoulder, as though Lewis were a cavalry of men pounding after him; he crosses three miles of open prairie at full speed, and disappears into the woods along the Medicine River.

Lewis realizes he is still holding his gun.

It is not even wet.

He gazes at his powder horn. He takes out his ramrod and puts it on the ground; picks it up again.

What happened?

He manages to get the rifle reloaded.

The rutting season must have commenced. Lewis was a rival to a sex-crazed male. Ho!

He shoulders his gun and walks after the suitor.

But the sudden retreat: unaccountable. The man stood his ground and said *Come on!* Death ran.

Lewis walks in the footsteps of the bear.

When he reaches the Medicine River, he explores its valley for an hour. More than once he stops, listens. No voice calls him farther on.

He turns back. It is six-thirty. He has about twelve miles to walk. His men fear him hurt or dead. They are debating whether to search for him now, or wait until morning. The sun is low in the west. The Medicine woods are shrouded in gloom.

The animal that suddenly appears before him seems in the twilight at first a wolf, then some kind of tiger, its rippling coat a tawny yellow. It gathers itself to spring and he fires, and at that instant it disappears, as though it had never been. He reloads and advances. He finds a burrow, but not a trace of blood. Impossible that he might have missed.

He emerges from the wood. The grassy plain is emerald in the yellow light. A herd of buffalo grazes a half mile distant on his left. Three bulls along the near edge lift their shaggy heads, stop chewing, stare at him, exchange a glance (did that last actually happen?), then charge.

No! he wants to shout with joy. I do not want *your* women, either! He alters his course to meet the bulls, *Come on!* He doesn't bother to raise his gun. It's only three against one. *Come on!*

A hundred yards from him, the animals stop. Is that all they're made of? Lewis keeps on. They stare at him, shuffling. "Yahh!" he shouts, leaping. They turn tail and flee.

Lewis walks on. He reaches the buffalo that he shot. He ignores it. He continues downriver. The sun is sinking, and he half believes if he spends the night on this enchanted plain, the sun will rise to disclose his gun and espontoon, the embers of his fire, but not a bit of him. He will have disappeared like that tiger, called away by the river-god and the buffalo-god and the bear-god, to join their conspiracy. So darkness falls, and he walks on, and his men are sure he is dead, but he decides he is not, nor even dreaming. The prickly pears are stabbing his feet. Fifth falls, fourth, third, second. The roar of the first. He can make out the white of the Indian path in the starlight. He turns down the slope. "Drewyer!" he calls down, "Gibson! Goodrich!"

Their voices float up to him out of the darkness. "God have mercy, Captain! Are you all right?"

"Never mind that!" A singing in his ears. Jubilation. "What's for supper?"

THE DISCOVERER, II
[June–August 1805]

1

So quick bright things.

Lewis asks himself, months later, when the gleam came off the world. It is midwinter. He cannot be sure; memory is so treacherous. Climbing the last slope of the continental divide, drinking from the Missouri where it sprang chaste from its source—surely that was a golden moment. Wasn't it?

But earlier. After he faced the bear alone, there came the sickness of the Indian woman, the portage around the falls, his iron boat. That boat mortified him. Surely it was then. Clark's justifiable anger—

It is midwinter, on the western coast. Raining. Lewis is confused.

The promised half-mile portage turned out to be eighteen miles, which made Lewis wonder if the Minetares had deceived him and Clark deliberately. But the Corps, regardless, would have accomplished the task and continued upriver within twelve days, had it not been for Lewis's failure. As it was, it took twenty-five.

Whose idea had been that boat? Lewis recalls himself and Mr. J sketching it at the long table in the President's library. A collapsible iron frame, to be assembled and covered with skins on the upper Missouri and used for—what, exactly? Even if it had worked, it was only one vessel out of seven; so how could it have sped them on? When he and the President sketched at the table and did sums in the margins and congratulated themselves on applying Reason to the problems of Missouri navigation, they were envisioning (Lewis seems to remember) a smaller Corps. But did they actually think the iron boat alone would suffice to carry men and baggage? Did they imagine picking it up and carrying it half a mile across the continental divide and climbing back in on the Columbia? It is inconceivable. Yet it must be true. When Lewis thinks of the three thousand river miles he lugged that frame; rummaged it out of the hold of the keelboat; oiled it, counted the screws; kept it in his own hut at Fort Mandan, so the Indians wouldn't steal the iron bars for hoes and war clubs; dragged its weight with the towropes. He recalls the delay it caused at the very beginning of the expedition, when he had it constructed at the Harpers Ferry Armory—the catenary he used to shape its hull—mathematically perfect! Oh, yes! A failed farmer turns his boundless ingenuity to boatmaking!

He recalls counting the pine trees on the hilltops as they dwindled and gave out, a week before the falls. He needed pitch to seal the seams. (There were a thousand pitch pines within five minutes' walk from the Harpers Ferry Armory.) He recalls gathering drift pine at the upper portage camp, which told him, what he could have guessed, that in addition to pine downriver, there was pine upriver. He had Gass and Shields dig a tar pit, but the driftwood yielded nothing. Either he hadn't enough of it, or it had been too long adrift, or western pitch pine lavished all its oils on its cones, and kept none in its core—Lewis did not know.

The other thing he needed was a dozen elk skins; the most durable leather. Elk had been fairly common in the past fortnight, but at the falls, they disappeared. Days were lost, hunting far afield. In the end, some of the boat had to be covered with buffalo. And there was no ash or elm for the interior braces, only weak willow, or weaker box elder, or weakest cottonwood. Then Lewis used sharp-edged needles to sew the skins together, instead of smooth; they cut the skins, causing the seamholes to gape as the skins dried. Then he made his crowning miscalculation: he had the skins shaved (this took three days). His experimental substitute for pitch—a composition of buffalo tallow, beeswax, and pounded charcoal—was applied; the boat was dried over a slow fire. God! it was a handsome vessel, smooth and gleaming and black. It was put in the water, where it floated like a perfect cork. For twenty minutes. Then the composition peeled away, and it sank. The only places where the sealant held was on the buffalo skins, which had retained some of their hair.

The men, while they toiled to build it, had dubbed it *Experiment*. And what in God's name was Lewis doing experimenting like a giggling schoolboy, when winter was coming on, and he had thirty men's lives on his hands? Clark, who accomplished the entire grueling portage while Lewis frittered away the work of six of the best men on his pet, his toy, never breathed a word of what must surely have been derision. And then Lewis wasted yet another day, dismantling and burying his boat next to the river.

In midwinter, standing at the door of his hut, he marvels at that inexplicable man. Perhaps his thinking was (he is confused; he struggles to remember) that they could retrieve the boat on the way back east. Packing it downriver would require little effort—all it needed was pitch to make it perfect—float like a cork—carry God knows how many thousands of pounds of unnecessary provisions. It is still waiting for him.

To replace the failed *Experiment,* the Corps needed two dugouts. Lewis had not seen a cottonwood anywhere near the requisite size since passing the Musselshell, over two hundred miles downstream. But some of the hunters noticed a stand about eight miles above the portage camp, and when Clark went with a crew of axmen to investigate, he found precisely two cottonwoods that were just large enough to be usable. This seemed like extraordinary good luck, and Lewis said so. But privately, he heard it as divine laughter. Yes, coming so soon after the bear, this orchestrated humiliation indicated once again that God simply would not have it that he be satisfied. This theory was an extravagance, he knew; it was self-pity; it was a fault in him. (He stares at the rain.) God had the planets to balance in their orbits, He had a billion seeds to usher toward their million forms of life, He had given Lewis a mind and a will of his own precisely so that he would not be hourly on His hands, clamoring for reward or punishment.

But He was such an ingenious craftsman. It would have been child's play for Him to lard His cosmic design with a few thousand automata—falling rocks, tipping carriages, sinking ships, showers of rain, misfired guns, thin ice, a turned blade, a pustule, a wrong word, a miscarried letter—armed to trip into action whenever a certain quotient of human happiness was exceeded in a certain locality. To borrow an apt phrase from Clark's journal, these moment's chances, these little ruinations of little lives, might collectively be termed *the choler of the earth.* (Clark had meant *color*—he was describing how the ravines flooded during rains and washed soil into the river, turning it brown; two days later a choleric gully nearly washed him and the Bird Woman into the Missouri and over the Great Falls.)

And the point of it all? Some might argue it was to teach men their craven dependence on God's saving grace. Mr. J would reject the thesis entirely, insisting that a benevolent Creator had given man a tool sufficient to his perfectability, if only he used it properly. As for Lewis—the President in his head discounted the theory, while the schoolboy in his bowels believed in it dreadfully. The schoolboy, naturally, could make more noise; that brat believed the deity had long ago convicted Himself of an unpleasant taste for pain. Therefore, Lewis's only recourse for a gram of solace was to pride himself on standing up to it. And he did stand up. If the gleam did remain after the failure of his boat, it was the one in his eyes (if he might indulge; he has nothing better to do), the one that said, *Do what you will, I will fight you to the last.*

2

The dugouts were completed in four days, and the Corps was again under way. It was now mid-July. Lewis noted, without surprise, that elk once more were everywhere. Ahead, he could see where the Missouri entered the first range of the Rockies, and as they toiled toward that point, the mountains grew. It was the identical phenomenon that had made a wolf a horse, a bear a mammoth: a small mountain five miles distant backed off ten as you approached, and tripled in size. The days were now excessively hot along the river, but snow still fell on the peaks that stood between the Corps and the Pacific. *(Who are you, to cross?)* The river was narrower, a hundred yards wide. The current was gentle, but the course so crooked the captains gave up charting every loop and meander. Instead, they took the general course and drew in the snarls by eye. No labyrinth could be more circuitous. *(Who are you, to seek?)* And monstrous hail fell, as it had done thrice during the portage, rocks of ice big enough to knock a man down, bloody his scalp; they were torn along by the wind with such velocity that when they hit the ground and rebounded, they fell again thirty feet off. They mounted up ankle deep, so that when the sun returned a moment afterward, like a theatrical lighting change, the plain sparkled, a dappled gray. The choler of the earth.

Yes, the gleam must still have been there, in some diminished capacity, because much of this shines in Lewis's memory. They passed a cluster of diminutive, deserted booths made of willow brush, and the Indian woman nodded, and Lewis remembered the Minetares called the Snakes *Bad Lodges.* This poor and weak people. The trick was to keep them from retreating. If they heard the hunters' guns, they would suppose it was their enemies. "Ask the woman what her nation's word for *white man* is," Lewis directed Charbono. The answer came back: *tah-ee-bo-nee.*

At last they reached the base of the first range, and after hundreds of miles of plain, there wasn't a hint of piedmont. Flat ground stretched behind, a mountainside stood before. The river flowed out of a gorge, which one might have taken for the gate of a walled city. *(Enter—)* They entered, dragging the canoes over a riffle, and beyond the river flowed peacefully between beige cliffs. Pine trees half-clad the upper slopes. An Indian road skirted the starboard bank. The captains agreed they must send out a party in advance of the sound of the guns. "I want to lead it this time," Clark said.

"Why, of course," Lewis said.

Clark chose Potts, Joseph Fields, and York to accompany him, and they set off up the Indian road, which climbed the mountain wall. It had been dug out in places, indicating more engineering than Lewis would have thought the Sosonees (the Indian woman's word for her people) capable of or willing to undertake. Inching along with the canoes, Lewis watched from below as Clark's party climbed throughout the day and disappeared over the top of the mountain at dusk.

Clark was gone four days. Meanwhile, the Corps pushed, pulled, paddled. Bighorn animals performed their flying ballet on the cliffs above, the stage machinery as hidden as ever. The mountains came closer until, for one stretch of six miles, cliffs rose twelve hundred feet sheer from deep water on either side. Towing or poling being impossible, the men had to paddle for all they were worth against the current, and dusk fell while they struggled. Lewis, looking back, watched the gate close behind them. Finally, in full dark, they came upon a small bottom, and Lewis would have given the men a dram, except they had consumed the last of their spirits celebrating their independence from alcohol on Independence Day. Now they were full citizens of Inner Louisiana, where rivers ran clear, and so did the blood of men. The Sosonees were somewhere in front of them, near, hidden, uncorrupted by whites, and if Lewis still had had ardent spirits, he would have poured them into the river.

The next day the gorge opened out into a bowl several miles across. There was a pile of fresh elk meat on the starboard shore and a note from Clark on a pole. Hanging in the western sky was smoke, which Lewis feared was a signal among the Sosonees to retreat farther into the mountains. The trader Heney at the Mandan villages had said their enemies called them Snakes because they had a talent for disappearing. Slithering away into a hole somewhere.

The river turned south. Hills crowded close again, opened into another valley, closed again. Antechambers; gate after gate. A bad rapid; towropes. Then the Corps emerged into an enormous valley, twelve miles across and stretching upriver as far as they could see. Charbono spoke up. "Wah-zoh say—"

"Who is Wah-zoh?" Lewis said.

Charbono conferred with La Page, who said, "The Snake squaw says she recognizes this country. We're near the three forks."

"Good." Lewis was not going to ask her how many days' travel it was.

On the second day in the valley, they caught up with Clark. His party had ranged far into the hills and found Indian tracks, but no Indians. Clark's feet were a mass of blisters, which he'd opened with his skinning knife. His face was the color of dirty water. Yet when Lewis suggested that the advance tour on the morrow be led by himself, Clark responded in what was, for him, a passion. "No! I can do it."

"Of course," Lewis said. "If that is your—"

"It is."

"Of course, of course."

Lewis picked over this in private. Some irritation still at the iron boat? Well, and why not? Lewis accepted his penance.

In the morning, Clark set off with a new party, and Lewis watched him endeavoring mightily to conceal his limp across the first half mile, until numbness apparently set in. Lewis turned to the boats humbly, gratefully. Now *he* would drag them, while Clark larked.

And it almost *was* dragging, because the Missouri was wide and extremely shallow in this valley, divided into many channels. The men poled up the riffles, the canoe bottoms scraping. Having long since lost their iron sockets, the poles slipped along the rounded stones, so Lewis rummaged out a parcel of gigs and had the men attach them to the pole ends with wire. The makeshift worked, proving that not all of his tinkerer's ideas were farcical. Still, the men's labor was excessive, and Lewis was inspired (humbly, gladly) to forget his epaulet for an hour at a stretch, and take up a pole and push with the rest of them.

"Hold it close in, sir, right along, if you please. Lean as she goes."

"Let's have a song, boys!" Lewis cried. In the evening he wrote in his journal, *I have learned to push a tolerable good pole, in their phrase.*

During the day, they hoisted flags over the canoes to show any Sosonees who might be covertly observing them that they were not Indians. But they saw no one. "Where are they?" Lewis asked of no one in particular. The valley stretched on. The mosquitoes were maddening. There was an endless cloud of gnats that pattered like rain, their bodies accumulating in a black scurf in the eyelashes. Along the shore, prickly pear was a torment. And something new—a species of grass with a hard, pointed seed armed with reversed bristles answering for a barb, and a tough, twisted beard on the opposite end which acted like a screw. The seeds caught in moccasins and leggings and proceeded to burrow inward through leather and flesh with all the determination of animal parasites. Lewis marveled at the simple mechanism, the brute intention. Choler. *I will fight you.*

Sun. Sore eyes. Dropping down dead at night. Seaman howling, biting at the seeds tormenting him. *Where are they?*

And then they came out of another gorge (the large valley had ended somewhere) and the broad handsome plain of the three forks of the Missouri lay before them. The first white men.

At the junction of the middle and the westernmost fork, Lewis found a note from Clark stuck on a pole: he was ascending the western fork and would rejoin the party at this place, unless he found fresh sign of Indians, in which case he would pursue them. He calculated on Lewis following him up the fork, and Lewis (surveying the plain from a high rock) agreed that its direction was the most promising.

A rest was necessary for the men, and Lewis wanted to fix the latitude, so they made camp. At midafternoon, Clark staggered in, fell to the ground by the flagpole, and puked gray foam. He had a high fever. Lewis ordered a brush bower made (the leather lodge being too hot in this weather) and helped carry Clark in. He pulled off his friend's moccasins. His feet were a horror. "These must be bathed at once."

"York!" Clark called.

Outside the bower, Lewis caught the negro's arm as he passed with a basin. "Your master is bilious. He has not had a passage for several days. I have prevailed on him to take a dose of Rush's pills. See to it that you don't forget."

In the morning, Clark couldn't rise, but felt recovered enough to discuss his reconnaissance with Lewis. The two men agreed that the middle and southwest forks were so nearly identical in size that it would be unjust to call either the Missouri. Clark acceded to Lewis's suggestion that they name the three forks after the Secretary of War, Mr. Gallatin, the Secretary of State, Mr. Madison, and the President. Naturally, Mr. Jefferson's name would adorn the southwest fork, which the captains intended to ascend, and which would form a part (unless Lewis erred grievously) of the transcontinental water passage. Clark said he had gone up the Jefferson twenty-five miles, then crossed to the Madison and descended. At no point had he seen any fresh sign of Indians.

Lewis left Clark to rest in his booth ("York!") and stood by the water, looking at the mountains in the west. Slithering away. Gate after gate had closed behind them. Game in these mountains would shortly grow scarce. Snow would come sooner than he had calculated on. If they did not find the Snakes, the successful issue of their voyage would be in doubt. Or to frame it in plain speech: they might all die here. Immediately after which, the Snakes would come out of hiding to strip them.

Lewis contemplated how it would appear to the people back east. Captains Lewis and Clark and their Corps of Discovery departed from the Mandan villages on April 7th, 1805, and were never seen again. A few remains of a flooded cache were discovered years later at the base of the Great Falls. A compass floated down the river and was recovered by the Minetares, who viewed it with religious veneration. A fur trapper in 1840 found a note on a pole, partially effaced by weather: *Meet me at—* No trace of journals was ever recovered. A year after the captains' mysterious disappearance, the Snakes began a war of conquest against the Blackfeet and the Minetares, wielding the best arsenal in the west.

"Charbono! Fetch me your woman."

She came up to him a pace behind her man, face lowered, so that as usual his view was of the top of her head. Which was not particularly expressive. He found himself irritated. "Ask her—*questionnez elle*—oh for God's sake! Where is La Page?" But once he had La Page in place, Lewis hesitated over how to put the question. *God damn your skulking bastard relatives, where are they?* "This is her people's country, is it not?"

The answer came back: Yes.

"I understand her people range over a wide area."

She gave a dull glance at Charbono, but offered up no response.

Badly phrased. "They range on both sides of the continental divide, isn't that right? Say something about waters flowing toward sunrise and sunset, La Page, you know how they talk."

Yes.

"And are they usually on *this* side, at this time of the year, or on the other side?" A simple enough question.

"She says, sometimes yes, sometimes no."

"La Page. I understand they are a roving nation. I fully understand that, *like the buffalo,* their whereabouts are maddeningly unpredictable. But surely she can drop us a little hint, a little word to the wise, about likelihood? Even nomads have *habits.* When she was a little girl, and it was July—not July, how to—when the sun was so high—when the currants were ripe—good God, these people need a calendar!—however you say it, *where was she*?"

This provoked an unusually long answer. Some pointing. Lewis was struck again by her tiny hands. A pickpurse's fingers. Her face lifted for a moment to glance in a direction. That straight severe nose. That effacement of expression. "She is describing her capture by the Minetares. She says it happened here."

Lewis exhaled. "Of course, that was not my question."

"I know, sir."

She was still speaking to Charbono. A regular harangue.

"However, it is not without interest. Tell me what she is saying."

That evening (sitting in the open, before dusk, feeding the mosquitoes), Lewis wrote,

> Our present camp is precisely on the spot that the Snake Indians were en-
> camped at the time the Minetares of the Knife River first came in sight of
> them five years since. From hence they retreated about three miles up Jef-
> ferson's River and concealed themselves in the woods, the Minetares pur-
> sued, attacked them, killed 4 men, 4 women, a number of boys, and made
> prisoners of all the females and four boys, <u>Sah-cah-gar-we-ah</u> our Indian
> woman was one of the female prisoners taken at that time; tho' I cannot dis-
> cover that she shows any emotion of sorrow in recollecting this event, or of
> joy in being again restored to her native country; if she has enough to eat and
> a few trinkets to wear I believe she would be perfectly content anywhere.

An observation perhaps equally true of her people, since Lewis had never got a clear answer regarding their accustomed whereabouts. Or had she been deliberately withholding information? There was another theory Lewis had heard from someone—was it Gravelines?—that these people were called Snakes because they were liars. (The Minetares had a colorful way of signing a lie; they indicated words coming out of the mouth and going in two directions; one could conceivably see a snake's tongue as a reification of this principle.) Perhaps she was in cahoots with them. Waiting.

Yes (he recalls, wondering if the rain might be stopping), he was angry. Because he was anxious, of course. Thirty men's lives on his hands. But he was also happy. He feels sure of that. He had done his penance for Clark, and he was five gates deep into the Rocky Mountains, and now he would conquer them, or disappear from the earth in the attempt. Who would not have been happy?

Other things rise before his mind, from those last days of searching. He recalls the berries that grew in incredible profusion in the upper valleys, red, yellow, purple, and black currants, gooseberries and serviceberries, superior in flavor and size to any variety in the east, whole hillsides colored like sunset. He and his little party (he'd gone ahead again to look for the Snakes) foraged through the bushes like bears, feasting, and it reminded him of his boyhood on a lazy summer's day, the gummy smell of berries wrinkling in the hot sun, and that made him think of the Indian woman again, because she had mentioned she was picking berries when the Minetares attacked. Mostly women and children killed, Lewis had noted, and none of the prisoners were men. The braves no doubt jumped on their horses and fled, leaving their dependents to shift for themselves. Lewis had heard of that despicable behavior among the Indians. The girl picking berries, the approaching enemy descried, the march to the woods, the men absconding, the arrow through her cheeks. Berry juice and blood on her leather smock. Dragged up on a horse. God knows what kind of violation. She might have picked up her venereal right then.

He recalls another gate and another valley (*come farther*), and the Jefferson forking into three parts (*choose*), and Clark behind with the boats, and the streams barely navigable now, almost all riffles and stones sticking up in lines clean across. One hundred yards wide; sixty yards; forty yards. Even Charbono could wade across now without gross mishap. And yet the flat valleys kept opening before them. This unimpressive creek kept dwindling into the distance under the broiling sky, snowy peaks in every direction. Lewis was forced to concede: this was a geography he did not understand. And its inhuman size had begun to—what was the word—oppress him? Perhaps even frighten. The foraging for berries, the pack on his back, the water he exclusively drank, that hint of fright; it was indeed like being a boy again, on the most glorious tramp, at that shivery moment when you first wonder if you have gone too far. And the phrase beat in his head with the swing of his stride, *too far, too far,* and he began for the first time to doubt the water passage whose doom he, like an emperor, was to pronounce, thumb up or down. Yet he clung to his foolish hopes. He had never known a river to penetrate so far into mountainous country without falls or major rapids. Some engineering would be required; removing stones, cutting through meanders. And they could use iron-framed boats sealed with imported pitch that floated like perfect corks—

He waited for Clark to catch up, who now had a boil on his ankle that Lewis opened and drained. Clark could not walk, so Lewis set out ahead once more. The Indian woman had recognized a rock outcropping and declared they were close to the creek's headwaters, where her people would be, or just over the divide, and Lewis determined not to return without a Snake if it took him a month. And still no sign of them, not even smoke, and another gate, and another fork, and suddenly, everywhere, there were rattlesnakes, but for some reason there was not a ring of fire, nor a three-headed dog. At last it was mid-August, and Lewis was heading up a valley some ten miles long, and the creek was a dozen yards wide (by no stretch of the imagination navigable) and the grass was tall, and there was an infinitude of grasshoppers. His party was trying to rediscover an Indian road that had disappeared, Drewyer searching a few hundred yards to his right, Shields away on his left, McNeal directly behind him, and Lewis looked up and saw, two miles distant, a figure on a horse walking down the valley toward him. Clapped his glass to his eye— sacklike tunic open at the neck—hair loose and unornamented—darker and shorter than a Minetare—the bridle a string tied around the horse's jaw—no saddle or gun.

"Oh, McNeal," Lewis breathed, "I believe we have discovered the gentlemen."

Lewis walked on at the same pace; the figure kept coming. When they were a mile apart, the horseman stopped. Lewis stopped. Lewis lowered his pack and took out his blanket. He flung it above his head and brought it to earth three times. *Come, sit, smoke.* The horseman did not move. He was looking right and left, toward Drewyer and Shields, who were still advancing. Lewis dared not signal to them; it would have looked suspicious. He could only hope they would gather their pennysworth on their own and stop.

They did not. "McNeal, take my gun and pouch." Lewis pulled from his pack the first trinkets that came to hand. A card of beads, a looking glass, a length of red ribbon. He stepped forward, holding the items in front of him. *We are white men. See.* Lewis was unarmed. The horseman had his bow, his quiver of arrows. *There is no danger.* The horseman had his *horse,* for God's sake. *I am a friend.* Three hundred paces. Lewis could see the fringe on the Indian's tunic. Two hundred paces.

The horseman turned his mount away, urged it into a walk. Lewis raised the red ribbon. "Tab-ba-bone!" he called. White man! But the Indian glanced again to left and right. Drewyer and Shields were still walking forward, in some witless amaze. Lewis, extremely vexed, risked a hand signal. Drewyer stopped. The Indian had reached the creek. On the opposite side was a willow brake. He turned his horse again, and appeared to wait. One hundred and fifty paces. *Please.* Lewis elevated the looking glass. "Tab-ba-bone!" He turned up his sleeve. *White skin.* One hundred paces. The Indian's nose was a straight severe line. His black eyes looked to the left. Shields was still coming on like a sleepwalker.

In a flash, the Indian whipped his horse about, leaped the creek, and disappeared into the brush. Lewis froze. He stared intently at the brake. Not a sign; not a sound. Then he saw the horseman galloping up a hill about three miles distant.

"Good *God,* man!" Lewis shouted, turning on Shields. "If I could have dropped you where you stood!"

And staring at the rain (which is not stopping), Lewis is not entirely sure he would not have done it, if he'd been holding his rifle. *For wrath killeth the foolish man.* Certainly it would have been an exquisite pleasure.

But no. Man is not born unto such pleasure. *Man is born unto trouble, as the sparks fly upward.* Saith the text.

And Lewis remembers the following day. At the western end of the valley, he found a large Indian road, running from the northeast toward the southwest along the base of the hills. There were two isolated rocks with high perpendicular faces on either side of the creek, for no discernible geological reason that Lewis could deduce. However, the literary reason was obvious: this was the final gate. The Missouri was five yards wide. Lewis breakfasted with his men on the last of the venison, and they followed the Indian road southwest for five miles along the base of the hills, at which point the main stream abruptly turned west and penetrated the hills through a narrow bottom. The Indian road followed it.

"This is it, boys," Lewis said. "I verily believe we will taste the waters of the Columbia today."

They turned into the little valley. Pretty green hills, pines on the upper slopes.

Lewis saw a strange animal. Drewyer fired, and hit it, knocking it down. But unaccountably, it sprang up again and disappeared. They found no blood at the spot.

Lewis hiked on. The more he mulled over his brief glimpse, the more he felt sure that the animal had been of the same kind as the one that had crouched leopardlike before him in the dusk of that enchanted day alone with the bear. His daimon. *Come on.* Up a crease. The creek was a yard wide, and McNeal stood crowing, a foot planted on either bank. Half a mile below the pass, they reached the fountain of the Missouri: three inches across, bubbling up, pure and cold. They drank.

And now Lewis could not resist another run. "Race you, boys!" Rifle in one hand, espontoon in the other, he was a spark flying upward. *I am at the headwaters of the Missouri.* The ground pounding beneath; grass and gravel; swollen wild rose hips. *You, Lewis, are our last hope.* The Minetares had told him what he would see: open and level plains descending toward the Pacific. He rose, and the ridgeline dropped, and Lewis won the race (probably Drewyer let him), and consequently he was the discoverer of the perfidy of the Minetares, of the immense ranges of mountains still to the west, their summits shining with snow.

Fourth Clark

Watching Janey swing Pomp in the skin lodge, singing to him under her breath, *ohh-wayy ohh,* it reminded Clark of home, of nephews and nieces at family gatherings where he got to play the big brother, here comes Uncle Billy!, hanging from his neck, riding his back. In this desert of toil, what a comfort it was to see.

She used cattail down to keep Pomp dry. It came out in matted balls, hairy-like, which she sniffed like a mother cat before tossing away. When she didn't have cattail, she pulverized buffalo chips. Clark could hardly believe his eyes, the first time he saw it.

Picking through his hair, crunching what she found. Greasing him. Gathering feet and hands all together between her hands and releasing them, *ohh-way!,* and his laugh. She played a sort of cat's cradle with sinew, showing the patterns to Pomp and saying something in her language, and then she could be any girl, white, black, or red.

Did white women nurse so often? Clark woke in the night and listened to the wet suckling, and her singing so quiet he wasn't sure he heard it.

Walking with that little drinking basket she'd woven reversed on her head, keeping the sun off, her bier on her back. If Clark was behind, he would have Pomp's two coal eyes fixed on him as though he was the most interesting thing in ten miles, which in this barren country maybe he was. In front, Clark would turn to see if she needed help when she struggled up a slope, Pomp invisible, but the top of the bier making a circle behind her head with the red triangles she'd painted on it, so big on her it seemed she was strapped to the board as much as her baby was. He admired her toughness. Her pace was three to his two, but she put one foot after another, and if she ever complained, only Shabono heard it.

Clark thought of Judith, of Martha. He was reminded of his delayed prospects. If you come back alive, Jonathan said, they'll make you a colonel, and the first thing Colonel Clark would do was get himself a wife and beget himself a family and lie awake at night and listen to his own wife suckle his own children in his own house. His days of living like an internant monk would be at an end.

The torments of the body. The human weakness Lewis lacked. Her darkness and lack of modesty reminded Clark of the negresses he'd had. He welcomed the day's exhaustion, even the sicknesses, they dulled the edge of desire. But he would dream of dandling Pomp, and Janey leaning into him, laughing, and laughing shrugging off her tunic, her breasts snuggling into his hands, and it was curious that the contrast between those pretty baubles and the ugly scars on her face screwed the pitch of his desire higher, and she with a carefree wanton look reaching down to put her hand on his jack, and he urging her back on the buffalo robe, spreading her willing legs, and he'd wake in the severest discomfort, and hear in the dark that wet suckling and her low singing half like breathing.

Living like a monk in Babylon. He remembered pushing her up the slope when the ravine flooded, his hand on her haunch. Not that he thought of anything at the time but getting them out alive. And anger at himself for not having seen the danger. And the result was, a good compass washed away. She sat at the top looking dazed from fright and Pompy bawling, and Clark hurried them back to camp to get them warm, at least he'd saved them when the moment came. And she barely over her sickness. He'd feared a relapse.

The squaw dies, Lewis had said at Fort Mandan, and you and I are up all night feeding Pomp buffalo milk. He hadn't said who'd go fetch it! And there she'd lain in a stupor (that was before the ravine), her pulse barely discernible, Pomp howling from hunger, her fingers twitching in a way that made Clark anxious. He'd bled her twice, but she only sank further. York held Pomp to her breast and the poor little fellow suckled while his mother's head lolled. She'd complained of pelvic pain, and Clark applied a poultice to her womanly parts, or should he say girlish parts, those tender regions, and he thought it was probably gonorrhea, acquired from her husband, the old Priapus probably couldn't count the squaws he'd had. It angered Clark, this good girl's suffering, while the man who'd infected her showed no ill effects, and meanwhile petitioned Clark to return to the Mandan villages, as though it was the Voyage of Discovery that was killing her, and not his pot-stirring prick. And loyal little Janey refusing to take medicine from Clark's hands, only from her roving husband's. But then, she also took from Lewis's hands, when he arrived. Clark didn't know why, she seemed in the main afraid of Lewis.

Lewis was of the opinion it wasn't gonorrhea, but an obstruction of her menses as a consequence of taking cold. Lewis was the better doctor, Clark would never say nay, but Clark had been around infants much of his life, and he had a suspicion from certain private signals his sisters made that nursing itself obstructed the menses. Whatever the cause, Janey started to improve almost from the moment Lewis touched her. He prescribed oil of vitriol and sulfur water, and checked her pulse every half hour until the crisis passed. Then she was up, and before either Clark or Lewis knew what she was about, she was out foraging for prairie apples, and ate too many, and Lewis reprimanded Shabono, but really, none of them had thought she would be active so soon.

She was tough, that was certain.

And . . . Clark sometimes had to ask himself whether he admired her toughness, or envied it. It was small of him. But the envy was there.

At least, if not of her, certainly of Lewis. And the irritation Clark had felt toward his undeserving friend was due at heart, he felt sure, to this.

He'd first felt a prick of annoyance at the mouth of Maria's River, when they were unsure which course to follow, and Clark had headed a party up what he and Lewis thought was the Missouri, while Lewis ascended the other fork. He and Lewis had agreed they'd explore for a day and a half. Clark had turned back on time, but Lewis had gone on for another day; he'd already determined the river wasn't the Missouri, but he'd gone on because he wanted to see how far north it went. He'd gone on merely to satisfy his curiosity. He'd gone on with his little party deep into Blackfoot country, and only his luck had preserved them.

Now if Clark had continued an extra day—yes, if he had, he would have discovered the Great Falls of the Missouri. He'd turned back only ten miles short. Yes, it was not annoyance at heart, but envy. Envy. It had to be faced. The Corps turned up the Missouri, and Lewis went ahead and discovered the falls. Lewis went ahead, even though he had dysentery, and Clark was healthy. And Clark's anger should have been directed at himself, since it was probably true that Lewis with dysentery could cover more ground most days than Clark could in his best health. So Lewis went ahead and discovered the falls, and then went farther, all by himself—this rashness he was capable of, Clark hadn't forgotten the circumstances under which he first met the young hothead—and would have been killed by that bear except for, once more, his enormous luck. He seemed to carry a sack of it with him.

Envy of his strength, envy of his luck. Nothing but envy. A dastardly sin. Clark must root it out. For one thing, it was the height of foolishness to resent the luck of his commander, since the success of the enterprise depended on it. But Clark had to face the fact that he found his friend, at times—what was the word— (Lewis would be able to tell him.) Overawning. Which was entirely Clark's fault.

History would call this the Lewis Expedition. Because Lewis was the captain, and Clark was his lieutenant. Envy, yes. This was the little brother squalling in him, saying, Lewis is the younger man, Lewis was my subordinate. This was the little brother stamping his feet and saying, It's not fair!

And none of it Lewis's fault. And consider his generosity. When Clark requested (of his commander) that he lead the advance party, after the falls, to find the Snake Indians, Lewis said yes. It was Clark's body that failed him. He remembered the miles of shattered flint they had to cross in the high country. He remembered pulling the prickly pear barbs out of his feet one night with a pair of pliers. He'd brought along York to help him, and then York tired out faster than he did. Clark remembered sitting by the campfire yanking out the barbs and angrily counting them and upbraiding York in the harshest terms for being unfit, fat, lazy. Seventeen.

The torments of the body. He limped into his last camp and waited for Lewis, and when Lewis saw how he was, naturally he proposed they switch places. His commander, on paper; his word, law. But Clark wouldn't have it. He couldn't bear the thought. The horse was galloping off without him, he would not let his body— He would punish it— He spoke harshly to his commander. Lewis responded as his friend. Clark would never forget that—how Lewis, despite his doubts and the importance of the mission, despite his right of command, bowed to what Clark wanted, without a moment's hesitation.

And punish his body Clark did, pushing his new party on, mile after mile, over mountains, through scorching heat. And his luck held. That is, he found nothing. And his body punished him back. By the end, he was in a fever dream, collapsing at the edge of camp, Lewis approaching at a run.

Clark was determined to give his body a purging such as it had never experienced, and he swallowed not one or two, but five of Rush's Thunderclappers, and the shit and bile and bitterness and green envy poured out of him all night, he shook like a leaf, spraying ugliness everywhere, until in the morning he lay on his bed of rushes damp and weak as a newborn.

And Lewis went ahead once more. Clark stayed with the boats, and the river became so narrow and shoaly that to call it navigable was no more accurate than to call Clark fit. If the Missouri was navigable to its source, as every last trader and Indian said, then the Corps had passed the source some miles back, in the dark, or in the fog of exhaustion. The work of hauling the canoes over the rocks became so bad that the men, for the first time since Fort Mandan, became restive, asking why they couldn't leave this damn creek and go by land. Clark remembered the night he almost had a mutiny on his hands. He urged and cajoled, and even propped his ankle up in view with the boil on it that kept him in such agony, because he knew the men liked him, and he wasn't above playing on their pity.

He agreed with them, but they couldn't cache the canoes before they found Lewis, or a note from him, directing them to do so. Lewis had rejoined them a few days before (having found no Indians), but then Janey had recognized an outcropping and assured the captain and the mock captain that her people and the divide were near, so the real captain had set out again. And *this* time, Clark and Lewis both knew, this time would be the one to succeed, if ever it was going to happen. Clark wrote in his journal, *I should have taken this trip had I have been able to march, from the raging fury of a tumor on my ankle muscle.* He had to ask himself: Whose raging fury?

The torments of the body and the soul. In this desert of toil and dispirit, Clark took what grateful refuge he could in the sight of Janey and Pomp, in thoughts far removed from the Corps of Discovery. By the campfire, unwrapping him from the sling (she'd lost the bier), and shrugging off her leather tunic to take a nipple squirting a thread of milk between two fingers and guide it to Pomp's mouth, then rocking, looking at her baby, a mother, a young girl, and every man in camp no doubt suffering equally all of Clark's baser feelings, but what of his more elevated ones? Thoughts of hearth and home and family and a woman's devotion. When Pomp was sated, she'd set him on the ground in front of her, and he'd look like a little drunken man, his eyes glazed, milk bubbling from his smiling lips, and he would sway and sometimes sink forward from the waist, and Clark would hoot with laughter.

He remembered the day she saw her people again. His ankle was better, but still tender, he was hobbling behind, near the canoes. A small treeless valley. From a hilltop the night before, Clark had seen a fork ahead, and he hoped to find a note from Lewis there, he'd had no account from him since he'd set out with Drewyer and Shields and McNeal eight days before. They'd just started; it was about seven in the morning. Little Janey was a hundred paces in front, trudging next to her husband, putting one foot after the other. And all of a sudden she started to dance. She flung her arms up. She whirled completely around. She was sucking her fingers, and for a moment Clark thought she'd blundered into a hornets' nest, but then he looked where she was pointing, and Indians on horseback came into view. Clark advanced and found that Drewyer was among them, dressed like an Indian. He reported that Lewis had discovered a band of the Snakes on a tributary of the Columbia, about forty miles west of that point, and had returned with a party of them over the mountain, and was waiting for Clark at the fork two miles farther on, with his compliments.

Of course Clark was relieved. His odds of returning home alive now were almost worth a sucker's bet. Maybe there was a spurt of envy, a gurgle of bile, but it was buried in the elation surrounding him, the Indians whooping with delight, and little Janey, little Janey, dancing out her happiness in a transport, and she'd brought Pomp around to her front and was cradling him, and Clark shouted back to the men, if they would just drag those God damned all to hell canoes two more miles, they would be free of them!, and he turned up the valley with Drewyer and the Snakes, and Janey and her kin sang a caterwauling song that sounded like delight and homecoming all the way to Lewis's camp, *ohh-wayy-ohh!*

Oh, he remembered. The next day, his ankle was well enough so he could now lead the advance party, while Lewis stayed behind to barter for horses and move supplies across the divide. Because there *was* a last little bit of something to discover: whether the Snakes were correct in saying the branch of the Columbia they lived on was not passable. And if it wasn't, how to reach the Pacific. In short, the passage.

Clark set out with a party, and on the second day he crossed the divide, and on the third day he reached the stream and the Snake camp Lewis had already been to. On the fourth, he followed the stream down toward the place where the Snakes said it entered the mountains and became impassable, and he came to a fork entering on the left and he saw that the two streams made a handsome river. He camped, and wrote in his journal, *I shall in justice to Capt. Lewis, who was the first white man ever on this fork of the Columbia, call this Lewis's River.*

A louse, a worm: envy.

lost woman

One of the stories this one heard on winter nights as a child, looking at the fire, wrapped in buffalo and the speaker's voice:

Two hunters were sleeping at night under a sticky-tree. A cloud came, and rumbling like thunder, and the young men woke up and saw Bird above them. They shot their arrows, but Bird took them in his claws and flew away toward sunbirth. Bird lived on an island in the water. When he came to the island, he killed one of the hunters. He tore open that one's belly and drank the blood. The other man remembered his knife of Coyote's blackrock. He threw it at Bird's neck. Bird flew up. He flew so high he was a speck, but then he fell. The earth shook when he hit the ground. Bird was dead. The hunter said, —Where will I go? He walked toward smoke and met an old woman. That one was Bird's mother. The hunter said, —I killed Bird. Bird's mother said, —My son was bad, he killed many people. Go and cut off his feathers. The man cut off Bird's feathers. The old woman wove the feathers into a boat. She gathered waterbird eggs and put them in the boat. She put many sticks in the boat. She prepared buckskins and made many pairs of shoes. She said to the hunter, —Now you are going back to your own country. It is a long way. It is dangerous. I will tell the waterboys to help you. The young man paddled away. The waterboys came to him and said, —Water-giant wants to eat you. You must keep a fire going, and he will be afraid. So the hunter kept a fire going with the sticks. The waterboys pushed his boat to shore. There was a sticky-tree, and the waterboys put the hunter high in the tree. During the night Water-giant came out of the water and climbed the tree to eat the hunter, but the waterboys pushed Water-giant down and threw him back in the water. The waterboys told the man he would have to walk for a great distance through country where thorn grew. That one put on many pairs of shoes, one over the other, and walked over the plains of thorn safely. The waterboys told the hunter he would have to pass many rattlesnakes, and must not be afraid. For a whole day, that one walked among snakes, but in the evening they were gone. The waterboys told the hunter he would have to pass through the land of Giant, who eats people. They said Giant would come and tickle him, but he must not laugh or move. When Giant saw the young man, he said, —Here comes man flesh. Giant tickled the young man's nose. He tickled his asshole. He played with the young man's cock and balls. He watched that one closely. The man did not move. So Giant went away. Then the hunter was coming into country like his own. He thought he was near to where people lived. The waterboys told him he would meet the owl-people. He came to a camp. The owl-people had no mouths. He watched them hunt, and when they brought deer back he wondered how they would eat it. They gathered the fat and put it on the fire and breathed in the smell. The young man felt sorry for them. He took his knife and cut open their mouths. There were teeth inside. Their mouths were all bloody, but they were happy. They ate and ate. Now they talked, and the young man could understand some of what they said. He went on, and soon he came to his own country. He stood by the sticky-tree where Bird had caught him and his friend. But his hut was gone. He went on and found some people. They told him that everyone in his family was dead. He went to live with cousins.

Maybe this one would tell that story to out of water when winter came. One of her hairs was wrapped tight around his finger, cutting. She picked at it, bit it. Tasted him all over. Her weakness, her strength, her waterboy. She made new shoes for forest bear and big knife and red hair, sewing the thick skin from a bull's neck on the sole to defeat thorn. Big knife felt the shoes all over. He looked at them closely. He tickled their assholes.

Before the sun-men entered the mountains, big knife made a rich offering to Knife-Metal Man. The other sun-men were making a pain offering, a Sundance, dragging the k'noos over the plain, bleeding, putting their spirits in the hands of Sun.

Big knife spent many days building a knife-metal boat. Enough knife-metal for thirty black weapons, worth thirty horses. Big knife sewed on elk and buffalo skins. He painted the boat black, like a warrior who returns from a raid with scalps. He floated it on the water. Knife-Metal Man lived on the water, the stories said. Maybe sun-men visited him in this kind of boat. Then big knife took the boat out of the water. He sang a mourning song. He cut the boat into pieces and buried it next to the river.

The headcutters and yellowlegs sometimes offered the war-horse of a bigman when he died, this one had heard. But big knife offered thirty horses.

They entered the mountains. This one looked at the sun and at the redberries and yellowberries and at the bow-horn young on the cliffs, and tried to remember when she was a child, and thought the plain of the three rivers was warmward. Big knife and red hair did not ask her. But the river led warmward. Camas flower, one thumb, rides ahead. She sang at night to out of water:

> *ice*
> *stopping the river*
> *come Sun, Father, melt it*
> *water take us to the good land*
> *you came*
> *out of water*
> *you came*

She held the big clear bead red hair had given her and turned it to look at Sun and the small sun was born that made fire. She gave the first bit of food to Sun, when forest bear was not looking. At night she used her firedrill. (Moon could not make fire.) The sun-men burned big fires every night. Wood-eaters, the undergrounders called them. They sat in the smoke and smelled less bad. This one called them salt-eaters. They had a pemmican packed in salt in wooden baskets. Their hunger for salt was like a horse's. When their sweat dried, salt whitened their faces. Salt was like smoking and sun-drying; the salt-pemmican did not rot. Did the salt the sun-men ate and the wood smoke they sat in and Sun who loved them protect them from the Small Man sickness, that rotted we-people, undergounders, headcutters, birds, but not them? Bear-men, wolf-men, horse-men without horses, planters and harvesters of knife-metal, changed-men who made long vows and did not die.

This one was walking ahead, out of water on her back in an undergrounder skin sack. A valley opened. She walked into it. She stopped, turned in a circle. She looked at the mountains on either side.

This one knew: she was two days coldward from the plain of three rivers. Halfway down this valley, flowing from sun-entering, was a stream with banks of white earth where this one had been with her band, digging in the banks for paint. When she was a child. This one sang names in her mouth: camas flower, one thumb, white elk skin, rides ahead, frog jumps in, tree frog.

Five days later, she stood holding out of water squirming at the place along the camp river where shouts broke out and one thumb galloped, pointing backward. She looked where he pointed and saw the turtle rock. She saw the middle river flowing quietly along its base.

She went to the redberry bushes. She eased aside branches, snaked in, stood on the spot. *Touched earth.* Out of water was pulling on a branch. This one picked a berry and offered it to him. He nibbled and spat it out. She picked a handful and ate. *Save her.* They would be sweeter later.

This one looked upriver toward the shed-fur trees she and the others had run to, but those ones were too far away. *Thrashing through, running.* She looked up the slope coldward. Horsemen had ridden down. *How do you think—?* How had this one reached those trees? She walked toward them. Climbs the hill's head came apart. She leaped over him. Did he try to grab her legs? Did she kick? Was it here? She looked up the slope. She wandered, looking in the grass. No shards of bone. No scrap of leather or porcupine thorn. She looked toward the trees, she looked back. Had it happened?

The next morning, big knife told her to come and he looked down at her with his wolf's eyes unsmiling and asked her where she was when bird rider captured her. Why did that one want to know? His power was great. He had made ohwa come. He had driven out her fever ghost. He had fought with Bear alone. He was looking at her closely. She could not look at him. She was only a woman. She had seen the way he looked at birds and plants, turning them over, sniffing. She had seen him run a knife in under a bird's wing and hold it in his hand, watching, counting, while it died. She told him what had happened, wondering if it was true.

At every fork in the river, big knife and red hair talked to Sun with the ring-metal bent pipe, and Sun showed them the way.

The land spoke to this one often now. A stream: sees the morning washed there. Jumps once sneaking up, stone in hand. A camp place: camas flower scolded small frog for too much water in the pot.

We-people did not have metal pots. They carved them out of whitestone or formed them from clay, or wove roots and sealed them with sticky and dropped hot stones in the water to cook the meat. Not much meat. Mealy-root, whiteroot, pebbleroot, snaproot. Goodfish, mountainfish, salmon. Ants, grasshoppers, lizards.

Was one thumb alive? Smells good had seen him gallop up the slope. Maybe protected by a spirit, by Buffalo, that one had flown unseen through the undergrounders riding down. Buffalo plucked him from danger, flew him to the shed-fur trees where thorn saw him ride in.

That small hill: red tongue coming over it with a hare, shaking his bow proudly. Then stick jammer popping up behind with four hares, and frog jumps in and cloud and this one laughing, and red tongue angry. Stick jammer and cloud were dead. Had smells good made it back? And jumps once and thorn? Those ones would be young men now. But drops the robe, changed by a changed-man in the undergrounder village, in five more years he would be a young man, too. He would come back to the tall grass valley, on a raid with undergrounders.

Two bears telling a story in the grass hut in winter. This one and small frog and small wolf wrapped in buffalo, listening.

Two bears and small frog and small wolf were dead. But her mother camas flower might be alive, and one thumb, who talked to her and showed her things, and her mother's brother fools eagle and her sister small moon, and rides ahead, and her father's younger brother white elk skin and his sister frog jumps in. And sees the morning, who died and lived again, and red tongue, who named her walks slow, and grass eater and spotted frog, who were younger and followed this one around, and crow flying who told stories and whose shoulder hurt him, and black cheek who chased this one and hit her with a rock and once burned her with a stick from the fire.

The land spoke again. Rattlesnakes. There were not many of those ones in undergrounder country. Red hair danced away from one that rose from a rock crack. This one almost stepped on one. But they got through the rattlesnakes safely.

This one was walking ahead each day, not wanting to wait for the k'noos, but that was the vow, so she waited. In the morning she walked ahead again, forest bear keeping her in sight, keeping close, thinking (this one thought) she might run away. Duck behind rock, touch earth, throw looks around, creep over mountain. Rides ahead, see! camas flower, hide!

—More firestick than small serpent people dream of, forest bear said again. —They soon paddle old serpent k'noo with firestick, you see. They use firestick for knife and spoon.

This one was walking ahead, forest bear keeping close, when she saw the we-people. Oh! This one jumped. A far-walking scout with news, a bird-stolen hunter returned! Foolish thoughts! *I am!* she cried, and they called back in we-people, words filling her like water, *you are,* and she turned toward red hair, who was walking an arrowshot behind, and signed that these were her people, she sucked nipple-fingers, she licked off the last smear of root stew when you reached into the pot, racing brothers and sisters. And the horsemen came around her and red hair was hurrying forward.

I am—
You are—
I was—
Who are—?
Walks slow—
Who is—?
Two bears' daughter—

This one recognized one of the men, a boy now a man, cut lip, and another, older, eagle tail. It was her own band, tall grass! —Camas flower? this one asked. They were off their horses, their faces bony and shining with starvation, their eyes owl-like staring, their hair cut short in mourning, and red hair had come up, and one of the horsemen was droor, dressed like a we-people warrior (so her band had been afraid of a trap, they had changed skins with the sun-men), and droor was shaking hands with red hair and signing, and the tall grass men were singing now, thanking Father and each his own spirit and vowing an offering, and hugging red hair, rubbing cheek to cheek, the undergrounders did not do that and red hair looked startled, his breath came out and red grease was on his cheek. They turned up the stream, and red hair's clawth hat with the strange hairy feather was off and eagle tail was touching his hair and exclaiming, and another man was looking at the strange feather and cut lip was asking, —Where is the black sun-man? Droor was waving them forward and forest bear was keeping close and murmuring, — Small bird do what old forest bear say, serpent people get plenty— The singing was settling, finding spirit voice, falling true like feet as they walked

> *sun-men come!*
> *thanks!*
> *black weapons come!*

This one had out of water in her hands and her own language in her ears and her face on fire and she came close to eagle tail, who was older, father's younger sister's son had taken a woman from his family (but she had not been a good wife), and asked, —Is camas flower alive?

That one looked up from a piece of red clawth that red hair must have given him. —No.

Camas flower was killed on the day this one was captured. Caught at the root place, dragged behind a horse, axed. One thumb was also killed, and sees the morning, and frog jumps in.

It was smells good who told this one. This one had recognized her among the we-people at the stream fork, when red hair's group came up singing. While tall grass men tied shells from the bad-tasting water in red hair's hair to call on spirit for friendship, smells good stepped forward and took this one in her arms. This one cried. Out of water squirmed and yelled and was brought around, and smells good looked at his skin and said, —Like dirty ash!

—The father is a sun-man, this one said. The words sounded good in her ears. Sun-woman, sun-child. Then smells good told her about camas flower, and she cried again. And she cried also for one thumb, who talked to her and showed her things. His buffalo spirit had not saved him. And sees the morning, who died and lived and died again. And frog jumps in, who had come back alive from the hardskins to be scalped by the undergrounders.

And all the people with hair cut short. —There was a raid in the grass moon, smells good said. —The hardskins killed twenty. And before last winter. The raids are worse than ever.

—Good small birdwife, forest bear said, appearing beside her, pulling her away. —Give bop-teest to serpent friend, robe chief want you *tootsweet*, time earn all those bad-smelling firestick.

This one walked into the brush shade, the council, the place of men and smoke, looking down, and sat in the circle on the empty robe. Lifting her eyes a little she saw: big knife and red hair and the tall grass men sitting on thin pronghorn, not warm buffalo. And: shoes taken off for the council, which is what we-people did. And: big knife wearing a we-people collar-robe and red hair with shells in his hair, and the tall grass speaker wearing big knife's clawth hat with the strange hairy feather. And: the tall grass speaker was this one's brother, rides ahead.

Oh! This one jumped up and threw the pronghorn around we-both and hung on rides ahead and wailed and thanked and sang grief for her long thoughts of his death, as spirit said a sister should, and she felt his short hair against her fingers and cried more, wondering whether it was brother or father who had died, and she cried for the starvation in his face. Rides ahead was a good brother (he was the son of two bears' younger brother, white elk skin, five or six winters older, a man already when this one was a child, not often speaking to her, but protecting her from black cheek and sometimes taking her up on his horse), and as a brother and a man should, he accepted her tears and let himself be fondled and hung on, and thanked for, keeping back his own tears, and his words. He said only, calmly, in the man's way (the ant-sting of hunger on his breath), —Walks slow, small mother, scar cheeks. We thought you were lost.

That council was short. The big council took place after straight-sun, after the k'noos had arrived with gifts. This one sat again on the pronghorn in the brush shade with a sun-man windcatcher stretched above, and big knife stood in his war clothes with the rows of metal suns and the tuft of shining hair on one shoulder and the big knife in his belt curving down past his knee. He spoke onglay. Rides ahead listened, and red tongue, and broken nose, and twelve other men. None of them had been speakers when this one was a child.

Between the councils, this one had learned more from smells good. Rides ahead's father, two bears' younger brother, white elk skin, had been killed by the hardskins in the grass moon. Two bears' sister frog jumps in's older daughter, grass eater, was killed in the same raid. So was camas flower's younger sister, small moon, and her ohwa was found beneath her, with her throat cut. Camas flower's older brother, fools eagle, had been killed in a blackshoe raid a winter ago. Black cheek had died of a fever ghost three winters ago. The winter before that, frog jumps in's younger daughter, spotted frog, had fallen off a horse on her head and died. Crow flying had made a vow to avenge the death of fools eagle and led a raid on the blackshoes, and he and the three tall grass men who went with him never came back and the shaved heads said later those ones had been ambushed and killed coldward from their country. Jumps once and thorn had not come back from the birds.

This one sat on the pronghorn in the shade, looking at the middle of the circle, where the grass had been torn out to make fire for smoking before the speaking, but it was ashes now. *Dirty ash.* The speaker's voice in her ears was big knife's.

This one died.

She turned her head away. —No. She talked back in her mouth to spirit. —You lie. The others died.

Big knife was speaking. Who was left of all her family? Rides ahead. And wolf tooth's older son, bowhorn bow. But he had run off with another man's wife and was living with the twoleaf people.

And out of water? this one asked spirit. Would out of water die soon?

Foolish person!

Now labeesh was speaking frahsay to forest bear. The others had died. And the ones left were starving, and all the tall grass men had only four black weapons, and no *bals* or black weapon powder to feed to them. White feather was still alive. He had stood in front of this one and turned to others and reminded all that he had given two horses for her when she was a child. And what had he received? Nothing. And now here was a woman with a sunman's child, and white feather had two other wives who gave him enough trouble (laughter), so he did not want her, but what about his two horses, what would the sun-man give him to show that he was not a man to be ignored? Others spoke against this. They said the sun-man had not stolen her, and must already have paid for her. If white feather wanted payment, he should go demand it of the undergrounders, they would not ignore him (laughter). White feather went off grumbling.

Forest bear was speaking to this one: —Frown say he and red hair come visit serpent children from seventeen big-knife tribe, big father live in bad-smelling big hut in so big village you not believe, on great water toward going-up sun where so many big-knife people live they like tree in forest, stupid robe chief always say that, he mean like grass on plain, he mean so many big-knife people, serpent people eye fall out of head. He and red hair want find best road to big water over mountain, need horse for bag, all what-all they carry, if serpent children help, trade horse for this-that, like bead, like coat, you know, good bird, say good, but not say firestick, frown and red hair say not got enough—if serpent children help, frown and red hair tell big robe father in big village serpent children good children, more robe come soon, bring so many good, make pile big like whole serpent camp, pot, ax, what-all, they bring so many firestick serpent children not believe, robe chief talk about make peace with minitadi, groh vant, what you call them, people who live in ground, make peace between all redskin tribe, but that load crap, you know, good bird, you say they get plenty firestick and no more hide like hare in mountain, eat root and berry, but go where buffalo, groh vant or pi-ay nwah show up, serpent children take out firestick, surprise!, shoot they bad-smelling ass off, say that.

After the council, big knife gave rides ahead one of the white-metal sun-disks with the face of Grayees-peert carved on it, and rides ahead thought the face was alive and pushing out from inside, she could see he was frightened, but he hid it. Big knife gave smaller disks to red tongue and broken nose. He also gave rides ahead a sun-man war-shirt with rows of metal suns, and red clawth leggings, and a knife-metal knife.

We-people were looking at the k'noos and the flat sticks and the wind-catching clawth. They were touching york and seemen. Big knife shot the black weapon that didn't need powder and made fire with one of the clear beads and held the black sucking rock that sucked the floating needle. People shouted. Red tongue had walked off angry because he had not got a war-shirt like rides ahead. Rides ahead was pleased with his knife-metal knife. Most of the we-people knives were made of Coyote's blackrock. Smells good was holding something. —It's like hard water! Sometimes it shows my face!

—Yes, this one said. *(How do you think—?)* —It is a kind of metal. The sun-men call it *loo-keen*.

The sun-men cooked undergrounder corn, and the band crowded hungrily. They thought it was sun-man food. They jostled to wipe the last smears from the metal pots.

Smells good was now jumping fish, because five winters ago when the undergrounders attacked, she had run into the river at the shoal place, trying to escape, and people had seen her, and they said she looked like a fish jumping through the water.

—You were caught that way, too? this one asked.

—I don't remember, jumping fish said. —I must have been.

Rides ahead was called holds black weapon. Because when big knife had first come to the camp by the salmon stream, he had asked we-people to come with him over the mountain to meet red hair on the other side. Many did not want to go. They thought this sun-man was a friend of the hardskins or the blackshoes, and was leading the tall grass band into a trap. But rides ahead and the brave ones went, and big knife said red hair would be waiting at the stream fork below the mountain, and there would be gifts, and a man all black with curly hair. But when they came to where they could see the stream fork, they saw no one. The tall grass people were uneasy. Red tongue said to rides ahead, —The sun-man has tricked us. But big knife handed his black weapon to rides ahead, and droor signed that big knife said rides ahead could shoot big knife with his own black weapon if this was a trap. So big knife became gives black weapon, and rides ahead became holds black weapon.

But it was not a gift, and when red hair came up, gives black weapon took his black weapon back.

Red hair was come and smoke. Because gives black weapon and holds black weapon waited for him at the river fork, and some of the people still thought it was a trap, but gives black weapon said, —He will come and smoke. And he came and smoked.

Gives black weapon and come and smoke called holds black weapon does not walk. Because when gives black weapon first met holds black weapon, he demanded, in the testing sun-man way, the gift of holds black weapon's name. Holds black weapon (who was still rides ahead) looked at this strange-eater with skin like ash, who might be a friend of the blackshoes and hardskins, and he said nothing. He got back on his horse. So red tongue said, —His name is does not walk.

This one was lost woman.

After sun-entering, in the dusk, this one went down to the stream below the fork. She cut off her hair. She made four cuts in each thigh and four cuts in each arm. She stood in the water and her mourning blood spread out like a thin robe, and was pulled into a red ribbon, and stretched and tore downstream.

This one watched gives black weapon trade for horses. For three good horses, he traded one sun-man war-coat, one pair of leggings, six small pieces of bright clawth, three small knives, six metal arrowheads, and three loo-keens. In the undergrounder villages, a good horse was worth a black weapon and a hundred bals and powder, plus three times what big knife gave. But the tall grass people were pleased with this trade.

The morning after the council, come and smoke and this one and forest bear and some of the sun-men and most of the tall grass people left the river fork and went up the valley toward the pass to the salmon stream. Holds black weapon had agreed to try to bring more we-people across the mountain with horses to help the sun-men move their baskets.

The tall grass was all around this one, up to her waist. It began at the stream fork and leaped in patches to the mountain foot a day away. Oh! The smell of the grass in the morning sun! No bottom or plain of the undergrounders had so strong a smell. Holds black weapon brought his horse beside her as she walked. —Is it true the sun-men don't have black weapons to trade?

—I think it is.

—What is in all those baskets?

—Gives black weapon had a dream, and the others are following it. They are following Sun. They have vowed to take a hard way from where the Sun is born to where it enters. Some of the baskets are filled with heavy things to make the way harder. Others have gifts for strange-eaters. And gives black weapon chooses his dream plants and birds to fill other baskets. That one is making a— This one had wanted to say clan bundle, but that was an undergrounder word. We-people did not have clan bundles. —He is making a power bag, a large one, not only for him, but for all the sun-men.

—But how could that one carry this bag?

—He can't. That's why he asks for horses.

Holds black weapon rode silently for a few moments.

—The undergrounders have something like this, this one said.

He was still silent. Then he said: —We will give them good horses for black weapons. The sun-men trade black weapons to our enemies.

—These ones are not the sun-men the birds talk about. They did not trade any black weapons to the undergrounders, even though they stayed with those ones all winter.

—They are like the mountain sun-men, then. We always get the wrong sun-men.

—But they say they will bring black weapons later.

Another silence. Out of water was asleep on this one's back. The turn in the path here, the arrow-tree brake beyond. Her childhood. Holds black weapon spoke again: —What did the undergrounders say about these sun-men?

This one had heard it said in her undergrounder village that the big knives were all fools. Except for the one who fixed black weapons, and the other one who made war axes. —I don't know, this one said.

Come and smoke had confused his name—kimma pahu'i—with the name does not walk—kimmia-wa'it. He thought that holds black weapon (whose name, he thought, was does not walk) had made him a gift of his own name, to make those-both name-brothers. So as the sun-men and the tall grass people headed for the salmon stream pass, come and smoke kept calling himself does not walk, and it made the tall grass people laugh in their mouths, because he was walking. Just where the valley ended and the climb to the pass began, a tall grass man (red tongue's father's sister's husband, but this one could not remember his name) was coming along the other road from coldward with two mules. He shouted to meet sun-men, and hugged them all, singing thanks.

—Hear the sun-man speaker's name, holds black weapon said.

Come and smoke turned to him and said, —Does not walk, while everyone looked serious. The tall grass man looked at come and smoke's feet, and everyone laughed. Then he offered one of his mules to ride. Come and smoke gave the man a sun-man shirt. He climbed on the mule. From then on, all the tall grass people called him does not walk.

Camped in the cold night, wrapped in pronghorn, this one told holds black weapon stories about the strange things she had seen: the earth huts of the undergrounders, the animal clans, the cuttings and stabbings of the Sundance, the trading fairs where birds brought three hundred horses and took away three hundred black weapons, the fields of corn, the yellow oily berries big as ohwas growing on vines, the frahsay sun-men traders, their sleds and dogs and metal pots piled high, the dog feasts, the onglay sun-men dragging the great wooden boat as big as a hill, the black weapon as big as a log, the footraces across ice floes to catch drowned buffalo. She took out the neck pouch she kept in her shirt and tipped the small hard pebble in her hand. She had dreamed about giving it to camas flower. —This is what sun-men eat in their country.

He put it in his mouth. She saw in his face her own astonishment.

—They call it shoo-gah, she said.

Holds black weapon was silent for a while. The stars had been brightening ever since this one left the undergrounder villages, and now they blazed. —I would like to live where people eat such things, her brother said.

He was silent now for a long time. When he spoke again, his voice was quiet and sad. —But I think some of what you say you are making up.

They passed over the mountain and across the lower slopes. This one knew every stream and root place and berry bush. From the top of a hill, she saw the camp by the salmon stream. Fifty huts. Her band. Only one was a skin hut. The brush huts looked like the wind had blown them here.

Does not walk and the sun-men were welcomed into the camp, but the only food for them was one salmon and a few sharpberry cakes. This one was hugged and cried over by brother's wife's sister's friend's mother. By friend's father's brother's daughter. She felt their short hair and cried. —Ash skin! they said, looking at out of water.

There was another council. Forest bear said, —Red hair talk load of crap again about peace, I skip that part.

Does not walk wanted to know more about the salmon stream. Where it went, and if k'noos could ride it. Holds black weapon drew lines in the ground to show him. He piled up dirt to show the mountains that were too steep to cross. He told does not walk the truth (unlike his sister, who made things up). No tall grass man had ever gone down that stream through those mountains, the water was too rough. But does not walk wanted to see for himself. He asked for a guide, and come down eagle agreed to take him. That old one had been coldward many times to visit friends among the shaved heads.

In the camp, the hunger was bad. This one looked at the dull eyes of the ohwas, the skin stretched and drying on skulls. She smelled the hunger smell. The salmon run had ended. There were only yellowflower seeds and redberries and sharpberries, and the camp had been moving every few nights up the stream, stripping every bush and flower.

Does not walk and the sun-men left after straight-sun to follow the salmon stream. This one and forest bear stayed at the camp. Now holds black weapon tried to persuade more tall grass people to go over the mountain with horses to help gives black weapon move his baskets. —Many said it was a trap, but I went, and the women cried over me and red tongue and broken nose, and we have shown the men who were afraid that it was not a trap. He was wearing the white-metal disk and the sun-man war-coat. But many still did not want to go. Winter was coming. They must hunt buffalo. The tall grass band was supposed to meet the red shell band and one of the twoleaf bands and the shaved heads at the three rivers. Riders said the twoleaf people were headed there already. —But these sun-men will give us black weapons! holds black weapon said.

—But not now, a young man said.

—How do we know they will come back? someone else said.

—The sun-man speaker says if we do not help them now, they will never come back, and they will keep other sun-men from ever bringing us black weapons.

Silence. Holds black weapon added, —And whoever brings horses to them now will be fed by them.

Half of the band agreed to go. In the morning, there was a hard frost on the grass. They set out across the mountain, with fifty horses.

In the cold night on the mountain, wrapped in thin pronghorn, huddling, she slipped her nipple into out of water's mouth.

Come Sun, Father, melt it
take us to a good land

She stroked his hair. *Ash skin.* The others had died. But not out of water. No! He had lost his birthcord. Wasn't that spirit saying he would grow into a man? That he would wander? He would not starve, he would never be found with his throat cut under this one's body after a raid.

Back at the stream fork, even the sun-men were having trouble finding game. Forest bear said their corn was running out. But droor and feelds went out early with their black weapons and gives black weapon said he had sent them far away, and they returned toward sun-entering with five deer. The tall grass people did not crowd around, they did not pat their bellies like starving beggars. But this one could see them sniffing the blood smell, she saw their owl eyes never leaving the carcasses. Gives black weapon offered the meat, and now they crowded, hacking with rough knives made of Coyote's blackrock, eating the meat raw. Their mouths were all bloody, but they were happy.

The horses were loaded with the sun-man baskets. Everything was ready. But holds black weapon had heard from a rider that the twoleaf people were half a day warmward, heading for the stream fork. He told gives black weapon they must wait. Gives black weapon drummed his wolf song on his teeth and walked in circles, beating the tall grass down. The twoleaf people arrived toward sun-entering.

—We will start for the three rivers in two, three days, holds black weapon told a twoleaf speaker, pock cheek.

—We can't wait, pock cheek said. —This winter is coming early.

—We will move quickly. We'll be there one day after you.

—We can't wait.

In the morning, holds black weapon watched the twoleaf people continue coldward.

—Old frown want know, can we finally get off ass? forest bear said.

—Old frown want know, they men keep promise?

This one was sitting in the circle, on pronghorn. Holds black weapon's face showed nothing. Red tongue and broken nose looked worried.

They had all left the stream fork yesterday, but had moved slowly, and would not reach the salmon stream camp until near sun-entering tomorrow. Gives black weapon had taken on his Bear spirit. He was looking closely at the others, and they were trying not to move. —Frown want know, why they send men on horse early morning over mountain, tell all serpent people meet tomorrow on mountain, all go hunt buffalo, leave robe chief stuck on mountain with finger up ass? Frown say, if they not promise help him with what-all, he not try cross mountain, he go back to bad-smelling big village on big water, no white men come again to serpent people. Frown say, if redskin children want white men be friend, help against enemy, give firestick, when promise, must keep promise. White men always keep promise. If serpent big-men keep promise, they send men after other, tell serpent people stay in village, wait for they come.

Red tongue said, —I didn't send the riders. Holds black weapon sent them. I thought it was wrong. I remember my words.

Broken nose said, —I also thought it was wrong. I also remember my words.

Holds black weapon was silent for a long time. His face showed nothing. He did not look at anyone, but at the empty center of the circle. Finally he said, —I sent the riders. I did it because my people are starving. But I was wrong. I will remember my words.

The council was over. Gives black weapon gave a small piece of bright clawth as a gift to the rider that went ahead over the mountain to tell the tall grass band wait.

Holds black weapon spoke to this one alone. —I said I would help the sun-men ten nights ago. Why do those ones move so slowly?

—It is their vow, this one said.

—It is not my vow.

—They have much power. If they are your friends—

—If we miss the buffalo hunt—

This one knew what that meant.

Holds black weapon said, —You told the sun-men I sent riders to the camp this morning. You shouldn't have done that, sister.

When they reached the we-people camp, holds black weapon told the band to be ready to leave for the hunt the next day. But this one was called to another council.

—Frown say, message come from red hair down stream. Red hair say stream not good, must go by land. Frown need horse. He got nine horse, one mule, he need twenty more horse, need trade tomorrow.

Holds black weapon said, —Tell the sun-man that I wish to be his friend. Tell him that the undergrounders, who he says wish to have peace with us, stole sixty of our horses in the grass moon. Tell him I will ask Father that enough of our men will spare him the horses he wants.

The next day, while the women gathered more yellowflower seeds, gives black weapon bought nine horses. This one watched him trade, and sometimes spoke between. For each horse, he traded three knives, red beads, scarlet cloth, a few metal arrowheads. Toward sun-entering there was another council. —We have taken him over the mountain as we said we would. We must leave for the hunt tomorrow.

—Frown say, red children promise help sun-men go where red hair build k'noos. Or if sun-men not need k'noos, red children promise trade horse he need. He need eleven more horse. If small serpent people want white men come back with firestick—

In the night, there was a buffalo dance. This one walked along the edge of the dance and sat next to holds black weapon. She said, —The sun-men are saying the tall grass people give their horses away for nothing.

The next day, gives black weapon had to trade twice as much for each horse. He walked away from most trades, and showed his empty baskets. He shot the black weapon that needed no powder. By sun-entering he had bought six horses. He called a council and said he needed five more. In the night, this one said to her brother, —I think he will trade a black weapon. With bals and powder. In the undergrounder villages, a horse always gets a black weapon.

The next morning, gives black weapon got two sore-backed horses for three times what he traded on the first day. After that, he could get nothing.

—Frown say, big knife white people many as tree in forest! They many as beaver on plain!

Does not walk arrived from down the salmon stream at straight-sun. He and gives black weapon talked to Sun with their ring-metal bent pipe, then called a council. Red tongue said, —We have traded too many horses already. We are late for the buffalo hunt. We cannot trade more unless we get black weapons.

—Red hair say, if serpent people help big knife reach big water soon, they come back here, spend winter with serpent people, shoot many buffalo with firestick.

Broken nose said, —You say we are weak. It is true. We must keep our horses, so we can escape from our enemies with our women and children, or we must have black weapons, so that we can fight.

At sun-entering, red hair traded a small black weapon, a *pist'l,* and one hundred bals and powder for a horse. —Red hair say, if good horse brought in morning, he maybe trade one more black weapon, big size.

The next day, the last horse was traded for a black weapon. Holds black weapon looked pleased.

This one embraced people and cried over her tall grass band. Then she tied out of water on her horse, and mounted, and started down the salmon stream with the sun-men. She turned to look back. The band was already leaving the camp to cross the mountain for the hunt. Men, women, children, horses, dogs, in a long line, dust hanging above in a cloud. Only old ones staying behind. This one looked at Sun, Grayees-peert, two hands past straight-sun. That way lay the mealyroot eaters, and the big river leading to the bad-tasting water, where Coyote first made people. This one and out of water would wander together like foolish ones, like the Foolish One, Coyote. The sun-men would find their spirit by the bad-tasting water.

And this one?

Shouts.

And where was that?

By the river.

She followed it.

THE FALLEN
[1806]

Now it has come to pass, and let it be bruited from the mountaintops: Lewis has heard the charming sound of a bullet whistling past his head. Hatless, he has felt its passage stir his hair. He has rushed forward in a melee. He has been surprised by the enemy. *Damn you, let go my gun.* The Indian fell on his knees and his right elbow. He raised himself and fired. Had he braced the gun better, the ball would have struck Lewis in the face.

Instead, Lewis has survived his expedition, which is over, or nearly. *The expedition which I have ever held in equal estimation with my own existence.* He wrote that 367 days ago; two days before his thirty-first birthday. Today is his thirty-second. Hard though it is to credit, he has had three on the expedition. *Two years,* he said, pumping Clark's hand in Louisville, his heart crowding his throat and blissful spaciousness spreading before his mind's eye—and in fact it has been closer to three years.

And yet it is over. Or nearly.

Lewis is lying on his stomach with a bullet hole through his left buttock and a trench (bullet-plowed) across his right. It is August 18th (his birthday) and he has not walked since August 11th. He is in the white pirogue, descending the Missouri River, which is hurrying him out of Louisiana at the rate of fifty miles a day. The Mandan and Minetare villages are one day past, the Ricaras are next, and if nothing intervenes, the Corps will arrive in St. Louis in a month. At which point the expedition will be not nearly over, but utterly so.

He is lying in the white pirogue across three elk-skin sacks packed with Indian tools, animal skins, and plant specimens, his head pointing upstream, so that the not infrequent spilling of the waves over the gunwales (a windy day) wets his moccasins rather than his face. The Corps' flotilla consists of:

five dugouts recovered from caches at the head of the Missouri, two of which are bound together to make them steadier for the Mandan chief Big White and his family; the white pirogue (in which Lewis lies); and a contraption devised by Clark on the upper Yellowstone River, where the trees were too small for regular dugouts: two trunks, each twenty-eight feet long and only twenty inches wide, lashed abreast, the gap sealed with buffalo skins, the resulting hump straddled by the oarsmen. All are present and accounted for, except Charbono, who was paid off at the Mandan villages, and his woman and child, and Colter, who received permission to reascend the Missouri with a party of trappers. Lewis has brought all his men home safe and (save himself) sound. A proud accomplishment.

Much, in fact, to be proud of: the Pacific reached; great tracts of land mapped and botanized and (can one say? probably not) geologized; a half-dozen previously unknown Indian nations described. A hero's welcome awaits. Balls, toasts, speeches, huzzahs. The adulation of all sorts of jackasses, whose only commonality is that not a one of them knows him. What makes it bearable is the thought of Mr. J, of Lewis standing before him in the library and saying, *This have I done.*

I am a philosopher, the President said. *If there is no passage, you will determine that.*

The Discoverer of Disappointment, the legend on Lewis's Masonic apron might read, the letters flowing along a ribbon, and beneath it might be depicted (except that its features are unknown) his heraldic animal, that leopard, or small tiger, or feline wolf, or ursine ermine, that appeared to him on the day of the bear, and again on the day of the divide, and in both instances slipped out of his grasp. Lewis's *incognitum.* But he should remember that finding what you hoped not to boasts a proud lineage. One need look no further than Cook himself, two of whose triumphs were the proofs of negatives: that there is no northern sea passage around the Americas, neither is there a large and temperate southern continent. *Who are you* to presume the world was arranged for man's paltry convenience? Thus the discoverer of disappointment merely carries out His unwinking work of chastisement.

Lewis is lying on three specimen sacks, his head resting on his left cheek. The only notable object in view is a set of small cracks in the third plank below the larboard gunwale. The wood is tulip-poplar. Because of the uniform grain, the dozen cracks are divided six and six, each group consisting of nested curves that partially interlock with their partners from the opposing group, so that the whole forms a sort of braid connecting the two halves of the plank. This braid flexes slightly, in time with (Lewis has determined) the stroke of the larboard stern rower. The regularity of the motion lends the appearance of breathing. At other times, one might fancy it a game of interleaved fingers, of hands (let us say) clasped in friendship. The fingers press each other and relax, press and relax.

The expedition which I have ever held in equal estimation with my own existence. Lewis jotted that down, or words very like it, on the gloomy evening he spent waiting with the Sosonees for Clark to arrive at the fork in the Jefferson River. He had gone over the divide and discovered the tribe, and had returned with the less fearful ones to meet Clark and the Corps, but their suspicions of an ambush were aroused when there proved to be no one at the point of rendezvous. Lewis was all too aware that if these capricious savages absconded into the mountains, he would never find them again, and his expedition (which he had ever held, etc.) would in all likelihood be doomed. The only thing that prevented them from decamping then and there was that Lewis had described York to them. White men might be damned, but they longed to see this black monster. Lewis slept with Cameahwait, their chief, bedded beside him, while most of the others hid in the bushes. But in the morning, Clark arrived, as he always arrives: stolid and steady, even if limping, or his face stiff with pain, but a light in his eyes and that ready smile widening in the spaciousness of his jaw, "Lewis!," he does always seem genuinely pleased to see him, and a characteristic gesture, a touch with his right hand to the side of his hat as he comes up, he might be adjusting it, or giving his hand something to do before extending it for the shake, or perhaps it is a private signal between them, meant to recall the lieutenant's salute that is technically Lewis's due, but has remained a secret from the men. A wink, then: *Yes, Captain?*

Lewis thinks of other arrivals, the notes left on poles at other river forks: *Meet me at—* And in all this wilderness, around this or that bend, there Clark would be. There was the time the beaver chewed down the pole with Lewis's note, and Clark took the wrong turning, but they found each other regardless. And the time Pryor took the note Clark left at the mouth of the Yellowstone, thinking Lewis had already passed; but Clark had thought to leave another note fastened to the horn of a buffalo skull, and even scraped a third in the sand: he'd gone farther down to escape the mosquitoes, and would wait where practicable. It was soon after that that Lewis was shot (the bullet drilling through the left buttock, searing across the right, spinning him around with the force of the impact), and he lay in surprisingly strong pain in the pirogue, and slept not a wink that night, and the next day, around this or that bend, there Clark was on the bank, huzzahs, the whole party together again, and Clark's voice approaching (Lewis could only hear from the bottom of the pirogue) and asking, alarmed, "What happened?" and Lewis lifted his head and said, "I'll be all right."

Clark is in the bow of the white pirogue. Lewis rests his head on his left cheek, looking at the flexing crack. He can hear Clark's voice, but cannot see him, no matter how he lifts or turns his head. Which is fortunate: such is Clark's solicitude, he would inquire after Lewis's comfort every time their eyes met, or describe the shore Lewis cannot see. But Clark has more important things to attend to, and anyway, Lewis would rather not converse. Thirty-two years old today. In all human probability, about half the period he will remain on this earth. (He will recover from this flesh wound, this trifle; and with no hero's scar to show the ladies, unless he drops his pants.) Half the period—he wrote something about that in his journal on his last birthday (sealed in tin and lead, stored somewhere near him, amidships, designed to float better than he would), something about *this sublunary world,* and regretting the many hours he has spent in indolence, and reflecting on how little he has done to further the happiness of mankind, or add to the store of human knowledge. *I dash from me the gloomy thought*— Lewis winces at the words' striving for effect. How blessed he would be if he could actually dash gloom, like water from his fingers.

He remembers that day, a year ago. Clark departed in the morning with ten or twelve men to cross the divide and reconnoiter the tributary of the Columbia that the Sosonees claimed was impassable. Lewis spent the day airing out stores and repacking them for the horses, until rain came on. In the evening, Drewyer killed a deer and one of the men caught a beaver, but provisions were short. Lewis's birthday supper (under a dripping sailcloth) consisted of half a pound of lean venison, a trout, a cup of corn, and water. He penned his gloomy thoughts in the failing light, while this Corpsman or that one (he did not see them, but he sensed it) absented himself awhile into felicity. Most of the Indians had departed with Clark, but two braves had remained behind with what passed for their wives, and Lewis felt sure they were hiring them out like ponies, to take his men up on their hardy rumps. Lewis had known from the first that he stood no chance of restraining his men from dallying with these tawny damsels, so he had confined himself to ordering that they should on no account engage in illicit conjugation. The Sosonee men were not so importunate in pressing forward their venerian chattel as the Siouxs, but willing (to say the least) they were, and Lewis assumed they shared with other western Indians the peculiarity of positively exulting in being cuckolded in public, while fiercely resenting it if performed in secrecy.

Why gloomy? He had conquered the Missouri. He had found the Sosonees. He had counted some seven hundred horses in their possession, and had little doubt he could acquire cheaply the thirty he needed, if the river proved unnavigable. The Sosonees had described to him a trail through the mountains to the north that they warned was difficult, but a tribe they signed Pierced Noses apparently used it regularly, and if Indians could do it, Lewis was sure the Corps could. Beyond, they said, lay navigable water. Therefore, the hard part was nearly over.

Then why gloomy? Sitting under the sailcloth, in the failing light, Lewis thought he knew (whereas now, lying ass-up in the white pirogue, he sees that what he thought then was only part of it): it had been the sight, when he first ran panting up to the pass at the divide, of those high mountains still to the west. Perhaps his hope for a water passage had not died completely at that moment; but the wound was mortal. He knew too well, if only approximately, how many feet of elevation Lewis's River (as Clark had named it) had to fall to reach an ocean that was not terribly far away. Perhaps a river that cut a course through gradually shelving land might be navigable over such a drop, but surely not one negotiating this titan's landscape. The Minetares (he suspected, outraged, in the first hours) had deliberately minimized the obstacles in the way of the Corps of Discovery, in order to instill in them an unwarranted sense of confidence, thus aggravating the possibility of failure.

Then Lewis found the Sosonees. *I take you by the hand,* he tried to say, but was pulled into a fierce hug by every man jack of them, *Ah-hii-e!* shouted in his ear until he was reeling. They led him to a leather tent, where the pipe was passed. Drewyer signed, and Lewis was struck by a comment made by their chief Cameahwait, Never Walks, to wit, that his band felt safe in this valley because their enemies had never yet penetrated it. Thus Lewis traded a new suspicion for the old: the Minetares had pretended to a greater knowledge of geography than they in fact possessed.

But a third, and very unpleasant, possibility occurred to Lewis while Drewyer was signing questions about the country to the west, and Cameahwait was making heaps of sand to represent mountains. Lewis recalled his interview with whichever Minetare chief it was when the country beyond the divide was discussed. Lewis remembered the chief signing (which must have meant Charbono wasn't present; why on earth wasn't he present?); he swept his hand around, palm up, inviting Lewis to note the landscape in which they sat. Then he shaped an angular peak, a knob, and gestured to the left and right. Then he pinched up a bit of sand from the ground. Lewis had occasionally watched Drewyer signing, and had noted the simplicity and admirable logic of the system. (Surely Drewyer was there. Or was he out hunting?) There had been many times before this, when Lewis had divined what a chief had signed before Drewyer told him.

Was Charbono not there? Was Drewyer neither? And had Lewis felt sure he understood? *Across the divide lies a country much like this one, with sandy knobs scattered here and there.* Was it possible that the Minetare chief had meant something else? *Across the divide, in every direction, lie mountains as numerous as grains of sand.*

Lewis watched Cameahwait form piles of sand like unmarked gravemounds: *Here lies a nameless fool.* There was a dance that night, which Lewis endured as long as he could, but he retired around midnight, telling his men to enjoy themselves. He was woken periodically through the small hours by the hollering.

Under the dripping sailcloth, gloomy thoughts. But now, lying in the pirogue, Lewis sees another, a deeper, reason for his disquiet that night, one year ago. Namely: the hard part was over!

Or nearly. He had no idea that the mountain route their Sosonee guide would lead them on would prove so grueling: the early snows, the horses butchered for their thin rind of meat, the candles the men ate in preference to the portable soup Lewis had paid so much for in Philadelphia. But dreadful as it was, it was completed in only eleven days. After that, it was all downriver to a sea not far distant. And everything after *that*, every footfall and paddle and heel in horse's rib, was a retracing of steps, a retreat to civilization. Balls, and huzzahs, and—

If that Indian had braced his gun the smallest fraction better, the musket ball would not have parted (whistling) Lewis's hair, and the charming sound would have been instead the splintering of facial bone, and Lewis wonders what that might sound like when it is your own face. (The cracks in the poplar plank open their mouths.) The Indian was either a Blackfoot, or a Minetare of the Prairie (the latter not to be confused with the Minetares of the Missouri River), allied tribes that preyed mercilessly on the Sosonees, the Flatheads, the Pierced Noses. When Lewis asked the party of eight young men by signs whether they were Minetares, they answered in the affirmative, but later it occurred to him that they had every reason to lie.

Whatever he was, the young savage needed to brace his gun better, but he had fallen on his knees and right elbow (his right hand holding the musket), and when he raised himself, he was forced to shoot one-handed, as his left hand was holding his guts in, so he tucked the stock of the musket in the crook of his right arm and fired, and the kick made the ball overshoot. The kick, and perhaps also a small breath from the Deity (gasping in delight), who wanted to save Lewis from a hero's death so that he might suffer a wound such as men who run from battle receive. And perhaps that second bullet, since it was shot half-blindly, required all five fingers of the divine right hand to guide it infallibly through Lewis's *derrière,* the fleshiest of mere flesh wounds.

But this is self-pity, a fault in him.

Lewis awkwardly dressed the wound himself until he rejoined Clark the following day, and since then he has allowed no one but Clark to tend to it. Clark is the only man in the party besides Lewis who has had much experience doctoring, but what is more important, it undermines an officer's authority to have a private or sergeant tend to his naked ass. (As for shitting, which Lewis can only do lying sideways, Clark has lent him York.)

To purge himself of self-pity, Lewis possesses a physic: the memory of an incident that occurred among the Sosonees. Lewis had gone ahead over the mountain and found them, and Cameahwait had smoked with him and made the piles of sand, and there was the dancing, and then Lewis waited a day to give Clark time to get up to the forks of the Jefferson River, and on the third day he had a devil of a job convincing some of the band to come with him back over the mountain to help with the portage, and by sunset they had crossed the mountain and reached the upper part of the valley that led to the

Jefferson fork some twenty miles away. All this time, Lewis had eaten nothing but a couple of handfuls of flour and a few dried berry cakes, and he was famished. He had the impression from the Indians' carefree countenances *(here lies a nameless fool)* that they found their cakes more filling than he did. In the morning, he sent out Drewyer and Shields to see if they could locate a deer in the hunted-out landscape, while he got the party on the move. Lewis was sharing a horse with one of the braves. About midmorning, a Sosonee spy came galloping up the valley. He pulled up long enough to shout a phrase, after which he wheeled and raced off, and the entire party, in a frenzy, gave the whip to their horses and followed him. Lewis was sitting in front of the other man, without stirrups, and he doubts his ass had ever taken such a beating (theretofore) as it received over the next mile. When he saw Drewyer up ahead, crouching over a deer carcass, and realized what it was all about—he had been fearing something far more serious, that through some mischance a real war party had been discovered—he reined up the horse and forbade the Indian to whip him, at which, without a moment's delay, the fellow dismounted and lit out at full speed on foot for the last mile. Trotting forward at his leisure, Lewis had in full view the scene, as the Indians converged, climbing over each other like a pack of famished dogs, on the steaming slurry of innards Drewyer had tossed aside. A confusion, a tangle; then they parted, turning their backs to crouch and hoard, and as Lewis rode up he saw blood runneling from chaps as the braves wolfed down raw gobbets of kidney and melt and liver, and there were two fellows who'd torn apart the paunch and were masticating black half-digested grass, and there was one—and this is the image that must never leave Lewis, that must rise unbidden every time he is tempted to wallow—who had got himself about nine feet of the small intestines and was avidly chewing on one end while using both hands to squeeze the contents *(pas bon pour manger)* out the other.

Lewis's first emotion was revulsion; but a pace behind it came pity and compassion. These were men, whose innate moral and intellectual faculties (he might as well bow to Mr. J's opinion on this point) were equal to his own. And he noted that, reduced though they were to this condition so closely allied with brute creation, they made no move to divest Drewyer of any part of the kill that he wished to retain. Lewis directed McNeal to skin the deer, and he presented all but a quarter to Cameahwait, who divided it among his people. Now, for the first time, women and children received a share, and like the men, they devoured the carcass raw, even down to the soft parts of the hoofs.

Over the next few days, as Lewis conversed and traded with this harmless and honest people, his compassion for their plight turned to ire at their tormentors, chief among them the Blackfeet and the Minetares of the Prairie. He knew that Indians had no concept of Christian mercy, and he recognized (what he had been ignorant of when he began this journey) that making war was, in a way, a reasonable necessity to them, as a method for choosing their leaders. But what he failed to understand was why, if they put so high a valuation on bravery, they showed no compunction about dispatching their enemies in an unfair fight, viz., when they possessed firearms and their victims did not.

Lewis had by no means ceased to accept that pacification of the Indian tribes was desirable, but he saw more clearly the obstacles to its achievement, and in the meantime, as he iterated promises daily to Cameahwait that he or other white men would arrive in the near future angelically bearing firearms, he found himself wishing that these assurances were not (as he thought likely) empty.

No; that wasn't quite what he felt. Giving the Sosonees their turn at overawing their neighbors was not the answer. Because one might take it as certain that, had they sufficient guns to engage the Blackfeet equally, they would also use them to abuse the Flatheads and the Pierced Noses. What, then, had Lewis felt? Perhaps nothing more defined than pity and anger, and a desire to punish a few cowardly bullies.

Damn you, let go my gun! That was how it started, the melee, the rushing forward, the bullet whistling over Lewis's head. That was months later, on the way back from the Pacific Ocean, in Blackfoot and Minetare country, along Maria's River. *Damn you, let go my gun,* and Lewis woke in gray light to see Drewyer scuffling with the Blackfoot (or the Minetare), Drewyer's rifle between them, and Lewis turned to seize his own gun, but it was gone. He had been surprised by the enemy.

He'd encountered this party of eight men the previous day. His own party numbered four: himself, Drewyer, and the Fields brothers. The nearest other Corpsmen were over a hundred miles distant. Lewis had sensed from the first (inspecting the Indians on an eminence through his spyglass) that there might be trouble. But flight would have meant abandoning Drewyer, who was separated from the other three, hunting; and in any case, the Indians had thirty horses, several of which were doubtless faster than Lewis's indifferent mounts. So Lewis and his men approached, and the Indians approached from their side, and Lewis and their leader shook hands, and Lewis signed a query whether they were Minetares of the Prairie, and they allowed as how they were. It was growing late, so Lewis proposed that they all camp together. Drewyer rejoined them, and they descended a bluff to a small bottom along Maria's River, where the Indians constructed a hemispherical lodge out of willow branches and buffalo skins. Lewis and Drewyer accepted their invitation to join them in the shelter, while the Fields brothers mounted guard by the fire outside the opening.

They were young men, dark, of a middling, broad stature. In the first moments of the encounter, they had appeared quite as alarmed as Lewis, and he had not believed their claim that three were chiefs, but he'd gone along, dispensing a medal, a flag, and a handkerchief to pretenders one, two, and three respectively. Number one fingered the medal around his neck as he parleyed through the evening. The skins they wore were smoked brown, and exceedingly well made. In addition to their bows (always surprisingly short, looking like boys' playthings) they possessed two trade muskets, which they said they'd got from a post on the Saskatchewan River. They seemed more fond of tobacco than the young Mandan and Minetare men (who said too much smoking made them poor runners), so Lewis plied them generously from his waning stores, while he told them, through Drewyer, that he had been to the great waters where the sun sets, had met many tribes, had restored peace among them, and had invited them to trade with him on the waters on this side of the mountains. He said that if the Minetares (or Blackfeet) wanted to be a part of this trading empire they should send their chiefs to meet Lewis at the mouth of Maria's River, where the rest of his men were waiting, a powerful force that would be damned upset if Lewis did not appear there soon.

It grew late; Lewis took the first watch. All eight of the Indians fell asleep. Near midnight, he roused Reuben Fields, and laid himself down.

Damn you, let go my gun. And there it was, the worst that could be said of a commander: Lewis had been surprised by the enemy.

The sound of a distant gunshot rolls up the river bottom, echoing between the hills. "Our dinner bell," Clark's voice comes from the bow of the white pirogue. "Venison, I wager."

You could say it was Joseph Fields's fault. He took the third watch, and at some point (the Indians all asleep) he foolishly laid his gun behind him. Around dawn, number one crept up and seized it. But it was just as much the fault of Lewis, who should not have been in a child's profound slumber during the surprising hour. Drewyer waked faster (or perhaps he was already awake), grabbing the barrel of his rifle at the same instant that a second thief took hold of the stock. It was his *Damn you, let go my gun* that roused Lewis, who sat up befuddled, asking of the world at large what might be the matter. Only then did he turn to see his own gun gone, and one of the Indians (number six or seven) running off with it.

The bullet in Lewis's ass, the ignominy, is no more than he deserves. The Indian ran, and Lewis, drawing his pistol, pursued him. The thief was hindered by trying to carry two guns, Lewis's rifle and his own trade musket, and after a dozen paces he saw it was no use. Halting, he dropped the rifle disdainfully, and walked off at a casual pace, to indicate that he was not afraid. At the same moment, the Fields brothers and Drewyer ran up, having recovered their weapons.

Now the Indians, having failed of their first objective, tried to run off the horses. Lewis's thief bolted and, along with another man, started hallooing mounts downriver, while the other Indians drove the rest of the herd in the opposite direction. Lewis sent his men after the main party, while he chased numbers six and seven. Among the horses they drove before them was his own. For such a small party as Lewis's to find itself bereft of horses in this hostile country was a serious thing indeed, and he called to the two men that he would shoot them if they did not give him his horse. But they kept on. Lewis pursued them for a quarter of a mile, during which he had opportunity to observe, for the dozenth time (though, in this case, with especial vividness) the Indian manner of running, toes turned inward, sparing the heel, which gave them a shambling bear's gait, and it still seemed to Lewis like a damned awkward way to cover ground (the Canadian traders claimed it was superior for distance, once you learned it), and it reminded him of the Sosonee fellow who had leaped off his horse and rolled a mile, starving for his meat, which these bully-boys in front of Lewis had robbed him of.

But Lewis, unlike the Sosonees, had a gun. A fair fight! The Indians reached a niche in the bluff enclosing the bottom, up which they turned, and when Lewis reached it, they were still thirty paces ahead, the horses laboring up the slope, and Lewis was out of breath. "My horse, or I will shoot!" he managed to shout a final time, raising his rifle. *You damned cowards; come on.* Number seven jumped behind a rock, while number six, holding the musket, turned to face Lewis. It was a cheap fusil, with a thin barrel prone to bursting and a niggardly charge (no doubt) of low-grade powder. The blast would sound like a shriek, the accuracy poor, the range less than it should be, but the ball was an ounce, nearly three times the weight of Lewis's, it would take his jaw off, and the musket could be reloaded faster than Lewis's rifle, and besides, Lewis didn't have his shot pouch, he'd left it in the lodge when he sprang up to give chase. So when the Indian turned and raised his gun, Lewis shot him through the belly. He fell to his knees and pitched forward, his left hand holding his guts in, his right (gripping the musket) extended, so that he landed on his right elbow. He struggled to rise, pushing himself back on his heels, and lifted the weapon, bracing the butt against the crook in his arm, and fired one-handed at Lewis's chest, but the barrel kicked up and the ball whistled half an inch above Lewis's head, where, hatless, he felt his hair ripple and his scalp shiver from crown to nape. The wounded man crawled behind a rock. Both Indians were now sheltered, and Lewis had only the one charge in his pistol, so the reasonable course was to return to the camp.

"Are you hungry, Lewis?" Clark asks. "I see the hunters on a bar ahead."

"Tolerably," Lewis lies.

When Lewis reached the camp, he learned about the other dead Indian. In the first seconds of the melee (while Lewis was drawing his pistol and giving chase to number six) the Fields brothers were catching number one, who had taken both of their rifles. In wresting his gun away, Reuben Fields stabbed the man, and the knife point must have pierced his heart, because he ran about fifteen steps and fell dead.

Lewis knelt by the body: the rich bead embroidery, the whiff of emptied bowels. The peace medal was still around his neck. Lewis did not take it, but straightened it and turned it over, leaving Mr. J face up. A little message: *These were not defenseless Sosonees, but Americans.*

Then flight. They rode 120 miles south and east, into the night, before they threw themselves down for three hours' sleep. Continuing at dawn, they traveled twenty more miles to the Missouri, where by good fortune they met up at once with Sergeant Ordway and the boats coming down from the falls. Lewis's eyes sought out and found Seaman, amidships in the white pirogue, barking with joy at the sight of his master, who would fain have echoed him (*Melee!*) if no one were there to hear, but as it was, he merely turned loose his horse, leaped in, and shouted, "Away!"

And here is Seaman now, still in the white pirogue, sitting by Lewis's feet (he can feel the dog's weight against his moccasins), maintaining the vigil he began the day his master was shot. Lewis remembers when the Wah-cle-lars stole him—

The oars are being shipped. Sand hisses along the pirogue's bottom. "Three deer," Clark says, as the men splash out and haul the boat farther up on the bar. His voice comes near. "How are you feeling, friend?"

"My age, dear Clark."

"In eight or ten days you'll be walking."

"My holiday over so soon? Would you tell York I require him?"

Had they continued half an hour more, Lewis would have had to signal. He lies on his side behind a willow brake, whither York and Hall carried him. The latter having absented himself, York holds Lewis's buttocks apart as his shit emerges so that it won't befoul the dressing on the humorously placed exit wound (the bullet struck him just below the hipbone, exited his left buttock an inch from his rectum, and plowed a mathematically perfect curve across his right buttock before coming to rest in a nest of bloody tissue inside his skin leggings, whence Lewis fetched it out and examined it with considerable interest). Now wouldn't this make—York is cleaning him wordlessly, he has the good valet's sense of when to simulate absence—wouldn't this private little moment make for a true-to-life portrait to hang in Monticello next to the President's Magellan and Columbus? *The Discoverer.*

Carried back, Lewis asks to be placed in the pirogue rather than by the dinner fire. He prefers not to lie enthroned on cushions among his communing men like an odalisque, he would rather be out of sight beneath the gunwales, where he can accept the roasted meat Clark brings him, assure him he needs nothing, listen to the camp talk if it interests him, or stare at his crack if it doesn't; where he can feel Seaman's weight against his feet, and speak to him, and feel the boat vibrate from the heroic thumpings of his tail.

A month to St. Louis. Then on to Washington, *This have I done.* And the

Mandan chief Big White and his family accompanying him, to meet Mr. J and be impressed with white power, and (God send) not sicken and die. None of the Minetares (of the Missouri, not the Prairie) agreed to go, claiming for their excuse that they feared the Siouxs. The Minetare chief, Le Borgne, had told Clark (Lewis spent all three days of the visit in the white pirogue) that as long as Big White went, it would be as if he himself had gone, he would hear all from Big White when he returned, and Clark gave Le Borgne the swivel gun to incline him more toward the U' States, but Lewis doubted the Minetares would give up their ways so easily. *We have opened our ears to you,* they solemnly apprised Clark; *we will make war only in defense.* Of their interests, they meant.

Lewis can hear Big White talking by the fire, Jessome translating. Something about the old Mandan villages that used to be in this area. He is an amiable enough fellow, but garrulous, even by the standards of Indians around a fire, and pompous, and Lewis is not entirely sure that, despite the ritualized crying, his village was not happy—particularly the younger, more active chiefs—to see him step into the double canoe and (following a speech) settle royally among the lap robes and wave himself downriver. Jessome and his cowed squaw and two children an unfortunately necessary entourage. (The younger one keeps spying over the gunwale at Lewis.) Lewis would have preferred to bring the Charbono *ménage,* could they only interpret Mandan.

The man turned. Lewis raised his gun and shot him through the belly. He fell on his knees and right elbow, he emitted a sound. *In all your intercourse with the natives, treat them in the most friendly & conciliatory manner which their own conduct will admit.* That was somewhere in the President's official instructions. Well, it is a nice question, precisely how much friendliness is admitted by a man who points his musket at you. *This have I done:* journeyed eight thousand miles, described some three hundred new plants and animals, hugged all the red men who wanted a hug, shot only the one who insisted on being shot.

Lewis contemplates for long minutes his demesne, his three square feet of poplar plank. Piles of sand, a finger tracing, *impossible,* a puppy landing with a whimper in his plate, *damn rascal,* turning in the thicket, searing pain in his side, his rifle soft and bending in his hands, *who's there—?*

Lewis wakes. The pirogue is being hauled off the sand. Leggings climbing over gunwales, the oars falling into rhythm. Where was he? Today is his birthday. He is twice sixteen, which sounds, does it not, barely out of boyhood. Home from a lark, tomorrow another. Surely he can dash from him his gloomy thoughts, if not like water from his fingertips, then through a more laborious method, weeding his mind of self-pity, cultivating (a happy farmer) his happier thoughts.

For example, he could reminisce about his diligence among the Sosonees. Anxious as he was, with so much to do, and fighting gloom, he nonetheless took extensive notes on the tribe. He remembers recording their vocabulary for Mr. J's collection, sitting in their single leather lodge on the next-to-last day, himself and Cameahwait and Labiche and Charbono and Sah-cah-gar-we-ah, Lewis filling in the sheet on his knees, head *pambi,* eye *puih,* and how about the mammoth? No, not the buffalo . . .

And their dress, which Lewis atomized at length in his notebook, and he wonders again whether a taxonomy based on clothing and decorative motif might be useful, not merely for distinguishing the Indian nations, but for determining the frequency of contact between them, perhaps even their degrees of common ancestry. Barton, in an appendix to his *Elements of Botany* (the complete text of which Lewis would have had time to get by heart during the tedious winter on the Pacific coast, had he not shortsightedly cached the book by the Great Falls of the Missouri), lists some dozen or so methods of classification devised before Linnaeus. Scientists who based their system on the fruit of the plant were called Fructists. Similarly, there were Corollists, champions of flower petals; and Calycists, who thumped for the lowly calyx. As Lewis is proposing a system based on decorative outer dress, he supposes that makes him a Corollist. Whereas a Calycist would perhaps classify the natives according to their smallclothes. And a Fructist would distinguish them by their deeds, would he not? *By their fruits ye shall know them.* In which case the Blackfeet, the Minetares of the Prairie, the Assiniboins, and the Tetons would be classed among the predator nations, the Pierced Noses, the Flatheads, the Mandans, and the Sosonees among the prey.

That harmless and honest people. Of course the Sosonees were capricious, and set little store by their word. (Could it be that, because savages had no notion of writing, words were not fixed for them?) For example, Cameahwait nearly abandoning Lewis and all his baggage on the mountaintop. But their natural talent for gaiety and unconcern, for living wholly in the present, in the midst of adversity, was admirable. Lewis and his men had the merest taste of the sort of hunger to which they were habituated—that was after the Corps had left the Sosonees, on their eleven-day trek through the mountains, when the early snows came. Lewis would never have believed a candle could go down so gratefully. Clark had taken practical notice of lizards and snakes when he was forced to fast while reconnoitering Lewis's River, but in the mountains, where the Corps would gladly have devoured anything that crawled, buzzed, or burrowed, there was nothing. Or rather, it was invisible under the snow; hidden in its midden. A portrait for Monticello: two dull-eyed scarecrows fighting over a salamander: *The Explorers.* Meanwhile, the Bird Woman turned candles and boiled leather and pine-tree underbark into mother's milk for her boy the entire way, with never a word of complaint. And Old Toby, their Sosonee guide, old enough to be Lewis's father, turned back to *recross* the mountains after he'd safely delivered the Corps to the Pierced Noses.

By then Lewis had stopped writing in the journal. Why?

Oh! Who knows, except unwinking Him?

His gloomy thoughts, Lewis supposed. The hard part was over, the passage did not exist, the Minetares were liars, Lewis was a fool, even uncorrupted Cameahwait's word could not be trusted, and the harmless and honest Sosonees had taken as ruthless advantage of the Corps' need for horses as any one-eyed Ohio frontiersman or grasping Yankee. When he left the Sosonee camp, Lewis had a sheaf of notes to write up, and by the time he managed to do that, he was days behind: the Corps had crossed the first mountain, met the Flathead Indians, and discovered the Flathead River (or rather, he should say, Clark's River). An oppressive sense of the enormous amount of information he still had in front of him to record joined forces with the equally oppressive conviction that his journey was nearly over—and he stopped. He stepped away from the boulder. He let it crash to the bottom of the hill, and he spoke skyward to the prison-keeper, *What do you think of that?*

The Corps struggled through the snowy mountains, and ate candles, and horses, and even the stinking bloodmeal sludge called portable soup, and thought they were starving, but to Old Toby they must have looked like children losing their nurslings' fat. And they tottered out of the mountains to a high prairie, where the Pierced Nose Indians (or Chopunnish, as they called themselves) took them in and fed them, and the river there was navigable and the pine trees were large, so they made dugouts, and it was downriver all the way to the sea. There were two or three falls down which they had to lower the boats with elk-skin ropes, but in the main it was onrushing water and rapid after rapid that, in earlier months, they would have scrutinized for a day and then portaged around, but now they merely called out to the canoes behind, *White water!*, and ran them, shooting out the far end with a feeling of being airborne.

From felling trees to tidewater, it was little more than a month, first through piney upland hills, then a broken desert, and suddenly (after the falls of the Columbia) a dark, wet land of moss and thunder and enormous trees. By early November they were back on the written part of the map, and a few mornings after that, the fog lifted on the tidal river and they saw ahead a steely lemon light, and they heard surf breaking on the rocks. Clark wrote that night in his journal, *Great joy in camp, we are in view of the ocean,* and Lewis witnessed firsthand the joy his friend spoke of, and wondered if he shared it. Was that thread of relief and resignation, that bone-deep watchfulness, in which nothing that might happen would ever surprise him—was that what men called joy? He threw a stick in the salt water, said, "Get it, boy," and Seaman leaped in and lived up to his name.

To congratulate them, witch Fortune sent weather worse than any had ever seen. They were trapped for days on a mat of drift logs beneath a cliff. Rain and whirlwind and lightning and thunder and massive waves; a chill, greasy chamberpot of a world, from which they crawled like mollusks into rock crevices (their tents had rotted long before, the leather lodge parting at every cinder mark). At last they managed to retreat to the head of the estuary, where they crossed to the southern shore; the Clatsop Indians had told them they'd find elk there. Three miles up a tributary stream, among cloudcapped fir trees near a spring, Lewis selected a spot of high ground nearly islanded in marsh. There they built Fort Clatsop.

Clatsop! The word will ever resound in Lewis's brain like an amalgam of *sop* and *clap,* of wet and filth and venery, of drip of drop, of clasp and slop, of clammy and close and

"Are you cold, Lewis?" Clark's voice comes.

Lewis lifts his head. "I'm fine."

"You were huddling."

"Merely experimenting with a new position. Something to amuse myself."

Fort Clatsop: two lines of huts facing each other across a small yard, a stockade at either end, a large gate, a small gate, a limp flag on a pole, a damp sentry by the gate, smoke from wet-wood fires. On the good days, rain needling down from low clouds; on the bad days, violent storms (flash and clap) and falling trees (crash and flop); on all days, day after day, all day, a dim dawn that never progressed to sun-up.

What do you do in a dungeon? You daub your name on the wall with your blood. You daily scrape a hatch with an iron spoon, so that strangers later may determine how long it took you to die there. A day after Lewis moved into his and Clark's hut, Joseph Fields hewed two slabs for the captains to write on (Clark's desk had been smashed when a horse rolled down a slope in the mountains; Lewis had cached his at the Great Falls). That was Christmas Eve. It took another week, of Lewis seeing his slab propped in the corner of the hut, and Clark's slab propped on Clark's knees, before, late in the evening on December 31st, Lewis noted down the weather (this monkey trick he never neglected) and cast his eyes along the column of his remarks for each day of the month *(rained; rained; rained; rained; rained; rained; rained; cloudy; cloudy and rained; violent wind and rain; rained; ditto; ditto; ditto; rained; rained; rained; rained and snowed and hailed; rained; some rain and hail; rained; ditto; rained; rained at intervals; ditto; rained with violent wind; rained; ditto; ditto; hard wind & rain; rained)* and told himself, self-exasperated, *For the rain it raineth every day,* and ground out a resolution for the New Year that he would once again keep his journal, his mood be never so foul *(Hey, ho, the wind and the rain!),* unless—and here he left his thoughts unspecified, but he probably meant something like unless he got a rifle bullet through his ass.

The following evening, January 1st, 1806, Lewis opened a fresh notebook and wrote, *This morning I awoke—* From lethargy, from torpor, from weakness, from the vapors; he awoke to duty, to self-respect, to a new year. What he actually wrote was something about being awakened by his men ushering in 1806 with a volley (which, in the first second, as he leaped from his bed, he thought was an all-out attack by the local Indians; but he didn't write that) and something else about the poor holiday repast of spoiled elk and wappato root and water. He wrote that he looked forward to January 1807, when in the *bosom of friends* he would participate in *mirth and hilarity.* The recollection of this horrific present would add zest to that future occasion, so that he would, *both mentally and corporally, enjoy the repast which the hand of civilization has prepared for me.*

If that sounded like a vow, it was. Lewis had hoped all his life for something that might imbue in him an unfeigned appreciation of civilized society, and he believed he had found it at Fort Clatsop. If he was going to suffer tedium and irksomeness and suffocation, he would far prefer that his dungeon come with decent light and a smokeless fire and a clean captain's coat with the lining and the cuffs just so, and linen on the table, and wine, and brandy, and a flealess bed.

And no Indians! Good God, what a—

The boat lurches, thick water rains down. Clark's voice: "Damn this headwind. Cruzatte, can we take her closer to shore without losing the current?"

An excellent waterman; a good fiddler. Myopic in his one eye, but absolutely nothing wrong with his ears. *I didn't hear you call, sir, I swear it, I swear!* Terror in his eyes. Was Lewis so frightening?

Clark calls, "We're making poor progress, Lewis. We'll be lucky to make forty miles today."

His birthday. "Wasn't the wind in our faces all the way *up* the Missouri?" Lewis tosses back.

He can hear a smile in Clark's words: "If memory serves." A phrase he's picked up from Lewis. When Clark gets home, his family will hardly understand him.

Damn rascal! Son of a bitch! That was how the Indians around Fort Clatsop proved to Lewis and Clark that the sailors who traded at the rivermouth in the spring spoke English. They squatted like frogs in the yard of the fort and cheerfully clarioned all the words they knew: *Musket! Powder! File! Bugger off! Damn Yank! Want fuck?* Holy Christ, what a collection of—

The thievery had begun as the Corps descended the Columbia River. A gunworm here, a knife there, a handkerchief, a striking steel. There was no escaping it, villages lined the river, one after another, the Indians were as thick as white settlers. Coming down the river was like leaving the upper air: trees closing in, clouds descending, plank houses hopping with fleas, people lining the shore, the stink of drying salmon, down and down. Echeloots and Skilloots and Cathlamets and Wahkiakums. *I take you by the hand,* Lewis said, and if he had worn rings, he would have found them missing after the shake. They smiled, they greeted. A knife here, a steel there. Short, ill-formed people, with bow legs and broad flat feet, flattish noses with wide nostrils, thick lips, coarse black hair. Their languages incorporated a clucking that made them sound like chickens. Down to the sea, watched all the way, down to salt water and endless rain and the Chinnooks and the Clatsops. And within a day of the Corps' arrival, the Chinnook bawds came to where his men huddled in the rain, old women with their young charges, who didn't care whether they retreated behind a bush, and the captains handed out ribbons to the men, to keep them from squandering every last file and awl in competition for the embraces of these deformed sirens.

Deformed: Lewis had seen (descending) the boards tied to infants' heads, so he knew how they achieved the crushed brow and the peak at the crown. (Here's a conundrum worthy of the subject of Indian names: the Chinnooks, Clatsops, Wahkiakums, Tillamooks, Cathlamets, Skilloots, and Echeloots all flatten their heads. The Flatheads, on the other hand, do not flatten their heads.) And he saw the tight cords at the women's ankles that swelled their legs to dropsical size. And he saw how his men cared not in the least. These creatures had the essential thing, the clasp and slop, and if men *in extremis* were capable of resorting to each other, or a folded elk's liver, or grease and a knothole, or poor dog Tray, then how better these objects, who possessed the name of *women,* and even to a certain extent resembled them?

Clap, and *louis venerea* (after which, surely, Louisiana is named), constant visitors, whom Lewis fought from his armamentarium, dealing out thunderous doses of mercury. And since the native men, in every weather, were stark naked below the waist, Lewis could tell at a glance whether a visitor to the fort had the pox. Coming to trade, squatting like frogs, clucking, their scabbed or ulcerated members dangling in the mud, *You like? Too much!* The females wore a petticoat of cedar-bark tassels, but as soon as one of them sat on her heels, the illusion of decency dissolved; she'd plant her spatulate feet and throw her scarred knees wide, and the tassels would fall to either side and you'd find yourself staring right up her battery of Venus, her *cloaca publica.* Good Holy Christ, Lewis has never—

All of them, men and women, wearing cast-off sailors' clothing, blue jackets too big for them, worn backward or inside out or upside down, and finger rings in their ears and earrings in their hair, and the women with sailors' names picked out in charcoal on their arms, presumably so that favorites could be located the following season, *Want fuck?*, excellent mimics, interested only in trade, smiling, waiting for you to turn around, a knife here, a steel there.

Lewis retreated into his smoke-filled hut to scrape another day in the wall with an iron spoon: *the stem is smooth, cylindric, slightly grooved on one side, erect about half its height on the 2 first branches . . . alternate pinnate leaves which are sessile, horizontal, multipartite for half their length . . .* Page after page, botany, zoology, wood smoke in the air and a plate of questionable elk, a cup of water, his specimen beside him, and Seaman by his chair (he had a chair now, and a table, too). Mindful of his instructions regarding native crafts, he examined Clatsop bowls and Chinnook spoons, nets and gigs and double-headed knives. Some of their productions were remarkable; for example, their carved canoes and woven hats. The hats were large cones topped with sinuous knobs, woven so expertly of cedar bark and beargrass that they never leaked rainwater. Lewis had two hats made for himself and Clark, and when they sat together outside the hut in the evening, in the rain, smoking crabtree bark after a game of backgammon, inhaling it into their lungs, Indian-fashion, perhaps they looked like a pair of Chinamen, ancient friends, thirty-one and thirty-five, incipiently rheumatic and intermittently febrile.

At other times, in the hut, while Lewis wrote at the table, Clark sat opposite, filling in the blank spaces on the map. By mid-February he had completed a draft of the Missouri River from its mouth to its headwaters, the multiple ranges of the Rocky Mountains, the Columbian tributaries—the Kooskooskee, Lewis's River, the Flathead River (or rather, Lewis reminds himself, Clark's River)—and the Columbia itself, down and down to the swamps and the sea. Indian information had been compared and included; celestial observations consulted; eastern and western longitudes linked up. Louisiana had been filled. At the same time, the most practicable and convenient water route across the continent had been found. It was not, however, the route Lewis and Clark had taken. By following the Missouri to its source, they had gone too far south, and had had to come north again to cross the mountains. A faster way appeared to lie in leaving the Missouri at the head of the Great Falls and ascending the Medicine River valley, which would bring you within four or five days to Clark's River (a tributary of the Columbia, but apparently not navigable); then from Clark's River you crossed the mountains through which Old Toby had guided the captains, until you arrived at the Pierced Nose villages on the Kooskooskee River.

And how long was the portage from Clark's River to the Kooskooskee, on this, the U' States' most practicable and convenient water passage? Clark consulted his figures. 184 miles. And the portage from the Great Falls to Clark's River? Perhaps another 150. Thus, to compare with Mackenzie's Canadian portage of 700 yards, God and Nature had generously supplied the Americans with—340 miles!

If there is a passage, Lewis, then a prospect opens before us—

Mr. President—

Gloomy thoughts. Lewis began to formulate a plan for the return journey.

Meanwhile, the Chinnook bawd came every few days to the fort with her infectious wares, and Clatsops and Chinnooks and Wahkiakums came to trade (and when the women traded, they closed their deals with whoredom), and every time they walked through the gate they brought with them swarms of fleas that later had to be picked out of the blankets. They traded wappato root and salmon and fat dogs, for which Lewis, and indeed all of the men except Clark, had developed a taste. The Indians were great hagglers; they could spend the entire day chattering and gesticulating over half a sack of wappato, and were never satisfied unless they thought they'd got the advantage of you. The more desperate you were, the happier they were. Amiable smiles, amiable refusals. And waiting until you weren't looking. A tomahawk, a coat.

Their great failing was, they had no warrior honor, no spirit. You could not goad them, as Lewis had done the Sosonees, when they hesitated to cross the mountain with him, by questioning their bravery. You could insult a Chinnook to his face and he'd be back the next day with a fat dog to sell you, smiling, waiting. Here, in perfect form, was the condition to which the grand American plan sought to reduce the more honorable Indian nations of the plains and mountains: a people who did not fight, who had no shame, people for whom trade was the be-all and end-all of existence.

Of course they valued blue beads above all others, and of course Lewis had no more of those. After that, they wanted white, and Lewis traded away the last he had. By mid-March, his entire stock of Indian goods consisted of three blankets and a yard of ribbon. He began to trade camp equipment.

Files, adzes, camp cups, wire. He and Clark moved forward their planned day of departure, from April 1st to March 20th. It rained. The fleas thrived. The store of mercury dwindled. Lewis was forced to trade his own lace uniform coat for a canoe, and when nothing he offered for a second canoe sufficed, he did as the Romans, he waited until the Clatsops weren't looking, and he took one. The day of departure arrived, but it rained and the wind blew so hard that ascending the Columbian estuary would be impossible, and the next day it did the same, and the next after that, and Clark and Lewis put on their Chinook rain hats and smoked crabtree bark. On March 23rd it also rained, but toward noon it let up, and they hurried the men into the canoes and escaped their dungeon, leaving the gate wide.

Now it was a matter of fighting up the Columbia, and every mile of the way, Indians crowded close again, Kathlamets and Wahkiakums and War-cle-lars and Echeloots and Skilloots, and items set aside for the merest instant disappeared, an ax, a lantern, a gun sling. It was like being tormented by insects, you turned to confront them and they scattered, you turned away and they crept back. The Corps struggled against the rapids, and Indians hid above and threw rocks down on them, and when they camped, the Indians crowded around in great numbers and smiled and picked up things and tried to distract you, or hoped to catch you alone so they might overpower you, but fled at the first resistance, and the tons of dried salmon on the scaffolds along the river in the Columbian gorge smelled (one could not avoid the thought) like a giant woman's pudendum, the cliffs trapped the odor, and the Corps flailed up through the gorge, slipping on the rotten fish skins that littered the portages. And three War-cle-lars stole Seaman, and Lewis sent three of his men after them with orders that if the thieves made the least resistance or difficulty in surrendering the dog, if they wiggled their fingers or emitted the merest hen-cluck, they should be fired upon. Fortunately, the moment they apprehended they were being pursued, they abandoned the dog and fled.

The river was high, and it was imperative that the Corps switch to horses at the first opportunity. When they reached the desert country, they attempted to trade, and the Indians (Skilloots and Eneshers) knew they were desperate, and though they had many more horses than they needed, their prices were exorbitant, and they made bargains and then canceled them, and they delayed through subterfuge, and they put forward brokenwinded nags, in short the offers were insulting, and they smiled and refused and waited until backs were turned, and tomahawks and knives disappeared apace, and Lewis traded away elk skins and coats and various pieces of camp iron and finally three large kettles and more knives, and clothing made from flags, and at last he had nine horses, and the morning before setting out, it was cold, and firewood was scarce, and the Indians refused to sell a stick, so Lewis, with joy in his heart, made a great fire of the Corps' canoes, paddles, poles, and every other wooden object they no longer needed (and for which the Indians had declined to trade, calculating that the white men would leave them behind), to warm his men in the morning, and one little Indian bastard crept in around the fire and tried to steal a makeshift socket off a canoe pole, and Lewis grabbed him by the scruff of the neck and beat him until he squealed and directed the men to kick him out of the camp, which task they performed to the letter, and Lewis now shouted to the Indians (crowded around the camp, waiting) that he would shoot the first of them that attempted to steal any item, that the white men were not afraid of them, that he had it in his power at that moment to kill them all and burn down their villages, but it was not his wish to treat them severely, provided they *let his property alone.*

And he must ask himself—lying in the pirogue, the hours of the first day of his thirty-third year heavy about him—he must be firm with himself—did he allow his anger, his gloom, to obscure his judgment?

Not in his treatment of the Columbia River Indians; they deserved far worse punishment than he had it in his power to deal out to them. But later. He means—

An unlooked-for consequence of the Columbian Indians' thievery and hard dealing was the ease with which the Corps now progressed. They traveled like Indians, on horseback, with scant baggage. They were dressed like Indians, in skin leggings and shifts and moccasins, and they used Indian saddles without stirrups, and elk-skin thongs tied around the horses' lower jaws for bridles. When they reached the Pierced Noses, they cut off the brass buttons of their dress uniforms to trade for roots, and Clark hawked his doctoring skills, and the braves and squaws lined up, and he dispensed harmless nostrums with a deal of palaver and solemn juggling ceremony, and the patients paid in horses, which the Corps could eat if they ran out of food again in the mountains. And the Pierced Noses (the great majority of whom, Lewis could not help noticing, did not pierce their noses) were on the whole an honest and trustworthy nation, so it must have been Lewis's gloom that made him impatient with them, irritated at their (trivial, in retrospect) bouts of stinginess and slipperiness, that indissoluble residuum of native unpredictability.

Impatient: Lewis tried to cross the mountains too early, when the snows were still high. The Chopunnish (as it was perhaps better to call them) had assured him it was impossible, yet he went forward, and risked the journals and his men's lives. They floundered in the drifts, and nearly got lost, before Lewis agreed to retreat, to wait like a reasonable fellow. He was gloomy. The hard part was over.

Therefore, he must ask himself—was it possible that he had wanted the return to be hard? To be dangerous?

He had formulated a plan. In order to ascertain whether he had really discovered the most practicable and convenient route across the continent, surely he needed to explore the route along the Medicine River. But then, what about the Yellowstone, which the Minetares said headed near the Three Forks of the Missouri? And what about Maria's River, which promised to extend U.S. sovereignty above 49° 37', and which Lewis had not had time to explore adequately the previous year?

Among the Chopunnish, Lewis waited, a simulacrum of a reasonable fellow. By the end of June, enough grass for the horses had emerged in the mountains to make a crossing just possible. Five young Chopunnish braves guided the Corps through in six days. The Corps split up at Clark's River, Clark heading south toward the Missouri headwaters and the Yellowstone, Lewis east. *(Meet me at—)* Lewis reached the Great Falls via the Medicine River, where he opened the caches (to discover that spring flooding had destroyed every last specimen he'd collected between the Mandan villages and the falls) and then divided his party a second time, leaving most of his men to portage goods below the falls while he, Drewyer, and the Fields brothers headed north to explore Maria's River. This would take them deep within the territory of two tribes that the Chopunnish, Flatheads, and Sosonees all feared, tribes that were attached to the British, and were rumored to be as vicious, lawless, and abandoned in their ways as the Tetons.

Lewis contemplates a potful of dirty water tipping back and forth (little ripples flitting in geese-formation from side to side) in the bottom of the pirogue. He must ask himself: did he want it? He means—

His exploration of Maria's River was a bitter disappointment. The river insisted on trending more west than north, and after several days he stood on a rise and could see where it came out of the Rocky Mountains, well short of the 49th parallel. The British had nothing to fear. Lewis called the spot Camp Disappointment. And on the day he abandoned hope, he needed to fix his position through celestial observation, but naturally it clouded up and rained, and it did the same on the next day, and his chronometer stopped, and the mosquitoes tormented dreadfully, and the food stores were nearly exhausted.

He wonders: was he reminded of Clatsop? (Oh, and, by the way, a river had destroyed all his specimens.) He turned south. Soon his party would reach the Missouri, and then it would be downriver all the way to St. Louis, where there would be balls and huzzahs and—

So—when Lewis looked through his spyglass and saw the party of eight Indians, what strange mixture of emotions might have been sporting, *sub rosa*, in his breast?

"I expect we will have some difficulty," he said to the Fields brothers. "If they attempt to rob us, we must resist to the last extremity, even unto death." His horses were inferior to theirs, so he could not outrun them, and in any case, Drewyer (who was hunting in the river bottom) could not be abandoned. So Lewis met them. He took them by the hand.

The reason he could not believe three of them were chiefs was that they were so young. Five were barely men—fifteen, sixteen. The oldest was perhaps twenty, and he the only one with scalp locks on his shirt. So the others had not yet killed their first man. They smoked Lewis's tobacco with delight, with abandon. Number one proudly fingered the medal around his neck. Their extra horses meant they had been out hunting. Fallen into this adventure by accident.

They fell asleep. *Damn you, let go my gun.*

If they had a plan, it was a foolish one. The fellow who stole Lewis's weapon ran off holding two guns, while his companion had none. And the others, trying to escape with the Fields brothers' rifles, left their own musket by the lodge. They must have acted on a whim: the watchman inattentive— the white chief in an abysmal slumber—guns—win their spurs. So they tried it. Why not? You test strangers, you make fools of them. Or if they catch you, you test them another way, you try to drive off their horses. You strut back into your village with their horses behind you, *This have I done.* This was a far cry from Chinnook pilfering; this was plains raiding, a sport.

When the boy who'd stolen Lewis's rifle saw he could not get away, he turned, and at that moment the Fields brothers ran up and took aim, but Lewis gesticulated, he shouted, "No!" The boy had not been raising the rifle. He dropped it. He did not even cast the priming before he dropped it.

Because it was a lark.

Or because he was too inexperienced to know better.

But Lewis was angry. He'd been surprised sleeping, he'd been made a fool of. The man had taken his gun, and now he took his horse. *His* horse. No matter that, with Lewis pursuing them so closely, the boy and his companion left a dozen of their own horses behind (a foolish plan, if they had a plan). No matter that Lewis knew the horses they left behind were better than his own. He was furious with these young men for having their adventure at his expense. He was enraged that, despite their heavy smoking, despite their short legs and ridiculous way of running, they could outdistance him, that by the time they reached the niche in the bluff, he was out of breath, and they were not. He was so out of breath, he could scarcely utter the words. *Let go my horse, or I will shoot!*

Of course they didn't understand. The one fellow jumped behind a rock and spoke to the other, who turned (what did Lewis want?), the man turned—no, it was a boy, perhaps sixteen—he turned with his fusil, which at thirty paces was near the extremity of its accuracy, whereas Lewis, with his rifle, could hit a sheet of letter paper at two hundred yards, he could choose which part of the quill pattern on the man's—the *boy*'s—shirtfront to pierce. Still, the Indian's ball was bigger, and he could reload faster (Lewis could not reload at all; remarkable, when you think about it, that the boy had not cast the priming), and no one, no one, would want a musket pointed at him from thirty paces. So Lewis shot him. The whistle, the shiver—

Lewis, lying in the pirogue, remembers: he shot the Indian, and came within half an inch of death, and sauntered back to the camp awash in a feeling of contentment and peace. He had had his melee.

The boys had left most of their baggage at the camp. Lewis cut the amulets off their shields for trophies and put the shields on the fire, along with their bows and arrows. He took their fusil with him, and their buffalo meat, and he took back the flag he had presented them with, but he left the medal around the neck of the brave Reuben Fields had killed. He selected four of their best horses, and rode hard south with his men. His Indian horse carried him much better than his own would have done; he had, he knew, little reason to complain of the robbery. He slept that night with perfect ease.

Lewis lies in the pirogue. The dirty water tilts, frets. Reuben Fields—or was it Joseph?—raised his gun to shoot the boy, and Lewis forbade him. Lewis saved the boy's life. Then he chased off the horses. He ran like a hare. You would not want a musket pointed at you from thirty paces, no you would not. The boy turned with the musket, his friend spoke to him from behind the rock, he turned—

Lewis rode hard south and told his men that if they were attacked by an avenging party, they must sell their lives as dear as they could. And they met the canoes coming down from the falls, and Lewis was swept downriver, and he was shot in the ass and, lying in the pirogue, still above the Mandan villages, he heard the voices of fur traders hailing his men, going upriver. So they were coming already. The blank space on the map was gone.

The question was—the only important, the very interesting question was—did the boy point the musket at Lewis when he turned?

There was no doubt he turned. Lewis shot him in the belly, Lewis saw the look of shock on his face. He clutched his belly and fell on his knees.

He turned and began to raise the gun. Of that there can be no doubt. Was it to prevent the boy from pointing the musket at him (his clear intention) that Lewis shot him?

Dissatisfied with bilgewater as an object of contemplation, he shifts his gaze to the crack in the plank. But that, too, seems unconducive, at this juncture, to philosophical speculation, so he tilts his head back (an awkward position) until he can see straight aft, where Cruzatte sits by the tiller. Isn't it wonderfully apt that the Lord's scourge should be one-eyed and myopic? Cruzatte avoids his captain's gaze. Lewis said: You go around that way, Cruzatte, I'll go around this way. *(Meet me at—)*

The Indian's friend spoke from behind the rock, and the boy turned. He was excited. He was young. He turned, holding the musket stock along his forearm. His arm swung as he turned, and the barrel of the musket swung. Lewis shot him. He was perhaps sixteen. He fell on his knees and right elbow, he emitted a sound of surprise and young pain. Lewis walked away. He had had his melee.

———

Evening on the shore. Wind sounding like foam in the cottonwoods, venison roasting (Lewis can smell it), Clark sitting with Big White a few feet away, asking him questions (Lewis can hear over the gunwale). Big White needs no encouragement, Jessome is translating his happy, digressive answers.

Thus does Lewis's birthday draw unremarked to a close. He is thirty-two. A mere one-third of ninety-six, the age at which his mother, wielding the shovel alone, and delving deep, will bury him next to her fourth or fifth husband.

Big White is relating some tradition of the Mandans. Jessome stumbles through it, Lewis listens: a story of their origins. It seems the Mandans used to live in a great village underground, on the bank of a river. A grapevine grew down through the earth, and some of the villagers climbed it to the upper surface, where they saw buffalo, and antelope, and prairie wolves, and grapes and berries and beans. They gathered grapes and took them down to their relatives below, who tasted them and resolved to go and live upon the earth. Many climbed the vine; they founded an upper village. At length, a pregnant woman, climbing, broke the vine, and the connection between upper and lower worlds was severed.

The underground village still exists, and when Mandans die, they go there. "If good, they cross river, reach village," Jessome concludes. "If bad, they no can cross river."

Being burdened by their sins, Lewis supposes, they are too heavy. Do the bad try to cross the river, and drown? Or do they merely gather in a wan crowd on the forsaken bank and—

Lewis had his melee and, well, God damn him, wasn't the younger man after the same thing? Hadn't he lain awake praying for what Lewis had prayed for when he marched off to the Whiskey Rebellion, what any normal man seeks out? And wasn't the young Indian granted what Lewis has ever been denied—a hero's death, his wound frontal, his friends present to tell the story afterward and embroider it with all sorts of dubious details, as, he charged forward, he saved a comrade, he picked up the flag, he blew the horn? So who is the luckier man? Lewis lives to tell his tale, which is that the young man turned, and something happened, and every time Lewis sees it, it's different.

Lewis went downriver and reached the mouth of the Yellowstone, where he was supposed to meet Clark, but Clark had gone farther downriver to escape the mosquitoes (he'd left a note, he'd scribbled in the sand), and

Lewis hoped to catch up with him that night, but didn't, nor the next, and Lewis was feeling his friend's campfires for warmth and hurrying on, and on the 11th of August he saw a herd of elk on a willow bar, and he got out of the pirogue to bag a couple, choosing Cruzatte to accompany him, and both men fired, Lewis killing his elk and Cruzatte wounding his, so they took different routes through the willow brake in search of the wounded elk, and Lewis spotted it and raised his gun and the bullet hit him in the ass. *Damn you, you have shot me!*

Big White is nattering on: "He say he born in old village opposite where we now . . . . He say Mandan people, when he born, live in seven village, big village, here, nearby, big, full of people, many Mandan, strong people . . . He say smallpox come when he just turn man, kill many Mandan. Then Sioux come, Mandan weak, kill many more . . . So they, seven village, they join, make two village, go upriver . . . But still trouble with Sioux, with Ricara, so go up farther, make new village near Big Belly, for protect . . . They weak now, turn to white father . . ." Lewis can hear the old chief crying, as Indians do when their tales require it. Real tears, even for old legends, or when visitors leave, whom the Indians barely know. Whenever their code says, Cry. Is it because they can't write? Every emotion is recorded through enactment?

He listens: the whine of mosquitoes, the chuff of the chief's weeping, a shuffling that might be Clark adjusting his notebook on his knee. Lewis saw the elk on the willow bar and landed the pirogue, and he turned to the four men with him and he selected the one-eyed, nearsighted fiddle player to accompany him. Lewis shot the more distant elk through the heart, while Cruzatte hit the nearby one in the shoulder, and the wounded elk plunged into the thick brake, and Lewis turned to Cruzatte and said, *You go around that way, and I'll go around this way.* Cruzatte entered the brake on one side, while Lewis, dressed like an Indian (that is, covered from head to toe in elk skin), entered it on the other.

And the bullet spun him around, and he called out *Damn you, you have shot me!* and Cruzatte didn't answer. So Lewis called his name several times, but on still receiving no answer, he concluded it was an Indian who had shot him, and perhaps there were a number of them in the thicket, so Lewis ran for the river, calling out to Cruzatte to retreat, and when he arrived in sight of the pirogue he shouted to his men, "To arms! I have been wounded, but I hope not mortally! Cruzatte is in danger! Follow me, and I will lead you to battle!"

Or words to that effect. And they followed him for a hundred paces, by which time his wound had become so painful that he could not go on, and he ordered them to proceed, and if they found themselves outnumbered, they should retreat in order, keeping up a steady fire. And he hobbled back to the pirogue and propped himself up against the gunwale, with his face to the field of battle, and he had his rifle at the ready, and the air gun beside him, and his pistol in his lap, and if they came at him, he would sell his life as dear as he could. And all the while, lodged in his breeches, was a .54-caliber ball from a U.S. Model 1803 army rifle.

After twenty minutes, the men returned. They reported no sign of Indians. Cruzatte was with them. Cruzatte swore he had shot an elk in the willows, he'd seen the rack as clear as clear, and no, he had not heard Lewis call his name. He repeated his story, his face white and his one eye closed, and by the time he opened that eye, he probably believed it.

Full dark, mosquitoes feasting on him, the smell of more rain coming, but overlaying it, the roasting venison, which must be ready. Clark will bring Lewis a piece. He is hungry now. This lying all day in the pirogue is harder work than it looks.

Thirty-two years old. When he and Clark are sixty-four, they'll sit wearing their Chinamen's hats under a cherry tree. Rheumatic and scarred, they'll watch the pretty girls run by, and Clark will put his head to Lewis's, and he'll say, *Do you remember the day Cruzatte shot you? Do you remember chasing me down the river? Do you remember the sound of my voice coming close?*

And under the tree, on that summer day, there will be mirth and hilarity.

Fifth Clark

Pompy danced in front of the fire and clapped his hands, piping, "Hot! hot!"
He fell plump on his backside and climbed manfully up again, and fell again,
and Clark squatted and pointed, "Fire, Pomp!", and swung him around. So
when Clark saw the sturdy square of sandstone standing by itself in a bottom,
he called it Pompy's Tower. He climbed up the one side that wasn't a cliff to
where Indians had scratched figures on a wall and he dug his name in with a
knifepoint, *Wm. Clark, July 25 1806*.

That was on the Yellowstone River. The Crow Indians had stolen half of
Clark's horses in the night. He sent Pryor ahead with the remaining horses to
trade for supplies at the Mandan villages, but the Indians, invisible as ghosts,
stole those ones, too. Clark had written a speech for the Crows. They knew
where he was (he saw their smoke), but they preferred the silent language of
trade. They gave him the Indian calling card, one worn-out moccasin, in exchange for all his horses.

*Children. The Great Spirit has given a fair and bright day for us to meet
together in his view, that he may inspect us in this all we say and do.*

*Children. I heard from some of your people some nights past by my horses
who complained to me of your people having taken twenty-four of their
comrades.*

Children . . . ?

You had to admire how they did it.

Not like the Columbia Indians. Clark remembered how they gathered
along the cliffs when Lewis pushed the Corps through some set of fiendish
rapids. They didn't want to miss the fair sight of white men drowning themselves. And all the goods to fish out afterwards. By then, Clark was annulled

to Lewis's rashness, he'd even started to believe his luck fed on it. The men believed the same, they'd follow their captain off a cliff if he shouted, "We must needs fly, men!"

Clark had only their liking; Lewis had their awe.

His friend's plan for the return trip was of a piece. When Lewis described it at Fort Clatsop, Clark thought it was as fantastical as an expedition with two captains.

But it worked! Each party did its duty on schedule, the cached canoes were safe, the falls portage went without a hitch, the grizzly bears didn't kill anybody, try as they might, Janey knew the way to the Yellowstone, the musket ball missed Lewis by an inch, he arrived at the Missouri at the *exact moment* Ordway's party was rounding a bend in the river. All four bands joined below the Yellowstone like a dance, take your partner, dosey-doe, played out over thirty thousand square miles of village green.

And Clark had to admit: Lewis's plan gave him (Clark) the chance to explore the Yellowstone alone. His credit, his river.

It was too bad it couldn't take his name. But Yellowstone was too entrenched among the traders.

At any rate, he had Clark's River in the west. It pained him to think how he'd been forced, in the end, to ask Lewis to put his name on it. Lewis had been the first to reach Lewis's River, and Clark had named it after him, even though he (Clark) explored more of it. So when the Corps crossed the mountain ridge separating the Choshonnes from the Flatheads and descended to another river, was it too much for Clark to expect Lewis to name it after his friend?

Clark was leading the party down from the ridge, he reached the stream in advance of anyone else. He wrote in his journal—he knew Lewis would read it—*I was the first white man who ever was on this river.* But they'd met a party of Flathead Indians, so Lewis started to speak of the Flathead River. A few days later Clark took the bull by the horns (or the captain by the nose!) and wrote *Clark's River* in his journal. But the same evening, Lewis picked up his pen for the first time after one of his bouts, and wrote *Flathead River.*

As though he'd gone out of his way. The Choshonne guide Old Toby said the river joined with another as large as itself and flowed far to the north before discharging into the Columbia. So it was a major tributary, and Clark could see the map in his head: the two principal forks of the Columbia, Lewis's and Clark's.

Lewis, as sole captain of the expedition, to whom all honors flowed, could afford to be inattentive in these matters. A subordinate must be vigilant.

Lewis did name a later river after Clark. Far down the Columbia, a southern tributary. Clark stood on an eminence to examine the country it flowed from. He estimated the river's volume. He knew from coastal maps that a great expanse of country to the south had no other outlet to the sea. He could see the map in his head: the Lewis curving ten inches up from the south, the Flathead arching ten inches over the north, and farther downstream this seven-inch addition, this lieutenant-sized river, the Clark.

You will observe that your rank has no effect upon your compensation, which by God, shall be equal to my own.

But that was the detestable little brother whispering in his ear. Clark accepted his fraction of renown. When he drew his map at Fort Clatsop, he put in a squiggle here and a wiggle there and the Clark River came out almost as long as Lewis's. But when the Corps went back up the Columbia in the spring, the Indians living at the mouth of his river informed Clark it didn't drain that large southern territory. It headed at Mts. Hood and Jefferson. So his river (he could see the revised map) was shortened to two inches. A sergeant's river.

Clark started referring to the river by its Indian name, Towannahiooks. He waited for Lewis to notice. He waited for Lewis to say something. To say, "I say, dear Clark, you deserve better than this." But as sole captain to whom all honors, etc., Lewis's attention was elsewhere.

Finally Clark was forced to speak. An unpleasant moment. But a moment only. Lewis saw where Clark was headed and jumped to the correct solution. And apologized handsomely into the bargain. No doubt he thought no more of it. But Clark could not forget he'd been forced to speak. Worse: he'd been forced to *ask*.

With the point of his knife: *Wm. Clark, July 25 1806.* He saw the Crows' drawings on the stone, but he never saw *them*, neither hide nor hair. Country to disappear into. *Children . . . ?*

But Clark and his men reappeared out of that hollow wilderness. They paddled into the Mandan villages in rags, dark as Indians. Clark tried to talk Charbono into continuing downriver, bringing Pomp with him. But since none of the Menetarree chiefs would agree to come down, Charbono couldn't draw pay as an interpreter. It was too uncertain for him.

Meanwhile, Lewis was laid up, all diplomacy was in Clark's hands. It was a catalogue of disappointments. The peace with the Rickerries hadn't held; the raids on the Snakes continued; the Mandans had quarreled among themselves; attacks by the Soues were feared more than ever.

The Menetarrees refused to consider moving to the mouth of the Yellowstone, because they said the Great Spirit had told them to remain where they'd always lived, or they'd die. Maybe death was on their minds because there'd been an epidemic that summer, it sounded from the chiefs' descriptions like whooping cough. Carried away over a hundred souls, most of them children.

All in all, it seemed a perilous place to be leaving Pomp. Clark had offered to adopt him, but Charbono said he wasn't weaned. Maybe in a year. Native women gave the breast ungodly long, Clark marveled it didn't create a nation of mama's boys. Janey carried Pomp up the bluff as the boats shoved off. That was Clark's last sight of him.

As the Corps descended the river, Clark's misgivings grew. He'd been with Pomp nearly every day of the boy's life. He'd spent more time dandling Pomp out in that great expanse of nothingness than ever he'd do with his own children. They'd be carried bathed and bonneted into their father's study by a mammy for an extended finger and a coo, and be spirited away again.

Pomp! Clark missed him terribly, his beautiful, dancing boy. Bright as a penny, he said *hot* to Clark, and *shoh* to Charbono, and whatever the Snake word was to his mother. What a future he might have, trader, interpreter, agent, diplomat. Clark would set him up; a word here, a favor there.

Then one night Big White talked about the smallpox that carried away two-thirds of his people, and Clark, with a wrench in his gut, thought of the vaccine he could get for the boy in St. Louis. And all the advantages of civilization, the education, etc. It was negligent of Clark to leave him to the "slingshots and arrows of fortune." A couple of days later, the Corps met traders coming up the Missouri, and Clark detained them for an hour to write to Charbono:

Your present situation with the Indians gives me some concern. You have been a long time with me and have conducted yourself in such a manner as

[*299*]

to gain my friendship, your woman who accompanied you that long dangerous and fatiguing route to the Pacific Ocean and back deserved a greater reward for her attention and services on that route than we had in our power to give her at the Mandans. As to your little son (my boy <u>Pomp</u>) you well know my fondness for him and my anxiety to take and raise him as my own child. I once more tell you if you will bring your son Baptiest to me I will educate him and treat him as my own child. I do not forget the promises which I made to you and shall now repeat them that you may be certain. Charbono, if you wish to live with the white people, and will come to me I will give you a piece of land and furnish you with horses cows & hogs. If you wish to visit your friends in <u>Montrall</u> I will let you have a horse, and your family shall be taken care of until your return. If you wish to return as an interpreter for the Menetarras when the troops come up to form the establishment, you will be with me ready and I will procure you the place—or if you wish to return to trade with the Indians and will leave your little <u>son Pomp</u> with me, I will assist you with merchandize for that purpose from time to time and become myself concerned with you in trade on a small scale that is to say not exceeding a pirogue load at one time. If you are disposed to accept either of my offers to you and will bring down your <u>son,</u> your famn Janey had best come along with you to take care of the boy until I get him.

Little did Clark suspect the Missouri was about to close to traffic for God knew how long.

The cause of it lay in news from those same traders carrying his letter up-river. Namely, the amiable Rickerrie chief Piaheto, who'd journeyed to Washington at Lewis's request, had sickened and died there. No one had yet told the Rickerries.

Neither did Clark, when the Corps reached their village later that day. They'd be none too happy.

The Corps got past the Tetons with nothing more than threats on either side. "You are bad people!" Clark hurled from the boat at the men on the shore. "No more traders will come to you!"

But that was empty; by the time the Corps reached the Kanzas River, they were meeting traders around every bend. Lewis was up and around by then. They heard news: the President had been reelected; England and America were on the brink of war. The traders were surprised to meet the Corps alive; they'd been given over long ago. Whiskey was passed across, the men had their first dram in a year, and sang songs in the night in the greatest harmony. The Band of Brothers was about to disband.

On September 20th, they passed the Gasconnade. They were nearing the first French settlement when they rounded a bend and saw cows on the bank. The men shouted for happiness, and Lewis (strange man) turned to Clark and said in a mocking voice, "Great joy in camp, we are in view of a cow." Then it was on to St. Charles, and a hero's welcome, and the next day, September 23rd, they rode into St. Louis. The whole town had gathered on the banks to huzzah three cheers. The Corps fired a volley, and it was a scene to remember, hats in the air, capers and handclasps, it was something for Clark to tell his grandchildren.

Now it was time for Clark's reward. For rank and recognition, a land settlement, back pay, a post, a wife. *If you come back, you'll be made a colonel,* his brother Jonathan had said. It was to him little Billy wrote the letter announcing his triumpeting return:

St. Louis 23rd September 1806

Dear Brother

We arrived at this place at 12 oClock today from the Pacific Ocean where we remained during the last winter near the entrance of the Columbia River . . .

Lewis was writing, too. But Clark's letter would reach Louisville before Lewis's reached Charlottesville, so it would be the one reprinted in newspapers across the country. A lesser man than Lewis might have ordered his subordinate to wait. But Lewis drafted Clark's letter for him. Clark wrote out the fair copy, and the letter made him famous. The newspapers called him Captain Clark. Clark folded his lieutenant's commission very small and addressed it to the Secretary of War with an ironical note:

St. Louis 10th October 1806

Sir

The enclosed commission having answered the purpose for which it was intended, I take the liberty of returning it to you.

I have the honor to be with every sentiment of the highest respect Your Most Obedient and Very humble Servant,

William Clark

St. Louis fêted Clark and Lewis while they paid off the men and settled affairs. Then they went up the Ohio River, torches along the shore, boats pushing off to greet them, more salutes than you could count. When they tied up below Louisville, Jonathan and Edmund were at the landing to meet them, and George (oh! he looked frail and witless!) and Ann, Lucy, and Fanny, and Clark's nephews and nieces and grandnephews and grandnieces, were gathered in Lucy's manor at Locust Grove, filling it to the rafters. William William William it was, and My boy! and By God!, captain, colonel, or general, who knew, but he'd done something grand, he'd climbed on his luck and won the race, and there was a banquet and bonfires, and ladies' attention (he found himself quite the gallant), and *Lewis & Clark* was the word of the day.

Lewis and Big White proceeded on to Washington, while Clark lingered. Everyone was clamoring after tales, and he told them, in the shops, by the fireplace. "It's a curious thing," he'd begin, puffing on his pipe, making them wait. There was the time. You wouldn't believe.

It was out of the question now for Clark to be attendant on George, his future was too bright, George's too dim, the family knew that. Clark was his own man. His old flame Martha had married in his absence (she seemed damn sorry about it, too), so his thoughts turned to little Judy Hancock, who'd be maybe fifteen now, and in mid-December he set off on horseback for the Cumberland Gap and the stage road up to her home in Fincastle, Virginia.

Her father was Colonel Hancock, a Congressman. They had a fine mansion on three hundred acres just south of the town. Clark still remembered the day in spring 1802, riding back from Washington with two of George's lawsuits settled, meeting Judy and her cousin on that balky jade. It was ignoring their love-taps, almost knocking them off as it cropped grass under a dogwood. And their pretty voices and slender forms and milky teeth as they thanked him, as he led them along, and then realizing she was a Hancock.

Fifteen now. Clark arrived, and found she wasn't married yet. She'd started to fill out to womanly proportions. She was pretty and lively. Clear white skin, black curls. Clark walked with her every day for a week. She was abashed in the hero's presence, but didn't spurn him. Her modest breast heaved with emotion. Clark daily felt more sure she was the girl for him, and he talked with her father. Then he told her he would know his prospects better when he returned from Washington. He hoped she'd wait for him (he said this with a smile, she was only fifteen, her father was delighted, Clark was the hero of the hour, the citizens of Fincastle had compared him to Columbus). Her family called her Julia now, she preferred it to Judith, which Clark hadn't known. So that river in the west—well maybe it was better, the Little Judy River, something private between them, an April day, a balky jade.

Clark went on to Washington, and that city of politicians was "no better than she should be," as maybe it was Shakespeare who said. Federalists were howling like prairie wolves, they said the bill of compensation for Lewis and Clark was extravagant. But it passed over their objections. Clark and Lewis were lions in society, and now that Clark was taken, the women flocked to him, he'd heard that happened and wondered why, but he didn't let his wonderment keep him from enjoying it. Lewis was made Governor of Louisiana Territory. The President put Clark forward for promotion to lieutenant colonel. The Senators rejected that, on the grounds it broke with seniority; but Clark wasn't too bitter, because they agreed to confirm any other nomination. So Mr. Jefferson appointed him Agent of Indian Affairs for Louisiana Territory, with the rank of brigadier general in the militia.

The compensation bill gave him sixteen hundred acres, exchangeable at two dollars per, plus double back pay, or sixty dollars a month for forty-three months, plus subsistence pay worth another eight hundred dollars, his pay as Indian agent would be fifteen hundred a year, and his opportunities for Indian trade ample, so General Clark was in a good position to press his suit in Fincastle. He'd told Lewis about Julia, and his friend confided he'd also developed an intimacy, with "a bewitching gypsy," and after a certain amount of winking and mystery, he pointed her out in a box at the theater. She was indeed a beauty, with a grand, empirical air. Lewis swore Clark to silence, "Else I am undone." Was it a question of a rival? The parents' wishes contrary? Clark never discovered.

Whatever the reason, the course would likely not run smooth, so when Clark was back in Fincastle he kept a brotherly eye out.

March 25th 1807

Dear Lewis,

I have made an attack most vigorously, we have come to terms, and a delivery is to be made first of January proximo, when I shall be in possession

highly pleasing to my self. I shall return at that time eagerly to be in possession of what I have never yet experienced. My friend, your choice is one I
highly approve, but should the thing not take to your wish I have discovered
a most lovely girl, beautiful rich possessing those accomplishments which is
calculated to make a man happy—inferior to you—but to few others.

Lewis had seemed discontented in Washington. A wife was what he
needed, a steadying hand. If only his romantic notions didn't get in the way of
choosing a proper mate.

As for the gypsy in the theater box, Clark never saw her again. Which,
come to think of it, would be just like a gypsy.

The general and his betrothed had a fond parting scene (her raven curls!
her downcast eyes!), and then Clark went to St. Louis to take up his duties.
There was much to do: purging the militia of Burrites, tracking down the
Corpsmen to remit their land warrants and extra pay, responding to agents'
reports on the ceaseless attempts by the Spanish and British to corrupt the
Indians against the U' States. Clark was also charged with the return of Big
White, and he sent the chief (intolerably puffed up by the attentions paid
him, he called himself brother of the President, instead of his son) off with an
escort. The commander was good old Pryor, promoted to ensign. Forty-eight
armed men, which Clark felt sure would be sufficient to deal with any hostile
band they might meet with.

Well—he was wrong! The Rickerries had learned of their chief's death
the previous October, and they attacked Pryor's party. Killed four, wounded
nine, one of whom was young Shannon, who lost his leg. Pryor had to retreat
downriver with Big White to St. Louis. Now the U' States had the friendship
of the Mandans in the balance, so long as Big White was kept from his people.
It was a sorry state.

But by the time Clark was informed of it, he was back in Louisville. He'd
left St. Louis in the latter half of July.

Yes, there was much to do, but he had other responsibilities. He had a wife
on the way. There was some business in Louisville he hoped to accomplish.

In St. Louis he'd felt like a man in exile. He was sleeping in a room of Mr.
Choteau's house like the whoriest bachelor. And Lewis hadn't shown up at
all. He was still in the east, arranging publication of the journals, and seem-
ingly in no hurry. To make things worse, York was vexing him no end about

wanting to see his wife in Louisville. Normally Clark wouldn't indulge him, but he had his own reasons to go home. In retrospect, it was a great mistake to give York the impression his petulance might be rewarded.

That was a painful subject.

And another disappointment: Clark had given a letter to Ensign Pryor to hand to Charbono, raising the matter of Pomp again, informing him he had 320 acres of bounty land and extra pay waiting for him in St. Louis. But of course the letter was never delivered. Clark wondered if the boy was forgetting his English. Or forgetting *him*.

At least he'd taken his first step toward acquiring his own family. And he took the second on January 5th, 1808, when the event of the winter season in Fincastle was carried off, and Brigadier General William Clark married Julia Hancock. Carriages lined the road, the house was festooned, the tables groaned. He pressed her hand (it trembled like a bird) and kissed her on the stairs. She was sixteen and radiant and unversed, a different thing entirely from negresses and wanton Chopunnish squaws (Clark at long last had indulged, not mentioning it to Lewis, when they were among the Pierced Nose Indians; doctoring the sick, Clark had had women thrown at him; "I believe I can say," he said in Louisville, filling his pipe by the fire when the women and children had retired, "they are not deficient in ardor"). This was different. Clark was gentle, and Julia's sweetness was more than he could describe.

He remembered York dressing him for the ceremony, still not himself, still worrying some bone. York was decked in finery himself, tailor-made clothes and ten-dollar boots, well-fed and glossy and nothing on earth to do except attend to his old master Clark. But still sulking, Clark knew him far too well to miss it, and maybe loading him with expensive clothes had been a mistake, too.

And what was Governor Lewis doing that winter? Clark hadn't heard from him in months. At the wedding, Colonel Hancock told him Lewis had been in Fincastle in November with his brother Reuben. He'd courted Letitia Breckenridge, the daughter of a general. A good match, but she'd played the gypsy, too, she'd decamped to Richmond. If she was being coy, she was the loser; Lewis didn't follow her. He departed the way he'd come, toward Charlottesville.

Which didn't please Clark to hear. When he'd become engaged the previous March, he'd asked Lewis, as a personal favor, to smooth the way in St.

Louis for his necessary absence to get married, and now he learned that his friend, ten months into his term as governor, had yet to set foot in the territory! Lewis's dereliction made Clark's own, briefer leave (though *his* was perfectly justified) appear more blameworthy.

Well damn it all, Clark was not going to lose sleep over it. He was his own man now for the first time in his life, with a wife and maybe his first child on the way, it was high time, he was thirty-seven years old, and "all the world was before him"—that was Shakespeare, he was sure of it—and he was going to enjoy himself a little. If Louisiana could manage without her governor, she could limp along without her Indian agent (who was, after all, only the second in command, or maybe he was the third, there was the secretary, Frederick Bates). Clark and Julia's honeymoon in Fincastle stretched into April. On the blessed day, Clark led her out to the dogwood tree, though they differed as to which dogwood it was.

Clark was busy preparing Julia's household for the move. By the end of April they were in Louisville, where Clark had to purchase a number of bulky items for the Indians, such as running gear for a horse-powered mill and portable forges. A letter had been waiting for him from Lewis, dated early March. It seemed the governor had taken up his post at last. Clark wrote back to say he'd arrive sometime in June with his bride and his niece Ann (a favorite of his, she and her three siblings had lost their mother, Clark's dear sister Elizabeth, when they were young; Clark could hardly believe Ann was a blossoming woman now, how old he was getting), and he must have added some reference to the "goods" or "merchandize" he was bringing, he meant the Indian goods. But Lewis, in his reply, decided to make a joke of it:

> I must halt here in the middle of my communications and ask you if the matrimonial dictionary affords no term more appropriate than that of goods, alias merchandize, for that dear and interesting part of the creation? It is very well, Genl., I shall tell madam of your want of Gallantry; and the triumph too of detection will be more complete when it is recollected what a musty, fusty, rusty old bachelor I am.

Clark was relieved to see that his friend was in good spirits again.

He and his household made their way down the Ohio to Fort Massac. There, to Clark's surprise and abashment (remembering his irritation with

Lewis all winter), they found two keelboats and a military escort waiting for them, dispatched by the governor. The gesture was welcome. Clark's progress had been slow, weighed down with dependents and furniture, and Julia was delicate. Her blessed condition had become apparent in Louisville.

On his arrival in St. Louis, Clark was again abashed (he really was ungenerous to his friend, what was it in him, what smallness?) to discover that Lewis had found a house for the married couple. No easy task, properties being scarce. It was cramped and dark, but probably the best Lewis could obtain at an affordable sum. Lewis took Clark and Julia through the rooms, pointing out the amenities.

Julia was touched. As they were settling in that night, she said, "People in Fincastle said Letitia Breckenridge found him alarming. I can't imagine why."

"Maybe she was intimated," Clark commented. "He's a formidable man."

"Oh, pooh. He's a dear. And he's good-looking."

"Now is he, now?"

So began Clark's life in St. Louis. Thinking about his angel (that *oh, pooh*! Curious and delightful how quickly the bashful girl becomes a wife!), his first child on the way, the city in which he was going to live, with its Choteaus and Lisas in their grand mansions, the high prices, the boom in land and trade—*Get on her, boy!*—the ground floor—Clark saw he must take on the mantle of a provider. Jonathan had said more than once, Billy's fault was, he didn't recognize there might be a rainy day.

The other Clark family men had long since set themselves up, while Clark had wandered hither and yon. It had been a grand adventure, but it was over. He had his sixteen hundred acres, and he bought twelve hundred more from Pierre Choteau. Buying lots in downtown St. Louis would be a sure investment. Maybe he'd go in on a venture with his nephew John to transport goods down the Ohio from John's store in Louisville, sell them in St. Louis at a clear profit of a hundred percent. And of course there was the Indian trade, that was the gold mine, as long as the redskins' warring didn't close the routes. Manuel Lisa had gone up the Missouri in the spring of 1807, bribed his way past the Rickerries, and returned with eight canoes loaded with furs, and a profit for each partner of three thousand dollars.

But the redskins *did* war, of course. At the moment, it was the Great Osarges who'd cast off allegiance to the U' States. The government had promised to set up a trading fort near them. General Clark's orders were to go up with a detachment of soldiers and advise on the location. He'd been planning to draw a line between the friendly Little Osarges and the vicious Great Osarges, but when he arrived at Fire Prairie he was met by the principal men of both divisions. All desired him to take them under his protection. So he drew up a treaty on the spot, which they cheerfully approved. They ceded near fifty thousand square miles of excellent country between the Missouri and Arkansas rivers, in exchange for the protection of the fort (which had been promised them in any case), a store, a mill, a blacksmith, and twelve hundred dollars' worth of merchandise. The treaty was so advantageous to the U' States, Clark had to assure the Secretary of War in his report that he'd taken no unfair means to induce their agreement.

Clark's Treaty, it might have been called. Except that when he returned to St. Louis, a few miscontents among the Great Osarges who wanted attention objected they hadn't been present. Clark assured Lewis every member of the Little Osarge Nation and a great majority of the Great Osarges were perfectly content, and Lewis said his trust in Clark was absolute. "However, if certain Osarges have even spurious complaints, we may be sure Mr. Choteau will encourage them. He has been going behind our backs, complaining of having been deprived of his lawful voice as their agent—not justly, but perhaps persuasively in the eye of the public, whose approbation he cultivates, if he does not downright purchase it."

So the governor saw fit to send Choteau back upriver to negotiate a new treaty. Which turned out identical to Clark's, except that it reserved a large tract of land, including the richest salt springs on the Missouri, in favor of— Mr. Pierre Choteau!

Lewis had taken a room at Choteau's mansion since moving out of Clark's overcrowded house in July, and Clark worried that his friend had come a little under that powerful and crafty man's influence. This was a town of weak laws and strong wills, unscrupulous people were making their fortunes, and Lewis knew more about birds and flower parts than men's dark hearts. Did he know what was said around town—that Secretary Bates coveted his position? Did he know how much bitterness he'd aroused among the settlers and traders by his attempts to regulate their conduct? The hatred of the Burrites he'd dismissed?

Clark saw Lewis frequently. He seemed in good enough spirits. But his temper was no more equable than it had ever been. Maybe less so. Maybe it was the intermittent fever he'd contracted, though there was nothing unusual about that, half the inhabitants of St. Louis had it. Clark had it. But then, Clark was used to it. There was the problem of Big White. A fur company Clark and other merchants were forming might serve in that regard. A friendly arrangement, to the benefit of all.

Anyway, Clark had other matters to concern him. Ann and Julia were homesick. His firstborn was due in January. And the slaves were sulky, they didn't like being hired out. But Clark had only a small garden to work, there was little for the slaves to do until a farm was bought, and the money from their hire was needed. He gave fifty here, fifty there, and soon they saw it was best not to cry about the whip, but do better.

And York. York! Oh, that was a painful subject! How could Clark have been so wrong about him? That's what shocked him to his soul—his being so deceived. He'd known York since they were children, they'd wrestled, eaten off each other's plates. None of the slave boys but York could be Clark's manservant, there was never a question. And all those years in Clark's service, the care, the understanding without being told, the pride in Clark, in himself.

Had it all been a lie? A deliberate deception? Could a fellow be so *fiendish*?

York knew things about Clark no one knew. But York didn't know him! Else how could he have expected for a moment Clark would agree to his demands? Because he seemed to expect. Expect and demand. It was outrageous! It was that trip west. York had done what was needed, what every man in the Corps did as his duty, but somehow he'd got the conviction that his services had been immense.

Clark remembered clambering out of that flooded ravine, York appearing a minute later, distressed (or so it appeared), nearly in tears, he'd been searching and feared the worst. He unscrewed his flask, tipped brandy in his master's mouth.

Was his only fear on that day that if he lost Clark he lost his ticket to freedom? Was that all Clark was to him? All his service directed toward? The moment when he would hold out his pink palm and say, "Now you owe me"?

Clark was determined to punish him, either thrash him or send him to New Orleans to be sold. But Lewis advised patience. He said to send York to Louisville, to visit his wife for a bit. Maybe he'd find his situation there not so favorable as he imagined.

Freedom and his wife: that's what York wanted. As if St. Louis wasn't full of negresses he could marry, whether he was free or not. If he cared so all-fired much about keeping a wife, why hadn't he contracted with one of the Clark family slaves? And how could he be such a damn fool to desire his freedom? That was something a field hand might sing about, who had no notion what a harsh world awaited the free negro. York knew better than that.

Except—he didn't!

Oh, Clark would never forget the moment. He'd concluded the Osarge treaty (the one that was stolen from him) and he was returning to St. Louis by boat instead of horse, because he was ill. Lying in the pirogue, feverish and puking and shitting liquid over the side. He hadn't brought York, because with the other slaves grumbling, and Ann talking about returning to Louisville, Julia needed a firm support. Clark was carried into the house, and there was York, who knew better than anyone how to tend him. Clark was in his power. Emptying the pot, wringing out the cloths: "Master William, I've been wanting to ask you something for a long time."

"Speak, York, speak! Open your heart!"

And York did, and a vulture flew out and commenced feeding on Clark's heart.

How dearly Clark wished his brother Jonathan were here. To hear his advice. He wrote letters to him. And with one of them, brokenhearted, he sent along York. Sulking. To be with his wife. York had looked Clark in the face and told him he preferred being hired out in Louisville. York had looked him in the eye and said he preferred being *sold*. So he could be with his wife. Clark had served his purpose, now he could be discarded. Clark wrote to Jonathan, *If any attempt is made by York to run off, or refuse to perform his duty as a slave, I wish him sent to New Orleans and sold, or hired out to some severe master until he thinks better of such conduct.*

All that winter York was in Louisville. Jonathan wrote that he didn't want to come back. As for Clark—a shave, a sleeve, a spoon, a shoe, a brush, a word, a hundred times a day, York was not there. Even Clark's old stock started giving him trouble. Scowl a little, pout a little, steal a little, lie a little. Fifty here, sixty there. He contemplated selling all but four. Turning his slaves into money! He'd always despised men who did that. He wrote to Jonathan, *Clouds seem to fly thicker than they used to do, and I think there will be a rainy day.* He wrote, *I fear you will think that I have become a severe master.*

Thank God there was a great light in his life. In January, his angel safely delivered. In the bedroom, Clark held the miracle, his son. He'd chosen the name long ago. Meriwether Lewis Clark.

And he had a gift for the mother, his pale, happy Julia. He'd carried it hidden all the way from Washington. A set of Shakespeare.

THE HERO
[1807–1809]

1

Lewis must concede that it was not entirely degrading, this adulation. His admirers would bow before a performing bear, if that were the nine days' wonder; yet the agent be ever so interchangeable, the phenomenon was real, and it was as heady as brandy: the breath of fame and fortune blowing from him, so that in every room he entered, along every path he trod, he saw it rippling outward across bodies and faces, a force, turning them toward him, flushing, a brightness sparking in the eyes. Lewis the burning glass, the striking steel.

But was his heart made of flint that even in this, his season of glory, he saw causes for derision and doubt? When he was served his first meal in heaven (if ever he got there), would he taste ashes beneath his nectar and ambrosia? He was a divining rod for ashes!

His metaphors were confused. Perhaps because the swirl around him was confusing: the offers, the sidling-up of favor-seekers, the encomiums, the emoluments, the impatience for tales, the importunings of scientists, for seeds, maps, measurements, skins, the world, the world, the world. Where was Clark? It was January; Lewis was in Washington City. The testimonial dinner had twice been postponed for Lewis's friend. When it was held at last on the 14th, Clark was not there. Could he still be in Fincastle? What was taking him so long? Surely Judith fell into his arms like a load of laundry the moment he appeared in her parlor, and what remained but to set a date? Lewis sat alone in the hero's seat. On his left hand was a lesser honorand, the vulpine Pierre Chouteau; on his right, Big White. Next to Chouteau sat the Osage chiefs, whom that merchant prince and Machiavel regarded as his personal property, along with every furbearing animal and mineral deposit in their immense territories.

Lewis had heard a thousand toasts by now, in every city and townlet between St. Louis and Washington that could scare up a table and a jug. He derived a certain (flint-hearted) pleasure from their predictable and blameless sentiments, as he called out Ho! and Amen! and downed his glass.

To the memory of Columbus! May those who imitate his hardihood never, like him, have to encounter public ingratitude!

To the Missouri! May it prove a vehicle of wealth to all the nations of the world!

Interspersed with the scheduled toasts were the volunteers, one of which it was incumbent upon Lewis to make. He tended to put this off, and therefore he'd be feeling his drink by the time he rose on his hero's legs (the banqueting hall or cowshed sinking to obsequious stillness), and there would pass an instant during which he was not entirely sure he wouldn't actually utter one of the phrases he'd been privately toying with.

To the sun! May it rise tomorrow, shortly after dawn!

That moment of standing, of sticking out his glass, filled him with panic, at what his audience expected of him. At what he half expected of himself.

To ladies' dresses! Which perform the inestimable public service of hiding their pudenda!

Of course he veered away; but on evenings when he'd neglected to drill into his head, ahead of time, some ironclad platitude, he emitted opinions that were a trifle obscure. As in Washington, where he intoned with perfect solemnity, "May works be the test of patriotism, as they ought, of right, to be of religion." The crowd expressed its preordained approval, and Lewis sat down, wondering where *that* had come from. Was it a swipe at his mother's Methodism? Or a glove thrown down to God: if You want me to believe in You, You damned well better *do* something?

The things Lewis heard about himself, in the edificatory preambles and exhortatory perorations of provincial dignitaries: he was a Touchstone, an Exemplar, a Cynosure, a Polar Star, a Standard, a Philosopher-Explorer, an Undaunted Leader, a Pearl of Manhood, a Prince of the Wilderness.

With the hardihood of a Virginian, born and bred, our own Xenophon conducted his Band of Thirty on this American Anabasis—

You have penetrated the gloom of regions yet groaning under unviolated forests—

Actuated by unsullied motives of genuine philanthropy, you have received in parental embrace nations still in the infancy of reason and government—

In Albemarle, where he spent three days on his way to Washington, Lewis learned new things about his childhood. As a young lad, he'd calmly shot dead a bull that was charging him. During a nocturnal Indian attack in Georgia, while his older campmates had scampered about in panic, he'd thought to douse the fire. When he was a mere sprout of a schoolboy, six or seven, he'd exhibited a scientific bent by jumping in the air and inquiring of his teacher, "If the earth turns, why did I come down in the same place?" He was particularly mortified by this last fib (peddled by the aged schoolmaster at every public gathering), because he remembered the anecdote, as surely others did: it hailed from the school's reader, an exemplum from the boyhood of a sixteenth-century astronomer.

At the gala in Washington, another new thing. Xenophon be damned. Someone read a poem by the famous Mr. Joel Barlow, in which Lewis was compared to—Apollo! Still, there was little practical fame in that; there was hardly a single working shrine to Apollo in Washington. The poem ended on a more helpful note, proposing that the Columbia be renamed the Lewis River.

But why stop there? (Lewis touched his heart, he pantomimed humility.) It was generally agreed that the Pacific Ocean was a misnomer. And who, after all, was Amerigo Vespucci?

The final toast, by inviolable custom, was dedicated to the absent ladies: *May they ever bestow their smiles on hardihood and virtuous valor!*

That was the hero's reward, was it not? Not what he did it for—the hero did it for Science!—but Science could not, in gratitude, sidle into his arms and turn up a humid face for a kiss. Every woman between St. Louis and Washington had now been put on notice: this hero lacked a wife.

Lewis rose, tottered, thanked. He escorted Big White (drunker) and Jessome (drunkest) back to their lodgings, then made his way in the dark to the President's House, whose illustrious occupant had retired hours before. Mr. Jefferson did not attend testimonial dinners. Lewis climbed the stairs to his room. He was going to be Governor of Louisiana. His Excellency, they would call him. John Pernier, a free mulatto he'd hired in St. Louis, rose from his cot to help him undress. "Pernier," Lewis sighed. "I'm tired."

"Yes, sir."

Lewis lay in the dark. Where was Clark? Pernier was in his nook; the President abed; Seaman in St. Louis, awaiting his master. Lewis had to admit—

But he'd overindulged. He fell asleep.

He had to admit (the next morning) that he was disappointed by his reception. That was the despicable thing. He might mock the attentions paid him, but in truth, he wanted more. It had infuriated him that the Burr conspiracy had come to light just as he and Clark were arriving in St. Louis, thus filling the newspapers with something other than *him*. England's impounding of American merchant ships, her impressment of American sailors, were personal insults. These trivial acts of war were stealing his thunder!

Thus raged the homunculus in the cave of his heart.

But he was being too hard on himself (he lectured himself, at other times). He was luxuriating in self-loathing. He didn't care a pin for the approbation of the crowd, only the esteem of Mr. Jefferson.

I received, my dear Sir, with unspeakable joy your letter of Sep. 23 announcing the return of yourself, Capt. Clark & your party in good health to St. Louis. Lewis had felt such anticipatory pleasure at the thought of his return to the President's House. He'd imagined—

Well, what *had* he imagined? Unconditional approval, he supposed.

No; that was too much. He'd expected (surely not unreasonably) a clear acknowledgment that he had justified his existence in this sublunary world.

It had not turned out quite like that. The first disappointment was, the President's House had changed. Lewis's office and cabinet had been pulled down. Instead, he had a bedroom upstairs, accessible via a new grand staircase. Along the same hall were the rooms of the three other young, or not-so-young, men of the household: the President's two sons-in-law, John Eppes and Thomas Randolph, and Lewis's replacement as secretary, another Albemarle man, Isaac Coles. *Five* mice in a church, now; a veritable congregation.

Coles, like the erstwhile Lewis, had nothing to do in the secretarial line. Thus he, like Lewis, carried messages to Congress, and rode with the President in the mornings, and closeted with him in the library. Unlike Lewis, he appeared to thrive in dinner settings, where his conversation perfectly married sparkle and reserve. He even looked like the President: tall and thin, with the same ruddy complexion and bleached hazel eyes. (And if he was Isaac, that made Lewis—ah, but he was self-dramatizing.)

[THE HERO]

The President had aged. He was more stooped; almost subdued. His second term was going badly. Trade had been devastated by the war between England and France. His enemies were losing no opportunity to point out that British depredations on American vessels could not be countered because the President had so drastically reduced the American navy. And the Burr conspiracy, this extraordinary personal betrayal, weighed heavily on his thoughts. Worse, while Lewis was gone, Mr. J's younger daughter, Polly, had died from complications of childbirth. The single time he referred to it in Lewis's presence, Lewis could see that the word for this emotion, too, was *unspeakable*. His wife long gone, now six of his seven children. "I feel as though, at my age, I should make Death my friend, Lewis; except that he has dealt so harshly with me." His sole surviving daughter, Maria, was in Albemarle with her children. Mr. J had always pretended to prefer retirement to public office, but now when he raised the subject (Washington was "intolerable," it was "sickening"), he sounded sincere.

Therefore the Touchstone, *et al.*, was a welcome distraction. But needless to say, when he'd envisioned his welcome, it had not been as a distraction. The President did evince enthusiasm. He detailed his own experiments with the seeds Lewis had sent down from the Mandan villages; he reported on the fates of the live animals (the prairie hen and three of the four magpies had died en route, the fourth magpie some months ago; the prairie dog lived on at Peale's museum in Philadelphia, but Peale thought it was pining from loneliness). Lewis took out the twoscore map sheets he and Clark had made of their route, and he and the President laid them on the floor of the library, aligning them according to the penciled arrows, so that St. Louis was by the door, Fort Clatsop was crowding the fireplace, Lewis's fight with the Minetares (or the Blackfeet) was hard under the geraniums on the windowsill. He and Mr. J ambled back and forth, and bent low, and even crawled, and Lewis told his tales, just himself and the President, and Mr. J (though disappointed at the absence of a water passage) was pleased with this hoard of new information.

What Lewis had not quite expected (he supposed, in retrospect) was that the presidential bravos would be interleaved with statements tending to characterize the expedition as the mere beginning of a process that must culminate in something far more important, viz., the publication of Lewis's findings. Of course Lewis had known all along that publication was the *sine qua non:* a fact unpublished was lost to science. It was just that— He considered the expedition itself to have been— Well—forgive his arrogance!—rather a signal achievement. And here was Mr. J, talking with more animation about lectures at the American Philosophical Society than he demonstrated for Lewis's attempts to evoke for him what the expedition was *like:* the dangers, the deprivations, the accesses of joy, the mornings, the air, the white light, the great spaces. For example, Lewis might speak of his first sight of the Rocky Mountains, that moment when, a far-off glint, his first wild—and the President would ask him to estimate their height.

Lewis had to remind himself: the President was no explorer, but a man of desks and papers. He had to remind himself: it was not just the President who could not understand.

Consider the dogs: he'd felt the need to be somewhat disingenuous about that. In his public letters from St. Louis, he'd written that the Corps, when among the Chopunnish, had been forced to eat dogs because the roots had made them sick, and the salmon were unfit. In other words, he'd made of it a conventional hardship tale: *we were in such dire straits, good citizens, that we ate dogs!* And the women hid their faces, and the men honored you for the sacrifice you had made. How could Lewis have written the truth? *The salmon were abundant, but we preferred dog. At Fort Clatsop, the elk were abundant, but we had come to love dog. We traded our brass buttons for dogs, pups that squirmed to ingratiate themselves, that we tomahawked and disemboweled. A dog on a spit, the oils bubbling, that heavenly smell, like beaver.* How could Lewis write or tell of the moment in a Chopunnish lodge, on the voyage back, as he tucked into toothsome loin of dog, when a brave scornfully threw a live pup on his plate (the Chopunnish did not eat dog) and Lewis, enraged, picked up the pup and threw it back against the brave's chest with great force, then speared a chunk of meat on his plate and held it up to the brave's nose, taunting, "Good dog!" and popped it in his mouth?

Consider (for a moment) what his public letters said: *The navigation of the Missouri may be deemed safe and good.* A falsehood. But as Lewis was forced to concede that no water passage existed, the President needed good news to protect him from Federalist criticism for the expense of the expedition.

The passage by land of 340 miles from the Missouri to the Kooskooskee is the most formidable part of the tract proposed across the Continent; of this distance, 200 miles is along a good road, and 140 over tremendous mountains which for 60 miles are covered with eternal snows; however, a passage over these mountains is practicable from the latter part of June to the last of September, and the cheap rate at which horses are to be obtained from the Indians of the Rocky Mountains and West of them, reduces the expenses of transportation over this portage to a mere trifle.

Highly doubtful. The Shoshones and Chopunnish were not fools.

The Missouri and all its branches from the Chyenne upwards abound more in beaver and common otter than any other streams on earth, particularly that portion of them lying within the Rocky Mountains.

Exaggeration, founded on ignorance.

We attempted with success those unknown formidable snow clad mountains on the bare word of a savage, while 99/100th of his countrymen assured us that a passage was impracticable.

Mere glory-mongering, feeding the public appetite for tales of adventure. The Shoshones knew Old Toby was right about the road through the mountains, because the Chopunnish used it every year. They spoke against its practicability for the transparent reason that they wanted the Corps to spend the winter with them, in the hopes of cadging more firearms.

Early in the morning of the 27th they treacherously seized on & made themselves masters of all our guns—in which situation we engaged them with our knives & our pistol recovered our guns & killed 2 of them & put the others to flight.

Oh, with what care had Lewis chosen those words! An exegete might write a commentary on them. Sitting in the hero's seat at banquets, Lewis had heard versions come back to haunt him—*with no thought of your own safety, you have braved the fire of ferocious savages to regain the steeds without which your little party was doomed to perish of inanition in that trackless desert*—and he had thought, staring placidly ahead, You fraud, you *miles gloriosus*.

In the early mornings in Washington, if he had not squandered the late-night hours, he went hunting. But the game had largely fled the woods. The stumps were gone from the avenues. The townhouses had been propagating. He submitted bills of exchange to the War Department; he drew up lists; he wrote recommendations. Astounding, the amount of paperwork that came bobbing in the wake of adventure. He paid a call on the Secretary of War, Mr. Dearborn, and informed him that in the matter of compensation, it was his wish that there be no distinction of rank between himself and Mr. Clark, and the man smiled with all the understanding in the world, and pursed his regretful lips, and said something about irregularity and impossibility. This was the man who'd blocked Clark's captaincy in the first place, this was the fucking idiot plenipotentiary, enthroned on his ziggurat of reports.

How wan, how anemic, everything seemed since the expedition, how sordid! From the moment Lewis and Clark had arrived in St. Louis, it was chits, bills, notes, bonds of conveyance, back pay, land grants—as though those three years had been a mere job, and now it was time to get paid. Of course they deserved it. But Lewis detested arguing for it. And the parties in Congress fought with all the decorum of a couple of Ohio bravos over the compensation bill. Senators who couldn't sit a horse, who hadn't spent a night of their lives out of a feather bed, said the proposal was exorbitant, unprecedented. Newspapers pontificated; ignoramuses wrote letters.

Big White and the Osage chiefs performed a war dance and calumet ceremony on the stage of a Washington theater, presumably not aware that, coming between yesterday's Turkish seraglio and tomorrow's Chinoiserie, they were nothing to the crowd but entertainment and novelty. Chouteau promiscuously professed his public spirit, while he fought behind the scenes (Lewis could detect the arras rippling) to retain his Osage agency—viz., his trade monopoly, i.e., his license to steal—in the face of Clark's superior claims. Eventually, the Indians and their interpreters were escorted to Philadelphia, to be further impressed with white power. But they were more impressed with the whores, and they all caught the venereal.

Clark at last arrived from Fincastle, and Lewis had so looked forward to quiet evenings with him reminiscing, but his friend was too full of Julia (this apparently being the designation of the winged creature that had emerged from little Judy's chrysalis), and of course this was natural, and Lewis rejoiced with him, but he was left with little consolation save the thought that a young (or not so young!) man's ardors inevitably waned; sweethearts became wives, while friends remained friends. Lewis had noticed before that men on the verge of marriage wanted the whole world married (it spoke volumes about their ambivalence), and Clark, alas, was no different. After he'd inquired twice or thrice about a possible lodestar of Lewis's own heart, one evening at the theater (the same house in which Big White had sat on an armchair-throne on the stage—the newspapers had called him King of the Mandans—and played himself, badly, and with his pale skin made paler by the footlights he looked as though he hadn't a drop of Indian blood in him), Lewis pointed out a woman whose name at least he knew, swearing Clark to secrecy, and thus, mercifully, to silence.

Besmirchment; soiling. Worst of all was the prospect of sergeants or privates from the Corps publishing their own accounts of the expedition. On the very day the Corps returned to St. Louis, Private Frazier had asked Lewis's permission to publish his journal, and Lewis, giddy, distracted, grateful to all, had given it, only recognizing his mistake when he saw Frazier's prospectus. The man was proposing not merely to narrate his own limited experiences *(another day hauling on the towrope, oh when will it end? . . . from a distance I thought I saw . . . I overheard one of the captains say . . .)* but to give an "accurate description" of the Missouri and its branches; the Rocky Mountains; the Columbia; the Indian tribes; the vegetables, animals, and minerals! the latitudes and longitudes!

Alarming and absurd! Was he going to compile his data from goat entrails? This shoddy product, rushed into print for a quick profit, would capture the public's impatient attention and diffuse its misconstructions far and wide! Lewis demanded that Frazier expunge from his proposal all pretense to scientific knowledge. The man blamed his publisher, and promised a retraction; but Lewis was now worried about the other men. Clark's Band of Brothers, oh, yes! The father's will and testament was about to be read, and backs should not be turned!

In early March, in Washington, Lewis's nightmare came true. Word reached him that a bookseller in Pittsburgh named McKeehan had bought Sergeant Gass's journal and was raising a subscription for publication. A draft prospectus claimed competence in all the scientific areas. Moreover, as this McKeehan was a stranger, who hadn't felt it necessary to request Lewis's permission—and being an Irishman, and even worse, a Pittsburgher—he was not likely to bow to demands.

"This is most unfortunate," said the President. "Some sort of warning must be published." Lewis withheld the comment that if the President hadn't instructed him to encourage the men to keep their own journals, they wouldn't be in this position.

Mr. J was concerned enough to work with Lewis on the draft of the public notice—in fact, the President mostly wrote it—and Lewis unwisely put his name to it. He published it in the Washington newspaper, the *National Intelligencer*:

Having been informed that there were several unauthorised and probably some spurious publications now preparing for the press, on the subject of my late tour to the Pacific Ocean by individuals entirely unknown to me, I have considered it a duty which I owe the public, as well as myself to put them on their guard with respect to such publications, lest from the practice of such impositions they may be taught to depreciate the worth of the work which I am myself preparing for publication before it can possibly appear, as much time, labor, and expense are absolutely necessary in order to do justice to the several subjects which it will embrace.

It was all true, all justified. But in this world, if you lied to the public, you were a hero. If you stated necessary truths, you diminished yourself.

Unwise; perhaps Lewis's judgment had been affected; he'd been ill. Clark had visited him in his upstairs sickroom, the day before returning to Fincastle to "secure his happiness" (as they say); then on to St. Louis. Even now the two old friends could not merely talk at their ease, as once they'd done on evenings along the Missouri and at Fort Clatsop, no, it must be a hurried visit, and money must raise its hydra head, and there must be receipts and signatures and tottings-up in the margins, because the Corpsmen's extra pay was in Lewis's keeping, and Clark had come to receive his, and to carry the rest to St. Louis. Lewis did steal a few moments to rib his friend, as friends did, about his coming trial in Fincastle. Perhaps Clark would *find* her *castle* closed to him! What, then, would the hero do? Swim the moat, scale the wall? Overcome her defenses with main force and vigor? Ha ha! Then Clark left, and Lewis swallowed some calomel pills, and spent the night with the chamber pot.

Toward the end of March, he made ready to go to Philadelphia. On the morning he left, the President (who'd been laid low himself, with one of his weeks-long headaches; he was squinting, heading for his bed) wordlessly handed him the latest issue of the *Monthly Anthology* of Boston, forwarded anonymously. A marked page, an anonymous poem:

> Good people, listen to my tale,
> 'Tis nothing but what true is,
> I'll tell you of the mighty deeds
> Achiev'd by Captain Lewis—
> How, starting from the Atlantick shore
> By fair and easy motion
> He journied *all the way by land*
> Until he met the ocean.
>
> Heroick, sure, the toil must be
> To travel through the woods, sir;
> And never meet a foe, yet save
> His person and his goods, sir!
> What marvels on the way he found
> *He'll* tell you, if inclin'd, sir—
> But I shall only now disclose
> The things he *did not* find, sir.

Lewis's eye skated over the next few stanzas—oh, it went on and on—it appeared he'd found no mammoths—no Welshmen, neither—nor a mountain of salt—and by gum, he was no Apollo at all! Then:

> We never will be so fubbed off,
> As sure as I'm a sinner!
> Come—let us all subscribe, and ask
> The HERO to a dinner—
> And Barlow stanzas shall indite
> A bard, the tide who tames, sir—
> And if we cannot alter *things*
> By God, we'll change their *names,* sir!
>
> Let old Columbus be once more
> Degraded from his glory;
> And not a river by his name

remember him in story—
For what is *old* Discovery
Compar'd to that which new is?
Strike—strike Columbia river out,
And put in—River Lewis!

The hero mounted his horse. Washington was the dust behind him, Philadelphia the haze of brotherly love ahead. There, he would arrange his own publication. *Ladies and Gentlemen, Lewis's patented expedition is guaranteed to chase away a gloomy day and simultaneously administer an emetic spoonful of accurate science! Accept no substitutes!*

2

Mid-December. A morning. The 14th, 15th? Fog. He lies, cover to chin, staring at the ceiling. He can't sleep. In his bed, in the house he grew up in, his mother's house; Ivy; Albemarle. Her hazel eyes, locust arms, oak endurance, she goes in and out, tending him with tinctures, decoctions, lavender for vertigo, marshmallow for acrimony, marjoram for agitation. Her boy come back with his tail between his legs. Tuck him in. That satisfies her pretty well, pretty well.

"Meriwether . . ." Her voice. The next room, this room.

A Journal of the Voyages & Travels of a Corps of Discovery, under the command of Captain Lewis and Captain Clark. By Patrick Gass. Proposal for publishing by subscription, by David McKeehan, Bookseller. A description of the country, inhabitants, soil, climate, vegetables and animals. To recommend the correctness of this work, the publisher begs leave to state, that at the different resting places during the expedition, the several journals were brought together, compared, corrected, and the blanks filled up.

Liar, poltroon! For the hundredth time Lewis slaps the rump of the horse, it bolts from beneath the publisher; the rope snaps taut, he kicks, kicks. *The price to subscribers will be one dollar.* No engravings, no maps, no vocabularies, under three hundred pages duodecimo, inferior paper, McKeehan promised it in boards, but it came out half-bound in leather, a lady's pocketbook, something to button in the bodice with sermons and sonnets.

All five thousand copies sold. Lewis has one in the trunk at the foot of his bed. A second edition planned.

Prospectus of Lewis and Clark's Tour to the Pacific Ocean through the Interior of the Continent of North America. This work will be prepared by Captain Meriwether Lewis, and will be divided into two parts, the whole comprised in three volumes octavo, containing from four to five hundred pages each, printed on good paper, and a fair Pica type.

Volume first, the narrative; volume second, geography and accounts of the Indian tribes; volume third, natural history. Printed separately, a large map. Ten dollars for the first two volumes, eleven for the third, ten for the map. Expensive; but necessary—the plates; the accuracy; the quality. *He therefore declares to the public that his late voyage was not undertaken with a view to pecuniary advantages.* The printing and binding alone will cost him $4,500. Out of his own pocket. *The first volume of the work will most probably be published about the 1st of January 1808.* About a fortnight from now. The journals are in the trunk at the foot of his bed.

"Meriwether, awake?" His forehead, wrist. "Drink this." She regards him. What would be the correct intrepretation of her expression? An herb doctor's objectivity, a mother's contempt? She is accustomed to this power. Lewis's father had fogs.

Lewis & Clark's Tour. The short title.

God Almighty!—when Lewis was handed the newspaper with McKeehan's reply to him printed in it—*it may perhaps be agreeable to Your Excellency to know the reasons of my interfering in this affair of the journals of what you very modestly call* your *late tour*—but his friend Mahlon Dickerson dissuaded him from riding posthaste across the Alleghenies with a horsewhip; "*Cher ami,* far wiser to ignore it; this pitiable lunatic will suffer the obloquy which his own words compel"—*by what high grant or privilege do you claim the right of authorizing or suppressing publications concerning this tour?*

It was good to see his old friend Dickerson again in Philadelphia. Lewis hadn't thought of him in years, but had always liked him; they'd met at the President's table; a Princeton man, a lawyer, the best of families, Clark's age, another fusty bachelor like Lewis, good-looking, sits a horse extremely well, loves company, a glass. The girls certainly had their eyes on the two gallants as they rode in the park—*it is alleged and believed you pocketed your pay as private secretary to the president during the expedition—while Your Excellency was star-gazing, Mr. Gass was taking observations in the world below—*

Lewis casts his eye cautiously around the room. His mother gone. A bowl of soup on a table by his bed.

—you are not a man of science, you are not a man of letters. I have information upon this point—

In Philadelphia, he attended three meetings of the American Philosophical Society. Of which he is a valued member. A clamor of questions. When would he publish? Barton held back his own paper on the antelope, in deference to Lewis's more complete account, forthcoming.

So much to do. Twenty dollars to the printer for the book prospectus. Ten to Varnum to distribute it. (Oyez, oyez, oyez!) Hassler was doing the longitude calculations. That was a hundred. Barton's man, Pursh, was arranging the plant specimens, helping with drawings; another sixty or seventy. Forty to Barralet for two engravings. All out of his pocket. And Brother Ordway reverted to a Yankee and demanded five hundred for his journal; Lewis cried him down to three, more than his sergeant's pay for the entire expedition, a pretty God-damned good premium for five minutes' daily scribbling, and not an iota in there Lewis might need, just to keep another McKeehan from crawling out of the woodwork. *I am afraid Captain Clark, who appears to have acted during the whole of the tour with the greatest prudence, firmness and courage, will be forced to blush for the man he has called his friend—*into the seventh circle of hell!—*a wag might insinuate that your wound was not accidental, but the consequence of design, so that the young hero would not return without more scars—*God!—*the young hero with his point of honor just past the point of a rock, with Cruzatte taking aim! Perhaps there will be a representation in the plates!* Oh, God! Dickerson was wrong! God! The bile is drowning him!

Lewis breathes, eyes shut. Locust Hill. December. He must go to St. Louis. His Excellency.

He opens his eyes. The soup is untouched. Or is it vomit?

So much to do in Philadelphia: trying to bring some order to his accounts, three years of bills of exchange he'd written, some two thousand in all, it was hard to credit the total, all the provisions, information he'd had to buy, Indian diplomacy, smoothing the way with Spanish officials, overpaying the Chouteaus for every gewgaw, gallimaufry, and Gallic shrug.

[THE HERO]

He stares: soup.

Sir: Upon examining your several drafts which have been paid at this office, I find the following among the number; and which upon referring to your accounts, I cannot discover that you have ever brought to your debit.

That was Simmons, the War Department accountant; his mild, remorseless pen.

Should you have any claims to oppose to the above-mentioned bills, or explanation to give, I beg you will have the goodness to state the same as early as convenient.

Sitting for his portrait by Mr. Peale, Lewis thought he could understand, of a sudden, the reluctance of Indians to undergo this procedure. Was that him, that embalmed three-quarter likeness that would be his ambassador to the avid world? Weak chin; beak. Peale showed him around his museum, the mounted skins Lewis had sent from Fort Mandan, the Indian weapons fixed on the wall. An antelope stared, devoid of its characteristic curiosity. A prairie dog sat up, guarding its hole. "Is that—?"

"Yes. The little fellow expired in February. Though he'd wasted, the pelt, as you see, was in good condition."

So much to do! *Sir: I am desirous to become a Subscriber to "Lewis and Clark's Tour," and I have taken the liberty of applying to you— Sir: Having been informed that it is your intention to publish a map . . . affords me an opportunity . . . an improvement I have made in the art of varnishing of maps . . . please to favor me—* Meanwhile, he was awaited with impatience in St. Louis; his secretary there, Frederick Bates, would not let him forget it. *Nothing but an actual experience could have fully informed me of the extent of those duties and responsibilities, which in your absence, it will be necessary for me to take upon myself.* Well, he was a pale, nervous young man, suited to office work, and suffering from a high opinion of his abilities—let him take them on! And as usual, the President had loaded Lewis with private errands: a watch to be repaired, a certain bauble to buy. This simple Republican, with his regal tastes. And while he was having Lewis augment his material cares, he was kindly reducing Lewis's own, sending twenty-five boxes of his western specimens to Albemarle *by water*; the ship (of course) was stranded by a wavelet on a grain of sand, and all was lost. *I sincerely regret the loss you sustained,* Lewis wrote, *it seems peculiarly unfortunate that those which had passed the continent of America, and after their exposure to so many casualties and risks, should have met such destiny in their passage through a small portion only of the Chesapeake.*

From Bates: *I have great cause to lament your absence. There are very many subjects which require— Contrary to my first expectation you must expect to have some enemies—*

Simmons: *You will do well to bring with you to Washington any papers or documents which may relate to your expenditures on the expedition, so as to explain such of the charges as may require it.* Of course. Now, where had Lewis put the receipts for all those dogs they ate?

In the evenings: rest, slow unwinding. Dinner with the governor, or toasts at a tavern, Lewis the guest of honor with Mr. Barlow, what was the name of that epic poem he was working on, the *Lewisiad*? Dining with Dickerson, talking late into the night about the coming war with England, or girls, or the horned lizard (on which Dickerson had decided opinions), accompanying him *chez* here and *chez* there, he knew everyone, riding out to some friend's farm and lounging all day in the heat, eating, drinking, shooting at trees. Perhaps Dickerson drank too much. Perhaps Lewis, as a friend, kept him too much company in it. In Dickerson's case, Lewis, from time to time, has suspected an irregularity in his passions, poor fellow. There was a hint of a scrape; Dickerson had had some fright. The girls! Lewis would say, pointing out the pretty ones. We may be bachelors, but mayn't we delectate? Amorites were everywhere, couples walking under the young elms, paddling palms on benches. Some mornings Dickerson confessed himself *bien chagriné,* and was it only partaking of too much spirits that he spoke of? The fellow needed a wife, a north to his compass. Lewis did, too, and he set his mind to it. There was a dark-haired Miss Ann with whom he'd traded a sentence or two. She had a self-possession that was not unappealing; she didn't pant in his face, or appear to be waiting quietly to devour a man (the wallflower that reveals itself to be a Venus flytrap); he thought he could imagine— But then he discovered her uncloying ways did not stem from self-possession, rather possession by another. She was engaged.

Love always played Lewis the fool! Then there was Miss Emily. But that was for show. When his hostesses were not asking him when his book would appear, they were wondering was there a lucky girl, or didn't His Excellency think the fair ladies of Philadelphia were as charming a gaggle as he might find anywhere? Miss Emily was a means of uncrowding himself. He paid compliments and court; her lower lip protruded with a glisten that he found obscurely repulsive; but they had quasi-witty exchanges, there was the touch of her shoulder to his upper arm as they both turned to view the scene. Then he began to fear she was taking it all too seriously, and he had to beg off outings. Fortunately, he was leaving for Washington.

I have made an attack most vigorously, we have come to terms. So simple for Clark! And that simplicity, one of the reasons Lewis loves his friend. Clark runs clear. Of course, Lewis noticed in his letter, announcing his engagement, that he'd again unconsciously borrowed from Lewis, in this case the notion of the castle—it was that ingenuousness, that openness, a frank quality—a boyishness, despite the fact that he was the older one, something unprotected, a poignancy with which he pursued his limpid way through the labyrinthine world. Lewis remembered (a small thing, but—), if York was engaged on some other Corps business, Lewis had often, before an Indian council, to stop Clark at the tent opening and fasten a button he'd neglected, pull his coattails straight.

"Meriwether . . ."

His soup. He is supposed to have eaten it. "I'm not hungry, Mother."

"Meriwether . . ."

Every time she utters his name, she is claiming him for herself, for her clan. Of course he is a Meriwether; but he is more a Lewis, and when is that mentioned? His height is from his father; his eyes, his temperament. The Meriwethers never flag; the women chirp, they rustle, they rule the roost; they go in and out with trays; they call advice from the next room. The Meriwether sisters said that William Lewis requested on his deathbed that he be buried at Cloverfields, the Meriwether farm where he'd turned up horseless and drenched, where they cared for him assiduously until he died under their care. Something about the bad roads, they said he said. So there he lies, among Meriwethers. He was the fifth of five sons, and his uncles were heroes from the Indian wars. He, too, had had something to prove. Volunteering early to fight the British; determining that a river would not stop him.

His mother is stoking the fire. *Although affliction cometh not forth of the dust, neither doth trouble spring out of the ground; yet man is born unto trouble, as the sparks fly upward.* Perhaps the line in all the Book that most sticks in Lewis's craw. God's unmanly shrug, His miserable self-exculpation: *It's your fault.*

He shuts his eyes. When he opens them, the room is empty.

She has been good to him. God knows, she knows what he is like. His lies to her over the years—how many has she seen through? She says she wants him to attend to the family's land claims in the Ohio Valley when he passes through Louisville on his way to St. Louis. What will he say about the claims he told her he'd filed years ago? Might he take refuge in irregular records? *I have found no trace—pages missing—fraud rampant—*

He should have been in St. Louis last fall. What he told Clark; told everyone. He returned from Philadelphia to Washington in July to settle his accounts with Simmons, then rode on to Albemarle in August. Some last family business; he would set out at the end of the month; be in St. Louis by October. What happened?

When he got on his horse, he rode to Richmond, instead.

Why?

(Think.) To observe the government's proceedings against Burr.

Why? The President had not asked him to go.

Burr's trial would afford invaluable insights into the secessionist intrigues of Louisiana Territory. Facts would come to light. The governor would be irresponsible not to avail himself of the opportunity.

In October, he was back in Ivy. Clark was in Louisville. He would be traveling to Fincastle toward the end of the year, to marry Julia Hancock. Of course, there was more family business to which Lewis was forced to attend, it never stopped: land speculation on behalf of his mother; arranging for his half brother John's education in Philadelphia.

Dear Dickerson . . . This will be handed you by my brother . . . I have given him letters of introduction to Wistar, Rush & Peale, and have strictly enjoined him to call on you frequently . . . we both know that young men are sometimes in want of such a friend . . . So much for business, now for the <u>girls</u> . . . My little affair with Miss A-n R-sh . . . I found that she was previously engaged . . . I am now a <u>perfect widower with respect to love.</u> Thus floating on the <u>surface of occasion</u>, I feel all that restlessness, that inquietude, that certain indescribable something common to old bachelors, which I cannot avoid thinking my dear fellow, proceeds, from that <u>void in our hearts,</u> which might, or ought to be better filled. Whence it comes I know not, but certain it is, that I never felt less like a hero than at the present moment. What may be my next adventure god knows, but on this I am determined, <u>to get a wife</u>. Do let me hear from you as frequently as you can, and when you have no subject of more importance talk about <u>the girls</u> . . .

He mounted his horse. The journals were in the saddlebags. It was November. He headed for St. Louis. His younger brother Reuben accompanied him, hoping to make his fortune in Louisiana. Lewis found no wife at Rockfish Gap, nor in Stanton, nor Lexington. The stage road seemed trapped-out of girls. Fincastle was the next town, and there Clark had found—

Wouldn't it be delightful—

However, on inquiry, there appeared to be no available Hancock girls. Lewis stayed at the colonel's house, where he made small acquaintance with the child-bride-to-be. Conventionally pretty; sepulchrally silent. The colonel, on the other hand, spoke with an old man's garrulity of his daughter's upcoming marriage. All of Botetourt County would turn out, and would His Excellency perhaps—?

The press of his duties, Lewis was sure the colonel understood—

The day after his arrival, he met Letitia Breckenridge. She was beautiful, it was uniformly agreed; one month older than Julia Hancock; just turned sixteen. The daughter of a general; unmarried; apparently sound of mind and limb. And not even engaged. Lewis could sense in the shadows the two clans, Lewis-Meriwether-Marks and Breckenridge, creeping together to form a ring around the future couple. The general dropped a line of comments like breadcrumbs. Young, callow Reuben told Lewis he would like to have Miss Breckenridge for a sister.

This sort of thing got Lewis's back up. "Marry her sister, then!" But he checked himself. Consider: if not now, when? Perhaps a double wedding. He spurred himself on. Spoke to her; called on her.

Oh, he tried! He was the simple soldier, the ramrod on the settee, decrying his eloquence while descanting eloquently on his "hair-breadth scapes, and deserts idle, and hills whose heads touch heaven." She was supposed to love him for the dangers he had passed. (See my wounds! On second thought—) And he had the impression, as he did with all white women, that she did not care a straw about a single thing he said, or that she said either, or for that matter, about any real thing in the wide world. Being courted was a stage role, and all her passion was reserved for the playing of it; the script was none of her concern. When she laughed or performed wonder on cue, he found himself struggling with rage. But he was determined to play his part, too. On her porch, he touched his heart; he turned to wave on the road. He was writing her a *billet-doux* from his room in the Hancock home when the news came: she had departed that morning with her father for Richmond. Sudden business was alleged for the general, and his desire for dear company on the way. Thus with sure feet did society move to smooth it over, to smile on. But Lewis knew perfectly well that she had fled from him. He'd played his part badly. As for her memory, lodged in his heart—well, Lewis "gave to Misery all he had, a tear." But Fincastle surely was talking about it today: how His Excellency chased the Breckenridge beauty out of town, and what was wrong with the man?

Reuben knew not to breathe a word. The brothers climbed on their horses. December 1st. If Clark was not already heading toward Fincastle from Louisville, he would start within the week. And with Reuben along, Lewis could not deviate from his promise to pass through Louisville. So they would meet. *My dear Lewis, wish me—! Why don't you—? There is no man on earth— A minor delay—*

Lewis turned his horse's head. "You may go on if you wish, Reuben. I am returning to Ivy. Pernier, come along."

What a relief to give in; he'd fought so long. He was so tired (though he couldn't sleep). Reuben tagged after, mutely inquiring, then resigned. Lewis rode up to his mother's door; she opened it to him. Unlike Reuben, she knew what to do.

And here he lies.

Two letters came while he was at Fincastle. From Bates: *When I wrote General Dearborn on the subject, he informed me that he should confer with you. I have heard no more—*

And from Peale. That very ingenious gentleman has completed a wax simulacrum of Lewis for his museum. The figure wears an elegant Shoshone tippet of ermine skins that Lewis donated to the museum; Cameahwait, when he feared the ambush, had given it to Lewis, he'd placed it around his neck. Peale wrote: *The figure has its right hand on its breast & the left holds the Calumet which you gave me.* There is a tablet below, on which Peale has composed a text, which he represents to the public as Lewis's words to Cameahwait on that historic occasion:

Brother, I accept your dress. It is the object of my heart to promote amongst you, our Neighbors, peace and good will—that you may bury the hatchet deep in the ground never to be taken up again—and that henceforward you may smoke the Calumet of Peace & live in perpetual harmony, not only with each other, but with the white man, your Brothers, who will teach you many useful Arts. Possessed of every comfort in life, what cause ought to involve us in War? Men are not too numerous for the lands which are to cultivate; and Disease makes havoc enough amongst them without deliberately destroying each other. If any differences arise about lands or trade, let each party appoint judicious persons to meet together & amicably settle the disputed point.

After which Lewis retired behind a rock, did he not, and stuck his ass out and asked Cameahwait to kindly shoot it.

He lies, cover to chin, staring at the ceiling. His soup is untouched.

His journals are in the trunk at the foot of his bed. *I have made an attack most vigorously, we have come to terms, and a delivery is to be made first of January.* A fortnight from now. Lewis closes his eyes.

"Meriwether . . ."

3

Only diligence made order; only vigilance maintained it. His Excellency Governor Lewis was ferried across the Mississippi River to St. Louis on March 8th, 1808.

They were waiting for him on the levee: his brother Reuben, who had preceded him with his carriage and furniture; his secretary, Frederick Bates; the merchants of the town, Auguste and Pierre Chouteau, Charles Gratiot, Manuel Lisa; a knot of the idle curious; early-bird seekers of vermiculate favors. He waded, nodded, warded off; accepted congratulations; turned aside gratification of thirst and hunger at sundry mansions. The press of business, gentlemen, he craved their indulgence, tomorrow evening, *avec plaisir.*

He gained his carriage and swayed up the short face of the bluff at a funereal pace, the merchants' finer equipages following, his saddlehorse led at the tail end by Pernier. Reuben was seated by his side, Bates facing (his knees crowding him), the glass raised against wheel-tossed slugs of mud. Bates spoke earnestly of pressing business, while Reuben glanced sidelong at his brother and Lewis gazed out the window.

Up from the boatmen's shacks along the shore, past the palisade of trading depots at the bluff's edge, into the town, the odd, crouching wooden houses Lewis remembered, single-story, begirt with frowning verandas, isolated among jungly gardens on the underbuilt blocks. That was the fault of the merchant lords, unwilling either to sell their large holdings in town or to build on them. Waiting for a more princely price, or was it pure French indolence? (Or in Lisa's case, Spanish torpor.) They passed the unkempt square by the old Spanish Government House, where the U' States flag had first been raised four years ago. Only four! Young, expectant Captains Lewis and Clark attending. The cortège of carriages had by this point dispersed. Lewis interrupted Bates to say to Reuben, "Tell the driver to take us up Main to the end, and down Second."

He studied the scene. His town; his responsibility. Still only three north-south streets, Main, Second, and Third. Some of the cross streets remained unnamed. Party, Faction, Discord, and Vine? Chestnut, Profit, Shady, and Deal? A new district was planned to the west, higher up, where the old fortifications were. The streets had grown more populated in the past year. Americans coming in. They'd mostly settled on the low land south of town, but they did business up here, speculating and peculating, insinuating themselves into the fur trade. Among the lower sort, it was easy to distinguish nationality. The French boatmen—*lard-eaters,* they were called—wore kerchiefs and gesticulated and smoked; the American detritus wore felt hats and slouched and chewed. Half the women were squaws, most of the children half-breeds. The prevailing language still French; it came through the glass as a tenebrous jabber.

Well guess what, *citoyens,* you belong to the United States now. There was Pierre Chouteau's limestone mansion; at two stories, looming like a cloudbank over the town. Hadn't it grown larger in the interim? Chouteau would prosper under any regime. Farther on was Gratiot's pile. Lewis had the driver circle past Lisa's grand residence; Auguste Chouteau's august château (if His Excellency may indulge). Liveried servants; standing groves of slaves; a glimpse of one of the French ladyships, topgallants flying, sailing down a veranda.

For lodging in town, there was Christy's Inn; lower on the scale, a half-dozen taverns with pallets under the eaves. There was no proper hotel. If you were a person of importance, you stayed with one of the lords. And be sure you sang for your supper. His Excellency might have nearly unlimited power on paper, but he knew he could not accomplish much, nor last long, without the tacit backing of Their Potencies.

Fortunately, they were eminently corruptible. Unfortunately, their price was damned high. God, he hated this place!

But that was a night thought. The sun was up. He turned from the window. Attention: "—therefore I would venture to suggest a reply to McKinney and Ramsay offering some assurances—"

"How many horses did they say the Sacs and Foxes stole from them?" Lewis interrupted.

"I believe I said six," Bates replied.

Sanctimonious little— "Is Dickson still trading with them?"

"Yes."

"He has influence. Tell him to distribute trinkets to chiefs with the standing to coerce the horses' return; have him remind them that our treaty allows us to deduct their robberies from their annuity. Which we will do."

"Very good. Turning to the subject of the lead mines, they are located in the District of St. Genevieve—"

"Mr. Bates, I know very well where they are."

"Of course, Your Excellency, my apologies, I spoke only in case—the long lapse of time— But permit me to expatiate; the profits from the mines are immense, a fact of which Your Excellency is, of course!, aware. Encroachments are daily occurring on public lands, fraud and rapine are rampant, specious claims are defended by desperadoes who refuse orders of removal; the lives of officials acting entirely within the lawful scope of their duties have been threatened, I myself have been the target of—"

Industry: At seven in the morning, Lewis sat at his work table, in his temporary office in Pierre Chouteau's house, Seaman blessedly at his feet again, less blessedly a midden of papers by his left elbow which it was his most excellent duty to digest leaf by leaf and deposit on his right: piteous complaints from quondam quasi-proprietors about irregular Spanish land grants that the American government had rightly disallowed; three volumes of the laws of the U' States recently enacted, in which all those pertaining to the Territory of

Louisiana might be found with tweezers and a microscope; a court ruling on what constituted legal tender in the discharge of a fee bill; reports of settlers squatting on Indian land and refusing to vacate; rumors of Great Osages invading frontier settlements and destroying property; a demand for justice from a notorious Burrite duelist; the Sacs refusing to deliver the man or men responsible for the murder of an American citizen eleven months ago at Portage de Sioux; Mr. Gallatin's entire correspondence for the past year on the subject of the lead mines; a citizens' circular charging that the irregular mails were the result of deliberate negligence on the part of the contractor; a dismissed officeholder proclaiming his loyalty to the U' States and denouncing the dictatorial Bates; a demand from the Sacs and Foxes for a blacksmith; applications for Indian trading licenses; applications for civil and military appointments; an insolent message from the Mahas; an implied bribe; an anonymous threat.

Lewis lifted his pen. *Sir: You would very much oblige me by drawing up articles of agreement between myself as Superintendent of Indian affairs in behalf of the U' States and Alexander Willard, a blacksmith whom I wish to engage for the Sac Nation—*

Dispatch: Before the close of the first week, Lewis had discovered a charming house of palisadoed timber on Main Street below Market, for him and Clark and the young bride to live in. There was a capacious, dry cellar and a good, wet well (both rarities in St. Louis); four rooms on the first floor, two of them finished in oil paint, instead of the usual whitewash, and the other two actually wallpapered, which Lewis believed was a first for the territorial capital; two carved mantelpieces; a garret with a tolerable floor for the servants to lodge in; a kitchen with two fireplaces; and a piazza, or veranda, along the whole of the east side, facing the street, where Lewis and Clark could sit of an evening and put their feet up on the banister and smoke. Lewis moved in on April 1st, and as the weeks went by, he liked the place better and better. There was a stable and six apple trees; Pernier was at work enlarging the garden. From the veranda, Lewis could see a wedge of the Mississippi between a barn and a paling opposite, and beyond, a vista of the low country; in the evenings, as the sun set behind the house, the surface of the river and the thickening haze glowed in roses and lavenders. Lewis smoked in contented anticipation. Clark had once spoken fondly of the view of the Ohio River flowing below his brother George's door. How he would love this!

Resolve: *A Proclamation: Whereas, the detached and scattered population of many parts of this territory, renders it extremely inconvenient and almost impracticable, for the public functionaries thereof, duly to execute the laws . . . this my proclamation, prohibiting all persons whomsoever . . . establishing dwellings on, or cultivating the Lands of the United States, to which the Indian Title may or may not have been extinguished . . . beyond or without the said boundary line to return within the same . . . the 15th day of June next . . . forfeit a sum not exceeding one thousand dollars, and suffer imprisonment not exceeding twelve months . . .*

Forbearance: Secretary Bates begged to differ, though in terms couched in deference and flattery. "—your acquaintance with the more remote regions of the territory far exceeds my own, and consequently your capacity in discernment, nevertheless, one might have thought an encouragement of white settlement more fitting to the aims of civilized—"

"It has nothing whatever to do with settlement *per se*, Mr. Bates, but with the application of the law—"

"You have defined the crux admirably, Your Excellency; and as promulgator of the law, the governor may—"

"Mr. Bates; this is an extremely complicated question bearing on the disposition of several powerful Indian nations, whom daily the English woo to their mischievous cause, and I will thank you to—" *One might have thought* that Lewis's own secretarial purgatory, spent dwelling in attentive, tombal silence, would have earned him a complementary reward.

Discipline: *Sir: . . . I hold it a consequence inevitable, that should we continue to pay the aggressors for their forbearance to aggress, and the injured to abstain from retaliation, we at once encourage war among the tribes . . . we cannot with complacency think of* <u>paying</u> *for* <u>disobedience to our will</u> *. . . Your present mission to the Sacs and Foxes . . . prevail on those nations to deliver us the murderer . . . Should the Sacs & Foxes on the contrary refuse to comply . . . all the traders among them, of whatever denomination, to depart forthwith . . .*

Sir: . . . I determined early in June to grant no licences to trade on the Missouri until a sufficient force was sent to establish permanent trading posts. The traders complained of this measure as arbitrary and injurious to the country; such is their blind infatuation for the possession of peltry and fur . . .

Sir: The band of the Great Osage, on the Osage river, have cast off all allegiance to the United States . . . I ordered all the traders, hunters and other white persons in the towns and country of the Osages to return . . . the nation is by this time no doubt destitute of ammunition . . . With respect to the malcontents, I have in several councils held with the Shawnees, Delewares, Kickapoos, Iaways & Soos, declared them no longer under the protection of the government of the U' States, and that they were at liberty to wage war against them if they thought proper, under this restriction only, that they should attack in a body sufficiently large to cut them off completely or drive them from their country . . .

Prudence: or should one say, Thrift (Horatio): Lewis was buying land. As he had foreseen, he'd been forced to prevaricate in his letter to his mother from Louisville about his supposed land purchases years ago (*I have experienced considerable difficulty and shall most probably lose the greater part—*). Writing untruths to one's mother—let it be admitted—was not a virtue. Lewis would stop it. Did Lucy Meriwether Lewis Marks want land? Well, she would have land. It would make his half sister Mary happy, too. Hills and dales! Mills and mines! Choice land that Lewis could have bought for a dollar an acre sixteen months ago was now going for two, but the price was still rising, so it behooved one to hop on that wagon. Eight or ten miles from St. Louis, dirt could be had for fifty cents an acre. Lewis rode out to inspect vales and swales, he rode back to inspect his accounts, he spurred himself on, he scratched his head, he scratched backs; by mid-June he owned over six thousand acres and was up to his neck in debt like any respectable Albemarle planter.

Foresight: Clark was coming. Lewis would happily have sent an Egyptian wedding barge, a corps of trumpeters, and a company of half-naked rose-petal-strewing maidens to bring him and his beloved on in grand style. But St. Louis was a frontier town, and he had to settle for two keelboats and a few pimply soldiers.

Conviction (most vital): *Your favor of the 11th instant from Nashville has been duly received*—Lewis was writing to an old Virginia aquaintance and fellow army officer, William Preston: the man who'd snapped up the *other* marriageable Hancock female, Julia's sister Caroline—*how wretchedly you married men arrange the subjects of which you treat . . . You run through a sheet of paper about your musty fusty trade, your look out for land speculations . . . a flimsy excuse about the want of money to enable you to come and see us &c &c before you came to the point. Then she is off. passed*—Lewis meant

Letitia Breckenridge—but that cruel name would never pass his lips more! No, nor his pen nib, neither—she had married—*off the hooks, I mean in a matrimonial point of view; be it so, the die is cast, may god be with her and hers, and the favored angels of heaven guard her bliss both here and hereafter, is the sincere prayer of her very sincere friend, to whom she has left the noble consolation of scratching his head and biting his nails, with ample leisure to ruminate on the chapter of accidents in matters of love and the folly of castle-building . . . I consider Miss E— B*—the Cruel One's sister, Elizabeth; Preston had thrust her stumbling forward as an alternative; what was she, thirteen? fourteen?, Lewis remembered nothing but bony arms and a hairpin about to fall out—*a charming girl, but such was my passion for her sister, that my soul revolts at the idea of attempting to make her my wife, and shall not consequently travel that road in quest of matrimony. So much for <u>love</u> . . .*

Industry, Dispatch, Resolve, etc.: these were Lewis's daytime virtues, a plaster colonnade erected on an ormolu slab of Conviction. While the sun was up; while the function demanded its functionary; while the dinner confronted the diner. Would his nights have been better if he hadn't drunk? A sterile question; he had to. It was a vice, yes; a weakness. But hadn't he, all day, exhibited greater strength than anyone could know, by gaining the evening shore without once having overturned a table, or stood naked in the square and spoken in tongues? Nightmares would come; better that they come at night. The bottle unlidded them. The ball, the tavern, the card party, unwinding; and when the mask began to slip, the whiskey and porter in his room alone, his candle, his trunks in one corner, his bed in the other and his chair to sit on, he put his feet on the table and tilted back, tilted the bottle back, his ass still ached when it was damp. Oh, and Seaman—good boy! Thump thump.

He didn't rave. He didn't weep. Hardly ever. He only needed to let his thoughts run; to let them out of the kennel, for God's sake. Expressions might pass across his face, words escape his lips. Lewis opened a trunk. He unwrapped oilskin, lifted out the journals; put them on the table. *August 31st 1803. Left Pittsburgh this day at 11 ock with a party of 11 hands 7 of which are soldiers, a pilot and three young men on trial they having proposed to go with me thoughout the voyage.* Three? Colter and Shannon—but who'd been the third? The weather had been hot. And two miles later, two out of five thousand, the very first day, Lewis handed the air gun to a man on the shore named Blaze, and Blaze blazed away and nearly blew a woman's brains out. Now *there* was something a proper explorer did not include in his proper, published narrative, no matter that it was fitting, viz., how much chance played in it all, how much of life was ridiculous.

But *Lewis and Clark's Tour* would not begin in Pittsburgh; rather, the departure from St. Louis. *On the 14th day of May, in the year of our Lord, one thousand eight hundred and four* (Lewis might write), *Captains Meriwether Lewis and William Clark embarked—* Except that they didn't: Clark embarked alone from Camp Dubois; Lewis joined him on the 20th, riding overland from St. Louis. But how awkward. Surely *Lewis and Clark's Tour* must begin with: Lewis and Clark!

This is what vexed him: the need to straighten, to smooth. Those small anomalies that were worth no one's attention, yet when you passed over them, you wrote a fable. *On the 14th day of May, in the year of our Lord, one thousand eight hundred and four, Lieutenant William Clark, posing as a captain (a capital offense, but no matter), embarked at Camp Dubois, while his fellow conspirator, Captain Meriwether Lewis, was in St. Louis disentangling himself from an intrigue with a female that he had entered upon from a sense of duty and was exiting with a sense of disgust (but no matter).*

Once lodged, the habit of small untruths (how well Lewis knew it!) led to larger ones. For example, those public letters he'd written when the Corps first returned: would he find himself forced to iterate in the published narrative the distortions he had practiced on the public to shield the President? (Doubtless some of the Americans now pouring into Louisiana, troubling His Excellency with their clamor for fur at any cost to diplomacy, their greed to settle on land, who cared whose, which they imagined would grow crops when they spat on it—doubtless some of them had first conceived the idea of descending on him from his own letters.) Thence it was but a step to the style, say, of the unblushing Parson Weems: *"Yes, father, you know I cannot tell a lie, I did cut it down with my little hatchet—" "Run to my arms, my dearest boy!"*—good Lord, what tripe!

On the 14th day of May, in the year of our Lord, one thousand eight hundred and four—but first let us fly on wings of fancy to the sweet scenes of childhood, where the reader may espy the young scholar and incipient scientist Meriwether Lewis jumping in the air and inquiring— Or the pamphlet he had, where was it? (he rummaged in a pile at the back of his desk) here,

Daniel Boone discovering Kentucky, imagined by one John Filson (a school-master! of course! tales for children!). —*I surveyed the famous river Ohio that rolled in silent dignity, marking the western boundary of Kentucke with inconceivable grandeur. All things were still. I kindled a fire near a fountain of sweet water, and feasted on the loin of a buck, which a few hours before I had killed.*

The worst of it was, some passages in Lewis's journals struck a false note not far from this. And now was it his duty to rewrite all his experiences in this perfumed fashion? He had (in fact) drunk from a spring on his way up the last slope of the divide; but if he included that detail, would it sound like embroidery? Or must he accept the falsity demanded of him, and subtract that mysterious creature that appeared to him and disappeared (a small anomaly, but it underlay everything) and must he add a mountaintop feast of buck's loin, good God, and while he was at it, what was to keep him from having twelve of his men up there with him, and he could pass out the loin and say, *Take and eat,* and then he could say, *One of you will betray me—and it will be you, Gass!* Of course putting a public face on things was *necessary,* just as it was *necessary* that Lewis find a wife under a rock somewhere, you couldn't very well put all convention to scorn, the result would be—for example, the President and "dusky Sally," Callender's accusations might well be true, but that was not the point, the point was that dusk *should* enshroud—

He stopped short. He'd been muttering. He rose, jarring the table. Like waking mid-snore. He paced to calm himself. Now if Bates was a proper secretary, he would stand in the corner with his damned yap shut, and Lewis could mutter in his general direction all he liked. He paced; paced. Perhaps it was for the best he wasn't lodging with the Clarks. (*The Clarks:* say it enough times . . .) In that small house, Clark would hear him. *Oh dear, it is quite a small house, isn't it?* Mrs. Brigadier General William Clark (sixteen years old) had ejaculated on her arrival, and two responses had occurred to Lewis (thirty-four), neither of which he'd said, to wit, number one, this is not Virginia, Madam, if the house strikes you as inadequate to the deserts of a Congressman's daughter, perhaps you should have declined marrying a man who must needs subject his wife to subpalatial conditions; and number two, perhaps the house would not seem so infernally small if Mr. and Mrs. Brigadier General had not brought with them a niece requiring a room of her own and—good God, ask them to stand still so that I may count them!— could it be *fifteen* slaves?

Oh, Clark! What had he got himself into? He stood there among the crates of china and linen, while a Juba carried a table this way, and a Venus took a sewing basket that way, and Tanner called to Scipio and Frankey needed to ask Mas' Clark a question, and the slave children milled like pullets, and Clark said nothing; or rather, he said the house was fine, he was glad to see Lewis, but he said nothing about all *that*. Had Madam insisted they be brought? Or—?

A married man.

And in a married household, there was no place for a bachelor and his dog. His *large* dog, as Mrs. Brigadier General characterized him. Lewis slept on the floor of the little office at the end of the veranda for one night only, then moved back into the house of the ever-receptive Pierre Chouteau. And here he was, at the end of an upstairs hall, a corner room to himself. His Exilency. Ha! That was a good one! "Eh, Seaman? You're not so large, are you? You're not too large to lift! Good boy, good boy!"

Morning; coffee; desk: *Sir: . . . I hold it an axiom incontrovertible, that it is more easy to introduce vice in all states of society, than it is to eradicate it, and that this is still more strictly true, when applied to man in his savage than in his civilized state . . .*

Sir: . . . The uncontrolled liberty which our citizens take of hunting on Indian lands has always been a source of serious difficulty on every part of our frontier . . .

Sir: . . . The love of gain is the Indians' ruling passion, and the fear of punishment must form the corrective; to this passion we are to ascribe their inordinate thirst for the possession of merchandise . . .

My Dear Friend: . . . The Indians have been exceedingly troublesome during the last winter and spring, but I have succeeded in managing those on the Mississippi; they have delivered three murderers to a party which I sent with a strong talk to them, they are now under trial and will no doubt be stretched . . .

Every time Lewis stepped out of his office (he'd rented a chamber on Main Street) he was surrounded in the street by Iaways, Sacs, and Foxes, beseeching him to show mercy for their compatriots. "Did *they* show any?" he tossed back at them, wading through the press. Now if Lewis could only stretch half the white inhabitants of Louisiana as well. He must be paying for his sins, he'd landed once more among the tribe of eye-gougers, there had been a horrific case the other day, the victim had been deprived of any hope of sight in either eye. The difference here was that the unwashed bipeds committing these acts called themselves gentlemen, and there was no one to gainsay them. Lewis had once thought of dueling as something grand, but in St. Louis it stood forth in its true colors: a ruffian plundered and defrauded, and when challenged, he cried Honor, he cried Satisfaction, and the next morning he murdered his accuser with all due ceremony at the edge of town.

Meanwhile, criminals were emboldened by the nearness of that great almost-nothingness that began at the city limits. Over the horizon waited British agents, happy to take outlaws in, add them to their network. Slaves, too, ran off into the void; one of Clark's negroes disappeared in August, while Clark was away, and Lewis sent York to search for him. In vain. Dead in a swamp somewhere, or at this very moment smacking his lips over a prairie chicken by a fire in the Iaway country.

Even when Clark was in town, Lewis hardly ever saw him. They occasionally played backgammon or cards in Lewis's room, but Julia was unhappy, and his niece was homesick and talking about returning to Louisville; Clark felt uneasy, leaving the two women alone. So Lewis mainly saw him at balls, where he could bring Julia and Ann, but that was hardly seeing him, business interfered, and there were compliments to pay, not to mention the irrepressible French ladies, who were worse than American ones, their histrionics of deportment (every moue, every arch of eyebrow) made the most affected American dame seem an Arcadian shepherdess. Oh, he hated the place! And the ironical custom was, Americans wrote home to tell friends and family to sell their farms and migrate to this paradise—why not? It was lonely and brutish out here, and if more people ferried across, the value of the authors' lands would go up! Lewis did it, too, he shrugged on his coat of conviction, *My Dear Friend . . . Louisiana at this moment offers more advantages than any other . . . in point of soil and climate it is inferior to none . . . I might fill a volume . . .*

Meanwhile, irritants from the east in epistolary form were migrating across the mountains on his desk. From the Secretary of War: *Sir: . . . Except in cases of the most pressing emergency detachments of the troops should not be made, to any distance from the established posts, without the knowledge and approbation of the Executive of the U.S. . . . Had Colonel Hunt remained silent on the subject, the department would probably have remained uninformed of the measures you have directed in relation to Mr. Boilvin's Expedition, as no*

*communication except some drafts for money, has, for many months, been re-
ceived from the Executive of Louisiana . . .*

Ho ho! Musty fusty bureaucrat, not true! On July 1st, Lewis had written
a long report on the matter (one might say, one might *carp,* that it was belated,
but he was infernally busy, did Dearborn want him to *govern,* or to spend all
his time reporting?), but his letter had crossed the Secretary's, in what
Louisianans were pleased to call their post. *Sir: Yours of the 2nd of July did
not reach me until the 14th Inst, a lapse of 42 days. From the tenor of your letter I am to presume that my communication of the 3rd of May had not reached
you, nor could you when you wrote have received my letters of the 1st and 16th of
July . . .* It was scandalous, how much mail was lost between Washington
and St. Louis. The Post Office Department sometimes did not receive one
newspaper in two weeks. Thus, practically speaking, it was all one whether or
not Lewis had actually sent the first and last communications claimed. *This
has been an extremely perplexing toilsome & disagreeable business to me
throughout and I must candidly confess that it is not rendered less so at this moment in reflection than it was in practice from the seeming disapprobation
which you appear to show to the measures pursued . . .*

And a letter from the President: *Dear Sir: Since I parted with you in Albemarle in Sep. last I have never had a line from you . . .* And another a month
later, from Monticello, where the Sage sat in his slippered ease, on his well-
tended holiday: *I am uneasy, hearing nothing from you about the Mandan
chief, nor the measures for restoring him to his country . . .* And a heartless af-
terthought: *We have no tidings yet of the forwardness of your printer. I hope the
first part will not be delayed much longer.* With something like nausea, Lewis
remembered having told his book collaborators in Philadelphia that he
would return to the city by May 1808: four months ago. He vaguely recalled
having received several letters from his publisher.

"Mr. Bates, I will doubtless be traveling to Washington and Philadelphia
this autumn to confer with the President and my publisher; I would speak
with you about certain matters that may fall within your competence while I
am gone—"

Bates did not like him, that was obvious. Having acted as governor for a
year in Lewis's absence, he'd behaved ever since like a displaced official. He
looked younger than his age, half-formed; a high, waxy forehead, something

weak and damp in the eyes. The sort of temperament that led either to fawning gratitude or to the other extreme, a hysterical sense of having been slighted, of the existence of plots against him. He was a veritable hothouse plant of rhetoric, his sentences were like the *convolvulus*—they coiled around you, the main stem all respect and deference, but the little tendrils twitching in the shadows with animosity and accusation. Lewis had heard that insanity ran in his family. And to think that Lewis had helped this toad of ill will to his post! that he had vouched for him to the President and sent him to St. Louis with letters of introduction, all for the sake of his poor brother, Tarleton Bates, whom Lewis had known years ago, and had loved, poor Tarleton! dead these thirty months, killed in a duel in Pittsburgh, while Lewis was at Fort Clatsop!

From the President: *With the Sacs & the Foxes I hope you will be able to settle amicably . . . as there was but one white murdered by them, I should be averse to the execution of more than one of them . . . their idea that justice allows only man for man, that all beyond that is new aggression . . .* Oh, yes! Second guessing and interference! From the retreat on the mountaintop!

Well, the President need not have worried *at all,* for the judge in the case, the Very Honorable John B. C. Lucas, Esquire, had already voided the conviction by the jury and obstructed the sentencing, on the grounds that the offense had been committed outside the jurisdiction of the court, to wit, out in that great almost-nothingness, viz., on what was carelessly and familiarly called "Indian land," and that the proper place to try those "sovereign" savages was on said "Indian land," according to the Indian laws (!) and customs prevailing. In other words, the Governor of the Territory of Louisiana was powerless to enforce the territorial laws over the vast majority of his so-called territory! So the three Indians sat in jail while the streets teemed with their red faction, and Lucas threatened to issue a writ of habeas corpus, and Lewis thundered his extreme displeasure, but beyond keeping the murderers behind bars, he could do nothing until such time as Mr. Jefferson might be pleased to hand down a decree on the matter that satisfied his exquisite sense of justice.

Mr. Peter Chouteau: . . . by these arrangements, we shall obtain a tract of country . . . Those of the Great and Little Osage who refuse to sanction this Treaty can have no future hopes, that their pretensions to those lands now claimed by them, will ever be respected by the United States: For, it is our unalterable determination, that if they are to be considered our friends and allies, they must <u>sign</u> that instrument . . .

At night Lewis swallowed an opium pill with his porter, and he spread out the journals, the maps, the loose notes scribbled in pirogue or on promontory. He chose a leaf at random, dipped: *the atmispr. became Sudenly darkened by a black and dismal looking Cloud . . . the Current of the River at this place is a Stick will float 48 poles 6 feet in the rapidest part in 23 seconds . . .* Clark's hand. If Lewis put Clark's notes in one pile, his own in another, it argued for the title *Clark and Lewis's Tour.* Captain Clark and Lieutenant Lewis. Why was there something attractive in that? What was wrong with him?

He turned a page; smoothed. The day poor Tarleton Bates died; what was Lewis doing? One of the red notebooks: the first page, January 1st, 1806, Lewis's hand, his New Year's resolution: *This morning I was awoke at an early hour.* That damp cell in Clatsop. His resolution. Resolve, yes, one of the daytime virtues: I resolve to write this book! Poor Tarleton died on the 8th; here: *Our meat is beginning to become scarce; sent Drewyer and Collins to hunt this morning.* Clark wasn't there; visiting the salt-making camp. *The Clatsops Chinnooks and others . . . excessively fond of smoking tobacco . . . appear to swallow it . . . many draughts together . . . in this manner becomes much more intoxicating . . . they frequently give us sounding proofs of its creating a dismorality of order in the abdomen, nor are those light matters thought indelicate in either sex, but all take the liberty of obeying the dictates of nature without reserve . . .*

There! Now *there* was a perfect example of the impossibility facing him. How could he write about that; even in his notes he'd not been—squatting like frogs, their virile members dangling in the dirt, and as they inhaled and gulped and inhaled again, the members becoming engorged, lifting (or the labia swelling, as the case may be), and at their full extent the savage emitting a soft grunt and, still holding the pipe with one hand, spitting and reaching down with the other, and Lewis turning his head away to look off into the tall trees, overcome with blank stupefaction at the variety of man permitted by nature. He supposed he might render it in Latin; except his Latin wasn't good enough; or bad enough.

Perhaps that was not the perfect example. A better one would be—what?

Never mind that, boys! What's for supper?—the bear stopping, wheeling—the next valley in the Rockies opening up; the next—the yellow foam he puked, his face green-white—climbing a pole where two rivers met to fetch his note—

Watermillions. Yes! Yes! How to express that? How to get to the *core* of that?

I hope the first part will not be delayed much longer. Wishing you every blessing of life & health I salute you with constant affection & respect. If the President really wished him life and health, why had he sentenced him to this hell? It was so easy for Mr. J; cushioned by established laws and procedures, a platoon of invisible slaves; not a moment's self-doubt. Lewis was not half the man the President was, he had neither the intellect nor the industry, but would Mr. J perform better here than his failed protégé, hadn't his own term as Governor of Virginia during disordered times ended in controversy and derision, Louisiana might have served Milton as a pattern of Chaos, had Mr. J *any idea?* he'd hummed and scribbled all his life about the west, but the Cumberland Gap had not once seen his back, nor the Ohio wet his feet, it was all on paper, in duplicate, filed away, and wasn't that perfect? wasn't it? Out here, Mr. President, out west, out in these *Trans-Mississippian* regions, as you call them, eyes are gouged for pleasure, Mr. President, and farther west, in Ultima America, in the transylvanian, Pacifician, nimio-pluvial piedmont, frog-men squat in front of you and mastur—

Lewis wondered. He got up; he paced; he wondered. Something had occurred to him. Those letters he published, with the exaggerations, the embroideries; it made perfect sense that he had done it; protect the President, etc.; no doubt also to assuage his own pains; he'd known that from the first. But here is what had occurred to him latterly: if it made such perfect sense to lie, then was any explorer's account true? Had Cook been killed in a skirmish with the natives of Owhyhee over a stolen cutter, or was he speared in the back by a cabin boy, his superannuated catamite? Did Washington ever, in fact, call the whistle of a bullet *charming,* or when the slug barely missed him did he urinate in his trousers, as Lewis (yes) did, a second's squirt, a shivering teaspoon?

The pill was not operating. Heat flared behind his forehead, cold was creeping down his spine. He opened his medicine chest. He might take another of opium. Or tartar emetic. Was this intermittent fever, bilious fever, hypochondria? He felt his pulse. Accelerated. Thoughts disordered; breath bitter. He opened another bottle of porter, chose a second opium pill. Three usually sufficed for night fevers. Sometimes in the morning he had to take two more. The slow sea settling, spreading to fingers, quieting what felt like a simmer of his sanguinary corpuscles. Slow . . . slow. Sleep. Not yet.

Why had the President picked him for the expedition? He tipped his chair back, drank. "Eh, Seaman? *That* is the question." Was it because the President never left the President's House, and Lewis was the only other white man in the building? Standing in the corner. Mr. J knew about Lewis's fogs. Clark at least had brought York along for his own illnesses. Perhaps Lewis owed everything to Mr. J's deep-dyed impracticality: tattooing a man's arms to make him a human cross-staff; picturing the Mississippi as an osmotic barrier through which red men would naturally separate from white; sending a periodic catatonic out to conquer a continent. Why not?

It should have been the Clark expedition. Clark deserved it. He'd never been adequately compensated for anything in his life. And he knew how to wear his laurels. A wife—

Lewis brought the chair back down with a smack, he aimed his bottle for a clear place at the back of his desk, he placed it pretty close, pretty close, he ran his hands over the leather journal covers, so new-seeming, almost pristine, those tin cases he'd devised, what a clever fellow!, surely this clever fellow could write a book, he could falsify the most important thing in his life, he only needed— He picked up his last journal; a few filled pages at the front, the rest blank, 12th August, 1806, *as writing in my present situation is extremely painful to me I shall desist until I recover and leave to my friend Capt. C. the continuation of our journal.*

But this was curious—Lewis had remembered those words as his last. But here was something else. Half a dozen sentences:

However I must notice a singular Cherry . . .

And suddenly Lewis was weeping. He had no idea why.

. . . is not very abundant . . . the leaf is peteolate, oval, acutely pointed at its apex . . . the fruit is a globular berry about the size of a buck-shot of a fine scarlet red . . . Had he saved a specimen? He couldn't remember. The great majority had been lost. Fresh tears came. *The style and stigma are permanent.* That man lying in the pirogue, in pain. His last words, in fact: *I have never seen it in bloom.*

[THE HERO]

Then blankness.

He took a third opium pill. Waited for the room to retreat a step; to uncrowd him. Checked his watch. Dried his eyes.

There—a slight wobble as the world came untethered from the glass surrounding him. Now perhaps he'd be able to sleep. "Seaman." Thump; a sugar-thread of drool from the lifted, groggy head; gray scattered across his muzzle. Eight years old? Nine?

Lewis lay in bed. If only the bear had killed him. If only, when the Indian boy had turned, Lewis had run full at him, arms spread. In a later age, there might be a stone marker (was this hubris?), a beaten path, Clark there bareheaded for the anniversary, an epitaph:

> He gave to Misery all he had, a tear,
> He gained from Heaven ('twas all he wished) a friend.

Morning; sour aftertaste of self-pity. Resolution: to wean himself from alcohol and other human weaknesses.

Coffee; desk.

Exemplum: For the territory's new newspaper, the Missouri *Gazette*:

The True Ambitions of an Honest Mind

Were I to describe the blessings I desire in life, I would be happy in a few but faithful friends. Might I choose my talent, it should rather be good than learning . . . I would have no master, and I desire few servants. I would not be led away by ambition, nor perplexed with disputes. I would enjoy the blessings of health but rather be beholden for it to a regular life and an easy mind, than to the school of Hippocrates. As to my passions, since we cannot be wholly divested of them, I would hate only those whose manners rendered them odious, and love only where I knew I ought . . .

Hortator: On rumors of war with England: *We are called upon, fellow citizens, to bear a part . . . defending our liberties and our country from the unhallowed grasp of the modern barbarians of Europe . . . this invitation to volunteer service . . . induce the young men of Louisiana to rally around the standard . . . thus prove themselves worthy of their fathers of '76 . . .*

Filius: A letter to his mother: *My life is still one continued press of business which scarcely allows me leisure to write to you . . .*

Agricola: Here was the idea. One: Louisiana was paradise. Two: Lewis owned part of it. Three: Reuben missed his mother. Four: His mother missed her son John, in Philadelphia, and her daughter Mary, in Georgia. Five: Lewis would never marry. Six: If Lewis did not get out of the room in Chouteau's house, he would be dead by forty. Ergo: The Lewis-Marks clan would migrate in its entirety to Cis-Mississippi and settle on a thousand acres Lewis had selected for the purpose. Lucy Marks would have John and Mary, and grandchildren on the way, and a new plantation to organize; Reuben would have his mother; Lewis would have someone across the table to keep him from seeing himself seated there. To pay for it, he'd decided to sell the family lands along Ivy Creek; he would cut his ties to his birthplace, to Albemarle. He wrote of his decision to his mother. *You wanted land,* he thought.

Amicus: Here was another idea. Lewis could not make it the Clark expedition; yet he had it in his power to help his friend. Clark's niece had returned to Louisville, but he retained his weeping wife, his slew of slaves, all that furniture and china, and now he had a child, a boy (whose name had pierced Lewis, his godfather, with pleasure and pain; but no matter), and the child had come into the world bawling and had not stopped since, and there would no doubt be others, Clark was a Clark; he'd bought himself a larger house, but he was deep in debt; Lewis had inexcusably been absent from Clark's wedding—

So here was the idea. One: The President was anxious that Big White be returned to his village *(an object which presses on our justice & our honor)* but the Ricaras stood in the way *(and farther than that I suppose a severe punishment of the Ricaras indispensible),* and the general government was too parsimonious to pay for a large enough force *(if it can be effected at any reasonable expense).* Two: Fur traders were also barred from the upper Missouri by the Ricaras, regarding which said traders howled to the governor, who (despite the court's opinion that he lacked jurisdiction over his own territory) was supposed to do something about it. Three: with trade to the upper Missouri barred, the British had a free hand among the Mandan and Hidatsa Indians, a situation posing grave dangers to the security of the United States. Four: Clark had formed a private company to reestablish trade with the Mandan villages, but this fledgling organization lacked the initial capital to fund the military might requisite to deal with the aforementioned Ricaras.

Ergo: *Articles of Agreement made and Indented . . . Twenty fourth day of February in the Year of our Lord . . . His Excellency Meriwether Lewis . . . within the same for and on behalf of . . . and the Undersigned members of and belonging to the Saint Louis Missouri Fur Company . . .* A joint venture, commercial and military, the company to organize the expedition and engage 125 militiamen, acting under the governor's orders; the government to pay the company for the safe return of Big White, after which the company would continue in its commercial capacity, with an exclusive license from the governor to trade with the Indians of the upper Missouri. Two birds with one stone: brilliant!

What remained to be decided was the just and *reasonable* amount that the government should pay the company, and Lewis, after much reasonable reflection (125 times eight dollars per month times six months times two for incidental expenses, or twelve thousand dollars, if the government did the job itself), decided that six thousand dollars was quite reasonable, then concluded that seven thousand dollars was rather more reasonable. The War Department might squawk, but war with England loomed, the frontier was in an uproar, the mails were bad, the governor must be allowed some Lilliputian agency of his own, and they had no idea of his travails, and perhaps he'd better say it was 140 militiamen.

Pater irae: That left the Ricaras, who treated the Missouri as their personal property and singlehandedly necessitated all this bother. (*I suppose a severe punishment*—) To the ever-available Pierre Chouteau, who would be commander of the expedition to return Big White: *Sir: . . . You may engage an auxiliary force not exceeding three hundred men from the most friendly and confidential Indian nations . . . you will promise them, as a reward for their services, the plunder which they may acquire from the Ricaras . . . you will demand of them the unconditional surrender of those individuals among them, who killed any person in their attack on the party under the command of Ensign Pryor; if they cannot ascertain the particular individuals who killed our citizens on that occasion they will in that case be required to deliver an equivalent number with those murdered . . . these when delivered will be shot in the presence of the nation . . .*

Lewis had a recipe somewhere for a stomachic. *Dear Mother:* . . . *I have been detained here much longer than I expected* . . . *you may expect me in the course of this winter* . . .

"Mr. Bates, I will be departing for Philadelphia in February or March to settle certain matters incident to the publication of my—"

There were rumors of an impending Winnebago attack on Fort Bellevue; there was a Prophet somewhere out in that wilderness, a half-blooded Shawnee; a counterfeit beard was alleged; he pretended to visions, the voice of the Great Spirit; he preached unity among the tribes, revenge on the whites; he was indubitably under British influence.

Lewis borrowed twenty-five dollars from Pierre Chouteau, for candles, bootblack, and porter. He took an antibilious pill. "Mr. Bates, beginning in May, as you will have in charge certain items of business that I must leave unfinished, you will please to—"

White squatters were settling illegally on land near the Shawnee village on the river Merrimack, *Whereas information* . . . *Now therefore* . . . *depart therefrom, at their peril* . . . Pernier was febrile, the doctor's bill exorbitant; Lewis borrowed the forty-nine dollars from Clark. Militia orders: *In consequence of the extreme reluctance on the part of the young men of Louisiana, to engage in the service* . . . Age of pygmies!

"Your Excellency, the merchants complain of restrictions beyond the provisions of the law; of arbitrary regulations established without a motive and relinquished without a reason—"

"Any measure that has a discernible effect, Mr. Bates, will inevitably draw objections in its train—"

"Sir, the people cry out—"

"It is ever the delusion of persons such as yourself, that if only they speak loud enough, it must be the voice of the People."

Snuff, in sufficient quantities, overcame his fatigue. Clark remarked in passing, "I have half a mind to—" It was one of his wife's locutions.

In consequence of certain information this moment received . . . *in relation to the hostile movements and combinations of the Indians on our northern frontier, the Commander in Chief has thought proper to order* . . .

"—complain that this incessant mustering of the militia requires too much of their time, how much must we attend to the clamors of those birds of ill omen—"

"Mr. Bates—"

An anonymous aviso: the soldiers along the Arkansas were trading whiskey to the Indians. A word to the wise: certain militia officers were marking trees on Indian land, informing the chiefs the land was theirs. A whispered warning: Captain Armstead was heard to say he would not obey an order given by the governor.

A rainy spring; the roads impassable. "As my trip to Washington has been delayed until June, I would request—"

Away to the east, Mr. Jefferson retired in comfort to Monticello, and Mr. Madison ascended to the presidency. Dearborn stepped down as Secretary of War; William Eustis assumed the mantle.

Lewis searched for his recipe.

White settlers were moving illegally farther up the Arkansas. The Sacs were at war with the Kanzas and Osages.

The rain continued. His wound ached. He tipped his chair back. Perhaps it had been a mistake to order Cruzatte to shoot him.

Big White climbed in a pirogue, settled a robe around his pontiff's paunch; the massive flotilla headed upstream. Reuben went along to make his fortune.

His Expellency gripped the chamber pot, vomiting bile and beer.

Chouteau carried a letter from Clark to Charbono; Clark's talk of Pomp had caused Lewis to wonder what he (Lewis) had been about that he'd never adopted an Indian child, *if any of them should wish to have some of their young people brought up with us, & taught such arts as may be useful to them, we will receive, instruct & take care of them* (the ex cathedra words of the ex-President), surely it would do a confirmed bachelor some earthly good; Jessome's boy of thirteen had expressed an interest in remaining in St. Louis, so Lewis *(pater indulgens)* adopted him; borrowed money from Bates for the first month of schooling.

"—a stranger to prevarication, and thus have made no secret of my support of Mr. Rhea's proposal to award a quarter-lot to every white male inhabitant—"

"And every time you *foolishly* make your support known, Mr. Bates, a hundred more grasping lowlifes occupy the best tracts of public land, in the expectation that their claims will be confirmed—"

It was positively comical to see how quickly his secretary could mount his little pedestal of rectitude, thence to leak appeals to his inviolable conscience, his ultimate arbiter on heaven's throne, etc.

"—no doubt, Your Excellency, the entrenched elite would prefer to retain its hold on the perquisites of trade—"

"Do not presume to lecture me about the influence of elites, when to converse with you is, as it were, to have Mr. Chouteau in the room—"

And the Iaway murderers escaped from jail, and Lewis offered a six-hundred-dollar reward and cut off trade with their nation, but all the while wondered why he didn't follow them; abscond into nothingness. But he took a pill, and morning came, and anyway, the nothingness was filling up, the pioneer willow that anchored the riverbank was crowded out by the cottonwood, the cottonwood by the ash.

"—you refuse to apprise me of the wishes of the general government—the law prescribes certain responsibilities—"

"And a damned fool I would be to leave them in the hands of a factious conniver who schemes to denounce me to the President and procure my dismission—"

You have wronged me—take your own course—I shall, sir—Clark, the poisonous toad has cut me dead in public view—speak to him, surely there is—contempt and insult, and I will not suffer it to pass—Lewis, a duel would be catastrophic, I cannot—the governor has told me to take my own course and I shall step a *high* and a *proud* path—apologize—if we give it time—fix the stigma where it *ought* to rest—patience, Lewis—

Meanwhile, the world waited, unwinking, for a moment's chance to wreck and destroy:

War Department, July 15th 1809

His Excy Meriwether Lewis.

Sir: After the sum of seven thousand dollars had been advanced on the Bills drawn by your Excellency on account of your Contract with the St. Louis Missouri Fur Company for conveying the Mandan Chief to his Village . . . it was not expected that any further advances or any further agency would be required on the part of the United States. Seven thousand dollars was considered as competent to effect the object. Your Excellency will not therefore be surprised that your Bill of the 13th of May last drawn in favor of Monsieur P. Chouteau for five hundred dollars for the purchase of Tobacco, Powder, &c. intended as Presents for the Indians, through which this expedition was to pass and to insure its success, has not been honored . . .

The return of the Mandan chief is an object which presses on our justice & our honour. Ah, but Mr. J was in his slippers at Monticello; planting cabbages and arranging his Indian museum.

The President has been consulted and the observations herein contained have his approval.

William Eustis

There was a sadistic, recurring irony to it all; Lewis's imp had arranged for the blow to fall on his birthday. He was thirty-five. He sat at his desk; he gazed around his office, which suddenly seemed precious. He lifted his pen.

Saint Louis August 18th 1809

Sir

Yours of the 15th July is now before me, the feelings it excites are truly painful . . .

Marvelous, really, how quickly word of a man's ruin spread. There must have been other letters in the mail packet; rumors from Washington, words to the wise. Lewis opened the Secretary's letter at eleven o'clock in the morning, and by three that afternoon all his private debts had been called in, amounting to some four thousand dollars. By four o'clock, Lewis had deposited with his creditors all the land he had bought in Louisiana. Now it was ten in the evening. A single candle burned on his desk. (It cost fifteen cents; three times the price in Washington City.)

I have been informed Representations have been made against me . . . I find it impossible at this moment, to explain by letter . . . the impressions which I fear, from the tenor of your letter, the Government entertain with respect to me, and shall therefore go on by the way of New Orleans to the City of

Washington with all dispatch . . . Be assured, Sir, that my Country can never make "A Burr" of me—She may reduce me to Poverty; but she can never sever my Attachment from her . . .

Lewis's last days in St. Louis passed in a blur. He packed four trunks with his belongings. At the bottom of one, his journals wrapped in oilcloth; his other papers—receipts, vouchers, letters—thrown in army-style. His clothing; a Mandan tomahawk (taken from the wall of his office); a dirk; his brace of pistols. He would wear his sword; he would carry his rifle in one hand, his espontoon—but he was forgetting, he'd snapped the shaft of the espontoon months ago, helping Pernier prise out a rotten fencepost in the garden of the house he'd rented for himself and Clark. He wrapped the blade in oilcloth and laid it on top of his clothes.

Haze. He remembered his smaller creditors flocking to his door. He said something to Clark about vultures. Clark had arrived at his office, saying, "I think I owe you money, friend." He and Lewis wrote out their account, passing a sheet of paper back and forth. $150 Clark owed Lewis, his half of the purchase of Ordway's journal; $125 for the rent of the house; $50 for Hassler's work on the longitude. Lewis's borrowings from Clark: October 7th, 28th; November 5th, 9th, 15th, 20th. Totted up, it proved Clark right: he owed Lewis $152.93. He paid the money in cash on the spot. Lewis could not hold back tears of gratitude. He remembered Clark saying, "You must not take this too hard."

Lewis said, "I'm going to Philadelphia to write our book."

Clark said, "Eustis has also protested some of my bills; it is not uncommon."

Lewis said, "I need a place of peace and quiet to finish it."

Clark said, "A show of thrift at the start of the new administration."

Lewis said, "I need a rest."

Clark said, "I am leaving for Louisville and Washington in two weeks. I will affirm to all, what you have done—"

Lewis said, "Meet me at—"

Clark said, "—return with flying colors—nothing dishonorable—I am fully persuaded—"

Lewis wept, "In this terrible world, an angel—"

On September 4th, 1809, His Excellency Governor Lewis waved his dog on board a boat bound for New Orleans. He stepped in after him. Clark stood on the shore. The boatmen shoved off, crying in French.

I have never seen it in bloom. Clark touched the side of his hat. He made a fist with his other hand in front of his chest, denoting Courage.

Lewis saluted him. Then waved goodbye.

4

Swampy heat; sky of tin; a thick white glare off the river. Fever. Whiskey at night to help him sleep, although he wondered if he ever did; snuff through the day to keep him standing. The crew spoke French one day, Latin the next. "What day is it?" he asked of a man he'd never seen before. "What is your name, sir?" He had the gentleman witness a document he'd drawn up. *I bequeath all my estate, real and personal, to my Mother, Lucy Marks . . .* "Mr. Trinchard, it has been a pleasure. My hand." Thump thump.

Was it that day he wrote to Clark? He'd made no copy. Sent upriver. A message in a bottle. *Dear Clark.* He tried to remember. He'd sent it to Louisville. *—sincerest hope—arrived safely with Mrs. Clark—find yourself—bosom of your family—* He had the unhappy feeling that he'd been indiscreet. "Pernier, what day is it?"

Your wholesome felicity—Creator—mysterious wisdom—determined ever to deny me— "Pernier, what time is it?" *—compelled to sell my tracts of land—destitute of hope for a place to call—*

"We are on the river, are we not?"

—enemies resolute—deprive them of the pleasure—

"What I mean is, not tied up. The brutes are working?"

—burden your happiness—

"I need you to find a certain document for me, Pernier. At the bottom of the large trunk, on the enclosure is written—"

—wretched and self-inflicted misery—

"Stay, Seaman." Lewis touched his patient head, closed the cabin door. Pernier was busy. Lewis strolled to the port gunwale. He glanced fore and aft.

There is no man on earth—

Like the Missouri, the Mississippi was always on a boil. What *was* the cause? Lewis had never discovered to his satisfaction. He glanced fore and aft. *Adieu.* He jumped; exhaled deep, relaxed. Cool dark.

However (he remembered), they fished him out. After that, they had their eyes on him. The second time, he was barely in the water before arms closed around him. Then it was a prison. "Pernier, where are my pistols?"

"I don't know, sir."

"Damn you! You're lying."

Gaining the shore. "What is your name, sir?"

"My God, Lewis—Your Excellency! It's Gilbert Russell. Commander of Fort Pickering."

"Am I at the fort?"

"Yes."

"It is imperative that I write a letter to the President, John Madison."

"James Madison."

"Of course. Pernier, where is my—?"

Dear Sir, I arrived here about 2 Ock P.M. yesterday was it yesterday? he crossed out "yesterday" *very much exhausted* was it two o'clock? he crossed out "2 Ock" *from the heat of the climate, but having medicine feel much better this morning* it must have been, he reinserted "yesterday" *My apprehension from the heat of the lower country and my fear* he inserted "taken" before "medicine" *of the original papers relative to my voyage to the Pacific ocean falling into the hands of the British* unhallowed barbarians insensate with *has induced me to change my route and proceed by land through the state of Tennessee to the City of Washington. I bring with me duplicates of my vouchers for public expenditures &c. which when fully explained* a further explanation when I see you *or rather the general view of the circumstances* Hell and damnation *under which they were made I flatter myself that they* he crossed out "that" *receive both* he inserted "will" before "receive" *approbation and sanction* he crossed out "and" *Provided my health permits no time* he inserted "sanction &" before "approbation" *shall be lost in reaching Washington. My anxiety to pursue and to fulfill the duties incident to the internal arrangements* he crossed out "the" *incident to* had he already written that? *the government of Louisiana has prevented my writing* writing, writing, was that right, it didn't look right, Lewis studied it for a moment, he added an n, "wrinting" *you as* he crossed out "as" *more frequently. Mr. Bates is left in charge. En-*

closed I herewith transmit you he crossed out "Mr. Bates is left in charge" *a copy of the laws of the territory of Louisiana. I have the honor to be with the most sincere esteem your Obt. and very humble* only so much self-abasement he could bear, he crossed out "and very humble" *Obt.* but unwise to send "very humble" crossed out, he could make it illegible, but wouldn't it look suspicious, damnitall *and very humble Servt.* but now it said "Obt. Obt." but wasn't that perfect, wasn't that? wasn't that? Perfect! *Meriwether Lewis.*

"Pernier, where is my—?"

"Captain Russell has told me, sir, to deny you—"

"Where am I?"

"At Fort Pickering."

"I wish to leave this room."

"Captain Russell has ordered—"

All that was murky and horrible. Five days, Russell told Lewis, once his head had cleared, five days in a log hut in which he was denied all spirits save claret and white wine, in which the fever slammed down on him from above, and he observed things crawling on the walls, *genera* that were perfect strangers to him.

But the fever had broken. Now he could think straight. Now he could plan. "My dear Russell, I candidly confess it, I have been guilty of gross and unmanly intemperance. That, and the intermittent fever, which has clouded many a man's mind, laid me low." One had to convince them. One had to be *obedient* and *humble.* "I thank you for those stern measures that my reduced condition required you to undertake. I assure you, I am determined never more to drink strong spirits or use snuff."

The watch was kept. The fever remained at bay. Lewis dined nightly with Russell. He made more eminent sense every day. "I must travel overland, the sea route is unsafe; war with Britain is imminent; I know this from certain confidential communiqués I have received."

"I am going to Philadelphia to confer with my publisher regarding final details—"

"Captain Clark is traveling to Washington by an alternate route, for safety's sake; we have agreed to rendezvous on—"

"I must leave two of my trunks in your care, two others will accompany me, they contain my public vouchers and the journals from my expedition. The British would happily murder to get their hands on these journals.

They have been tracing my movements, I pray you tell no one, else I am undone—"

One evening, Russell said, "Perhaps someone could accompany Your Excellency."

"I have Pernier," Lewis said reasonably.

"Yes, but surely . . . the amount of your baggage, someone to help—"

"An excellent idea! I welcome it."

In the event, it was a Mr. James Neelly who was assigned the job of Lewis's keeper. Russell sold Lewis two horses and loaned him a saddle.

Attention: On September 29th, 1809, His Excellency Governor Lewis set out overland from Fort Pickering, at Chickasaw Bluffs, on the east bank of the Mississippi River, with his *fides Achates,* Seaman (a dog of the Newfoundland breed) and his half-French, half-negro servant, John Pernier. Accompanying the lunatic, in the role of Argos, was James Neelly, United States Agent to the Chickasaw Nation, and accompanying Neelly, in the role of slave, was a negro, first name Tom, surname lacking. The intrepid band had five horses in their train: the agent's two, plus the governor's two, plus a fifth that His Agency had loaned to His Excellency to carry his extra baggage. The four men, five horses, and one dog traveled southeast along a well-marked Indian road leading to the Chickasaw Nation, approximately one hundred miles distant. Thence they would follow the Natchez Trace 170 miles northeast to Nashville. The journey would take them, *in toto,* nine or ten days.

The weather was excessively hot. The atmosphere was notably humid, but there was little rain. The governor's journals were packed in his saddlebags. His rifle was on the cantle. He wore his pistols. The Newfoundland, walking, suffered in the heat. Twice or thrice daily, the governor called a halt so that the dog could lie for half an hour in a chance stream. His Excellency drank water. In the evening, in his simple half-faced camp of mosquito netting, he allowed himself a small amount of claret. He swallowed an opium pill to stave off fever and invite sleep. On rising, he took nothing save coffee. He made eminent sense. "I wonder at the lack of rain," he said to the agent. And: "We will arrive at the Chickasaw Nation on the third." And: "I warrant you, there will be war with England by spring." He could not forbear a measured comment or two about his protested bills. Nor did he impose on himself an absolute injunction against occasional animadversions to the malign stupidity of William Eustis, Secretary of War. In the mornings, the mulatto checked the powder. The governor wore his pistols. His journals were in his saddlebags behind him. He drank water. He was a ruined man.

Perhaps it was fatigue; perhaps the heat: on the night of October 2nd, the fever returned. The governor took a second opium pill. When that did not operate, he took a third. He could not remember arriving at the Chickasaw Nation.

What he did remember:

Lying down; Neelly standing over him. "You have agency business to conduct here, Neelly, and the press of my own affairs militate that I be getting on. It grieves me to conclude that we must part ways."

"Your Excellency is too sick to travel. A day's rest, perhaps two—"

"Damn you! God *damn* you! Pernier! Where is—?"

Lewis experimented with a larger dose of claret, as a carminative and soporific. He was forced to resort again to snuff during the day, as a tonic, but in strictly limited quantities. On the evening of—"Pernier, what day is it?"— Lewis's fever had lessened, and he stood up straight and looked Neelly in the eye and assured the Devil himself he was well enough to travel on the morrow, and by God he would go, and Neelly could accompany him (Lewis would welcome it!) or he could go to hell, but Lewis would proceed on regardless, his papers were too important to suffer more delay, at any moment England might declare war.

In the morning, they left; northeast along the Natchez Trace; swampy heat. Lewis, his keepers, five horses, a dog. Behind him, his journals. He wore his pistols, but he had no powder.

Along the trace, there were stands to sleep in: rough cabins offering infested bedding for a reasonable sum. Lewis slept on the cabin floors with his yellow bear skin and buffalo robe. At Perry's Stand, Lewis met a traveler, a young man on his way to Nashville. The following morning they traveled together. The young man exuded youthful admiration for the hero, and Lewis made excellent sense, and at noon, when youth incarnate pressed on (Seaman submerged in a rivulet), Lewis presented him with one of his prospectuses. "The book is being printed this very moment in Philadelphia; I have taken a liking to you, sir, and I will send you a copy gratis, if you will furnish me with an address."

In the morning, Lewis had his coffee and a pinch of snuff and a small glass of whiskey to clear his head. Pernier inspected the powder. Lewis wore his pistols, and his rifle was on his cantle, but he had no powder, and wasn't that perfect? "I should tell you, Neelly," Lewis said reasonably, "in case there should befall some accident, the papers in my trunks must be forwarded with all dispatch to the President."

He inquired casually of Pernier, "Has word arrived yet?"

"Of what, sir?"

"Of Eustis's dismissal."

"No, sir."

In the late afternoon, in a hickory stand at the top of a rise, with his head perfectly clear, he stopped his horse and said, "Listen."

Pernier reined in. "What, sir?"

"Silence, damn you! Listen! Don't you hear?"

"No."

"Shh!" He waited, hand out, motionless. "*There!* Did not you mark that?"

Pernier looked unhearing. Land of the deaf and dumb.

"Clark's voice. He has heard of my difficulties. He's coming after me."

5

Diligence: It is easily done in the night. Seaman (obedient and humble) stays. All the previous day, Lewis urged the party on. After fording the Tennessee River (low in this dry autumn) at midmorning, they labored through the hill country for thirty-five miles. Camped out by the trace. Now the others sleep the sleep of the tired innocent. Lewis unearths the powder canister from the bottom of Pernier's bag. Measuring by touch, he removes a smaller amount than Pernier would likely detect. The priming powder is where? It takes him a while, but he is patient. Here. Two pinches.

He picks his way down through honeysuckle and polecat tree to the grassy verge of the creek. He pats the necks of the two horses he has previously selected. Whispering to them, comforting, he leads them down the trace in the direction they have come, a mile and a half, then up an abrupt valley he noticed before. He finds a laureled, sheltered spot with good grass. If Lewis were a horse, he would stay here. He walks back.

They mean to control him. But he has it all figured out.

In the morning, the animals are discovered missing. Neelly is unwilling to entrust his slave Tom with the search for his best horse. Thus he remains behind, while Lewis, making unimpeachable sense, promises to wait for his keeper at the first house he comes to that is occupied by white people. The day grows hot, under a pearly sky. Black clouds lie low in the east. Now it is three horses, three men, the baggage. As the other horse that strayed was Pernier's, he must walk with the dog. Lewis has it all planned.

The trick is not to listen to irrational voices.

He urges his band on. Nashville is a hundred miles. They must make it in three days. Seaman and Pernier pant up the hills. The midday break is short. In late afternoon, the black clouds mass and loom, and instead of passing on, as they have done for days, they tarry, rain thunders down, a squall sweeps through the forest flattening bushes and whirling up dead leaves. Then it is gone in a moment. The sun breaks out, the air is fresh, The trick is not to—

Such as this irrational voice: *What a beautiful evening.* The sun drops below the tops of the trees; the road is in gloom, and yellow light walks above, and Lewis remembers, out west, looking up of an evening and seeing an armada of white cottonwood seeds sailing down, sunset-lit, from a deep blue sky, miles from any tree. A miraculous snow.

In other words, his hiding God has popped up for a brief appearance, to plant mischievous seeds of doubt: *How beautiful, how brief.*

When the sun is a hand's breadth above the horizon, they arrive at the foot of a ridge, and Lewis spurs his horse up the trail, leaving the others behind *(race you, boys!),* calling back, "I will press on ahead to see if there is a stand near." A spark, he rises. He has his pistols, he has powder. At the crest he finds—

A clearing. In fact, there *is* a stand: a crude log cabin; a small kitchen beside it. A barn is visible down a path through the woods, some two hundred yards off.

As Lewis approaches, a woman appears out of the cabin. He leans on the pommel. He is the soul of logic: "As evening has found me here, Madam, I wonder might I stay the night." Three or four or five children peer at him through the door.

The woman assents; he dismounts. He carries his saddlebags into the cabin, the children scattering. A dark, airless room. A table; two beds. The woman is standing in the doorway. "Are ye by yourself?"

He comes close to study her. She is not pretty; coarse-featured and hirsute. She smells of curds. She's put an extra foot between them. "Where is your husband?" he demands.

"Mr. Griner'll be coming directly."

"You, I conclude, are Mrs. Griner." She nods. "Mrs. Griner, I am Meriwether Lewis, Governor of the Territory of Louisiana. I have two servants behind, who will come up shortly. They will sleep in the barn. I will sleep in the house. I will have some spirits. After that, I will have some supper."

The woman herds her children into the kitchen, and returns with a black betty and an earthenware cup. Lewis leaves the cup on the table and fetches his silver tumbler from his saddlebags. He sits in a chair outside the door, the black betty at his feet. The sun is just down. A love-sick sickle moon is swooning to follow. An artfully placed cloud on the left is an inevitable pink. "Madam," Lewis comments, with one hundred percent accuracy, "this is a very pleasant evening." Lewis is rather upset about this evening. God laughs and laughs; He makes Lewis badly, then blames him for it (was the word *mistake* in Lewis's letter to Clark? was the phrase *mistake of nature*?); then He sends a beautiful evening. He whispers like a pander: *This world, a flower.*

Lewis has it all figured— Oh! And yes! There's His canon 'gainst self-slaughter—He designs the prison, then stands at the only door a man can open himself and commands Thou Shalt Not, and the punishment He threatens is so dire, you know this is what He fears most—that you will dress yourself in your petty divinity, take hold of the only valuable thing He has ever given you (the rest is gaud and trash, even He admits it), look Him in the eyes, and throw it away. *Go ahead.*

The trick is—

Pernier and Tom and Seaman are crossing the clearing. Lewis is out of his chair, mid-snore. His tumbler lies on the ground. The woman has disappeared. "We will lodge here tonight," he proposes unanswerably to the men as they come up. He fills the earthenware cup with water for Seaman and sets it down. "You two will sleep in the barn with the horses. We cannot afford to lose another one." Pernier glances at the distant barn. "By the way, Pernier," Lewis asks, assuming the forced casualness that the powderless lunatic's question would logically require, "I wish to check the powder, after today's rain. Where is it?"

"I'm not sure, sir," Pernier mumbles, turning away, disarmed.

He has it all—

[THE HERO]

The servants unload the horses and take them to the barn. Lewis paces in the yard, while the earth rotates through seven and a half degrees of arc. Supper is served. Root stew with memories of mutton. Lewis sits at the table, Seaman's weight against his leg. He manages two swallows. He rises impatiently. Seaman groans. Irrational voices—such as the one that sounds like Clark. (He just heard it again: *Lewis.*) A poor-will's call; breeze through branches; a squirrel's claws on treebark. In the past few days they've all said *Lewis* in Clark's voice, clear as clear, and it is Him, planting mischievous seeds, whispering lies. *Clark is coming. Clark has heard.* But Clark is not coming. Clark is in Louisville. Clark has read Lewis's letter—

"A long day!" He strides into the yard, hailing his fellow inmates, eating their dinner on stumps; negroes, powerless, equal (some say) in the sight of— He brings out the black betty, pours generously into their obedient and humble tin cups. "A hard day."

"Thank you, sir."

"Much obliged, sir."

The sky is mauve. "I wonder how Neelly is getting on," Lewis wonders. He goes to the kitchen door. The children melt into the corners. "I desire an ember," he says to the woman. She makes way for him. He takes one up with the tongs and lights his pipe. He returns to his chair outside the door and— no! the plan!—he turns to the servants. "Another one!" He pours. He sits.

Seaman has fallen asleep by his chair. The woman reappears. This time she is holding a crying baby. Plucked from some inexhaustible fund. "What is it?" he asks, with truly marvelous patience.

"Do you want me to fix you your bed?"

Lewis puffs once or twice, considering. Vermin, certainly. But no matter. But she might suspect— But then Pernier would expect—

"No, my excellent Madam, you shall not make up my bed. I will sleep on the floor in my buffalo robe and my bear skin." He studies her deaf and dumb face. "I have been to the west, you see." He perceives that she is frightened of him. Weak vessel. Of course she lied about Mr. Griner returning soon. Comfort her. He gestures toward the western sky, now gray. "It is a sweet evening," he says in a kind voice.

She doesn't look. "Yes, sir."

Yes, sir. Yez, mas'. Yes, Your Excellency. Yazzuh! They come running. "Pernier! Spread out my robes!"

"Yes, sir."

See?

Lewis takes his last puffs. Sweet tobacco. The woman retires to the kitchen. Lewis, all-seeing, sees the latchstring disappear through the hole. He observes Pernier coming out of the cabin. The man is tottering with fatigue; half drunk. "Is that all, sir?"

"Yes, Pernier, that is all. Good night."

"Good night, sir."

He has it— Lewis watches Pernier and Tom walk gingerly across the clearing toward the barn. It is dusk, as tradition demands.

All-remembering Lewis remembers:

> A shepherd and milkmaid are walking home:
> But far about they wander from the grave
> Of him whom his ungentle fortune urged
> Against his own sad breast to lift the hand
> Of impious violence.

Thou shalt not.

But then comes the sweet voice of Reason, God's mistake: *Why not?*

Far about they wander. Clark will never stand bareheaded at Lewis's grave. Impious. Well, he wouldn't in any case. He's read the letter. *No man on earth*— Lewis was in a fog when he wrote that. What was the complete sentence? He knocks his pipe against his bootsole. Fetches out his pick; cleans it.

He rises. Brings his chair in. The woman has lit a candle for him. His buffalo robe and bear skin are on the floor. Seaman is asleep (exhausted) beside them. He returns to the door to look out. Custom has spoken: it is dark. Mosquito whine. He closes the door.

Vigil: By the light of the one candle, he paces. Seaman groans. The world rotates. Humans sleep. What was the sentence? He has copied all his letters except that one. His journals are in the saddlebags next to the bed. His letters are in the small trunk on the floor by the table. Clark is in Louisville. God is in heaven. He doesn't need to look at the letters. Lewis, all-loving, has reread them. Looking for evidence.

A curious finding, a datum: in the sixth month of 1803, Meriwether

Lewis sent a letter to William Clark, inviting him on an expedition to discover the most practicable water-route across the continent of North America. He wrote: *My friend, in this enterprise, if there is anything which would induce you to participate with me in its fatigues, its dangers and its honors, believe me there is no man on earth with whom I should feel equal pleasure in sharing them as with yourself.*

In the seventh month of 1803, William Clark sent a letter back to Meriwether Lewis, accepting his invitation. In this letter, William Clark wrote: *This is an undertaking fraited with many difficulties, but My friend I do assure you that no man lives with whom I would prefer to undertake Such a Trip &c. as your self.*

To pose the question as a man of science, with a head unclouded by emotion: Why does this bother Meriwether Lewis?

It is the voice of friendship (comes the whisper).

Or (ungentle Reason must ask) is it wind in the branches, is it a poorwill's call?

"Clark," Lewis says out loud. He attends to the sound of the word in the room. "Clark."

Who is asleep in Louisville, with his legs drawn up and his hands between his knees, who will never forget that sentence, which Lewis cannot remember. He goes to his things on a chair. He takes out his pistols. He examines the powder he secreted in his tinderbox.

He has—

Less than he thought. Insufficient for two regular charges. But he divides it. The bullets do not have to travel far. He cleans out the touchholes, loads and primes. A fine pair of pistols, well balanced.

Life: the vagitus, and a moment later, the quietus.

And then the undiscovered country, from whose bourn—

"Seaman." The old dog groans. "Seaman, come on." Lewis opens the door, Seaman's head lifts. "Come on." By the Missouri: the Indian scaffold he saw, the dog sacrificed beside it. Barbaric! Who is he? Seaman's immortal spark. Running young again in fields of asphodel. "Come on, old boy, go on out." He pats the patient head, pushes the rump. *That warm touch* (whisper); *never again*—

He closes the door. The smooth maple stock in his palm; the cool muzzle against his forehead. Dear Mother: Today I am to be married to the heaviest musket in the magazine. (Whisper:) *never again*—

The trick is not to listen.

The sentence. He—

Pulls the trigger.

On the floor. Ears ringing. Warm blood in his eyes, blinking. His other pistol. He's on his stomach. He drags his elbow up in front. He lifts his head and tries to turn the pistol against his chest. A damned awkward position. He raises his head higher, rolls half on his side. The pistol fits into place. He fires.

He lies there for a while.

Then he gets up.

He looks at the candle. He looks around the room. "I have done the business," he says, to no one in particular.

He goes to the door. He opens it. He steps out into the clearing.

It is very dark. He falls on his knees. He is thirsty. He has made a mistake.

He crawls toward the black hump of the kitchen. "Madam," he says to the logs. He puts his face against the door. "Madam."

There is a water bucket by the door post. He lifts the gourd and scrapes in it, but it is empty. "Madam, give me some water." The door does not open. He has made a terrible mistake.

He turns about. He crawls in the direction of his room. *A place to call*—

He must rest for a while. He props himself against a tree. Where is Seaman? On the trail of a deer or squirrel. Lewis has shot himself in the head and breast, and he sits against a tree, thinking.

He thinks of the yellow bear. *These creatures being so hard to die it rather intimidates us all.* Shooting the bear in the head was not a good idea. That thick frontal bone. He has made a mistake, he sees that now.

Now, for the first time, he sees: nothing since the expedition has seemed real. He knows that now (he sees that) because *this* is real. This clearing. This tree he is leaning against. Orion, rising in the southeast. The Pleiades overhead. About 3 A.M.

He picks up a leaf. His hand is bloody, but— Red maple. *Acer rubrum.* He turns the leaf over. The feel of it in his hands. He will miss this. That pin oak over there. *Quercus*—? So real. And that bear, standing under the wild cherry. Looking at him. Lewis is surprised. A yellow bear in Tennessee. They are dangerous. He had better move off.

He gets up. He is extremely tired. And thirsty. Terrible thirst, actually. He must have strayed from the river. He walks for a while across the plain. He's on his knees. He crawls up over the lip of a bluff. Surely from here, he could see— The river?

Then darkness. Then Pernier staring down at him. He is in bed. Thirst. Gray light. The yellow bear is in the room, behind Pernier. "I have done the business," Lewis points out. To make it clear. That there be no doubt. "Now give me some water." The silver tumbler comes close. He sips. His arm is bleeding. He was doing some work with his razor. He wants to make something else clear. "I am no coward," he argues invincibly.

The bear is looking at him. "I am so strong," he says, "so hard to die." The conclusion is inescapable. "I would appreciate it, Pernier, if you would take my rifle and blow out my brains."

Pernier looks frightened. Lewis wants to reassure him. He wants to tell him: Don't be afraid of the bear. Because he has realized (of course) that this is *his* bear; the one he met, when all the gaud and trash of the world fell away.

The bear is looking at him. Lewis thinks, You are a man of science. Ask a question.

He endeavors to think of a useful one. Unfortunate that. So tired. Lost opportunity.

He asks, What was the sentence?

The bear looks at him.

Ask again. Repeat the experiment.

What was the sentence?

Pernier is saying something. Lewis waves him down. He is trying to hear the bear. The bear is turning. It walks away over the plain. It looks back. Lewis picks up his rifle, his espontoon.

He follows the bear toward the mountains.

Then darkness. A motion. Something . . . something. A vital thought bumps, slips away. He hears, *Lewis*. He opens his eyes. "Lewis," Clark says. "Throw the stick."

"What?"

"Throw the stick." Clark is holding the chronometer in one hand. In the other, he has a slip of paper and a pencil. Lewis looks down. A cottonwood stick is in his hand. He looks up. He and Clark are on an island. The cherry trees are blossoming in pink clouds. The river flows by. "Throw the stick, Lewis."

Lewis throws the stick. His young, fluid arm. It lands in the Rivanna exactly where he wanted. O, the joy!

"Thirty-five," Clark says, writing with a pencil.

"Isn't it thirty-three?" Lewis asks.

Then something else. Then water.

"It runs so fast," Clark says.

Lewis wants to say something about that, so fast, does he mean the chronometer, he thinks, so fast, and he turns to speak to Clark, but Clark is gone. Instead, there is an Indian. An old Shoshone. Lewis is standing in the wind at the crest of a treeless ridge; snowcapped mountains all around. He is at the divide.

The old man wants to tell him something. He gestures for Lewis to sit next to him. Lewis does so. He can smell tobacco on the old man, and grease, and sweetgrass. A pleasant smell. The old man raises his right hand in front of his eyes and points two fingers straight out: *I see.* He cups his palm in front of his mouth, tips it toward his lips: *Water.* He gestures wide, forming waves and troughs with his hands: *The sea.*

I have seen the sea.

He rocks back, smiling. A marvel, deep in these mountains. An old man's pride. Telling the children.

Lewis smells the sweetgrass, the tobacco, the grease. The wind is fresh. He blames himself for never having taken the time to learn the language of signs. So simple! What was he—? The language of nature. Speak to all. I take you by the hand.

The old man's hands are moving again. With his right finger, he draws a line from his heart to his mouth and extends it, straight out. A bird's flight. He touches Lewis's chest.

Lewis is struck hard by the extreme beauty of the gesture.

I speak true.

The old man smiles. The sea. A marvel. Watermillions.

Yes, Lewis says. *I understand.*

[THE HERO]

Second Charbonneau

He come down river for reward, America grateful old Charbonneau, she say, what, this beau vieux walk ten thousand mile for me, he sleep in rain, freeze ball off, run with grizzly nose two inch up ass, lose best damn skillet in river when pirogue tip over, he get only four hundred dollar? That disgrace! Give old lion four hundred more dollar, give old hero big piece American land! So he come down with Chouteau, first Chouteau bring back Big White, Big White bigger fool ever, he say all gift from government all his, no hand out, other Mandan angry, Le Borgne want kill him, but old Le Borgne kill other Mandan chief week before, maybe he got quota, Big White not get tomahawk in head for now. But that other story. Old lion Charbonneau come down river, Red Hair letter in pocket, good friend, Red Hair, he look out for old Charbonneau, he got something here, there, interpret job, trade this for that, Charbonneau save his ass from flood in ravine, he not mention it, that between him and Red Hair. He come down river in big Chouteau boat with Bird wife, little Jean-Baptiste, first time in St. Louis, big town, good trade, but Red Hair not there, people say he always leave, he away four, five month, he not like St. Louis, he east city boy.

Everybody talk about Big Knife, Governor Big Frown, they say whole town not like, maybe he feel bad, cut throat, Charbonneau little surprised, but what he know? he just say yes, sir mon capitaine grand-couteau, he stay out of way. He know Red Hair better, where damn Red Hair now, old conquering lion Charbonneau down for grand reward, for America kiss all over, Red Hair in east, Chouteau say, he in Philadelphia, he in Washington, he in Louisville, old Charbonneau wait patient, but Bird wife not happy, she want go back Minitadi village, in meantime, old Charbonneau not sit with thumb in ass, he talk to Chouteau, brother Auguste, Monsieur Lisa, they powerful trader, he play faithful servant, blink, yes sir, he play Indian expert, he do good job, when he baptize Jean-Baptiste in St. Louis church, godfather is Auguste Chouteau, man built St. Louis, grand papa of Louisiana, now little Jean-Baptiste have Red Hair and Chouteau for protect, plus Itsikamahidish, happy smoke all tobacco Bird wife give, plus Mother Church, Father, Son, what-all, black robe (who sooner later take everything, you wait), black robe Père Somebody put power-water on boy forehead, brave Jean-Baptiste expect pain, burning iron, such, like Minitadi, he surprised, he maybe think what-all stinking power this? Old Charbonneau put mark on paper, black robe hold feather, say, what mother name?, old Charbonneau not like Père Who-Fuck, he remind old North West Company partner, smooth hand, talk low, but eye say, carry me to tent, donkey, so Charbonneau answer, Tsakakawia, he say, what?, old happy Charbonneau say, Sakakamia, Tsakakabia, he say what again, Charbonneau say, Oiseau, Boitseau, Moitseau, he shrug like idiot, leave blank, Charbonneau say, helpful, she little Serpent squaw, he write that.

Wait for Red Hair, stay with Chouteau, Bird wife not happy, afraid big white man town, but not brave Jean-Baptiste, he five winter old, speak Minitadi perfect, French pretty good, little Mandan, little English, he stare at horse carriage, want spend all day watch carriage, up, down street. Charbonneau cash last bill Red Hair give three year ago, buy little this little that, for bring upriver. Wait, get bored, get drunk, little Bird wife ask go upriver, he say, soon, you wait, you see, old Forest Bear know what he do, he ask Chouteau, where damn Red Hair now, Chouteau say, he in Paris, France, he at north pole, he on moon. It summer before Red Hair show up, Bird wife sick in heat, thank Father, Son, Itsikamahidish, she get better, she good woman, she all old Forest Bear got in cunt department, white bead dead, he and Bird wife like Mother Church man wife now, old Charbonneau not fuck nobody but little Bird wife, she only fuck him, they live forever in buffalo robe kiss all over, too bad someday she get old ugly, he buy young slave girl in four, five year, Bird wife have help around lodge, someone yell at.

Red Hair final show up with wife, little son, Little Frown, Charbonneau worry he forget promise, but he good friend, old Red Hair, he write such in letter, letter in Charbonneau pocket, Charbonneau save his ass, he not forget, Red Hair say, Pomp, Pomp, Red Hair smile, wife smile, brave Jean-Baptiste shake hand, bow to white lady like old Charbonneau show, he say in English, *good day*!

Red Hair got himself good life, big wood house on big street, big garden, he live like pasha, he no idiot, he want drink, little piece cake, chair bring, pillow plump, stinking little china doll on mantelpiece move one-half inch to left, he call, Ruba!, he call, Juba!, five, six negro come in, do what-all he want, old friend Charbonneau say, Red Hair, you need bigger house, all these slave bump each other, Red Hair agree, he build brick mansion, Charbonneau look at Bird squaw sit quiet off side, say in Minitadi, you see? you wait.

Now Big Knife off in spirit world, Red Hair write book about Minitadi-Mandan, but Red Hair not know much, he stuck in Fort Mandan all winter, freeze ball off, he also forget, he turn to old expert Charbonneau, he ask what game they play, what Minitadi word for this, for that, how tell time, what-all. One thing Red Hair ask when white lady out of room, he wonder about papoose, Indian squaw have one, two, white lady have seven, eight, what go on? Charbonneau say, funny you ask, wise old friend Red Hair, I wonder same since twenty year, I think, what wrong with men, they spend too stinking much time on horse bareback? I see berdache, Indian men dress like women, I think same, maybe some true, they not have hair on body, maybe relate. But squaw also keep baby away, do what-all, pardonnez-moi, use hand, use mouth, they know herb, cook mess in pot, only damn thing they know how cook, make sick, run against rock, friend jump on stomach, they say, too many children, hunt give out, crop give out, old Charbonneau think of ten, eleven brother, sister in Montreal, poor dead maman, he think, damn good idea, old Itsikamahidish not say, act like stinking fruit-tree. Mulatto interpret, maybe get all wrong, but Red Hair write, Charbonneau help so much, no way Red Hair forget.

Red Hair back late from moon, stupid question, what-all, it October before grateful America give old hero Charbonneau his big piece bottomland, une belle pièce, Charbonneau assume, anyway, he never see, Red Hair pick, Charbonneau not care, he not break back like donkey farmer, he want live like pasha, like Red Hair, secret is trade, plus government job, like Red Hair promise. Season too late for boat upriver, Red Hair say company boat in spring, Charbonneau stay for winter, get bored, get drunk, trade little more, little Bird wife get sick, probable white man disease, town dangerous for her, he want go back upriver, he worried about little Bird wife, Jean-Baptiste stay healthy, he get white-man power from old strong horse Charbonneau, he go in shop, he watch carriage, watch boat, ask question, learn English.

Red Hair company boat ready in grass moon, after first spring flood, Charbonneau buy bisquit, powder, ball, vermilion, he sell belle pièce bottomland to Red Hair for one hundred dollar, he wink, Red Hair wink, he know, Red Hair know, that piece worth five hundred dollar, easy, but it *friendly arrangement*, as Red Hair say, he keep promise, Charbonneau get job with Red Hair fur trade company, he engagé, not paddle stinking canoe, he sit on ass, intrepret, say, exact so! get two hundred fifty dollar in year, guarantee, for long company last, trade on side like always. Good for Charbonneau, good for Red Hair, good for Jean-Baptiste, he say to Bird wife, you see? old Forest Bear know what he do all along. Bird wife cry, it hard for little maman, but Jean-Baptiste strong white boy, he not turn into berdache in woman clothes, better for him, he learn English, they American now, he get school, Red Hair grateful, Chouteau for protect, he grow up powerful man, old Charbonneau hundred year, little Bird wife what-all, they lie happy in buffalo robe, powerful hopini medicine son, Jean-Baptiste, maybe governor Louisiana, take care of old ugly parent. Bird wife still cry, she feel sick, but old Charbonneau say, you get strong after leave white town, we make other boy, you be like white woman, like Red Hair wife, who wave from door with brave Jean-Baptiste, she already got Little Frown brother, must be Littler Frown, cook inside.

Coyote went down to the bad-tasting water.

This one is wrapped in buffalo. A fever ghost is in her. Or what sharbono says: she breathed bad air. Glue stink. Her throat hurts. Or what the under-grounders say: sun-men bring sickness with their blood-tasting knife-metal, their iron.

This one died.

Maybe it will happen now. Wrapped in buffalo, shivering in a corner of a sleeping hut in a sun-man fort.

Fort is an english word. This one listened for two winters in red hair's town, in saint-looiss. Four worlds, the number of spirit, of the winds. Bad air blowing through her.

Coyote went down to the bad-tasting water. He saw a pretty girl.

This one saw out of water. Then she didn't see him. She turned away. There were horses and people moving back and forth. Noise. Sharbono pulled her. He spoke angrily. Down to the boat. Her waterboy! His taste, his smell. She turned away.

Down to the water. She sat in the boat.

Coyote saw a pretty girl. Her name was water girl.

She came up the mizoori with sharbono.

Many days, sitting in the boat. Every day the same. The boat was there. The river was there. Out of water was not there.

She is wrapped in buffalo. *This one died.* Maybe sharbono is right. Maybe it is good for him, her sun-child, to be among sun-men in saint-looiss. White men. Maybe this one's misery is foolish. Her longing.

She pined for him in the night, and her spirit left her body, searching for him, and maybe it was then the fever-ghost entered. The empty hut, the untended fire.

This one and sharbono came up the muddy river, the mizoori, with red hair's man, missyer-lisa. They came to the village of the undergrounders, the minitadi, the bigbellies, the groh-ventr. They spent a bad winter there.

Coyote chased water girl. He caught her by the shore.

The traders from coldward, the c'nadyans, the british, told lies about the americans, the big knives. The minitadi listened to northwest-kump'ny band; the light-skinned undergrounders, the mandans, listened to mizoori-fur-kump'ny band.

Bad winter. Sharbono was in mizoori-fur-kump'ny band, his speaker was red hair. Minitadi speakers le-born and spirit buffalo robe were angry with red-hair-people. Two hunters were killed with arrows. Red-hair horses were stolen. In the redberry moon, missyer-lisa came with men and black weapons. He stole back some horses and took away mizoori-fur-kump'ny band furs. Mizoori-fur-kump'ny band followed missyer-lisa five nights downriver, to this place, near the big earrings, the ricaras, the ree.

Water girl took Coyote on her back across the water.

The red-hair-men were building a fort. This fort, fort manyul.

Where this one lies shivering and throat-stuck and rotten-breathed in a buffalo robe in a corner.

Across the water is the island where water girl lived with her mother.

She is a child, wrapped in buffalo and the speaker's voice.

On the way to the island, Coyote slipped down and stuck his cock in water girl.

Sharbono does not tell stories. By the fire in winter, he says, today, I. Tomorrow, you must. He does not tell stories about the french Woman Above, Mother Aygleez, or how french sun-men stole iron from Great Spirit, or when english sun-men broke away from french sun-men, and whether they fought over hunt-spoils, or who would be speaker. Or as english say, prezdent, like prezdent clark.

This one longs for out of water. She longs for listening to stories.

Water girl dropped Coyote in the water. She left him to drown.

For father and son and ghost-spirit, said the man in black in the med-sanh hut when he put the water on her son's forehead. He made the sign of four directions, four winds, which maybe meant, you will wander, foolish one.

But Coyote crawled up like a water-strider and swam to the island.

She lies in the brush hut, a child, wrapped in buffalo with small frog, listening, laughing. They knew Coyote could not die! Or, when he did, he came back to life, like all the animal-people. When he stole fire, and Crane's people killed him, Hare hit his dead body with a whistle, and he jumped up. When he climbed the cliff, chasing the two young women, and fell down and died, the women waited a while and then asked him, what are you doing down there? and he said, I am eating the marrow of a mountain-lion! Come join me! But the women were not tricked.

Ohwa! Ohwa!

This one turns in her robe. Sharbono wrapped li-zet in a separate skin. This one was too hot.

She pulls her ohwa close, slips her nipple in her mouth, turns her own mouth away, her rotten breath. Bad air. Ohwa chews and cries. This one holds her breath (she feels faint), looks down, pinches her nipple. Her milk is drying up. *This one died.* And her ohwa, her li-zet?

There are two women in the fort who have milk. And li-zet was born four moons ago; she can live without milk, if she must.

Tomorrow, you must. Today, I.

The water trickled down out of water's forehead, and the man in black in the med-sanh hut said, for father and son and ghost-spirit. Sharbono was the father, and out of water was the son. Maybe this one was the ghost-spirit?

And the spirit water explained his name, because zhonh-bopteest means (this one had learned after many questions, many shrugs, sun-men do not like to speak of these things) he who puts water on his forehead, and spirit must have told sharbono in a dream long ago that this would happen. The water made three streams trickling down out of water's forehead, and the man in black looked at the sign but said nothing. This one wondered if it was a sign of the plain of three rivers, where she was captured, where all this foolish wandering began.

Her ohwa is crying. This one tries to swallow, and a rawhide bag is glued to the inside of her throat, the pain is hard to push away. Her crying ohwa will not take the little milk that comes. (Sharbono will not tell her what li-zet means.) It is daytime and only one gard-man is in the hut with her, on the other side, asleep, and she says, please? (she feels very faint) and missyer? but he does not move. She says, please? louder to the door, but it stays closed. Her legs are too weak to support her, her ohwa is crying louder.

Please?

Then a dream. *The river is frozen.*

Then she must be only half asleep, because she wonders, was that a dream?

Because (she is almost awake) she remembers that the river outside the fort (in this below world, now) is frozen.

She opens her eyes. Night. Sharbono is holding her hand. Li-zet? she asks. There is hardly space in her throat for the word. It floats up through a crack.

The river stopped flowing ten, fifteen nights ago.

She good, sharbono says, wah-zoh not worry. Ree squaw nurse her, she drink like whiskey. She wait p'ti twah-zoh get better.

Sharbono gives this one water to drink. It trickles down hot and rotten-blood-tasting through the crack in the rock of her throat.

One winter evening, when Coyote was outside squatting to shit, he looked down and saw a fire below. He thought the fire was in his asshole, so he jumped up. But then he saw it was far down the mountain. He asked his asshole, what's that fire for? His asshole said, another tribe owns it. Crane is their speaker. Why don't you go and steal their fire?

She is burning, wrapped in her buffalo robe. She tries to pull it off, but is too weak.

He thought the fire was in his asshole, so he jumped up.

Two bears, telling the story, jumps up, throws frightened looks around. In the brush hut with small frog, this one laughs and laughs.

But wasn't she telling a different story? It is bad to tell a story wrong. Or to start a story and not finish it. The animals listen, the tall grass creeps to the hut-door to hear.

Coyote crawled up like a water-strider and swam to the island. He went into the hut where water girl and her mother lived. He was eager for the night to come. But when the women pretended to eat the waterbird eggs, they let the eggs slide down to their cunts, where Coyote heard the shells cracking. He went outside to ask his asshole for advice.

[s]

They lowered two bears, wrapped in elk skin, into the crack in the rock.

It is bad to tell a story outside winter. It brings bad weather.

This is winter now. The river is frozen. How will out of water lift his head out of the water if the river is frozen?

He does not need her; he must learn to be strong.

Li-zet came hard. She was too big. That was just before missyer-lisa came with his black weapons to take the mizoori-fur-kump'ny band away from the minitadi village. That was a hard trip. Five days. This one's blood dried in mats on the horse.

Bad summer. They arrived where sun-men were cutting trees. Big earrings (ree) and undergrounders (minitadi and mandan) and dog-eaters (shyanh) and headcutters (soo) coming to see, to trade, to steal, to fight. Sharbono went back upriver to trade with mandans for horses. This one was helped by spotted cheek, a twoleaf woman. That one had been captured by the minitadi and sold to a french-speaker, a trader, who now worked for prezdent clark, for mizoori-fur-kump'ny.

Coyote picked up his elkhorn scraper. He stuck it into water girl's cunt. Water girl cried out. —Something is wrong with my teeth.

One day sharbono came galloping, pointing backward, shouting *o-zarm!*, meaning the enemy is attacking, and the sun-men ran where he pointed. When they came back, they said big-bellies had stolen seven horses.

Later, a man the horse-thieves captured and let go returned to the fort. That one said they were not big bellies. They had told him they were birds. Sharbono said, —Which mean one bad-smelling thing we know, they not bird.

The next day spotted cheek died of bad air. Or of fever-ghost. Or sunman nearness.

Sharbono left again, for the bigbelly village, to try to get the stolen horses back (if it was them, not some other tribe that was not the birds). This one pushed away her weakness. She nursed her small ohwa and tasted her all over. Pining, she tried to love her like her first ohwa.

Bad summer. Every day *indyans* (the english word for the french word, *laypóh-roozh*) came to trade at the unfinished fort, bringing many skins and robes, beaver, otter, wolf, fox, buffalo. They took away vermilion and whiskey, black weapons and powder and ball. When a band of soo came they fought with the ree, and two soo were killed, and three ree were wounded, and a band of shy-anh stole horses from some mandans, and threats were traded.

Coyote talked to we-people. He said, I saw fire from the mountain last night. Why don't we go steal it?

We-people had never seen fire. Coyote took a shit, and asked his shit for advice, and his shit said, go have a feast with Crane's people.

Night. Sharbono is asleep in his robe near her. Where is li-zet?

Wasn't she telling a different story?

Wolf said, people should be born out of fingers, without pain, without fucking. Coyote said, no, fucking is good. People should fuck, and they should be born with pain, through women's cunts.

She is a child in a brush hut, wrapped in buffalo, laughing. People born out of fingers! Crazy!

But she is also frightened. How much will it hurt?

This one listens, in the sun-man fort, in the winter night. The river is frozen and silent.

Camas flower kissed her. She said, it will hurt, but you will be strong.

One thumb put his maimed making hand on his chest and said, the salmon finger points to the heart. This one was just a child, but she loved him, she wanted to be his woman. But two bears had given her to white feather, who was old, and never spoke to her.

The winters that age you. How many winters?

Sun-men count their winters carefully, like beaver skins going in the pack.

Maybe ten when this one was captured (jumping fish, foolish one), then two, or was it three, before forest bear bought her (sharbono), and the winter when red hair and big knife came. Then the long winter of rain. Three more, or was it two, with the undergrounders again (minitadi), two in saint-looiss, last winter (bad winter), and this one, her last. Ten; three, four, five, seven, eight, nine, another ten; and one. Ten and ten and one.

Camas flower said this one smiled when she first heard thunder, and that meant she would live long. But she never believed it.

The ree woman told this one about three med-sanh stones across the river from fort manyul, a day's walk on the prairie. Long ago, it was said, a man was in love with a girl. But the girl's father would not give her to him, so the man went off alone onto the prairie, to meet spirit. To ask, to wait, to starve. The girl followed him. Then a dog followed. Sorrow turned them all to stone. Beginning with their feet.

This one dreams: The river is frozen. She is standing on the still ice. You can see the wind. It lifts thin snow off the ground and stretches, spins it, against an empty blue sky.

The dream is strong and clear. This one knows. This is the dream of her death. She sings:

> ice
> stopping the river
> take this one to the good land

She wakes. Night. Shivering. But where will she go? (They lowered him wrapped in elk skin into the crack in the rock.) People say different things. To Wolf's house, or underground. Or Great Spirit's council room, where maybe this one will interpret. Or to Coyote's wandering campfire.

Coyote will say, my daughter, foolish one. Then he will try to fuck her.

Wolf said, people should not die.

Coyote said, they must die, or there will be too many of them.

This one, in the dark, unable to swallow (her throat is rusting iron), feels spirit near. Where will I go? she asks.

Bird.

When?

Shouts.

She sleeps again, and wakes. Sharbono is holding water to her lips. It pools in her throat.

She held out of water, she carried him, she tasted him all over. He danced by the fire. She turned away.

Wasn't she telling a different story?

Crane's people were dancing the nuakin dance around the fire. Coyote joined in. He was wearing a headdress that reached the ground. When Crane's people were not looking, he let the end of his headdress drag near the fire. He pulled some of the fire off. He hid the fire under his robe.

This one is walking slowly, her hand high. She is holding two bears' hand. The grass is as tall as she is. But there is a path through the grass, which leads to a bush. Redberries come down to her, from high up, in two bears' hand.

Her throat is singed and crushed bone, leaking marrow. Her breath speaks to the dead.

When sharbono came back from the bigbellies, he held her hand. —I worried, p'ti twah-zoh.

The arrow burrowed. White bits flew.

Sharbono said, —British and american have war now. Minitadi angry at old forest bear, they say I big knife now.

In the morning, Crane's people tried to start a fire, but they couldn't. Where are those visitors? they said. We must chase them, and get our fire back.

Sharbono said, —I think they maybe attack fort, but big knife not believe, they say I try scare, I do for minitadi, I traitor, I maybe hang from tree.

She opens her eyes. Missyer-lisa is holding her arm over a bowl. Her blood is in the bowl. He is making another cut with the iron. She cannot feel it.

She hears her ohwa crying. Li-zet, she tries to say. (She can hardly breathe.) Sharbono's ear comes close. Li-zet, she thinks she says. Doesn't he hear her crying?

Crane's people saw Coyote ahead of them. He was the last in the line of we-people, running away. Crane's people shot arrows at him, but missed every time. They shot all his hair off, but could not hurt him. Then he grew tired. When he came to an old footprint, he hid in it.. They could not see him. —Where did he go? they asked. Then they saw the footprint. —That's him! They threw a rock at him, and he ran away. Then he came to an old pile of shit, and he hid there. The enemy could not see him. Then they saw the shit and said, that's him. Coyote ran again. He was very tired. He gave the fire to the we-people in front of him. The enemy caught up with him. They killed him and skinned him.

Bird, spirit said. Does that mean this one will fly up to Wolf's house?

Or will she go underground, cross the river to the undergrounders' village, become again a bird-girl, protecting the corn?

Her blood has filled the bowl. Missyer-lisa presses her flesh around the cut (she cannot feel it), he mutters something. This one wishes looiss were here. He would not save her (it is her time) but maybe he would send her on her way a little stronger.

She is thirsty.

Now Hare came out of the hole he had hidden in during the chase. He hit Coyote with his whistle. Coyote woke up. Why did you wake me? Coyote asked. I was dreaming.

In the brush hut, water speaks and small frog shout, we knew it! we knew it! They roll against each other, laughing, under the buffalo robe.

Small frog, who kicked. The arrow burrowed.

But wasn't she telling a different story?

Coyote went down to the bad-tasting water. He broke the teeth of water girl's cunt.

But looiss is dead. Sharbono said he let his own fever-ghost out. Having spirit-power is dangerous. It can be too strong. Other spirits are jealous. They send bad luck or craziness.

They lowered him into the crack in the rock. Someone said:

> *reach a good land*
> *don't come back*

But where was that good land?

—Where is li-zet? she tries to say again. There is a rushing sound in her ears (she cannot move her legs), but beneath the sound she can hear a long, unchanging ohwa wail.

Her throat is frozen. —Li-zet, she maybe says.

Camas flower kisses her. Camas flower says, don't be afraid.

She runs through the shallow water. Water drums behind her. Water glitters, bright white.

After he'd broken their teeth, Coyote fucked water girl and her mother. They were pregnant. They told Coyote to go outside and fetch water.

Sharbono held her hand and said, —I worried. Three ree hunter killed by soo.

She swung out of water in the skin lodge. She watched him walking. She turned away.

She is very thirsty.

ice
stopping the river
take this one to the good land

She opens her eyes. Bright day through the chinks in the logs. Sharbono is standing with the ree woman. This one cannot move legs or arms now. She cannot turn her head. She tries to move her lips. Air whistles through the ice-crack in her throat. She is no longer shivering. She can hear, under the roar in her ears, the abandoned wail of her ohwa.

But she can see her ohwa asleep in the ree woman's arms.

The waterboys put the hunter high in the sticky-tree. During the night Water-giant came out of the water and climbed the tree to eat the hunter, but the waterboys pushed Water-giant down and threw him back in the water.

This one listens closely.

Ohwa!

It is not li-zet she is hearing. It is out of water. She slips her bursting nipple in his mouth. Water-giant rises in the ravine, chewing rocks, he sweeps ohwa downriver in his holder. He must be strong. Her misery means nothing. This foolish one is only a woman.

No, fucking is good, Coyote said. And people should be born with pain, through women's cunts.

Sharbono is weeping. But it is good for him. He must be strong.

But this foolish one was telling a different story.

As soon as Coyote was gone, many babies pushed out through the women's cunts. Water girl and her mother took the water brought by Coyote and washed the babies, except for one tribe. They said to Coyote, —We have left these for you to wash.

Those ones were the we-people babies. Coyote washed them.

He said to them, —You are my children. I will stay with you. Do not be afraid.

Camas flower kisses this foolish one.

ice
stopping the river
take this one to the good land

She is standing on the frozen river. No people, no trees. Bright empty blue sky, bright ice. She waits for a long time. Wind lifts snow, drops it. Then she sees, far across the ice, a figure walking toward her. It shimmers, stretches. It is spirit. It comes closer. It is a man. He is one thumb. He is taller than one thumb. Slender. He is looiss. He comes closer. He is more graceful than looiss. He flashes silver like a fish. He is pronghorn. He comes closer. He is a beautiful young man. He comes up to her. He stops. He is a strong, brave, beautiful young man. He is her son. She opens her mouth to speak to him (her good throat, her free voice). Does she say it? Or does he?

Why did you wake me? I was dreaming.

Clark and Company

He arrived by steamboat at the St. Louis landing at eleven in the evening, September 12th, 1832. He slept on board.

He was a ghost. He was Rip Van Winkle. So much had changed in the years he'd been gone. Steamboats like floating castles. Forests felled. Democracy louder, patriotism uttered like a threat: "I'm an American, I am!" The thrust-out jaw, the implied challenge: *And what are you?*

He? He was a famous writer, a well-traveled man (which, he admitted, made him suspect). A "spectator of other men's fortunes and adventures" (Burton's *Melancholy* was his bedside reading). He was an addicted theatergoer. He craved amusing company. He was adaptable. He was visited with skin rashes and obscure internal ailments, for which he took pills and drafts. He'd appeared in the following roles: New York City lawyer; businessman of Liverpool, England; colonel in the Iron Greys; diplomat in Madrid; Secretary of the American Legation in London. He spoke English, French, German, Spanish.

But he was an American, he was, he reckoned, sure as shootin'.

Back home in America; homesick for Europe. He was half a year shy of half a century. In his youth, he'd been a japer, a trickster, one of the Lads of Kilkenny. He'd been a dandy, a roaring blade. He'd cut a figure. His motto was: To Be Pleased with Everything, and If Not Pleased, Amused. He was genial, kindly. A friend of the family, a favorite uncle, an intimate in homes away from home. He held umbrellas, counseled moderation, invented amusing tales for the children. He was a lurker in libraries, a lover of folklore, a seeker-out of the quaint and curious.

He was plagued with insomnia. (1:30 A.M.) He was renowned for his felicitous style, his sensibility. He was the Essayist, the Tale-Teller, the sweet-voiced Nightingale of Melancholy. He was the author of "The Broken Heart," which made Lord Byron sob. His other motto was: In Hoc Est Hoax. He was an absolute old bachelor. The Wandering Jew. A second Boabdil, exiled from paradise, the gate walled up behind him. He was the biographer of Columbus, the mythomancer of Gotham. He could call spirits from the vasty deep (however, they declined to come when he called). Returned to America after seventeen years, he was the hero of the hour, fleer from banquets held in his honor, quailer at announcements from the stage that he was in the theater. He was author of the lines:

> For even thus the man that roams
> On heedless hearts his feeling spends;
> Strange tenant of a thousand homes,
> And friendless, with ten thousand friends.

Long ago, when a trickster, he'd loved a girl. She had smiled at him one day, coughed on the second, died on the third. Years later, he loved another. But by then he was too old (honorary uncle, friend of the family, holder of umbrellas) and she fled from him.

He did not believe in heaven or hell. God was a word, an overworked rhetorical device. Life was a mystery.

Relentless seeker of new sensations, generous applauder when the curtain came down, fits-and-starts keeper of journals, from which he excluded nothing save his feelings. In all his tale-spinning, scene-painting, lore-mongering, only once: as lap-robe-arranger of a certain family, one of his homes away from home, he'd written to the young mother (had he loved her? had there been a series of young mothers that he had loved?) a letter revealing his deepest wounds. He bound her to secrecy. He made her promise not to copy the letter (after all, he was famous), and to return it to him after she had read it. Then he burned the most confessional pages; locked the rest away. The last words on the last surviving page: "Do you want some of the _real_ causes? While at Dresden I had repeated . . ."

Ah, future biographers! Forgive him his teasing (In Hoc Est Hoax), his little puff of talcum-smoke before the black velvet backdrop. Life was a mystery. Shouldn't a _Life_ be?

Whim-follower, wayward, traveler incog. Being of the air, flute player, vessel (some mornings) of incapacitating horror, quester for and perpetual misser of war, floater on the surface of occasion, weary of everything and of himself, the man of the weathercock mind, possessor of a heart that would not hold on. Emulator of Herodotus, Father of History, Father of Lies; namesake of the Father of His Country; pilgrim seeking spiritual fathers. As for his real father (the excellent, grim deacon): nothing occurred to him.

Hoaxer, hider, dodger, Proteus. He'd read in small-town newspapers (he was glimpsed at the theater; he was said to be the guest of) that his eyes were blue; that they were brown; that they were gray; that his hair was black; that it was chestnut. If you caught him and held him, perhaps he would tell you your own history. Or your own fictions. Old Man of the Scene; his time had gone by. A writer of "literary anachronisms," according to Mr. Hazlitt. Seduced by the pleasure domes of Europe, crabbed the harpies of patriotism. When he'd been young, his scribbling had been a lark. Now it was all that kept him going, a shield he held up. Life was a joke, you might as well tell it properly.

He had come west on a whim. He was searching for an American theme. (This prodigal nephew might find it convenient to embrace his favorite uncle, Sam.) In the newspapers, it was rumored; anecdotes of America from the agile pen of; portraits of the prairie; scenes of savage life. If not for his pen, he would have floated away by now like a dandelion seed. His public might have glimpsed him going, it would have exclaimed, "How pretty, when the light catches him just so!"

His names were: Jonathan Oldstyle, Gent., epistolar of times gone by; Launcelot Langstaff, infallible editor; Linkum Fidelius, unheard-of writer of folios; Jeremy Cockloft the Younger, travel-writer, greenest scion of the Cockloft Cocklofts; Mustapha Rub-a-Dub Keli Khan, Tripolitan ketch-captain and husband to twenty-three wives; Diedrich Knickerbocker, half-cocked old man and missing person, historian of New York; Seth Handaside, Landlord of the Independent Columbian Hotel; Geoffrey Crayon, Gent.; Fray Antonio Agapida, skeptical chronicler of the conquest of Granada.

He signed his letters "W.I." The correct pronunciation would be with an American "W," a European "I."

In the morning, he perambulated St. Louis, jotted in his notebook: *Mixture of French & american character. French billiard room—marketplace where some are Speaking French some English.* The scrape of a fiddle heard from a dim interior; an old French song. Ancient air. The happy Gallic turn for merriment. No, the happy Gallic turn for *gaiety.*

He put up at the Union Hotel. The clerk asked him when the book he was writing on this great state of Missouri would be out. He was introduced to Mr. Pierre Chouteau; to a Dr. O'Dwyer; a Judge Peck, a Mr. Bates. His traveling companion, Commissioner Ellsworth, naturally desired an interview with Governor Clark, so in the afternoon, Judge Peck obligingly drove them to a farm a few miles out on the prairie, where the governor took his ease. W.I. was freshly shaved and bathed. Under his frock coat he wore a crisp white shirt and a red vest of watered silk. He felt well.

Flowering & fragrant shrubs—The Govs. Farm. small cottage—Civil negro major domo who asks to take horses out, invites us to walk in the orchard—& spreads table with additional courses—lovely day—golden sunshine—transparent atmosphere—pure breeze—fine nut trees—peach trees grapevines Catalpas &c &c—fertility of country

The plain facts, around which he would weave his fabric, tease out his filigree work (if he allowed vulgar rumor to dictate the writing of a book). He wrote sitting on a rustic bench, waiting for the general to return from an outing.

The bench: a thing of Arcady. This glorious view—grassy sea; no, a cliché; the verdant main; the pristine prairie. The broad merry laugh of the negro. The pendant apples shining in the light of. The rich domestic rewards of this hero of the wilderness. Perhaps he should place it later in the day: shining in the light of the setting sun. Pleasing rhythm. Appropriate backdrop for the general in his golden-maned retirement. Sun setting, resplendent something; full moon rising; soft gaze, or benign visage. Diana, regent of lakes & woods—beautiful phrase; pity there were neither lakes nor woods. "Excuse me, sir." The major domo was standing over him. "The general is approaching." The darky gravely indicated the direction to take out of the garden. These ramrod-straight old negros. Stately as grandfather clocks.

And here came the general, trotting up on horseback, his gun on his shoulder, two dogs in his wake (portrait of a sylvan seigneur), a young boy on a calico pony, must be his grandson. A setter bolted out from the house and commenced bullying the other dogs. The general and his grandson laughed, hallooed their guests. The general swung off his horse, extended his hand.

"Commissioner Ellsworth, Mr. Irving, Judge Peck, welcome! You'll dine with me, won't you? Commissioner, my congratulations on your appointment. Mr. Irving, this is an unlooked-for honor, I have read your books with pleasure these many years—"

The usual: Ichabod Crane; Rip Van Winkle; the Christmas Dinner. Yes; how kind of the general. Writings from a dozen years ago. They should put it on his tombstone: How Kind of You to Remember! But of course he meant well. W.I. examined his host. A fine, healthy, robust man; tall, mid-fifties, perhaps more. His hair, once red (didn't the Indians call him Red Head Chief, or Red Head Father?), was now gray, swept back from a high forehead, falling on his shoulders. A wide, amiable mouth; prominent muscles in the jaw. He still wore an ample white stock around his neck, twenty years out of fashion. Eyes turned down at the corners, exactly like George R. Clark's, in his portraits. Gave the brothers a chastened, worldly-wise air. What a family of continent-striding giants, these Clarks! Alas, America would not look upon their like again.

Half a dozen negroes were converging: two to take the halters, two others to relieve the master and young mas' of guns and gamebags, two last to take orders, which the governor gave. He urged his guests toward the dappled bower where the tables groaned. Ripples spread outward, negroes hurrying forward, popping out of the kitchen, a boy (teeth flashing) brushing a just-fallen autumn leaf or catalpa pod from the waiting chairs. The sheer number of negroes in America continually surprised W.I. One would swear they were half the population. And after all the promises of the old Virginians, the demands for northern patience. After all that, Missouri was a slave territory! Where would it end? Jefferson, in his last years, supporting the extension, a damned cowardly performance; tired old man. But you couldn't deny it, there was something charming, something picturesque. Shining black faces; the governor undoubtedly a kind master; a big family. W.I.'s chair was held; he sat. A rustic feast, a veritable wedding by Breughel: fried chicken; bison and venison and roast beef; roast potatoes, tomatoes; cakes, bowls of walnuts, bread, sweet butter, honey. Something about the abundant blessings of a clear conscience, the rewards of a virtuous life. Venerated equally by redskin and paleface, the old warrior (or statesman, rather), snowy locks, the lion in winter, the Nestor of explorers.

It was his turn to speak; to thank. He opened his mouth. He hated speak-

ing. "This cornucopia—delightful—lacks nothing for the complete gratification of a grateful American—grateful to your illustrious services, I mean—
save the presence of Meriwether Lewis." Inwardly, he winced. Inviting a
ghost to the banquet. No doubt a painful subject. Lewis had been uppermost
in W.I.'s mind (still, it was no excuse) since the ride out in the carriage. Judge
Peck had regaled him with rumors from his native Tennessee about the man's
death.

Meriwether Lewis: for a long moment, during which he proudly mar-
shaled facts, Clark thought his famous guest had meant *his* Meriwether
Lewis, his eldest son, on whom rested so many of his hopes (William and
George Rogers both had capacity, but lacked application; it was too early to
tell about Jefferson—who should know better than to be slouching like that in
his chair—he was only eight). Lewis had done well as a cadet at West Point.
He showed every sign of being a first-rate soldier. Now he was aide-de-camp
to General Atkinson (who had nothing but praise) and he'd just been
blooded in a decided manner, in the campaign against Black Hawk. Everyone
said he came off with much credit. He'd returned to St. Louis (unhurt, thank
God) only last week.

"Yes," Clark said. "Would he were still among us. A great man." This Irving was an odd fellow; a bit of a peacock; fresh and plump as a new-hatched
chick. His voice was strangely halting; husky and weak; as though he'd damaged himself. Raven curls, pale face, large eyes; gave him a surprised look. Or
maybe it was watchfulness. They said he was writing a book about this tour.
That was his notebook sticking out of his coat pocket. A Meeting with the
General. Have your cake and write about it, too. Something self-pleased
about him. Still, why not, he'd done well for himself. Clark had wept like a girl
over his "Broken Heart." That was the year after his dear Julia had died. Ah!

"Have you read my book on the Lewis and Clark tour?"

"I am reading it now—Mr. Ellsworth has kindly loaned me his copy—
fascinating!"

Loaned him. Irving probably couldn't find one for himself anywhere. It
had taken Clark himself two years after publication to procure a copy. The
1812 war with England, trade all to hell, the first publisher bankrupt just before going to press, the second just after. Fifteen hundred copies, but who
knew where the bulk of them were, moldering in some depot. Clark had been
unable to assume the financial risk of buying them all. All he had was the

copper plates, and the right to lose more money by publishing again. He'd had such hopes for the profits. Ironic, that he'd quarreled with the government over who owned the story, when it ended up worthless. Lewis not writing a damn line; then his death delaying it more; Mr. Biddle hesitating over accepting the editorship, then taking longer than he'd promised; spurious editions all the while, making good money; then the war. The thing was cursed. And to top it all, Lewis's mother, that old dragon, intimidating that Clark had seen a profit and was keeping it all to himself. He'd had to send her a statement of accounts to shut her up.

Now there was an American theme, W.I. thought. Such a pity it had already been written. And not well, either; the book was deficient in both charm and excitement. *We left our camp on Monday, May such-and-such, and proceeded upriver, passing two islands, one of which was a mile long and half a mile wide, the other half a mile long and a mile wide, and camped by a stream that was 53 yards across.*

What he might have done with it! *St. Louis, at the time of which we treat, was yet a wild frontier town of motley population—that singular aquatic race, the hectoring, bragging boatmen of the Mississippi—vagrant Indians loitering about the streets—now and then a stark Kentucky hunter, a true Leather-stocking, strode along—scrape of a fiddle, an ancient French air, the click of billiard balls arguing the happy Gallic turn for gaiety—here arrived the two tall, robust American captains, carrying the hopes of a young nation on their shoulders—*

Cursed! Barton dying, leaving the scientific material all ahoo in a mass of unrelated papers; the Indian vocabularies missing; Mr. Jefferson's own copies stolen off a boat, dumped in the James River by the disappointed thief (who'd chosen that one trunk out of dozens, as though directed by Misprovidence); Hassler unable to make head or tail of Lewis's lunars; Pursh decamping to London with the surviving botanical material, publishing it himself. What little botany and zoology got into the book was mostly wrong; that was Paul Allen's doing. And yet he demanded five hundred dollars for his labors. Ah, Lewis! Cursed! Cursed! Pursh named the bitterroot after him, *Lewisia rediviva.* Something about living again. Because the dried root, soaked in water, put forth flowers. His poor friend. "It would have been a better book, if only Governor Lewis had lived to write it," Clark said. Not a damn line.

What Peck had told him during the carriage ride had filled W.I. with longing to ask the general what he might know of the circumstances of Lewis's death. Was it true that over a hundred dollars in cash had disappeared from the governor's saddlebags that night? That *three* pistol shots were heard, even though Lewis carried only two pistols? What about the rumor that Lewis had discovered a gold mine out west, and was carrying a map indicating its location? And wasn't it suspicious that the innkeeper, Grinder (who was said to be of Indian blood), seemed to have a good deal of money in the years following the incident?

"I saw him," W.I. said.

"Who?"

"Your co-captain—Governor Lewis."

The general gave him a startled glance. "When was that?"

"The trial of Aaron Burr—Richmond—I was unknown, then—not known—that is—before Knickerbocker's *History*—of course *he* was famous—all eyes on him."

What a romantic sketch it would make! Something for a magazine. (Yet W.I. held off from asking; prying, rather.) His tragic life, in a dozen pages. On the steamboat down the Ohio, W.I. had met a man from Lewis's native county, who'd said that when Lewis was a mere eight years old, he'd gone hunting alone at night with his dogs, even in the icy depths of winter. The man had said Lewis's family could track him by the blood in the snow that trickled from his bare feet. And Peck had said that on his last day on earth, in the Tennessee woods near the inn, Lewis had heard a mockingbird singing its own song; a thing folklore held to be an omen of death. Wonderful!

Carrying his saddlebags with their valuable secrets into the rude cabin, where Grinder waited, black eyes glittering. The desperate struggle in the darkness, the muzzle flash; the mighty heart stilled. October 1809. And wasn't it curious that in the same month, W.I. (all unaware) was concocting his hoax about Diedrich Knickerbocker, who (he had pretended) arrived at the Columbian Hotel in New York City, carrying his mysterious and valuable saddlebags; that he subsequently disappeared; that the saddlebags were opened, and found to contain the manuscript of his History of New York; that another hand edited them, after which they were published to acclaim. That was the real beginning of W.I.'s writing career.

"My family and I have enjoyed a hearty laugh over Knickerbocker many a time," Clark was saying. In truth, he'd only dipped into it. He'd been shocked by the rough treatment of Mr. Jefferson, whom Irving called William the Testy. The mountaintop retreat he was always riding off to was Dog's Misery; could someone tell Clark what *that* was all about. Of course, Irving was a New Yorker; snideness was mother's milk to them.

"How kind of you to remember," the plump, pleased Fed said. Dog's Misery brought Pompy's Tower to mind. Writing his name on the rock. Trappers up the Yellowstone told Clark his signature was as clear as if he'd carved it yesterday. Which sometimes it seemed; at other times, a different life altogether. His Pomp was the other reason (besides Lewis) for Clark to feel paternal pride. The boy had turned out well. A fine hunter and scout; sharp as a tack; spoke English, French, German, Spanish, Menetarree, Mandan, Kanzas; proficient in sign language. Everyone who met him could see he was a cut above; he drew people to him; that German princeling, Paul Wurtteburgh, or Wertenburgh, who decided after two days' acquaintance to take Pomp to Germany with him; his traveling companion. That was 1824, the year Jefferson was born; Pomp was eighteen or nineteen; Clark missed him so much (the boy had been up the Missouri for months at a time, but Germany was so far away), he nicknamed Jefferson (another February boy) Pomp. The first Pomp came back, what was it, three years ago. Now he was trapping up around the three forks of the Missouri, with Jim Bridger (Clark hoped there'd be no run-ins with Blackfeet). His second Pomp had settled down to his plate of buffalo and potatoes.

"Have you visited my Indian Museum, in town?" Clark asked his guests. "It's on the corner of Main and Vine, just south of my townhouse. I have calumets, painted buffalo robes, tomahawks and battle-axes, a Chinnook rainhat, portraits of all of the chiefs who've visited me in St. Louis, two Indian canoes, much more. I'm told it's the best Indian museum in America. When Lafayette's secretary saw my three grizzly-bear-claw necklaces, he said the London Cabinet of Natural History had only a single claw, which it pronounced a great rarity." In the book, Mr. Biddle changed Pompy's Tower to Pompey's Pillar. He'd thought Clark had mistaken a classical reference; some column in Alexandria. Supposed to contain Pompey the Great's head! So that's what traders up there called it now. A pity. And apparently Lewis's River was a goner. (The book and Clark's map so delayed; copies moldering somewhere.) Trappers were calling it the Snake. Poor Lewis! His lonely grave, with its wooden marker, its fallen-in fence (Lewis's half brother John Marks had visited it; he'd written to Clark). No one to mourn him there but his dog. Too early to know about Clark's River; the Blackfeet too hostile for any whites to venture that route. Still furious over the deaths of their two braves. Clark inclined his head toward the commissioner, who was asking a question about the Panias. *Your co-captain,* Irving had called Lewis. The book was titled *History of the Expedition Under the Command of Captains Lewis and Clark.* No one would ever know. Except Mr. Biddle, who'd noticed the discrepancies in the papers; Clark had conjoined him to silence. That was perfectly correct; he *had* been captain. And he *had* been the first white man ever to set eyes on Clark's River. It said so in the book.

Ellsworth was pressing Clark for more information about the territory he and the two other commissioners would be inspecting. Mr. Irving was planning to trot along with his notebook. "My opportunity—" he quavered, "—behold herds of buffalo scouring their native prairies—remnants of those Indian tribes—about to disappear—amalgamated—some new form of government."

Gentlemen, you had better hurry. But Clark didn't say it. Instead, he tried to recant on the subject as though there was something reasonable to say. Ellsworth seemed a decent enough fellow. But he was an easterner; inexperienced, uninformed. He seemed to have no notion of the impracticality of his assignment. President Jackson's Indian Removal Act was all hard realism for the country east of the Mississippi, perfectly doable; get rid of the last damn Indians. Something like fifty thousand of them; last of the Ohio tribes, plus Choctaws, Chickasaws, Cherokees, Creeks, Seminoles. The children's fairy tale was reserved for the west: send three commissioners out to determine which lands to grant to the immigrant tribes. As Superintendent of Indian Affairs, Clark was already knee-deep in displaced Indians. Destitute, diseased; every winter, practically on his doorstep, hundreds starved. Ellsworth and his two worthy comrades were supposed to settle disputes over land, mark boundaries, make peace between the tribes. Three men; a six-legged creature. Clark had grown up calling that a bug. It was all flapdoodle; anyone who knew a thing knew it; it was to make the Removal Act appear humane to the people out east. Whereas out here, where the dirty work was done, the whites had no humane feelings for the Indians. Out here, the whites had a word: jacksonize. It meant, hightail it to the nearest Indian camp and kill everything that moved.

Clark was a relic, he knew that perfectly well. That was why he'd lost the governorship of Missouri, as soon as it came to a state election. They'd called him an Indian-lover. A cabiner was in the White House now. *His* museum had articles made of Indian skin. "While you're here," he said to his guests, "you should go see Black Hawk, the Saukee chief. He's being held at Jefferson Barracks, ten miles south of town." Chained, arms and ankles, to a cannon. Give them a little idea. The Indian chiefs who came to Clark in his council room still called St. Louis Red Hair's Town. Whereas half the whites would run him out on a rail, if they could. His Lewis had told him about the last battle in the Black Hawk war. There'd been about a thousand Indians left, after they'd been chased to the Bad Axe River; out of food, short on ammunition. Lewis said they showed the white flag, but General Atkinson said, We're a little too old for that trick, and ordered an attack. Lewis said it was what you might call a massacre. Some eight hundred Indians killed; many of them women and children. Lewis had gone off to win his spurs, and he'd come back mighty bothered. Clark didn't know what to say. He stood there with his hand on the boy's shoulder. Then a phrase came into his mind from somewhere: *The world is what it is.* So he said that.

Irving was hesitating to interject; he'd been mewing the last three sentences. "Yes?" Clark said.

"General—very much appreciate your excellent information on the Indians—very helpful—Mr. Ellsworth, I'm sure also—but—forgive me—an unrelated topic—forgive the curiosity of an American—or perhaps, a writer—I was wondering—doubtless many would like to know—in your opinion—do you think—did Governor Lewis—is it plausible to you—knew him so well—do you believe—did he die by his own hand?—I apologize—"

Clark signaled for coffee. "Pompy, you're excused." The boy shot off toward the kitchen like an arrow off the string. Probably to see if the prairie hen he'd shot was getting dressed. That one's mine, Chloe! Happiness such a simple thing at that age; any little scrap blazed; it was enough to start tears in Clark's eyes. That letter from Lewis; he'd received it at his brother Jonathan's house. His fever had deranged him. Clark wasn't surprised when Pernia said later that Lewis conceived Clark was on the trail, coming to his relief. Insanity was a terrible thing. Ran in Lewis's family. His half brother John had had to be confined for a while. Must have come from the old dragon; the common element. Not one of her sons ever married. Poor Lewis! The first thing Clark did, when he heard of Lewis's death, he got Jonathan to forward him that letter. Clark saved everything. He was his family's historian. But he burned that letter.

Then there were Lewis's other papers. The journals. Where were they, what condition? Clark was terribly anxious. His book! What on earth was he going to do? Lewis had shirked his duty; left him to struggle on alone. "A moment, gentlemen," Clark said. "Forgive me." On the mountaintop, in the woods, Lewis's neglected grave. Only Seaman, who refused to leave; touched no food offered him; died on the mound. Clark received his collar from the innkeeper in the post, with the letter telling him. Now there was loyalty.

Oh! Why did he have to think of this! Just so a jolly little writer could amuse himself— "Chloe! Where's that coffee?" Maybe it was only a story; sort of tale people liked to peddle. Maybe the innkeeper sold Seaman. He was getting old, but still worth a dollar or two. Some people said he was a suspicious character.

The coffee was on the table; the most famous writer in America sipped from his cup, his large, pretty eyes averted. Lewis's memory besmirched; the shame of suicide. Surely it was better; the only way Clark might overtake Lewis on his trail, come to his relief: "I have always believed," he said, "that something nefarious happened that night."

Yes! W.I. thought. Young man in his thirties; governor of a vast territory; hero crowned with laurels; life before him. What motive—? W.I. felt relief.

The meal was over. Spanish cigars. Glorious repast. He was full to bursting. The silver-maned general's domestic felicity; riches of the rustic table; light of the setting sun. But really, it still shocked him a little (this European) to see the meat still heaped on the platters, the full bowls. A sort of gross plenty seemed to prevail throughout America, in hotels, on steamboats, in country cottages; food was wasted, as if it had no value.

Last advice from the general; Indian anecdotes. Everyone rose; thanks expressed and dismissed; the general ushered his guests toward the drive, while negroes converged to clear the table. Perhaps that was the explanation: all across America, superfluous negroes ate superabundant leftovers in kitchens and pantries.

At the front of the cottage, the general hallooed for his grandson, who came running. He told the sprightly boy to fetch his pony and escort the gentlemen's carriage back to town by a certain picturesque route he knew. There followed a silent moment, while the men waited for the carriage to be brought up. Perhaps W.I. had eaten too well; perhaps he felt too comfortable. He ventured some observation to his host about the remarkable number of negroes in America. A mistake. He could see the general stiffen. The skin folds at the outer edges of his eyes descended. "In many ways, I assure you," he said, "they're more trouble than they're worth." The general had taken W.I.'s comment as an implied criticism. Which had been far from his intention. He opened his mouth to speak, but the general went on: "I've freed three, you know. And do you know, the law makes it difficult. You can't just turn them loose in the world, you must set them up. An expensive proposition."

"Oh, I am sure—"

"I placed one on a ferry. I put another on a farm; I gave him land, horses, a plow; I built the man's house for him! And the third—I bought him a large wagon and a team of horses. Not two. Not four. I bought him six horses. And I pointed his nose toward a drayage route that guaranteed good business, the Nashville–Richmond road."

"Believe me, I—generous—"

"And do you know what? All three of them repented their freedom. They all wanted to come back to me. And here's something else you don't know— the wagoner was York. You've heard of York. He's in the book. Famous York! Hero of the Missouri expedition! Adviser to the Indians! Well, it turned out the *hero* could not get up early enough in the mornings. He drank too much and landed in the calaboose. He didn't take proper care of the horses I gave him. Two of them died; the others fared poorly. So he sold them. But he had no head for business, so naturally he was cheated. He entered into service, but did badly. The family didn't take to his lordly ways. Finally, he said, do you know what he said?, he said, 'Damn this freedom! I have never had a happy day since I got it! I'm going to go back to my old master and I'm going to beg his forgiveness and I hope he takes me in.' So he set off to come here. And I would have taken him in. But he choked on a partridge while he was traveling through Tennessee, and he died."

The carriage had arrived. "My goodness," W.I. said.

"A damn sorry tale," the general concluded. "Gentlemen—"

Farewells; a grandfather clock handing them up into the carriage. The general tapped on the window. Mr. Ellsworth lowered it. The general's pink face spoke past the commissioner to W.I., on the far side of the bench: "A last tidbit for you: some of the traders think they've met traces of York's brood along the Missouri. So you see—he lives on!" He raised the glass with a snap, stepped back smartly, signaled to his grandson to set off.

Clark watched the carriage go. Damn it all, why? That had been beneath him.

He was tired. It was four o'clock. Time for the old man's nap.

He went into the cottage; passed through the sitting room to his small bedroom. Ben helped him out of his coat, shoes, stockings. He shuttered the window; put fresh water on the bedside table. Clark lay on the bed in the darkened room. Sunlight made a square glow around the shutters. A fly buzzed.

Waiting for sleep was when unease stole around him. Why must he think about those long-ago things? York and Lewis. Both men changed utterly; gone. And here he still was. He'd done well enough, hadn't he? A general, even if only in the militia. Governor of Missouri Territory. Until the election. His book hadn't made a cent; the fur trade had never been his friend; his mercantile business hadn't prospered. Meanwhile, other men of St. Louis had grown rich as Procrustes. But he had his brick mansion in town, his council house and museum; this cottage; he owned thousands of acres in Missouri, Indiana, and Kentucky. Bulwarks against debt; he hoped not too frail. (He breathed deep, tried to settle himself.) Those years he'd ridden thousands of miles, fighting George's creditors. Names and figures still burned in his memory. Bazadone: a Spanish merchant, whose goods George had impressed. $20,500: the amount the Virginia legislators failed to honor in 1791. Vigo, Legra, Jiboe, Thooloe, Trusseron; £434, $2,100, $4,680. Clark was the family historian. Safe in a trunk in his brick townhouse, he had George R.'s memoirs. No one else was interested. The great man he'd once been shined out of those pages. In his last years he'd been no more than an animated clod. Dead eyes; paralytic; one leg a stump, because one day, alone and drunk in his cabin, he'd fallen into the fire. Oh! And Lewis's ruination was like a nightmare returning. The drink, the debt, the derangement. His creditors killed him! Clark remembered them circling like vultures around

Lewis's door the last day he saw him. Poor Lewis! Poor Lewis! Was there no human feeling? Was there no simple goodness?

There were his angels: his Julia, his Harriet. (Wasn't it curious that he'd ended up marrying both those little girls he'd met, on an April morning, on a balky jade.) But both were dead. And poor John Julius, born deformed; and Edmund, eleven months old. And little Mary. That was the hardest. Clark kept everything (trunks and trunks): he had her last letter, from her aunt's place in Kentucky, where she'd been sent after the death of her mother. *Dear Papa, I hope you are well. I want to see you, and my brothers. Kiss them for me. I am a good girl, and will learn my book.* Seven years old!

Oh, his Pompy, may heaven protect him! Jonathan dead. Clark had always hoped, in vain, that his big brother would come to live with him in St. Louis. *All* his brothers dead. And many of the Band of Brothers. Clark kept those records, too; he wrote letters, asking; he made lists. Those who had died of "the natural shocks that flesh ails to": Ordway, Pryor, Colter, Gibson, Goodrich, McNeal, Shields. And those ushered out by their fellow men: Drewyer, Potts, Weiser, and Thompson, all killed by the Blackfeet; Crusat, killed by the Tetons; Collins, by the Rickerries; good Joseph Fields, stabbed in the eye in a street brawl on Main Street, St. Louis. Of course, as a man grew old, the dead crowded. Yet no old man had communicated to Clark, when he was young, this horror awaiting him. He guessed the young never listened to the old. The Indians of the plains, on the hunt, left their old and infirm behind to starve to death. Every generation was struck all over again by the horror. The death of everyone you knew, their replacement by young strangers who didn't understand you (because the young never listened to the old).

—flowers—Hazel nuts—&c pass by a little farm—everything in abundance— The return route across the prairie was indeed picturesque. *— pass by a circle of Indian mounds, on one of them Genl. Ashley has built his house so as to have the summit of it as a terrace in the rear—* But W.I. was aware that he had nothing yet that would serve for a scene in a book. It irritated him. Those damned expectations! Well, dear readers, one could not simply order up a sentimental encounter, a hairsbreadth escape! Where were the Indians?

Clark lay on the bed, and the dead crowded around. Manuel Lisa, too, and Auguste Choteau, and Charles Gratiot; and Big White (killed long ago by

Le Borne; all the trouble Clark and Lewis had had, returning him to his people; and when he got there, no one believed his stories, he lost respect; complaining to anyone who would listen that he wanted to go back and live among white people). And Janey. And her little girl, whom Clark adopted; his dear Lizette; dead before her first birthday.

Clark lay on the bed in the dark room, and he wanted to sleep. But he could only think, *Why?*

And those words came to him again, from somewhere, they sounded in his mind, spreading calm (a little), peace (a little):

The world is what it is.

Last Charbonneau

He look at man behind desk supposed be Red Hair, what, this not St. Louis? this not Indian Office? but he know, Red Hair dead, this man Pilcher, old Charbonneau know him slight, he work for Astor-Chouteau company, he superintendent now. It since one month I hear, Charbonneau say, he not mean Red Hair, he mean end job, I come down straight, I not know, six month, I interpret like donkey. He wheedle, he good at, he play old man, totter, look lost, poor fellow, wasn't he Lewis-Clark tour?, America grateful, not got dollar to name, that disgrace!, what-all. Pilcher sign note, first, second quarter 1839, hundred fifty dollar, say, *you understand,* say, *service no longer required,* that English for no job, old man. *I understand,* Charbonneau say, his English better all time, maybe stay St. Louis, interpret French-English, maybe tell story, get on table, paint sign, finger point, twenty-five cent, Oldest Man on Missouri!, say, when I first come on Missouri, it so small I straddle it.

He pocket note, go out on street. He eighty. Outlive everybody. Hundred fifty dollar. He not like St. Louis, not stay here. Trader say Jean-Baptiste on Platte somewhere. Go back upriver. Where? All Mandan dead. Twenty left? Half Minitadi dead, run from Fort Clark, little band here, there. Charbonneau never see smallpox so bad. Come on steamboat. Mandan rot in village, kill self, kill children, want kill white dog, say, white dog bring, even chief Four Bear, friend, he say, kill all white. He dying, face rot, say, he so ugly, wolf on prairie run away, say other wolf, see stinking dead body? he Four Bear, friend white people.

Charbonneau speak Mandan good, better old Jusseaume ever, believe, Jusseaume final go bother spirit world, four, five year ago. Smallpox come, white people hide in Fort Clark, even old Charbonneau worried, he take powder and ball for trade to Minitadi village, go at night, Mandan not see.

Minitadi not have smallpox yet, post brave around, keep out who-all from Mandan village, Fort Clark, but old Forest Bear safe, he get little case hundred year ago in Athabasca, he never get. He take squaw to Minitadi, try save, too late, she get fever, break out, horrible, rot, die, horrible.

He outlive everybody, no Minitadi-Mandan, no job, no Clark, no protect. Hardly no this for that. Charbonneau look at street, look at people. Men wear stinking silk hat. Hardly no beaver, anyway. Buffalo gone soon. Company take hundred thousand robe in year, all cow, how buffalo last no cow, all stand around, sore asshole? All over. He love Minitadi-Mandan village, Knife River. Now where he go? Find little band runaway Minitadi, say, here Forest Bear, old Many Gourd, he still alive? They say, old man, time you die. They maybe say (it not true, other trader visit, company not like quarantine, bad for trade), they maybe say, old man, you bring smallpox wife, dead spirit want revenge, time you get tomahawk in head. Oldest Man on Missouri!, he stand on table, thirty-five cent, say, time I save Captain Clark, time I discover Rockies.

Old Charbonneau walk street. Easy play old man, rheumatism, ass ache. Say, time I try fuck Saulteaux girl. Hundred fifty dollar. Old Many Gourd in whore capital, pocket full, like throw money in river. He stand on table, Oldest Man!, say, time I marry Assiniboin slave girl, I eighty, she fourteen, I take out big old stiff happy cock, push in young cunt like tight hand, stinking lie, he give feast, like stinking chief, make friend, make poor, friend whole stinking fort, cook meat pie, pheasant fricassée, boil tongue, coffee, drink six, seven cup, think maybe help, go in room, strip slave girl, she young, hard, thighs feel so good, ass feel good, he look at young cunt wait, he wait, cunt wait, he wait, cunt wait, people out door bang pot, pan, wait. Cock nod little, shake head, sorry boss, little lump at base, like lump in throat. Five, six year now. He outlive cock. Give slave girl rest fort, easy be stinking give-chief when.

Next morning, news come on steamboat: Red Hair dead.

He reach corner. Where he go? Remember first time he fuck Bird, she not like, he feel little bad. What problem? He got cock, she got cunt, fit together like First Made plan. Later, she like. She best woman he ever have, always do what he want, never try run away, she give him Jean-Baptiste, poor Lisette. (Maybe he wait Jean-Baptiste come back from Platte, next year, two year?) He miss her many year, little Bird, scar-cheek. He remember (time I) when she die at Fort Manuel. Month, two month before Sioux burn fort. He remember two, three trader squaw carry out gate, rattle gourd, moan, cut leg (old Charbonneau give squaw tobacco, blue bead, say, more moan! more rattle!), take down in bottom, put in branch tree, his Bird, he wonder where she go, if go, he wonder if anything after. Squaw rattle gourd, what-all, talk to First Made. But they stop, hear all shout, up at fort, think attack, run up bluff. Only bunch Ree come all excite, news stinking trader robbed, but squaw not go back down, Charbonneau say, give blue bead back, stinking bitch refuse.

He still on corner. Main and Vine. Corner not move one stinking inch. Well, First Made? Where old Charbonneau go?

THE EXCELLENT MAN
[1840]

Leads Woman-Hearts up the Hill tells the children, Once I swam a river, and the children chorus derision, they've all swum rivers. He says, You never swam a river as wide as the river I swam, and a boy asks, How wide was it, and Leads Woman-Hearts up the Hill answers, Fifty winters wide. They look interested now. He says, I'd seen fifty winters when I dived into that river, and when I crawled out the other side, I was a newborn baby.

He lets them ponder that for a while. Chilly and wide. Pokes the fire. Caught 'em. He says, After I crawled out of that river, I walked toward the cold land, many nights. I wore out eight pairs of moccasins. Had to kill a whitehorn—that's the whiteskins' buffalo—to make more. He throws his arms around the cow's neck, slits its throat. I was going to where the whiteskins who trade with the Blackfeet live. During the day I slept hidden, so the Big Knife whiteskins wouldn't find me. If they did, there'd have been a fight, and if it was more than ten of them to one of me, they might have beat me. They'd have made me go back across that river, where I'd be fifty winters old again. I'd be drinking that whiteskin water that makes you a fool.

Some smart alec challenges, How did you do all that, if you were a baby? and Leads Woman-Hearts up the Hill says, Fuck you! I was a big, strong baby! The children laugh, and he stands up. Don't you believe it? He plays the bear, cuffing. They scatter. A girl with bright eyes and a scared mouth says from a safe distance, You're making that up!

He is a batse-tse. Their word for chief. *Excellent man.* You might say, a fellow who beats others hollow. He was the first, yes he was, to run up the hill, where the Blackfeet were dug in behind rocks. His people had been pushed back three times. Fifteen men lay dead, and a dozen horses, and now they hung back. Some counseled returning to camp. Three whiteskin trappers were along for the show, and Leads Woman-Hearts up the Hill couldn't bear to see these filthy whiteskins thinking his people were cowards. So he jumped up on a rock. He said the Crows' hearts were small, the whiteskins wouldn't trade with such women, if redskins were afraid to go among the enemy, he'd show a blackskin wasn't. Putting his soul in the hands of Lord Above, not looking right or left, he ran up that hill like a crazy-dog-wanting-to-die. And the Crows followed him, maybe thinking, that old man ain't gonna show *us* up, or maybe trusting the crazy-dog to bring them back. Not only was he first over the rocks, he made the first strike, he crushed a man's head, he grabbed a gun—and ever since, he's been a bona fide batse-tse, ask anyone, and when they hold council, he stands and speaks anytime he has something to say.

He sits in front of his leather lodge, and he tells the children, When I was a boy, I was a bear cub.

In the Ohio country, the redskins called negroes bearskins. He remembers the first time he told the bear story, among the Ricaras. Redskins touching him, feeling his muscles. Maybe like an auction. Except the expressions on the redskins' faces weren't like any whiteskin's he'd ever seen.

He says, Where I come from, the bears are as black as night. They make the bears you have around here look like rabbits. A black bear could tuck one of your bears under each arm and dance a scalp. But the whiteskins captured me when I was a cub, and first thing they did, they shaved my hair off.

The boys flinch. Worst thing you can do to a Crow man. Hair down to their feet. They hate his hair. He says, A bear cub can't grow properly without his hair, so I'm only as big as you see me.

After his people beat the Blackfeet, they tortured the wounded to death, tore the bodies to pieces. The women and children paraded heads and hands and entrails on sticks. That's something he'll never get used to.

He gathers the children round in the evening and says, I was a great medicine man among the whiteskins. The children are ready to believe it from his mouth alone. Years of sucking out bad spirits gives their medicine men swollen lips. He says, But my medicine only worked on whiteskins. Damned if he'll be spending his days sucking wounds and venereal sores.

When it's winter and hot in the lodge, and he's wearing only his loincloth, he can point to the scars on his back and thighs. So much good happened to the whiteskins every time I cut myself, they didn't want to let me go.

[THE EXCELLENT MAN]

That's why I had to swim the river. I'd whip myself, my blood would fly, and their corn grew, the rain came. Cut yourself some more, York, they'd say, it hasn't rained in a week! York, lay a big gash down the middle of your back for me, I feel a little fever coming on!

Dance, York! York, get on up here!

He was fifty years old when he ran away. Runaway slave. He didn't like that phrase; a disobeying child. He was fifty years old when he stopped begging for his freedom, and took it. Letty and Rose were gone. He had nothing to lose. When Master William first beat him, that shocked York to his soul. He was no thieving field hand, he was—well, he was one deluded blackskin, is what he was.

Good old York! He was sent to look for Caesar, when Caesar stopped begging, and took. The governor gave him money for expenses, and a pass, because good old York could be trusted. Render Caesar unto. Good old York would go to the very edge of white settlement, he'd stare at three thousand miles of freedom, and turn his back on it. And he did. He didn't see yet that every good service he'd ever done Master William wasn't a laying up of treasure in his account to buy his freedom with, but another hoop of iron binding him. Trusty York.

He sits in the morning outside his leather lodge, while one of his wives cooks, and the other works on a new pair of leggings for him, and his fifteen-year-old son is probably out berrying with his girl, which means poking her behind a bush, and his eight-year-old boy is round about somewhere, he's gotten tired of the old man's tales. He tells the children a story from the time he traveled from Red Hair's Town up the Muddy River and over the mountains to the Bad Lodges and on to the Big Water, with the famous Red Hair himself and another whiteskin chief. He tells about how, on the way back, when he and Red Hair and ten other whiteskins were coming down the Elk River, the Shit-along-the-rivers stole every goddamn one of Red Hair's horses, he had over fifty, and they stole them all, and Red Hair and the whiteskins never saw a feather off the head of a single brave. That's one of the few stories those Shit-along-the-river Crow tell that are true, he says. And Red Hair said, York, I sure would like to see some of those horses again, so York cut himself all up and down the legs and danced, and walked on his hands, and shook his woolly hair at the sky. But Lord Above wasn't listening that time.

Three years of storing up treasure. He was just a big buck blackskin manservant when he started down the Ohio in 1803, but he carried a gun, he shot buffalo, he poled the boats ass to ass with the soldiers, and after a few months he could sit down by the fire without it always turning to nigger jokes and Dance, York. When they reached the Pacific Ocean, there was a vote on where to build the fort, and after Master William polled all the whiteskins, he said, You, York? and York gave his opinion, and his name went on the list. Sure, it was put last (none of those rivers he'd crossed was Jordan), but it was there. Only little Tsakakawia came after.

Leads Woman-Hearts up the Hill tells the children about how he first learned a little we-speech. The whiteskins didn't want a powerful bearskin medicine man like me speaking, because I was supposed to be listening to Lord Above's mumbles, and keeping an eye out for Old Man Coyote's tricks. A mute man is like a blind man, or a we-man naked on the mountaintop not drinking water, you can hear the prairie dogs farting. On this three-winter trip I made with Red Hair, there was a Bad Lodges woman and her whiteskin man, and the only speech they both knew was Earthlodge. Leads Woman-Hearts up the Hill breaks into Earthlodge dialect, exaggerating it and making it sound stupid, like a whiteskin speaking nigger talk, the children always love this part, he does it while scraping an invisible hoe over the ground, the Earthlodges are all women, working in the fields.

They came into St. Louis, guns firing and cheering, and the first thing York saw was a whiteskin whipping the tar out of his slave in the street. But York had hopes. The main thing he'd regretted those three years was not seeing Letty and Rose, but he would soon, he'd stored up all that treasure, and Master William wasn't a bad master. That blind, deaf, and dumb blackskin had hopes.

But why was the whiteskin cutting the blackskin medicine man in Red Hair's town? one of the children asks. Why wasn't the blackskin cutting himself?

Not every blackskin is as good as I was at cutting my own back, Leads Woman-Hearts up the Hill says. It's hard to do, reaching around, try it yourself. Here's a switch. You have trouble, come back, I'll help.

Rose had been five when York went west. She was eight when he got back, and twice as tall. The thought of living far away from her and Letty was worse than the thrashings Master William gave him. York got himself hired out in Louisville. His masters were vicious men. The Clark family saw to that. He was the slave who thought he was grand. His masters horsed him up and whipped him regularly, sometimes so bad he couldn't stand afterward. Master William's brothers wanted to sell him south. But the Master must have still had a touch of feeling for his untrusty York. Kill him up here slow, instead of quick down there.

Then Letty and Rose were taken down to Natchez by their master. That was 1812, and it was the last York saw of them. *Till death or distance do you part.* And then you jump over the broom. And Lord Above's got his own broom, and he sweeps his dust around any old time he feels like it. Rose was about to turn fourteen. If she's alive today, she's forty-two. Letty in her sixties. York should have jumped in the Ohio the night after their boat went around the bend.

Instead he drank. For eight years, he was half dead. He landed in jail; the guards beat him; he begged Master William's forgiveness; he would have crawled back and licked his boots. Master William and one of his nephews started a drayage business, and they told York he was the wagoner. To test him. See if he'd become trusty York again. Reforge those hoops of iron. When the drayage business failed, Master William blamed him.

This is some of the hair that was shaved off me when I was a bear cub, Leads Woman-Hearts up the Hill tells the children, taking the leather pouch out of his shirt. This is what made the Blackfeet bullets fall at my feet like elk shit when I ran up that hill. He opens the pouch to show the two locks. When his people come back from a raid, the bravest warrior paints his body black. But after he ran up that hill, York just threw off his shirt. He danced, showing his honorable scars. Black is night, black is mystery, and whiteskins hate mystery, but redskins love it.

It's a mystery why York, one ordinary morning, woke up in his animal misery and saw in the sunlight and heard in the birdsong that he could keep on the way he was going until the other half of him died, or (since he had nothing to lose) he could run. A mystery and a vision. York was half a century old. Maybe that inspired him. Maybe jumping in the river was a prayer for the second half. He crawled out dripping water in Indiana. It was lucky this dried-out slave had spent three years in the wilderness. Detroit was three hundred miles. He made it in three weeks. Some whiteskins helped him. He tries to remind himself of that, whenever hatred for the lot of them rises in his heart.

Let me tell you about the redskins who live near the Big Water over the Shining Mountains, he says to the children. They're about yay high. They don't have heads. Their faces are on their chests, their eyes where your nipples are, their mouths at your navel, right *there*. What are you afraid of? So when it's cold, and they have their shirts on, they can't see anything. They bump into the trees. And the trees, they go up as high as the clouds . . .

He was fifty years old when he crossed into Canada. Fifty-one when he came up the Assiniboine River as an engagé with the North West Company (with ten whiteskins and three other runaway blackskins, paddling for the Promised Land). Fifty-two when he crossed the plain to the Minitadi-Mandan villages. He worked for a season for Mackenzie's outfit. But that was risky. A trader up from Red Hair's town might recognize him. The companies got their licenses from Red Hair. York didn't know what his old master might ask them to do, if he knew. So when a Crow band showed up to trade, and York realized he could understand some of what they said, he cut himself up and down his thighs, he shook his woolly head at the sky, and Lord Above was listening that time. He took out his broom and swept this little piece of black grit along with the red dust bunnies into the mountains.

Crows, Bird-People. They say Bi-ruke: *us*.

He's seventy years old. When he stands in council, his people look at his black skin, and his rope scars and switch scars and belt scars, his thick medicine lips, and they see power and majesty. (But they hate his hair, and they think his nose is the ugliest thing they've ever laid eyes on.)

The whiteskins are coming. There's a trading fort at the mouth of the Elk, another at the mouth of the Big Horn. Lord Above alone knows why he's not going to stop them. York's people have no idea what's coming, and they wouldn't believe York if he told them, and they wouldn't be able to do anything about it if they believed. But he won't live to see the whiteskins come, and he's thankful for that. When he dies, if he's lucky, the Mumbled-About Land he's swept to will look a lot like the one he's been living in for eighteen years. Plus Letty and Rose.

Leads Woman-Hearts up the Hill sits in front of his leather lodge, and he sees his eight-year-old son coming along the path with his bow and arrow and a rabbit for the pot, and he tells the children, There was a fish washed up on the shore of the Big Water that was bigger than ten horses lined up nose to tail. A hundred redskins lived off that fish for a month. The same little girl with the bright eyes and scared mouth pipes up again, she hoots it, scared but happy, You're making that up!, and Leads Woman-Hearts up the Hill pauses for a moment, choosing, because sometimes he growls at them straightfaced, Everything happened exactly as I've said, and other times he laughs and cuffs, he plays the bear (but they run faster every year), and he calls after them, You're right, it's not true, not a word.

AUTHOR'S NOTE

In this novel I have nowhere intentionally falsified history, but have sought instead to take the record as I found it and fill in gaps. The journal entries, letters, and other written documents quoted (with two exceptions, noted below) are real. My interest throughout was to imagine character traits and unrecorded incidents that I believed provided plausible explanations for certain historical questions. In particular, I wanted to dream up a Meriwether Lewis who fit all the puzzling facts and still breathed on the page.

The novelist's privilege is to play the fool, rushing in where historians refrain from treading. For example—to take a small but well-known crux—the record tells us only that when Lewis invited Clark on the expedition, he wrote that Jefferson had authorized him to offer Clark a captaincy. As there is not a shred of positive evidence to contradict this, the historian properly accepts it. However, there is circumstantial and negative evidence that a novelist finds intriguing: the fact that Jefferson signed off on Clark's commission as lieutenant without a word of complaint; the fact that no mention of the "wrong" commission appears in the surviving correspondence between Lewis and Jefferson; the fact that Lewis, in his letters to his mother, sometimes presented as true what his subsequent actions suggested he only wished were true.

A larger crux is Lewis's suicide. In the absence of clear evidence, the historian's job is to keep the question open, whereas the novelist's preeminent task is precisely the opposite: not only to choose an answer, but to make it an expression of character, thus implying a certain inevitability. In the past, many writers shied away from the suicide theory entirely, and of course it is *possible* that Lewis was murdered, but the weight of evidence has always been on the other side. Even with today's more tolerant notions of bipolar disorder and depression, explanations are sometimes put forward that suggest a desire on the part of the theorist to find a cause extrinsic to Lewis's personality: for example, that he was suffering dementia caused by tertiary syphilis or by an acute phase of malaria. One thing everyone can agree on is that Lewis was a lonely man. In making his curiously insoluble loneliness the center of my explanation (with malarial fever, writer's block, and financial embarrassment as contributory causes), I naturally looked for its source. The hints in the record are circumstantial, negative, and wholly inadequate for historical probability, let alone certainty. But the fact that they have never, to my knowledge, been added up to form even a speculation suggests that tolerance still has other territories to open up.

Regarding York's later life, I'm out on a branch. In 1832, a fur trader named Zenas Leonard did meet an old black man among the Crow Indians who claimed to be York. (Leonard witnessed the fight with the Blackfoot, and the black man's leading role in it, that I have described.) There have been traditional arguments for the "real" identity of this supposed imposter, but they all turn out to have rather large holes. However, most historians accept as true Clark's statement to Washington Irving in 1832 that York had died in Tennessee. Again, the novelist is free to concentrate on character, and thus to wonder about the sad elements of wish-fulfillment that seem to pervade Clark's story. There is no evidence other than Clark's 1832 claim that he ever freed York (or any other slave), and the surviving Clark family correspondence gives no hint of an abatement in Clark's bitter feelings toward his former manservant; whereas it does show that York was set up as a wagoner while still a slave. (A note for Lewis and Clark buffs: most references to Irving's record of the 1832 conversation draw on John Francis McDermott's transcription, in which York dies of "cholera." But Irving's handwriting was notoriously bad, and Sue Fields Ross, in her painstaking edition of his complete journals, thinks the word looks more like "choke." If my Clark was going to be fashioning York's end as poetic justice, his choking to death—as though eating his words—seemed a more fitting punishment.)

I have most risked foolishness in the Sacagawea chapters. As an Anglo-American, born and raised in the Boston area, I can claim no personal or familial knowledge of Shoshone, Hidatsa, or Mandan culture. I have only a novelist's conviction that the poverty of a narrative excluding Sacagawea's voice would be worse than the presumption required to include it. I've based my portrait of her band's culture on the anthropological studies of Robert H.

Lowie and Julian H. Steward, a number of early travelers' accounts, and the more recent overviews by Brigham D. Madsen, Virginia Cole Trenholm, and Maurine Carley. I do not speak Shoshone. The unusual elements of Sacagawea's syntax and vocabulary were inspired by perusals of Beverly Crum and Jon Dayley's *Western Shoshoni Grammar* and a *Shoshone Thesaurus* by Malinda Tidzump, as well as various vocabulary lists by early travelers. Some of my etymologies are no doubt incorrect, but I was trying to suggest the spirit of the language, rather than the letter. The lack of capitalization of proper names is my way of indicating that many Native American personal and geographical names are in the nature of ad hoc descriptives, arising from practical circumstances and liable to change. (The names in York's chapter are an exception, because York would not think of them this way.) The tales Sacagawea remembers are recorded in Lowie's *The Northern Shoshone,* with a few small additions from Anne M. Smith's *Shoshone Tales*. I have paraphrased them, using words and sentence lengths that conform to Sacagawea's voice, and omitted some details.

Geographical isolation kept the Shoshone hidden from whites longer than most other North American tribes, and when white contact did come, it so quickly disrupted the native way of life that much about pre-contact Shoshone culture (which varied, in any case, from band to band) will forever remain unknown. The Sacagawea chapters in this novel are best thought of as an outsider's fantasia on Native American themes. To paraphrase Clark: the most I can hope for is to be only half wrong.

Regarding the text, I've tried to avoid anachronistic terms, but have intentionally chosen modern American forms of words and phrases that have altered slightly since the early nineteenth century: *toward* instead of *towards, whence* instead of *from whence,* etc. My aim throughout was to suggest older forms of thought without distracting the reader with archaisms.

The spellings of Indian tribal names differ throughout the book, to suggest the difficulty Lewis and Clark had in hearing these strange new sounds. As for personal names, if Lewis and Clark consistently used a nonstandard spelling that doesn't suggest a different pronunciation, I've generally ignored it. If a different pronunciation is implied, I've followed it, reasoning that this was the name Lewis and Clark *thought* the person in question had. So, for example, I've rendered Robert Frazer as Robert Frazier; George Drouillard as George Drewyer; Reubin Field as Reuben Fields. An exception is Charbonneau; I've retained Lewis's consistent spelling of Charbono because I liked its suggestion that 1) Lewis would never have seen Charbonneau's name written down and 2) he made little effort to understand this Frenchman. Clark had an almost comical difficulty with foreign names, especially on first hearing them, and the text reflects this. (It also reflects Lewis's imperfect Latin.)

Where journals and letters are quoted, I've modernized Lewis's spellings, so that his writing would not contrast strangely with the modern spelling of what the reader is to take as his thoughts. I've also corrected trivial mistakes and eliminated redundancies. As for Clark's misspellings, I've retained some of them, following the principle that Lewis would tend to notice them, whereas Clark, naturally, would not. I've marked omissions with ellipses in cases where I want to call readers' attention to the fact that they are seeing partial versions of documents. In a few other cases, where I want to present a passage as full, but there exists in the original some clause unrelated to my concern, I've omitted it without ellipsis. The quotation from John Evans's journal in section 4 of "The Captain" has been converted into the present tense.

Here and there, I've represented as thoughts phrases that appear in the relevant person's letters or journals. For example, in Jefferson's library monologue, some of his statements regarding Indian policy are taken from his February 1803 letter to William Henry Harrison.

As two of the documents quoted no longer exist, I had to make them up. The first is Lewis's letter to Henry Dearborn in section 3 of "The Captain." The War Department's Register of Letters Received lists a February 10, 1804, letter from Lewis, "relative to an appointment for Capt. Clark," but the letter is missing. I wrote one that would, among other things, explain the puzzling reference to the Corps of Engineers in Dearborn's response. The second document is the letter Lewis wrote to Clark shortly before he killed himself. On first hearing of Lewis's death, Clark wrote to his brother Jonathan Clark, on October 28, 1809, "I fear this report has too much truth, tho' hope it may have no foundation—my reasons for thinking it possible is founded on the letter which I received from him at your house." Two days later, Clark wrote his brother again: "I wish much to get the letter I received of Govr. Lewis from New Madrid, which you saw, it will be of great service to me. Pray send it to Fincastle as soon as possible." No further mention is made of the letter, and it has never been found.

I've scavenged ideas from all over. Books that have particularly influenced me are James P. Ronda's *Lewis and Clark Among the Indians*, John Logan Allen's *Passage Through the Garden,* Donald Jackson's *Thomas Jefferson and the Stony Mountains*, and W. Raymond Wood and Thomas D. Thiessen's *Early Fur Trade on the Northern Plains*. Stephen E. Ambrose's *Undaunted Courage* provided an excellent overview of Lewis's life, and a guide toward sources where I could probe deeper. John Bakeless, though biased against Indians, otherwise proved helpful in his *Lewis and Clark: Partners in Discovery*. In particular, his chapter "Lieutenant Clark Fights Indians" gave me much material for my own chapter "First Clark." My portrait of Thomas Jefferson owes a great deal to Joseph J. Ellis's in *American Sphinx*. Thomas P. Slaughter's *The Whiskey Rebellion* formed my view of that conflict. My conception of Charbonneau's experiences and attitudes was influenced by Richard Glover's superb introduction to *David Thompson's Narrative*. For Clark's later life, I've drawn on Jerome O. Steffen's *William Clark: Jeffersonian Man on the Frontier* and James J. Holmberg's series of groundbreaking articles on the recently discovered letters of Clark to his brother. My cameo of Washington Irving derives largely from Johanna Johnston's biography, *The Heart That Would Not Hold*, with some additional help from Edward Wagenknecht's *Washington Irving: Moderation Displayed*. The indispensable work on York is Robert B. Betts's *In Search of York*, along with the epilogue by Holmberg, which appears in the revised edition.

I've already listed my sources on Shoshone culture. For the Hidatsa and Mandan, in addition to the relatively extensive accounts of early visitors such as George Catlin, Alexander Henry, and Maximilian, Prince of Wied-Neuwied, I've drawn on Alfred W. Bowers's *Hidatsa Social and Ceremonial Organization* and his companion volume on the Mandan; *The Way to Independence* by Carolyn Gilman and Mary Jane Schneider; Washington Matthews's pioneering work *Ethnography and Philology of the Hidatsa Indians*; and *Waheenee: An Indian Girl's Story told by herself to Gilbert L. Wilson*. Robert H. Lowie's *The Crow Indians* was my main source on the Crow.

The only other author I have read who speculates about Lewis's sexuality is Clay Straus Jenkinson, in his *The Character of Meriwether Lewis*. This insightful monograph came to my attention late in my own writing, and Jenkinson's guesses are slightly different from mine. However, I was gratified to see someone else pointing to those places in the journals that cry out for a little attention.

Other writers whose scholarly articles on various aspects of the expedition have been indispensable to me are Irving W. Anderson, Robert N. Bergantino, E. G. Chuinard, Rita Cleary, Paul Russell Cutright, Ruth Frick, John D. W. Guice, Robert R. Hunt, Arlen J. Large, Grace Lewis, Joyce A. McDonough, Bob Moore, William Nichols, Ernest S. Osgood, Dennis R. Ottoson, Donald W. Rose, Lawrence A. Rudner and Hans A. Heynau, Bob Saindon, and Eileen Starr. Many of these articles appeared in *We Proceeded On*, a quarterly published by The Lewis and Clark Trail Heritage Foundation, which deserves special mention (and gratitude) as a forum for wonderfully detailed information on a wide variety of Lewis and Clark subjects. When I wanted to find out exactly what kind of hat an infrantryman of 1804 would have worn, or when the Corps most likely ran out of whiskey, or what phase the moon was in on the night Lewis died, *We Proceeded On* often provided the answers. Particular mention should be made of Dayton Duncan's article in the November 1998 issue of *WPO*, "Meriwether Lewis's 'Curious Adventure.'" Duncan's perceptive reading of Lewis's journal entry on the day he met the grizzly bear above the Great Falls has influenced my own view of the incident.

Most of the primary documents I've consulted and/or quoted appear in Donald Jackson's *Letters of the Lewis and Clark Expedition*; Gary E. Moulton's meticulously edited thirteen-volume edition of the expedition journals; James J. Holmberg's *Dear Brother: Letters of William Clark to Jonathan Clark*; A. P. Nasatir's two-volume compilation of documents pertaining to Louisiana, *Before Lewis and Clark*; Clarence Edwin Carter's *The Territorial Papers of the United States*; and Thomas Maitland Marshall's *The Life and Papers of Frederick Bates*. Additional material resides at the Missouri Historical Society (The Meriwether Lewis Collection); the American Philosophical Society; the University of Virginia; and The Filson Historical Society in Louisville, Kentucky. I thank those institutions for making this material available to me. Additional thanks are due to the curators, archivists, and other experts who have been generous with their time: Elizabeth Chew at Monticello; Carolyn Gilman and Kristina Perez at the Missouri Historical Society; Robert Cox at the American Philosophical Society; Ann Southwell at the Alderman Library, University of Virginia; and Billy Maxwell at the Lewis and Clark National Historic Trail Interpretive Center in Great Falls, Montana.

I owe a special debt of gratitude to James J. Holmberg, Curator of Special Collections at the Filson Historical Society, who took the time to answer quite a number of my questions about Clark and York while he was hard at work finishing his own book, *Dear Brother*.

To the careful and loving work of all of these historians, both amateur and professional, I owe a great deal. As I have lived with this large subject for a mere four years, an insufficient depth of relevant knowledge on my part has no doubt caused me on occasion to misinterpret their findings. In other words, all howlers are my own.

Readers of the manuscript, from whose wise counsel and words of complaint I benefited, were Geraldine Brooks, Paul Cody, David Hall, Tony Horwitz, and J. Robert Lennon. Thanks also to Stephen Marion, for his advice on Tennessee speech patterns; and Larry Moss, *socer superbus*, for help in translating the quaint Latin of certain fastidious anthropologists (since my Latin is even worse than Lewis's).

Finally, thanks to Paul Slovak, for consistent support and intelligent suggestions; to Madeleine and Cora, for existing; and to Pamela, for (as always) patience.

FOR THE BEST IN PAPERBACKS, LOOK FOR THE

In every corner of the world, on every subject under the sun, Penguin represents quality and variety—the very best in publishing today.

For complete information about books available from Penguin—including Penguin Classics, Penguin Compass, and Puffins—and how to order them, write to us at the appropriate address below. Please note that for copyright reasons the selection of books varies from country to country.

In the United States: Please write to *Penguin Group (USA), P.O. Box 12289 Dept. B, Newark, New Jersey 07101-5289* or call 1-800-788-6262.

In the United Kingdom: Please write to *Dept. EP, Penguin Books Ltd, Bath Road, Harmondsworth, West Drayton, Middlesex UB7 0DA.*

In Canada: Please write to *Penguin Books Canada Ltd, 10 Alcorn Avenue, Suite 300, Toronto, Ontario M4V 3B2.*

In Australia: Please write to *Penguin Books Australia Ltd, P.O. Box 257, Ringwood, Victoria 3134.*

In New Zealand: Please write to *Penguin Books (NZ) Ltd, Private Bag 102902, North Shore Mail Centre, Auckland 10.*

In India: Please write to *Penguin Books India Pvt Ltd, 11 Panchsheel Shopping Centre, Panchsheel Park, New Delhi 110 017.*

In the Netherlands: Please write to *Penguin Books Netherlands bv, Postbus 3507, NL-1001 AH Amsterdam.*

In Germany: Please write to *Penguin Books Deutschland GmbH, Metzlerstrasse 26, 60594 Frankfurt am Main.*

In Spain: Please write to *Penguin Books S. A., Bravo Murillo 19, 1° B, 28015 Madrid.*

In Italy: Please write to *Penguin Italia s.r.l., Via Benedetto Croce 2, 20094 Corsico, Milano.*

In France: Please write to *Penguin France, Le Carré Wilson, 62 rue Benjamin Baillaud, 31500 Toulouse.*

In Japan: Please write to *Penguin Books Japan Ltd, Kaneko Building, 2-3-25 Koraku, Bunkyo-Ku, Tokyo 112.*

In South Africa: Please write to *Penguin Books South Africa (Pty) Ltd, Private Bag X14, Parkview, 2122 Johannesburg.*